Cut and Deal

Cut and Deal

Ben Beazley

First published in Great Britain in 2014 by DB Publishing,
an imprint of JMD Media Ltd

© Ben Beazley, 2014

British Library Cataloguing in Publication Data
A catalogue record for this book is available from the
British Library

ISBN 978-1-78091-415-2

Printed and bound in the UK by Copytech (UK) Ltd Peterborough

Chapter 1

Watching the rain pattering against the window pane and bouncing off of the glistening pavement outside, Lisa Abbott stood deep in thought. She liked rain, it was restful and helped her to organise her thoughts, something which at the moment was of paramount importance.

Three months ago on a similar day to this, she had stood amongst the tightly packed crowd in the Town Hall Square and listened whilst the Mayor of Leicester, Councillor Walter Lovell, balancing precariously on a brewer's dray in front of the Town Hall steps beneath the unfurled flags of Great Britain, France, and the United States, told the assembly that the war to end all wars was over. At eleven o'clock that morning, Monday 11th November 1918, hostilities had ceased and the celebrations could begin.

The 'celebrations' lasted for almost a week before the clamour of church bells pealing and factory hooters blasting died away, and the street parties finally wore themselves out. Now in late January some of the realities of the newly found peace were beginning to be realised.

For the hundreds of soldiers trickling back into the town after four years in the trenches, the realities of post war Britain were not nearly so bright as the promises had been. The crippled and disabled were finding things particularly bleak. Some - those able to perform limited tasks - were being found basic work in warehouses or factories. Many able bodied, men were finding that the jobs they had left no longer existed. In some cases small firms had been absorbed by bigger companies whilst others, stripped of their workforce first by the ethic of 'volunteerism' and later by conscription, had simply closed down and disappeared. Where a man was lucky enough to be offered back his old position it invariably meant that the woman drafted in to temporarily replace him was now out of work. With foodstuffs in short supply the cost of living was escalating dramatically, whilst the absence of the war bonuses and overtime that everyone had come to rely on meant that plummeting earnings brought further misery.

A prime example of those hardest hit were the housewives and single women who for the duration of the war had filled absent men's places working on the tramcars. Now because of the Corporation's naïvety they were amongst the first to be thrown out of work. In a flush of patriotism, in August 1914 the town fathers, anticipating a quick return to work, allowed any Corporation employee – policeman, fireman, teacher, gas fitter or tram driver – to join the Colours on full pay for the duration of the war. By the time the truth sank in, that the war was going to be a prolonged affair, it was too late, they were in a self-created circle of financial ruin. Not only was the Corporation paying the wages of men who were away at the front, they were also paying their replacements - who by the middle of 1915 were without exception women.

It was now, thought Lisa grimly that the piper must be paid. Rates on houses were already going up to meet the fiscal deficits, which meant that landlords were putting up rents. It was not for this that the soldiers returning from France had spent four years fighting. The men who left in August 1914 were clerks, factory hands, farm workers – on their return they were battle hardened veterans, many of whom would be prepared to achieve lawfully or otherwise what they had fought for. There would be an upsurge in crime – and an upsurge in crime would create unprecedented opportunities. Opportunities that Lisa did not intend to let slip her by.

The young woman gazing pensively out of the window of the tiny terraced house decided that it was now time to implement certain plans that she had been making during the last few months.

The time was right for her to move on, and it was this that was occupying her mind.

Lisa Abbott, whose real name was Ada Manners, had come to Leicester three and a half years earlier in the summer of 1915 in a move driven by expediency. On police bail for the theft of money from her employer in Kelsford, she did not have to think twice about accepting the offer made to her by Frank Kempin, a soldier who was wanted for the murders of a nurse and a local carter, to take the hour's train journey south to Leicester and begin a new life. The new life that Kempin proposed involved her working from the house that she was presently living in at 42 Mansfield Street as a prostitute, a role which, whilst not filling her with enthusiasm, she had quickly realized she was not in a position to argue about.

Not in the initial stages that was. In April the following year the situation changed dramatically when Frank was arrested during a conscription dodgers check at a local cinema by the police, and taken back to Kelsford before being hauled off to serve a long prison sentence in a military prison.

None of the women who worked the streets in the Belgrave area of the town were allowed to operate without the consent of the licensee of the nearby George III pub Nobby Armstrong, who controlled all of the criminal activities in the district - and Armstrong had taken a very strong fancy to Lisa. With Frank out of the way, the gang boss made her an attractive proposition.

She could remain in the house at 42 Mansfield Street and he would arrange for well-to-do clients to visit her at the address for sex. His exact words ran through her mind. *'You're a presentable girl and you keep your place shipshape. How would you like that little house to yourself? You would work direct for me. There are plenty of high class gents in this town, businessmen and the like, who get piss all at home and would pay ten bob a time for you in a nice comfy bed. Let's say you get three quid a week, and you don't have to go outside your front door.'*

In the time that had elapsed since that conversation Lisa had done very well for herself. With her cut of the earnings plus the 'little extras' that her clients were only too willing to pay for - services that Armstrong had no idea about – she now had just over five hundred pounds stashed away in the bank. Also, she had worked very carefully at becoming indispensable to the Irishman.

When he said that she was a very presentable girl and kept her place shipshape, Armstrong was telling the truth. At twenty four years of age, Lisa Abbott was a very bright young woman who had no intention of spending the rest of her days entertaining men for a living, far less handing over the proceeds of her efforts to someone else.

Her present situation was she reflected, due entirely to circumstances. Having left school at thirteen she spent the next three years helping her mother doing cleaning work in some of the big houses in the Cranley Park district of Kelsford before taking a job at the newly built Criterion Hotel in the centre of the town as a chamber maid. Tired of making beds for a living, just after the war broke out, in September 1914 she was offered a permanent position as a housemaid with Mr and Mrs Sutton in Lyndon Terrace.

From the outset it had been an unhappy experience. George Sutton was a stout middle aged man with a taste for young girls, and Lisa - or Ada as she was then - with her long blonde hair and slim figure, was a very attractive young woman. It was not long before her employer was finding every opportunity to brush past her in the hallway or on the staircase.

Matters came to a head during the first week in June the following year, when catching her unawares polishing a table in the dining room, Sutton put his hand up her skirt and between her legs. Startled, Lisa let out a sharp scream just as her mistress, Elspeth Sutton was coming into the room. In the ensuing confusion, Lisa was ordered to go to the kitchen from where she and the cook Mrs Herbert, listened attentively to the tremendous row that took place between their employers.

Strangely, after things quietened down Lisa was not sent for by either Mr or Mrs Sutton - not as Mrs Herbert warned her for Mr Sutton to apologise, but because it was inevitable that she would be sacked, simply to remove temptation from his way.

After about an hour of sitting in the kitchen drinking cups of tea, Lisa was presented with the sight of Mrs Sutton standing in the doorway accompanied by a tall young man in a dark suit and bowler hat who told her that he was a police officer. To her amazement, Elspeth Sutton then accused her of stealing a half guinea from the dressing table in her room, and before she knew what was happening the girl was being taken by Detective Constable Cleaver to Long Street police station, where despite her emphatic denials, she was charged with larceny.

It was very obvious to the young woman that despite her innocence, to await the foregone result of her case being heard in the police court was not an option. Next day she slipped quietly away and changing her name to Lisa Abbott took a job as a barmaid at the Generous Briton in Kirkstall Street near to Sevastopol barracks. It was there that she became friendly with Frank Kempin, a soldier who came into the pub regularly, and when he suggested to her that they should catch a train to Leicester and begin a new life she readily agreed.

Life with Frank Kempin however was not quite what she expected. A petty thief from Manchester, Frank joined the army – from which he had so recently deserted – in order to avoid arrest for beating up a local prostitute whose performance had not met with his expectations. The reason for his hurried departure from Kelsford was that he was strongly suspected of two having committed two brutal murders in the town, and from the outset it was his intention that his new traveling companion should go out onto the streets and earn her keep. It was at this point, on their arrival in Leicester that they first made the acquaintance of Edgar Armstrong, and once Frank, by virtue of his being arrested in April 1915 was taken out of the equation Lisa came to be working for the Irishman.

By mutual agreement, turning tricks exclusively for Armstrong, Lisa never went back on the streets. She discretely entertained well to do clients obtained for her by Nobby whose needs were not being met elsewhere. Most came to the house after dark and by prior arrangement, however there were some who preferred daytime assignations, and they usually booked a room at one of the numerous commercial hotels in and around the town.

A shadowy figure passing the window, followed by a knock at the front door interrupted her train of thought, and opening it she saw the hunched figure of Gimpy Todd leaning on his crutch in the doorway attempting to avoid the rain pouring down from a leaking gutter overhead. He glared at her, the usual dour expression on his face enhanced by his dislike for the woman.

'Nobby wants to see you,' he grunted.

She frowned at him, 'is he coming here or does he want me to go over to the pub?' she asked.

Since in addition to their 'business' arrangement, taking Lisa on as his own woman, Armstrong was nowadays a regular visitor to the house, usually twice or three times a week, and always during the afternoons. The arrangement suited Lisa, the fact that she did not particularly like the big Dubliner with his uncouth ways and perpetual smell of stale sweat, was so far as she was concerned irrelevant, she merely regarded him as another customer.

A basic premis of Lisa's lifestyle since moving to Leicester was that so far as she was concerned, this was a very temporary interlude in her life. Lisa Abbott had no intention of spending the rest of her days as a whore – albeit when the going rate was two shillings, a high class ten bob a time whore – consequently she never fell into any of the traps that proved the undoing of so many of her sisters in the trade.

Always smartly dressed, she kept her house immaculate and when not working, cooked and baked regularly. Whilst most of the street women were drink sodden slatterns, Lisa seldom touched alcohol. Consequently after three years as a 'working girl' she still looked as good as the day she arrived in the town.

Her influence over Nobby Armstrong did however give her a degree of power that was not appreciated by his other minions, and this was the root of the dislike towards her presently evinced by the man at the door.

'He says come over to the pub now,' Gimpy muttered.

Your day will come you fancy bitch, he thought. Standing out here in the soaking rain, whilst you hitch your skirts for the entire local Council! It won't last though – everyone knows that Armstrong isn't the man he used to be. When Nobby's gone your days will be numbered and you will be back out there flogging it with all the rest of them.

Lisa Abbott disliked the one legged Todd as much as he disliked her. 'Gimpy,' as he was known in the Belgrave district always told the story that he had lost his leg in the South African War, the result of a Boer bullet, but everyone knew that he had been run over by a milk cart when he was a child.

'Tell him I am on my way,' she said and closed the door.

Shaking the rain from her umbrella the young woman pushed open the unlatched door of the lodging house in Abbey Street next to the George III, and went in. Although the pub was only just around the corner from where she lived, the walk was sufficient in this weather for the hem of her dress to be soaking.

'Got your nice dress wet have you Lisa?' cackled the old crone sitting in the broken down rocking chair, peering out of the window at the passers by.

The girl eyed her speculatively. Even in these rundown surroundings, Sadie Riley - otherwise known as 'Mother Clipstone,' due to the practice in her younger days of clipping gold coins and smoothing them back down on an oilstone – was a hag.

Still wearing the same black crêpe bonnet tied under her chin, and matching shawl wrapped around her skinny shoulders that she was dressed in the first day that the girl ever saw her, she resembled a bundle of rags dumped in the chair. A thin curl of pungent blue smoke rose from the bowl of the stubby clay pipe protruding out of the corner of her toothless jaw. A chipped stone jar of rum sat on the uncovered boards within reach of her hand. Mingled with the odours of years of neglect and accumulated filth, the room stank of stale tobacco and unwashed humanity, much of it emanating from the old woman herself.

Gimpy might not like Lisa because of her influence over Nobby Armstrong, but Sadie recognised in her a spark of something that she herself had been many years ago, and it meant that the two women were implacable enemies.

'Yes,' Lisa replied coldly, 'but I've been out in the rain - I haven't just pissed myself.'

Ignoring the old woman's stream of imprecations that followed her, Lisa made her way through into what served as the eating room for the lodgers, and up the narrow staircase to the first floor dormitory. Despite it only being early afternoon, the short miserable winter's day made it almost dark in the long room which served as the sleeping accommodation for the lodging house occupants. None of the sparse gaslights were lit as the place would be empty until early evening.

To her left was a doorway that led through into the upstairs living quarters of the George. It was an arrangement that had on more than one occasion proved it's worth when an unannounced visit to the pub by the police had allowed whoever they were looking for to slip quietly away through the lodging house and over the back wall into the next street. Similarly, this was the route by which any stolen goods were transferred back and forth.

After tapping quietly on the door, Lisa turned the handle and entered the adjacent bedroom.

Edgar Armstrong, sometimes known as the 'Baron,' or more usually 'Big Nobby' was a large Irishman in his early sixties, although drink and a lifetime spent in bar room brawls made him look considerably older than his years.

The bed that previously stood next to the door had been replaced by a battered old desk that was used more to house bottles of Bushmill's than anything else. Summer or winter, Nobby Armstrong always wore the same dirty vest and trousers along with a pair of heavy boots that had kicked many an opponent into submission. He was sitting next to the desk, chair tipped back on two legs, the back resting against the wall, waiting for her.

'Sit down lovey, we need to talk.' The thick Dublin accent was laden with whiskey fumes, and she realised that he had probably been drinking for most of the day. Lisa looked at him thoughtfully. She agreed with the general consensus, the old gang boss was not the man he used to be. It was not just booze, he had a bad colour and his breathing was laboured, also of recent his visits to Mansfield street were not nearly so frequent as in the past.

'There's trouble coming, and I think it best if you were not here for a while.'

He took a cigarette from the packet of Gold Flake next to his elbow, and scraped a match along the surface of the desk. The intake of smoke resulted in a paroxysm of coughing that sent his face a deep puce colour.

After a minute, the spasm subsided and the Irishman continued.

'Terence Shaughnessy is a different man to his uncle. When Michael was alive we kept our territories separate and didn't interfere with each other. But young Terence is greedy. Yesterday one of Giordano's 'hokey-pokey' men had his cart turned over in Argyle Street. Fuckin' ice-cream all over the place, kids scraping it up into paper cones, the van man took a slapping and lost his money bag!'

'I'm going to have to sort things. Put a few of the lads together and kick some shit out of Terence's runners. Thing is if it gets out of hand I don't want him thinking he'll get at me by taking a razor to you.'

Lisa felt a surge of elation run through her body. It was not the concern that Armstrong was apparently showing her. She knew that she was merely a prized asset so far as he was concerned – something to brag about in his cups. Inadvertently he was giving her the perfect opportunity to put the first stage of her plan into place.

Michael Shaughnessy, until his unexpected death through an heart attack just before Christmas, was the boss of the Wharf Street area, the boundaries of which ran alongside those of Nobby Armstrong's domain. Similar to the Belgrave, Wharf Street was a slum district that ran from Humberstone Gate back across the east side of the town to the edge of Belgrave. Shaughnessy and Armstrong were related – cousins she thought – and had for years existed side by side, taking the rake-offs from all of the petty crime in their areas, with little dispute between them. Michael's nephew Terence was however a different matter. Young and brash he had always been Michael's acknowledged successor and was now greedy to expand his territory. The 'hokey-pokey' men that Armstrong was referring to worked for the Italian ice cream manufacturer Enrico Giordano who paid his dues regularly for the privilege of selling his wares around the streets in the Abbey and Belgrave area. The 'runners' upon whom Armstrong was intending to take his retribution, collected bets in the maze of pubs along Wharf Street and deposited them with the handful of bookmakers who similarly paid their dues to Shaughnessy.

'I have been doing some careful thinking of my own Nobby, and I reckon that if you trusted me, we could do ourselves a bit of good outside of this town. If you want me out of the way for a while, I could be doing something useful.'

She watched his reaction carefully, a wrong move here and she could be in trouble. Armstrong's eyes locked onto her's the popped red blood vessels working overtime.

'Go on,' he said quietly.

'Things are happening here,' she said slowly. 'There is going to be a lot of shit going on soon. Look around. Soldiers coming back who are going to be out on the rob as soon as they find that there is no money about for them. Shaughnessy trying to take over your territory – now we both know you can deal with that, but the thing is while you are sorting him it is bound to attract the attention of the coppers. There will be grief and they will come down on both of you. It will quieten down, but in the meantime so will business. The girls will be frightened to work, the lads who should be out robbing will be too busy watching Terence's boys, and the police will be picking off everybody for farting in the street.'

She paused to allow him to turn over what she was saying. That he would emerge the winner in a turf war with Shaughnessy she seriously doubted and was in fact counting on it. He was too old, sitting watching him she could see that his breathing was laboured and he appeared she noticed for the first time, to be losing weight. She wondered if there was something physically wrong with him.

'What have you got in mind?' he asked. Lisa was bright, of that he was aware, possibly a bit too bright though. He would listen to what she had to say then decide how far she could be trusted.

'There are also a lot of 'good honest citizens' about who have made a deal of money in the last year or two –right?' She paused again and waited for his nod of acknowledgement.

'So we need to tap into the market and relieve them of some of that cash. My idea is that I go up to Kelsford and have a look around for a suitable premises where we can set up a nice little gaming house.'

A frown creased his brow, before he could interject, laying her hand gently on his, she leaned forward confidentially, allowing him an unrestricted view down the loose front of her half unbuttoned blouse.

The frown persisted but his eyes dropped automatically to the deep cleft between her breasts.

'Listen a minute,' her voice dropped to almost a whisper as she leaned in even closer. 'A premises right on the outskirts of the town, we bring clients in mid-week on the train from Derby, Sheffield, and here - lay some girls on for them. It will be away from their own turf, they tell their nearest and dearest they are away on a business trip, and you clean up.'

'What's your cut?' he demanded.

Inwardly she breathed a sigh, his gaze moved back to lock once more onto her eyes. *He was interested.*

'I move up there and run it, you will I am sure give me a nice little bonus to make things worth my while, and I only have one 'gentleman friend' – you.'

'What about the local police, they are not just going to let you walk in and set up in business?'

She gave him an enigmatic smile. 'Two things. First, no one apart from you and me must know what we are doing. That way there can be no interference, and you have got a nice little insurance if things go wrong down here.'

'Second, I have got some experience of the Kelsford police, and there are those amongst them who are bent – leave that one with me.'

With the weekend over, at half past ten on Monday morning, Lisa stood in the doorway of the buffet on London Road railway station watching the lightly falling snow that had replaced the weekend rain, waiting for the train from London to pull into platform one and take her to Kelsford.

The meeting with Armstrong had gone even better than she could have hoped. She was certain that her assessment of his physical decline was correct and that in offering a bolt hole in Kelsford she was throwing him a lifeline. If things went wrong in the impending gang war with Terence Shaughnessy, he now had somewhere to slip away to, in the process of which Lisa knew he would also ensure that a substantial amount of the ready cash that she needed went with him.

Where, she wondered not for the first time was his money? For thirty years he had run all of the criminal activities in Belgrave, nothing moved in or out of the district without passing through his hands. Although she recognized that it was only petty crime - a two bob prostitute now was only sixpence when he started out - and brokering minor burglaries along with the extortion of local traders would not have brought in a fortune, he still must have a substantial amount of hard cash somewhere. It definitely was not in any bank, so the big safe in his upstairs office had to be the place she decided.

The young woman smiled to herself, and a middle aged businessman about to enter the buffet to escape the inclement weather, mistaking it as a polite greeting, touched his hat and smiled back at her.

She watched idly as the businessman ordered a cup of tea from a bright young girl in an apron who was standing pad and pencil ready, by the table at which he had sat himself. Half open by his elbow she noticed a special edition of the Leicester Daily Mercury carrying the news that, with the increased number of influenza deaths and hospital admissions, the Medical Officer for Health – Dr C. Killick Millard - had declared an epidemic.

Lisa shivered, it was cold in the buffet but it was not that which caused the small spasm. The Spanish flu that started last year amongst the soldiers in France was once more sweeping across the country and hundreds, young and old, were already dying. Hopefully Kelsford would have escaped the ravages of the virus and remain relatively safe.

Momentarily the thought crossed her mind that if the epidemic continued there would be a goodly amount of medical supplies included in the barge cargoes that she had her eye on. As soon as she had acquired the premises that she was looking for, she would have to talk to Gilbert Manton as a matter of urgency.

Staring out of the window Lisa's attention returned to the matter on hand. From the outset she knew that Armstrong would go for the idea of a gambling house and high class brothel. The proposition was pitched accurately at his level of thinking. She also knew exactly what sort of property she needed for her own plans, and it was not going to be what Nobby was expecting.

By the middle of the previous year, once it was clear that the war was won, the young woman had occupied her mind with how to move away from the life into which she had been so unceremoniously thrust, and at the same time secure her future. It occurred to her at an early stage that one of the seemingly stupid things about the way in which the Edgar Armstrong's' of this world operated was the fact that everyone – including the police – knew about them. On the other hand some of the clients who Nobby had steered towards her during the last two and a half years, were she knew businessmen who were secretly making fortunes out of the war effort by dealing in contraband goods and other crooked deals. There were two members of the Town Council who she had discovered through careless pillow talk, by using inside information, had purchased areas of farm land on the edge of the town at a fraction of the true value, which they were now preparing to sell back to the Corporation for property development at a vast profit.

It was the activities of one particular man that interested Lisa. Gilbert Manton was a middle aged haulier who ran a fleet of ten canal barges operating out of the Belgrave Gate wharf. Lisa had a regular arrangement with him which Armstrong was unaware of, for Tuesday afternoons in a small upstairs room at the Sailor's Return pub on West Bridge, the landlord of which was a friend of his. Since early 1915 Manton had been moving barge loads of government supplies from his warehouse at the Belgrave Gate depot, north to Sheffield and Manchester. Everything from food and clothing, to machine parts and rifles. From an early stage he had an arrangement with the munitions controller at Leicester that somewhere along the route a certain amount of the cargo was diverted and transferred onto another barge, or a lorry waiting on a secluded pack horse bridge under which the canal passed.

It was the fact he, and those like him were never going to be found out - because they were clever enough to conceal their activities in the first place – that fired Lisa's brain. What she speculated, if rather than the risky business of diverting the goods en route, they were simply taken direct to an anonymous warehouse a safe distance away on another branch of the canal where the loading and unloading of cargoes was part of the daily routine, to be taken off and stored until the optimum time for disposal. With the war now ended there were going to be massive amounts of government stores being bought and sold, it would be possible with careful planning to hi-jack entire cargoes that would never be missed.

Unless things had changed since she came down to Leicester, there was a location on the outskirts of Kelsford that could in Lisa's opinion be perfect. On the north side of the town was the canal basin, a group of large warehouses, built thirty years ago. Initially a very prosperous development, the site suffered badly when a rail link taking goods directly into Manchester was built just prior to the war. The situation was compounded following a Zeppelin attack in December 1915 when two out of the three main buildings sustained direct hits and were destroyed. The purpose of the young woman's present journey was to see if there was still a viable premises left standing.

The sound of a train approaching interrupted her thoughts, and a few seconds later, steam hissing from between it's wheels, the locomotive shuddered to a halt and the handful of waiting passengers moved quickly from the shelter of the station buildings to climb aboard.

Finding a window seat Lisa, her small suitcase stowed in the overhead netting, wiped the condensation away from the glass with the back of a gloved hand. The businessman was still drinking his tea oblivious to his casual observer. As the train began to draw noisily out of the station she saw him signal to the young girl who was now working behind the buffet counter. Lisa wondered if he was going to order more tea - or a breakfast even - simply to create an opportunity to begin a conversation with her.

Armstrong was going to be a problem she realised. In her purse was £20 that he had sent round to her at the house in Mansfield Street. It was for traveling expenses and accommodation – as she told him, if they did not want to attract attention, then from the outset she needed to stay at a decent hotel. Just how she was going to play it she was not certain. She would have to convince Nobby that a warehouse could, with the right amount of money be converted into a gaming den, he was not stupid and he did not like spending money without a guaranteed return. Her real difficulty was not going to lay in convincing him that the plan as discussed was workable, it was going to be later removing him from the equation - after he had supplied the money - that would be problematic.

One thing at a time she decided, perhaps either nature or Terence Shaughnessy would resolve the problem for her - look for a property first.

Whilst Lisa Abbott was boarding the train at Leicester, fifty miles away in Kelsford a meeting was taking place in the Chief Constable's office at Long Street police station that would have interested her greatly.

Seated behind his highly polished and remarkably empty desk, Sydney Hall-Johnson fixed Detective Superintendent William Mardlin with what he considered to be a steady and authoritative gaze.

'I have had a request from the Home Office Will for you to be seconded for twelve months to their police liaison department with immediate effect.'

He paused in order to gauge the head of his detective department's reaction. From the darkening of the Superintendent's heavy features, Hall-Johnson decided that the proposition was not well received.

'Do I have a choice in this?' asked Mardlin.

'Not really.' The Chief Constable needed to tread carefully he decided. Since the death of his wife in an air raid, Will Mardlin had become something of an introvert, with few friends and immersing himself totally in his work. Work that he was exceptionally good at and would not now want to be taken away from. Hall-Johnson on the other hand had been delighted when he read the contents of the letter which bore the signature, *'Sir Rowland Leigh-Hunt on behalf of the Secretary of State for the Home Office,'* stating that it was necessary to second certain senior police officers from various forces throughout the country to central government in order to assist in the implementation of various post-war measures, and as such the services of Detective Superintendent Mardlin were required forthwith.

His mind working overtime Sydney Hall-Johnson read and re-read the letter several times before summoning the new station office boy Thomas Bowler and instructing him to find Mr Mardlin. For Kelsford police to have a senior officer working at the Home Office and instrumental in the formulation of national policy could potentially have huge advantages for the force in general, and Hall-Johnson in particular. Once Mardlin was *in situ* the Chief Constable would be in direct receipt of early decisions, and able to act upon or influence them in such a way as could only reflect in the eyes of the police world, upon his own vision and perspicacity. First however he needed to convince Mardlin to accept the position with good grace.

'I don't think that either of us has a choice. This is an Home Office instruction. I am assuming that you have been selected because of the success that you had in sorting out the Soldier Murders, and then with resolving the fraud at the War Hospital. It really is a great chance for you Will, and a year in London would be an excellent break.'

Mardlin scrubbed a hand across his jaw, a habit he had when he was thinking. That he could not refuse the secondment was obvious, and if he was perfectly honest the last two years had been less than good for him. A spell away in London might not be a bad thing.

The loss of his wife Susan, in an air raid just before Christmas 1915 had been the first blow that he had to absorb. That he and Susan – with her wandering eye and wayward lifestyle – were no longer in love was a fact of life, but like so many couples who had been married for twenty years they enjoyed a companionable relationship. The 'Soldier Murders,' that Hall-Johnson was referring to were so named by Gilmour Bathurst, the attention seeking editor of the Kelsford Gazette because the original suspect was a soldier by the name of Frank Kempin, who had been eliminated from the enquiry at an early stage. In eventually tracking down the killer, Mardlin and his deputy, Inspector Harry North were also able to clear up a major fraud involving the management of the local Kelsford War Hospital.

What Sydney Hall-Johnson was not touching on – primarily because it was something that he did not know about – was that few people were aware how complex the enquiry had been, and the effects that it wrought upon Mardlin personally.

Hall-Johnson was never told that the enquiry also involved Mardlin working alongside the Intelligence Services in identifying and eliminating a spy network that threatened the entire war effort. Nor was he ever aware of Mardlin's disastrous affair with Irene Deladier, a wealthy young widow, who had come to England early in the war as a refugee from France.

Still turning over the proposed move, Will eased his position in the armchair by the fireplace and steepling his fingers under his chin, considered his response. The reason that Sydney Hall-Johnson had not been a party to these things was that in common with the majority of his brother chief officers up and down the country, Hall-Johnson was not actually, and never had been, a working police officer. Consequently so far as the Detective Superintendent was concerned the Chief Constable was generally told no more than he needed to know.

Whilst men such as Mardlin joined the service and worked their way up through the ranks, the office of Chief Constable was one which was advertised in the *Times* and the *Gazette* for the perceived elite of the nation's great and good to apply for. This process invariably either attracted elderly candidates who were at the end of another career, such as the army or civil service, or as was more often the case, younger men whose aspirations in such a career had come to nought.

In Mardlin's eyes Sydney Hall-Johnson fitted firmly into the latter category. A regular officer in the King's Own Yorkshire Light Infantry the Chief Constable had, following the restructuring of the army in 1906 found himself on the retired list drawing a half pay pension. In Will's estimation had he been any good as a soldier, then he should in any case by the age of forty nine, have risen to a higher rank than that of Captain. As it was, unable to manage on the meagre stipend that he received each month, Captain Hall-Johnson successfully applied for the post of Head Constable of Kelsford Borough Police the following year.

Since that time, so far as Will could see , the man regarding him from across the desk, had led a charmed existence attending all of the correct social functions, becoming a member of the local golf club, and of course stepping onto the square of the Kelsford Masonic lodge, thereafter doing as little as possible and understanding only the basics of how a police force was run.

Heaving himself out of the depths of the armchair, Mardlin stood up and adjusting his waistcoat, eyed the spare sandy haired figure behind the desk.

'Alright Sir ... there is just one thing though.'

'I was intending to retire.'

Detective Inspector Harry North carefully wiped away a trace of foam from the heavy white moustache - which along with his carefully barbered, snowy white hair, had many years ago earned him the nickname of the 'Silver Fox' - and glared balefully into the pint of Winstock's best bitter on the table in front of him.

As usual, the bar of the Pack Horse Hotel was crowded at this time of day with farmers and horse dealers who having completed their morning's market trading were now crowding the noisy tap room. From their seats in the alcove by the window the two detectives could watch the various comings and goings whilst enjoying a sufficient degree of privacy to enable them to talk without being overheard.

'I am fifty four, I have been walking the streets of this town for almost thirty five years – I want to retire!'

Mardlin knew that this would be his friend's reaction. Having agreed to move to London for a year, he had made it clear to Sydney Hall-Johnson that he would only do so on the understanding that his deputy took over the running of the detective department in his absence.

Harry was without a doubt his best - and probably only - friend, but that aside he was also a talented detective. If Will were going to London he knew that he was the only person capable of temporarily replacing him.

'And what are you going to do if you retire? The idea is wonderful … the reality is that you would be dead inside six months.'

Mardlin knew that what he was saying was true. A lifelong bachelor Harry lived in digs with a widow Laura Percival in Tennyson Street, and other than his one and only interest in motor cycles, giving up work would kill him.

'Unless you and Laura are thinking of doing something else together …?'

For years there had been speculation at Long Street as to whether or not Foxy and Laura Percival were an item, but not even the two senior sergeants in the department, Bert Conway and Clarence Greasley, North's colleagues of over twenty years, would have dared make a joke about it to his face.

'We just might have - it wouldn't be the first time for either of us, but that is our business, nothing to do with anyone else. Enquire not what boils in another's pot!'

Lighting a cigarette from the packet of Players next to the pint on the table, he inhaled deeply.

Will took a sip of his own beer, 'listen, I don't know what this job is all about, it might be interesting, in which case I will stay for the twelve months. If it is simply pushing paper around, I will be back in a fortnight.' Both men knew that North had no intention of retiring and that this could be the ideal excuse for him to stay on for a while longer.

'Meantime, you get to run the department as acting Superintendent and earn a hat full of extra money.'

North continued to glare morosely at the pint pot. 'Alternatively, you bugger off out of the way to a nice cushy number in the hallowed halls of Toy Town, whilst I pick up all of the shit that's going to be happening here.'

Will nodded glumly, he had no answer to that.

With the war now over it was inevitable that the return home of thousands of battle hardened men was going to mean trouble. After previous conflicts, because of the relatively small numbers involved, and the fact that the economy of the country had never been substantially affected, the demobilised soldiers had presented relatively few problems This time it was going to be different. Women were occupying places in the labour force, money was becoming short, food supplies were not as yet fully restored. Crime rates were going to soar.

Looking up Harry grinned at him, 'You can get me another beer.'

Chapter 2

Three days later strolling along Gray's Inn Road, Mardlin checked the directions that he had been given for the Calthorpe Arms. He was slightly puzzled. Having obtained Harry North's agreement to take over the running of the detective department, Will, in accordance with the instructions contained in the letter concerning his secondment - handed to him by a very smug Hall-Johnson, who already saw himself striding purposefully through the corridors of power - telephoned the number supplied in the letter for details of where to go on his arrival in London. To his surprise he was instructed by the young man with whom he spoke, that on his arrival at St Pancras he should make his way to the Calthorpe Arms in Gray's Inn Road, where he would be met by a Home Office courier.

Although he was not familiar with Home Office procedures, Will could not see how a secondment to a police liaison department would begin by being met in a pub by a 'courier.' However, in the absence of any other information, leaving the railway station he set off on the ten minute walk to the rendez vous.

Waiting a moment on the edge of the kerb to allow a motorised taxicab to pass, he crossed over and went through the corner doorway of the pub into the tap room where he paused to orientate himself, it was an almost subconscious action, the consequence of years of police work. A long mirror behind the bar on the Gray's Inn side of the room provided a clear view of the passers-by on the pavement outside. To his right, tall windows looked out into Calthorpe Street. The single doorway set at the corner of the building where the two roads joined meant that no one could enter or leave without being seen by everyone in the room.

His gaze came to rest on the figure of a tall dark haired man in his early forties seated behind a table at the far side of the room. The immaculate suit and carefully knotted Guards tie were at a variance with the rough clothes of the one or two workmen enjoying an early lunchtime pint at the long polished bar.

Will gave a slow smile, and nodded an acknowledgement to the hand raised in welcome. Things were beginning to fall into place, whatever the true reason for him being summoned to London, if Ralph Gresham was involved, then this was certainly not going to be an office job.

Having bought a pint of the flat bitter favoured by Londoners, Will settled into the chair opposite to Gresham and nodding towards the tie said, 'I always thought that you were a Sapper.'

It was two and a half years since their paths last crossed. Whilst investigating a series of murders which were linked to an extensive fraud enquiry involving the Kelsford War Hospital, Will had become involved in the highly secret 'Project 19' being conducted at the Old Water Mill on the outskirts of the town. Ralph Gresham, employed by Military Intelligence, was at the same time hunting down an espionage network which was leaking information to Berlin on Project 19 through a spy codenamed *Nemesis*.

In some ways thought Will, looking speculatively at the man opposite him, it had been a most successful association. Between them the murders were resolved, and *Nemesis* eliminated. On the other hand, Will's wife Susan was killed in an air raid, and he had subsequently become entangled with Irene Deladier, whilst Ralph's partner Ted Bayliss, lost his life when the destroyer *Dunfermlin* was torpedoed with all hands in the North Sea.

At the time that all of this was taking place Gresham's cover had been that he was a Colonel in the Royal Engineers.

Touching the knot of the elegant maroon and navy striped tie with the thin gold line running through it, as if checking that it was adjusted correctly, Gresham gave a knowing chuckle.

'Nothing wrong with the Engineers my dear chap – Kitchener was a Sapper. It seemed more appropriate at the time, everybody involved in developing gas warfare was in the Engineers, so it fitted nicely with Project 19. Actually, I joined the 5th Dragoon Guards – 'Princess Charlotte's' - as a boy soldier in 1892 and I am still on their books.'

Mardlin continued his quizzical appraisal, 'what is this all about Ralph?'

A slight twitch pulled at the side of Ralph Gresham's jaw, as taking a packet of Passing Cloud cigarettes from his pocket he flicked open a gunmetal cigarette lighter and applied the flame to one.

'There is a lot going on at the moment Will. All of those good people passing by out there who think that the war is over and everything is now going to be wonderful, when in fact, whilst the shooting might have stopped for the time being, I can assure you this is the intermission not the end.'

'There is still bitter fighting going on in Russia. The revolution against the Romanovs signalled one of the biggest upheavals in history, since overthrowing the Tsar the country has been in turmoil. At present it is being ruled by a gang of brigands called the Bolsheviks. The disintegration of the army has served two purposes, neither of which are good. It took Russia out of the war whilst at the same time supplying these Bolsheviks with thousands of armed men.'

'Six months ago they executed the Tsar and his family in a cellar at Yekaterinburg – an event which I can assure you has frightened the wits out of every royal household in Europe.'

He paused to stub out his cigarette before continuing very quietly. 'Something that you will not know is that last summer, in sympathy with the Russians the French army also mutinied.'

A look of stunned surprise crossed Mardlin's face.

Ralph Gresham cast his eyes around the bar, no one had come in since the policeman's arrival which signified that he had not been followed.

'It has been kept very secret. The French commanders never told Haig or the British government. The only reason that we know about it at all is through French Military Intelligence.'

'Last year their Spring offensive collapsed with massive casualties, the mismanagement by Nivelle as Allied Commander brought down two successive French governments in a matter of months. Between April and June elements of fifty four Divisions of their front line troops staged mutinies and there were extensive desertions.'

In answer to Will's unasked question he continued, 'it was to some degree inevitable with the attrition levels and the conditions that they were living under.'

'From the battle figures now beginning to surface, it looks as if Britain will have lost – killed, wounded and missing - during the last four years in the region of three million men, the same figures for the French come to around six million. For every man that we have lost, they have lost two.'

His beer forgotten Gresham paused to allow Mardlin a moment to assimilate the enormity of the numbers. Whilst listening intently to what the intelligence officer was saying, part of Mardlin's brain was occupied in trying to work out how this affected him personally and why he was being given the information.

'Have you any idea Will what is going to happen next – the peace settlements I mean?' Ralph lit another cigarette and tapped the lighter gently against the table top as he gathered his own thoughts.

Mardlin shook his head, 'not really, I suppose that we will exact some form war reparations from the Germans as compensation, and then keep an eye on them in the future.'

The Colonel gave a hollow laugh. 'Good Christ, if only! You have no idea what the stupid bastards are going to do.'

'Again, this is classified information Will,' his voice once more dropped to a little above a whisper, so that Mardlin had to lean forward to hear what was being said.

'They want revenge, especially the French. At present the details are still being worked out, it will be the middle of next year before things are sorted. The French want the return of the territory of Alsace-Lorraine – that one goes back to the middle of the last century for God's sake! Belgium is claiming territories on it's eastern borders – Eupen and Malmédy. The Rhineland and the Saar are going to become occupied Allied territory. Half of Prussia is going to Lithuania, the Sudetenland goes to Czechoslovakia.'

He paused, 'You don't fully understand what I am saying do you Will?'

Never a political animal Will shook his head slightly, so far as he could see these propositions simply divided up the German Empire and ensured that those who had suffered achieved some compensation.

The twitch was more pronounced now. 'What it does Will, is it completely fucks up their economy, making it impossible for the government to rebuild a society destroyed by the Kaiser and his team of donkeys. It ensures that for the next twenty years German industry will be totally bankrupt, which in turn means that every German – not just your working man - is going to be living at subsistence level.'

'That happened in Russia and they had a revolution – a revolution that, believe me - in future years will influence the power balance of the entire world.'

'What they are proposing will either result in the dissolution of the entire German nation, or if they find some way of climbing back out of the abyss, ensuring another war.'

Will had difficulty in comprehending what Ralph was saying. How with this – the war to end all wars – being ended only weeks ago, was it possible to comprehend the possibility of another.

'Alright,' he said slowly, 'so now tell me why we are sitting here.'

Ralph Gresham returned to the table with two more pints of bitter and whisky chasers. The policeman had reacted as he had expected. Interest followed by disbelief, and then questioning.

'I work for a government department which takes an active interest in protecting our national security.' He needed to choose his words carefully, fuller explanations could come later if Will Mardlin decided to accept the job that he was about to be offered.

'At present the prime source of our 'interest' lays with the Russian situation. The revolution is by no means over. At present there is a major opposition force, the White Volunteer Army, based in Siberia under Admiral Kolchak that is fighting the Bolsheviks and which I am reliably informed is at present being reinforced by a joint French and British Expeditionary Force.'

Gresham did not feel the need to mention that whilst acting as a military observer during the Russo-Japanese War in 1904 he had met Aleksandr Vasilyevich Kolchak at Port Arthur. A dark, thin faced, austere man, Ralph doubted if Kolchak, whose entire experience had involved naval encounters, would prove successful as a land based leader of counter-revolutionaries.

'You see the thing is, with the appalling conditions in the trenches it was not just the French and the Russians who have taken matters into their own hands. Since late last year, when things were at their lowest ebb, there have also been a series of mutinies in our own forces.'

'The Bolshevik propaganda has reached our men, there are quite a few subversive elements amongst the troops who are trying – not unsuccessfully – to ferment discontent. Fortunately they are being hit hard by our commanders and have as yet been unable to get a sufficient toehold to achieve their aims – but the indications are that it is nowhere near over.'

Seeing the disbelief on the other man's face, he lit another cigarette from the stub in his hand before continuing.

'Last September there was a serious incident amongst our own troops at Étaples near to Boulogne. It is one of those depots that, rightly or wrongly was being used as a training camp for new recruits coming out from England and at the same time a rest camp for wounded men waiting to be sent home. Unfortunately it was also an acknowledged hell-hole by anyone who had been there, and a hotbed of dissent. On a Sunday afternoon a New Zealand artillery man was arrested on some jumped up charge by the Military Police. It provided the flashpoint that the agitators had been waiting for, the entire depot erupted and one of the MPs' opened fire. He killed a corporal and wounded a French woman who was in camp.'

'That was it, the situation developed into a riot, and the Tommies took over the town. It went on for three days before troops from other units were drafted in and took control.'

'During the week prior to that, two companies broke camp down the road at Boulogne, twenty three men were shot down by our own troops and as many again wounded. You have to believe me Will, things are serious over there and it is about to begin right here soon if we don't do something about it.'

'Why though Ralph, is this happening now? Surely the war is over, the killing is finished – it's time for a new beginning.'

The two men were strolling through a quiet stretch of parkland a ten minute walk from the pub. Mardlin never a lunchtime drinker, needed some fresh air and time to digest the implications of what he was being told.

'Ah yes, *'land fit for heroes'* - *all for one and one for all !* It simply can't happen Will, and there are those who know how to exploit that fact.'

'Since well before the war there has been a ground swell amongst the working classes across Europe for changes to be made in living conditions. The war has provided the catalyst for the fuse to now be lit under the powder keg. You only have to look at what happened in Ireland in 1916.'

'In other words, communism,' put in Mardlin.

'Exactly,' indicating a wooden bench, Gresham took a seat and huddling down in his overcoat against the chill February air continued, 'it is a very strong movement here in England Will, and it has been deeply infiltrated by dyed in the wool Marxists who are absolutely steeped in the Bolshevik ethic of achieving power by force.'

'Can the organisation not be proscribed by parliament and closed down'? asked his companion.

'No, you are thinking like a policeman. They are gaining the support of a huge proportion of the working classes, to drive them underground would be fatal. The problem is not the aims of the party but the fact that it is being used by those who have their own agenda. What we need to do is identify the subversive element and trace it back to it's roots. Once we have identified individuals we can work at destroying their influence.'

Sitting on the bench musing, Will was beginning to have an understanding of why he had been seconded to London.

'So where exactly do I fit into this'? he asked.

Ralph Gresham sat for a moment in silence watching a nursemaid pushing a baby in a perambulator along the gravelled footpath a few yards away. The girl, who was in her late teens, looked cold and was obviously performing her task with little enthusiasm. He wondered idly why the carriage was commonly referred to as a 'mail cart.'

'From a practical standpoint we are bracing ourselves for massive social unrest. Thousands of men are returning from the services. Part of the unrest in the army is the tardiness of the authorities now that the fighting is over, to demobilise men. Those arriving back are struggling to find employment. Add into the mix a civilian population that for four years has been in full employment earning more money than ever before in their lives – increased wages, overtime, war bonuses – who are now back on basic money. Women who have been working in factories and the transport industry are being thrown out of work entirely – because the terms on which they were given jobs were simply that they would be temporarily filling in for men who had been conscripted.'

'A key factor in controlling civil unrest is the police – and there is strong evidence that they are no longer reliable. For some time there has been a movement throughout the country for a police trades union to be formed. That movement is stronger now than ever and it is being propelled forward by subversive elements dedicated to destroying the one key organisation that can deal with them.'

They stood up and began walking again. Mardlin pushed his hands deeper into his overcoat pockets. He knew that what Gresham was telling him concerning the unrest amongst the lower ranks of the police was true. Last year in August a strike in London by Metropolitan officers had caused havoc for several days. In his own force there was an undercurrent of disaffection amongst many of the men, who now that the war was over were looking for the promises made by the government to become reality.

He gave a brief nod, 'So where do we go from here?' he asked.

Gresham touched his hat politely to an elderly couple passing in the opposite direction before replying. 'I have been given the task of monitoring what is going on, identifying subversive elements, and dealing with them. In order to achieve that I need to work closely but covertly with the reliable elements of the police, and that my friend is where you come in.'

'We need a police officer who is totally reliable to work with me on this. You were the obvious choice. Had it not been for you I would not have been able to crack the identity of Nemesis and put a stop to him before the Germans were in a position to produce MD 19 gas and wipe out half of the Western Front. Plus the fact that we get on and are comfortable working together.'

Will turned over what Gresham was saying. This was the offer, the reason that he had been brought down from Kelsford, now he must decide whether to accept and be brought into the inner circle, or get up and walk away.

He was curious though. Ralph Gresham lived in a shadowy world of which Will had, during the Nemesis affair been allowed a brief glimpse through the curtain of secrecy that surrounded it.

'If this is a government issue, would it not be more beneficial for someone from the Metropolitan Police to be seconded rather than me?'

The nanny and her charge were disappearing out of sight through the tall wrought iron gates that led back out into the busy world of central London, a large wet snowflake settled on the lapel of Gresham's immaculately tailored overcoat.

'No, I don't want them involved. We both know that with last year's strike and your own experiences in Whitechapel that the Metropolitan force is tainted.'

'Consider the consequences of a national police strike William ... now, are you in or not'?

The following morning Will came down to breakfast in the small but well appointed hotel tucked away in a side street at the back of Wellington barracks, to find that Gresham had already finished his bacon and eggs and was studying a copy of the Times.

'Morning,' he said brightly over the top of his paper. 'I can recommend the kippers, or if you prefer, the bacon and kidneys are excellent.'

Despite it's rather grandiose title, the Clarence Hotel, hidden discretely away off of Buckingham Gate was, Will would have thought, too small an establishment to be able to make much of a living in a district such as this where the overhead costs must be extremely high. The room that he was occupying on the first floor was comfortable to the point of being luxurious with a wide double bed, fitted carpet - which he guessed to be Wilton - and something he had never seen before, a bathroom and toilet through a connecting door.

His curiosity aroused, after dinner the previous evening - served by an impeccably dressed waiter in evening suit and tails - Will took a look at the fire door at the end of the landing near to his room. Gently pushing the release bar he stepped out onto a fire escape which in the illumination of a street lamp below, he saw gave out into a tidy yard typical of all such establishments, complete with an array of dustbins and a couple of beer barrels awaiting collection by the brewery.

Pausing in his appraisal of the yard Mardlin noticed that the bins and the two barrels were actually set out carefully, with a narrow pathway between them. He saw immediately that if anyone running the few yards from the fire escape to the tall yard gate, were to tip the barrels over, they would roll towards the fire escape and into the path of a pursuer.

Stepping back into the passageway he allowed the fire door to close once more, then pushed the bar to re-open it. It did not move, confirming his suspicions. The door was designed to open once, then closing back on a heavy spring become deadlocked.

'An interesting place Ralph,' he said quietly, although looking around he realised that it was not necessary, they were the only people in the room.

'Did you know Will that politicians read the Times and policemen read the Telegraph,' Gresham asked absently.

'It is more like a club than an hotel,' continued Mardlin refusing to be deflected.

'Fine dining, rooms and staff that would not be out of place in the Savoy, and an escape route on every floor. I would wager that the kitchen leads out into the next street. And ... most interesting of all ... we are the only guests.'

Gresham folded the newspaper and laid it carefully beside his plate.

'It is owned by the government. The man who we work for 'acquired' it during the war as a place where certain highly secret meetings could be held, and rather sensitive guests could be accommodated.'

He grinned widely, 'Vernon Kell would have an apoplexy if he knew of it's existence.'

Seeing Mardlin's puzzled expression he continued. 'Major General Vernon Kell. He was originally in charge of the home section of the Secret Service Bureau which is now MI5. As Head of the department he likes to be known as 'K' – all good *Boys Own* stuff!'

Mardlin speared half a kidney onto a bacon laden fork and holding it in mid-air between the plate and his mouth said, 'rather naïvely, I had thought that you were part of MI5.'

Gresham shook his head and drawing a cigarette case from his pocket selected a Passing Cloud from it. He made a questioning gesture with the cigarette and Will having shook his head, applied a match to it.

'No,' he said pensively. 'No, Vernon Kell runs MI5, the official intelligence arm of the British security forces dealing with threats on the Home Front. It's sister organisation, MI6 on the other hand deals with overseas intelligence gathering.'

'As with most loudly and proudly proclaimed organisations, MI5 is lightweight. For starters, to be one of K's people you need to have the correct background. Public school, good regiment, everybody off Friday afternoon for a weekend's shooting. Even for a secretary, Daddy needs to be at least something in the city and preferably a baronet. Consequently they all have the same outlook on life. 'Play the game, keep a straight bat, it is the playing not the winning that counts - all terribly incestuous ...' Needless to say, the people on the other side of the fence who are dedicated to bringing down society don't adhere to these rules – which is where we come in.'

He paused to stub out his cigarette in the ashtray which, on clearing away his breakfast plate the waiter had placed unobtrusively at his elbow.

'Prior to the war, I and one or two others with a military background were employed by the government on intelligence work such as the Nemesis thing that you and Harry were involved in. When things became more structured we were relegated to the background, Kell knew about us and frankly did not want to be involved. We don't have the correct social pedigree, and in his opinion the work that we are involved is, 'not at all acceptable.'

'What exactly do 'we' do?' asked Mardlin.

'Basically, the dirty work. K's people see themselves as intelligence officers recruiting agents and then sending them out to do their bidding. We work under a different régime, if a job needs to be done, then it will be done personally - if you see what I mean.'

Will nodded slowly. He was thinking about the Browning Modèle 1900 automatic pistol he found laid out on his bed the previous night alongside the hotel's complementary dressing gown and box of fifty Abdullah Turkish cigarettes. Smaller and more compact than the automatics that he had seen before, it fitted snugly into the soft leather shoulder holster that accompanied it.

He was beginning to wonder exactly what it was that he was getting into, but at the same time found his new situation intriguing and not a little exciting. It would be a change he thought from the regular daily routine of police work. He was alone with no family or commitments, and even if Susan were still alive, with her wayward lifestyle they virtually went their own ways before she was killed.

'And 'the man we work for,' who is he?'

'That at present you don't need to know,' replied his companion with an air of finality. 'Now eat up, we are off to France this morning, and I need to get you into the tailor before we go.'

The tailor's, in contrast to the Clarence Hotel, was by no means hidden away from the public eye. Descending from the taxicab that dropped them in Savile Row, Will found himself staring up at the four storey edifice of a premises that described itself simply as 'Gieves and Hawkes.'

'Best tailor's in town,' declared Gresham breezily, 'come along, this on expenses.'

Passing beneath the crisp Union Jack flag fluttering over the main entrance, Will soon found himself in a fitting room the size of a small lounge being measured by two elderly gentlemen in shirt sleeves and waistcoats.

'The suit will be ready next Thursday Sir,' the older of the two - a tall, thin, silver haired man - who must, Will guessed be in excess of seventy, murmured deferentially.

Before Will could respond Gresham spoke from the depths of a red leather armchair in the corner of the room.

'You will need an allowance in the jacket Cyril if you please.' It was obvious on their arrival that he was known to the establishment and that they were expected.

'Ah, yes Colonel Gresham,' the tape measure hovered momentarily before flicking up to chest height.

'Left or right handed Sir'

'Right,' Mardlin wondered how much the suit was going to cost and whether, despite Ralph's jaunty assertion that it was on expenses he was going to find himself presented with a bill equivalent to half a years salary.

The second tailor - a rotund little man who with his shiny bald head and well modulated tones, bore a remarkable resemblance to Mr Pickwick - gave Gresham an enquiring look.

'Seven point six five, Browning, Hubert.'

Hubert gave an approving nod. 'Ah yes Colonel, nice and compact. Very neat if I may say so.'

The two fitters thought Will, bore a marked resemblance to a music hall duo, an impression that was emphasised by the fact that each seemed to prefix every sentence with an aspirated 'ah.'

'Your uniform has been pressed and is ready Colonel, and from the measurements you gave us I think Mr Mardlin's should be a suitable – although not perfect – fit.'

Gresham gave Will his most charming smile and waved a hand casually in his direction.

'Best if we go in uniform today Will - you'll look very smart.'

Chapter 3

The collar of his army greatcoat turned up against a biting wind, Will Mardlin watched with interest as the boat edged it's way in alongside the long stone pier that led into Boulogne harbour. The port laid out in front of him was much larger than he had anticipated with tall white buildings stretching along the quayside and back up the steep hill into the town. Over to the right in the distance he could make out the dim outline of the cupola of the medieval cathedral presiding over the scene. At the furthest end of the jetty a three funnelled warship was tied up, smoke rising lazily from two of it's stacks to mingle with the grey afternoon sky.

As the mail boat glided into it's berth he saw that the broad quay was crowded with a host of vehicles, canvas sided ambulances, supply lorries, and motorcycles. The few soldiers that he could see moving around them looked cold and dispirited in the inhospitable winter weather.

With a gentle bump the *Invicta* touched the side of the harbour wall and a sailor deftly threw a line from the bows into the waiting hands of a French docker. Looking back along the side of the ship Will saw that a similar process was going on at the stern.

Within minutes a broad gangplank was in place and sailors began unloading the bags of mail and supplies they had brought with them on the two hour crossing from Dover.

As the only passengers, Mardlin and Gresham made their way down onto the wharf and picked their way through the stacks of mailbags towards where the army vehicles were parked. Apart from themselves and the dock workers, the only others on this part of the jetty in the growing gloom were two military policemen armed with slung rifles.

His mind drifted back to the one and only time that he had been in the port previously. Christmas 1887. It seemed a lifetime ago, he was fifteen at the time and travelling back to England with his parents. His father, a sergeant in the Royal Field Artillery had for the past eleven years been stationed in the various garrisons across India in which Will had grown up. Pulling his greatcoat collar up around his ears against the biting wind, Will remembered how bitterly cold Northern France had seemed to him after the heat of India, even to this day he did not like cold weather. The town was a riot of coloured lights and Christmas decorations, the red's and gold's' of the illuminations glinting off the oily waters of the harbour. It was the night when the locals celebrated the festival of 'St Nicholas, le Père Noël.' Standing with his mother and father on the deck of the ferry boat surrounded by suitcases, he remembered watching, fascinated as a red robed Father Christmas, having descended a ladder from an upper storey window of the Mairie, was carried off by a procession of brightly decorated fishing boats from the mouth of the River Liane and out to sea. As the flotilla of tiny boats disappeared from view along the coast, a sudden hush fell on the harbour and the crowds began to quietly melt away, workmen slipping into the warmth of nearby cafés, parents taking excited children home to discover what small gift had been left for them by le Père Noël.

The hush that now pervaded the dockside was a different one, oppressive and heavy.

'Transport should be here any minute,' Gresham cupped his lighter against the wind whilst he lit a cigarette.

Mardlin felt distinctly queasy after the journey across the Channel, through what in his opinion was a decidedly rough sea. The cloud of cigarette smoke, caught on the wind and blown into his face, did nothing to ease his nausea.

'Hopefully the situation won't arise, but avoid getting into conversation with any of the officers here, should it happen, let me handle things.'

It was Will knew sound advice. Both he and Gresham, courtesy of Gieves and Hawkes were wearing the uniform of Guards officers. Whilst he was no stranger to being in uniform from his early days in the police, plus the fact that he had been brought up on army camps, Mardlin was uncomfortable wearing one to which he was not entitled. Ralph on the other hand, dressed in his own uniform, freshly cleaned and pressed by the outfitters, looked totally at ease. He had of course, Will remembered served during the early part of the war with his regiment in the trenches and was at liberty to wear the campaign ribbons on his tunic - something which 'Captain' Mardlin was not.

Gresham had been somewhat vague about the reason for their trip across the Channel, simply saying that it was in response to an urgent request for a meeting with a French intelligence officer of the Sûreté Générale, with whom he had been in contact for some time. Will decided that the sharing of information between the two of them was something that would have to be addressed – he was not used to being treated as the hired help. Either Ralph told him exactly where they were going and what they were doing, or on their return to England he would be on his way back to Kelsford.

Will's train of thought was interrupted by the sound of an engine, and looking along the quayside he saw approaching, a small open backed Daimler lorry that would normally be used to mount an anti-aircraft gun. The gun had been removed and the flat tail section was now empty.

The vehicle pulled up next to them and Gresham's face showed mild annoyance as throwing away his cigarette, he put his head into the cab and spoke to the man behind the wheel.

'Do we not have such a thing as a car here Percy?' he demanded.

The driver, a square featured young man with dark eyes and a slightly pug nose returned his gaze evenly. 'Not a good idea at present sir. Staff cars attract a bit of attention – one got trapped in a side street a couple of days ago by some 'overdue-demobees' and turned over. The two officers had to leg it into a house and away through the back yard. Could I suggest that you keep your collars turned up until we get out of town.'

Gresham gave a brief nod, 'apologies, should have known.'

Seating Will between himself and the driver, Gresham climbed into the open cab and they set off across the uneven setts towards the end of the quay, the vehicle's wheels clattering noisily over the concrete surface.

Will stole a glance at the soldier. He and Ralph had spoken, if not as equals, certainly not as a private would address a Colonel. He was trying to place where he had seen the man before. Then it came to him, although he had put on a little bit of weight in the last two years, Percy was the man who had driven the taxi on the morning that Gresham rescued Harry North and himself from the gang in the Whitechapel pub.

As they lurched uncomfortably onto the cobbled road that led up the hill out of the town Gresham spoke again.

'What does Tessier want Percy?'

Their driver took a final draw at the cigarette he was smoking before deftly flipping it out of the cab into the roadway.

'He has picked up some information that a man named Vasily Petrov, who is a high ranking member of the Bolshevik party is due to arrive here soon. Petrov apparently is on his way to England and André wants you to be present when they interrogate him.'

Gresham grunted, 'First catch your fish. What else do you know'

Percy made a face, 'Other than that we are meeting at a farmhouse five miles outside of town – the location of which I was given ten minutes ago – nothing. You know what the French are like, they only tell you something by accident. André is playing this very close, I have been here two weeks and I don't know any more now about what they are doing than I did when I arrived.'

Ralph lit two fresh cigarettes and handed him one. 'What about our side of things. What is the situation with the troops?'

Percy drew on the cigarette and inhaled deeply. 'Volatile. On a day to day basis, highly unpredictable.'

'Since the riots here in Boulogne, and then the big one at Étaples, there have been several smaller incidents up and down the coast – mainly in Labour Units. The brass are dealing with them by bringing in armed MP's and Guards companies – I never thought I would see it, but they have actually opened fire on a couple of occasions, one or two of our own men have been killed.'

'That is why I didn't collect you in a car, plus you are wearing Guards uniform, and the Guards are anathema here at present.'

He sniffed loudly. Will was not sure if it was due to the cold, or a mild censure of the officer who perhaps should have known better, with the uniforms of the entire British Army at his disposal, than to adopt that of the brigade which along with the military police was identified as its enemy by the common soldiery.

Gresham studied the end of his cigarette, the icy slipstream blowing through the cab was causing it to glow like a beacon and burn down fast.

'I take it that it is the Guards who have been putting down the riots?'

'With a vengeance - and a few Vickers machine guns,' the driver cast a look out of the cab and swung hard right onto a side road.

Ralph's face twisted into a deep scowl. 'The stupid bastards can't see it can they. All they have to do is ask for volunteers who want to stay in the army, keep some of them here to run the ports, send the others to Germany to make up an army of occupation, and let the rest go home. But no, that is too simple, and now they are frightened of our own men. Did you know that they are talking about making Haig an Earl and giving him and immense amount of money, *for services to the Empire.*' Jesus, he would do better to open a business in Smithfield – 'Douglas Haig, Family Butcher Since 1916.'

He lapsed into a morose silence and no one said anything more until a mile or so out of the town, reaching a narrow gap in the pavé road Percy turned the lorry onto a dirt track that led up to a large white painted farmhouse.

In the fading light the farmhouse looked like so many of the other buildings that they had passed on the road since leaving the harbour, and so unlike any of those in England. White painted with a slate roof, entry was gained through an archway wide enough to allow a horse and cart to pass under, cut through the centre of the house and bisecting it into two exact halves. Driving through the arch they found themselves in an enclosed stock yard flanked by stables and grain stores. All of the windows Will noticed were invisible behind tightly closed green shutters.

The man waiting for them in the arched gateway that cut the building neatly in two was in his mid-forties, very tall, standing over six feet, and gaunt looking. As he politely greeted them Will noticed that the cold air brought on a spasm of coughing and wondered if he had at some time been gassed. Having shook hands with the new arrivals André Tessier led them through into the spacious kitchen at the back of the building which looked out into a neat stock yard where Will could see their driver parking the lorry.

Looking around with interest Will saw that the room could have been a farm kitchen anywhere in the world. A long plain table was flanked on each side by a wooden bench intended to seat a dozen people. A black wood burning stove stood at one end with cooking pots on it, from which the tantalising smell of a casserole and a variety of unidentifiable vegetables seeped. The atmosphere was redolent with the smell of drying washing and the tang of hams curing. Glancing up at the ceiling he saw half a dozen flitches of bacon hanging from heavy iron hooks, along with two lines of clothes airing on wooden slats that were attached to the ceiling by a system of cords and pulleys tied to the wall.

He realised that his nausea from the crossing was easing and that he was extremely hungry, they had not eaten since leaving London some ten hours ago. Glancing around he was disappointed to find that the room did not have a timepiece, and had to guess from the darkness outside that it was probably about seven o'clock. Through the window he could just make out the shadowy figure of their driver deep in conversation with two men in sleeveless fleece jackets and caps pulled down tight on their heads. Both carried heavy calibre rifles on bandoliers slung casually across their shoulders.

Once they were seated at the table a stout middle aged woman wearing a long white apron appeared from the next room and placed a tall green bottle bearing the legend *Ricard* on the table along with a jug of cold water. Before leaving she poured two inches of the dull coloured liquid into four tall glasses and set one in front of each of the men. Their host poured water from the jug, filling them to about an inch from the top. Will noted with interest that the contents turned to the colour of metal polish and gave off a distinct smell of aniseed.

'So Ralph, how are things?' although the Frenchman was speaking to

Gresham, his eyes flicking quickly onto Will, held an unspoken question.

'Good André, everything is good. This is Will Mardlin, his department is working with us now – don't worry, you can trust him.'

The question in Tessier's eyes was replaced momentarily by something else that Will did not understand. *'L'aimant d'Irène ?'* It was said softly and in French, but Will caught the name Irene and immediately was on his guard.

Gresham held up his hand and responding in the same language replied, 'Yes. He is very good, and very safe, now trust me.'

Seeing the anger beginning to rise in Will's face Gresham said to him quietly, 'I will explain this to you later, there is a small matter of history. Believe me it is of no concern, let's get down to business.' At this point he did not want to go into details of how during the Project 19 operation, in order to ensure French cooperation, André Tessier had been quietly infiltrated into the Paris offices of the Kosminski Company, of which Irene was a family member.

Picking up his glass, he pushed Will's towards him. 'Santé,' he murmured.

Deciding that this was yet another issue to be resolved later, Will gave him a hard stare and took a sip of his drink.

'You said that you wanted an urgent meeting André, what is this all about?'

Gresham wanted to get down to business, he was also curious. Like himself the Frenchman was a professional intelligence officer and would not have sent the urgent message to London requesting a meeting without good reason.'

Tessier took a sip of his drink, the pastis was refreshing and felt smooth on his throat as it went down. Will Mardlin he thought looked distinctly the worse for wear after his recent trip across *La Manche*. The aniseed would he decided with quiet amusement soon resolve his nausea - one way or another. He was he realised, probably being over cautious about Ralph Gresham's partner. Once French Intelligence had been alerted at the beginning of 1916 to the fact that the Kelsford gas project was being funded from France by the Kosminski diamond empire, he had, because of his previous association with Major Samuel Norton who was a member of the family that owned Kosminskis, been instructed to use their friendship to infiltrate the organisation. As part of his background work he had quickly found out that Sam's sister Irene, was having an affair with the head of the Kelsford detective department – Superintendent William Mardlin.

'Have you heard of a man named Vasily Petrov?' he asked.

Gresham nodded slowly. 'Vaguely, he was an officer in the Tsarist Okhrana. His name came up a year or so ago when the monk Rasputin was assassinated. I would have thought that he would have been one of the prime targets for the revolutionary firing squads.'

Tessier smiled and swirled the smoky liquid around in his glass.

'That in itself is very interesting, and as yet we do not understand why he not only survived, but crossed over and is now an important figure in the new secret police – the *Cheka*.'

'Since the revolution certain figures have begun to emerge as leaders - primarily Vladimir Ilyich Lenin, and a Georgian by the name of Josef Vissarionovich Djugashvili, who calls himself Josef Stalin. The whole thing is in the melting pot, it looks very likely that this Georgian may attempt to seize power from Lenin, which might be a good thing for us. Irrespective - in true Russian style, having dismantled the Tsarist secret police – the Okhrana – they have immediately set up one of their own - the Cheka - under a Pole by the name of Felix Dzerzhinsky.'

'We don't know how he has done it, but Vasily Petrov has been made a senior officer in the Cheka. The most likely reason could be that either he was a long time supporter of the revolutionary cause and was already secretly working for them, or he simply had access to so much information that he was an asset that Lenin and Dzerzhinsky could not afford to turn down.'

'Or,' suggested Will, 'amongst his files he has got something on one or both of them.'

André Tessier nodded in agreement. 'Precisely, and if he has, then it is vital that we find out what it is. Which brings us to why we are here.'

'The problems amongst your soldiers here and our dock workers, are mainly being fomented by a communist cell that is based in Calais. Some months ago we managed to put an agent into the cell. He is a Ukrainian by the name of Fedir Yurkovich, and as a result we have been getting back some very useful information. We were ready to close in on them when our man found out that a high ranking officer, who he identified as Petrov, is coming through here on his way to England.'

'It is all very secret, but from talk that Fedir has picked up, the situation in England is almost right for a general strike led by the police to be called. Petrov is going over there to organise it.'

'Where exactly in England is he going to?' asked Gresham.

Tessier shrugged, 'at present, other than that it is somewhere in the Midlands or North West, we do not know.'

'Liverpool,' grunted Will. 'With the failure of the strike in London last August, Liverpool is the next target. At present it is illegal for police officers to belong to a union, but there is a strong movement to alter that, and the most militant district is Liverpool.'

'And if a strike in Liverpool succeeds,' Gresham said pensively, 'he is geographically in an ideal position to orchestrate follow-ups in the other industrial towns such as Sheffield, and the North East – Newcastle for instance, where unemployment is highest.'

'Can your man identify Petrov?' Ralph looked across the table at Tessier.

The Frenchman shook his head. 'No … but I can.'

The others waited attentively for him to continue. Tessier got up and stood looking out of the window at the snow flakes gently drifting down, he hoped that the snow would not interfere with his plans for the evening. Turning his attention back to the men at the table he continued.

'For thirty years the Okhrana used Paris as a base for monitoring the activities of Russian dissidents and activists across Europe. They maintained a presence in the Imperial Russian Consulate on the Rue Grenelle. It was very much an open secret, we knew all about it, but it suited us to allow them to continue. Obviously whilst they watched the activists, we watched them. With the war coming, we closed them down in 1913, but prior to that for about twelve months, Vasily Petrov was stationed there as head of operations. He was a very shadowy figure, no embassy receptions or diplomatic dinners, he succeeded in being almost invisible.'

'The fact that we closed down the section working from the Consulate simply meant that they moved to a more discreet location – the *Agence Bint et Sambain*, which employed a couple of French ex-policemen and posed as a detective agency.'

He paused to light a Gauloise. Blowing a thin plume of acrid blue smoke towards the ceiling, the smell of which instantly caused Will's nausea to return, he continued.

'It is somewhat ironic that I didn't come into military intelligence until the beginning of the war, prior to 1914 I was an officer in the Chasseurs à Pied, yet I was the only one who got a good look at him. I was in northern France until late summer 1915 on tactical evaluation work but after Yprès I was posted to Paris and transferred to the Sûreté. Early in 1917 with the revolution brewing we got word that Petrov was coming back to Paris in order to close down the agence. He obviously knew that once the revolutionaries came to power the Okhrana was finished, and wanted to personally clear out certain files. That was exactly what he did. I was responsible for the surveillance operation and followed him for two days before he caught the train back to St Petersburg. Whatever the documents were that he came for, they fitted into a briefcase, and because he had diplomatic immunity we were forced to let him leave unchallenged.'

'Where is your man - Yurkovich now ?' asked Will quietly.

Tessier gave him an approving glance. 'As a Ukrainian he can pass as a Russian. Knowing that once we have taken out Petrov all of the members of the cell will be arrested, we arranged for him to leave for England a couple of days ago. He will make contact with the cell in Liverpool and report back through your people.'

He gave Mardlin a wry grin, 'that is the only reason that I have given you his name.'

'So,' said Gresham, 'when is Petrov due?'

The Frenchman placed his glass carefully on the scrubbed table top, and nodded approvingly to the woman who, apparently oblivious to what was being discussed, was busy placing deep boules of steaming mutton casserole in front of each of them.

'Tonight.'

The snow was now falling heavily, covering the darkened streets of the old medieval quarter in a ghostly luminescent blanket that took the entire scene back to a distant time. Replace the guttering gas lamps - the shades of which were sizzling and spitting, as icy snow flakes landed on the hot glass shutters - with rush lights and you could be in the thirteenth century Will thought.

Huddled in the shelter of a deep shop doorway he checked across the street to where Ralph and André Tessier were similarly ensconced in the entrance to an undertaker's. Next to him Percy blew on his hands and quietly moved his feet in an endeavour to bring some feeling back into his frozen limbs. A clock nearby chimed eleven. They had been waiting for over two hours. According to the information that Yurkovich had given to André, Vasily Petrov should have arrived across the road at the Bar des Pêcheurs an hour ago. Will wondered how much longer they would keep up the surveillance. It was becoming obvious that either something had gone wrong or they had deliberately been given false information. Two of Tessier's men were watching the alley at the rear of the café, and another pair were further down the street near to the cathedral in the car that was to be used to make a getaway out of the town with their prisoner.

The sound of a group of men approaching noisily from the direction of the old town gate let into the curtain wall that ran around the quartier, attracted his attention. Was this what they were waiting for, a party of revelers going past the café giving cover for the Russian to slip unseen through the door and into a back room?

Will watched carefully, the group was made up of about ten British soldiers all apparently the worse for wear, out on a noisy drinking spree. He held his breath as the man at the front, a thickset Fusilier pushed open the door of the café and went in. Shouting noisily the rest of the soldiers attempted to follow him.

In the light spilling from the open door onto the street Mardlin saw that a dispute was taking place at the *caisse* just inside. Either the owner was not prepared to have a bunch of drunken Tommies take over his premises, or it was part of a pre-planned diversion. Movement from the shadows opposite caught his eye, Gresham and Tessier obviously of the same mind as himself were also paying close attention.

It was apparent that the argument was escalating and the sound of breaking glass was followed by the shrilling of whistles blowing as a nearby military police patrol, alerted to the disturbance came running down the road. As they plunged into the fracas a second patrol breathing hard from their exertions, came pounding up from the opposite end of the street.

Next to him, Percy drew his revolver from the holster at his hip, and gripping Will's arm pointed urgently to the figure of a man in a dark overcoat slipping quickly from the doorway of the café into the shadows. Without looking to left or right, he turned and hugging the shadows of the building line began to walk swiftly away.

Across the road André Tessier and Gresham, guns in their hands were moving to follow him. It was perfect, he was heading straight towards the team waiting in the vehicle.

As Will and Percy moved out of from their hiding place, the street behind them erupted into a mass of men, as soldiers and police spilled out of the bar into the roadway fighting. Suddenly a shot rang out, one of the soldiers – the Fusilier who had been the first to go into the bar – had fired a revolver. It was followed by two of the military policemen returning the fire with their already drawn weapons.

Startled, Gresham and Tessier spun around to see what was happening behind them. Another of the military policemen now opened fire, and bullets spattered into the doorframe of the bar sending splinters of wood flying into the night.

Their quarry was now clearly illuminated in the pool of light cast by an overhead gas lamp mounted on the wall of the shop next to the undertaker's. The moment was brief before he was lost again in the darkness. Now it was Tessier, caution thrown aside running to catch him, who was for a fleeting second starkly illuminated.

At first Will thought that he had lost his footing on the treacherous surface of the footway as he stumbled, then dropping to his knees the Frenchman fell face forward to lay prone in the snow.

Throwing himself against the wall of the building Gresham dropped to a crouch and pistol held double handed in front of him swung back and forth seeking a target. Percy took up a position kneeling on one leg in the doorway that he and Mardlin were occupying covering the street behind them.

Frozen in an eerie tableau they waited, the seconds ticking by, the only sounds those the running feet of the fleeing soldiers disappearing into the depths of the old town, pursued by the MPs.

Cautiously, the Browning held close in to his body, Will moved to where the inert form lay on the narrow footway. Kneeling beside the body he saw that Tessier had been shot in the head, blood was oozing from a small clean hole just above his left temple.

He made a negative gesture towards the others, who leaving their cover moved to join him, the sound of a car engine starting up caught their attention and they saw the Renault reversing down the road towards them.

With the assistance of the two Sûreté men, Tessier's body was lifted onto the back seat of the car and before the first Gendarmes arrived at the scene, they were speeding off out of the old town towards the farmhouse. The entire incident had lasted less than five minutes.

'What a total bloody mess!'

Ralph Gresham glared disconsolately over the ship's rail as the harbour wall glided silently past them. The snow had been replaced by a light sleet which none of the three men appeared to notice.

'Total and utter, bloody mess,' he repeated gloomily. 'Have you got any decent cigarettes Longman – I can't take any more of those fucking French things?'

It was Will realised, the first time that he had heard Gresham refer to Percy by his surname.

A packet of Black Cat, produced from the depths of a greatcoat pocket were handed over. Gresham lit one in silence and passed the cigarettes back.

On their arrival at the farmhouse, in answer to Ralph's terse questions, Tessier's men confirmed that the shadowy figure who left the café had not passed their position, and that he must have disappeared into one of the unlit alleyways that led off of the street. He had not been picked up by the watchers at the back of the café.

Leaving the French intelligence agents to deal with the aftermath of the evening's events, the three of them quickly gathered together their belongings and taking the Renault, just managed to catch the late night mail boat to Dover.

'Stating the obvious, we were obviously set up. The town is ready to explode, so the whole charade was easy to engineer. Selected Tommy Atkins who are sympathetic to the cause, big fight which gives them an opportunity to kick the shit out of the MP's, and our man the opportunity to confirm that we are waiting for him before he slips away to cover.' He said bitterly.

'Pity about Tessier. One of their senior operatives stopping a stray during a fight between British soldiers will not endear us to the Sûreté Générale.'

Will pulled the collar of his greatcoat up further against the rain, sometimes he wished that he smoked, it would probably help him to work things out, which was exactly what he was attempting to do now.

'I think that you have got this wrong Ralph,' he said grimly.

'If I am right, we have been set up from the very beginning, before we even left England. I don't think the man who left that bar was Petrov, because Petrov was not in Boulogne at all tonight, and never has been. I think that this was all about André Tessier.'

Gresham watched him intently. 'Go on,' he said quietly.

Will paused, gathering his thoughts. 'Those MP's were on the scene too quickly. The fight had hardly begun when they came running. They were part of the setup - I doubt if they were really military police at all.'

'We were intended to see our man leaving. Think about it, in the circumstances any trained agent would have slipped out the back way and quietly disappeared. That was done to draw us out onto the street.'

'The French Sûreté Générale have information that Petrov is coming to England to organise a major operation involving the police that if successful will result in national chaos. The only person that they know of who can identify him is Tessier - and that is what this is all about, Tessier had to be eliminated !'

'One other thing that makes me certain that I am right. Tessier was under a street light when he was shot, making a perfect target. When he went down, in the rattle of the gunfire, I heard the distinct crack of a rifle being fired. My bet is that when they do a post mortem on the body, he was shot from an upstairs window.'

'That gives us something of a problem then doesn't it,' put in Percy Longman. 'Tessier's man Yurkovich is somewhere in England and we don't have any means of contacting him.'

Gresham nodded. 'We have got to rethink one or two things,' he said deep in thought. 'We need to make contact with Yurkovich - or rather we need to persuade the French to get him to contact us. With any luck, André being taken out of the equation will render him extremely isolated in England, and we will be able to run him ourselves.'

'Not of course that we will put it as simplistically as that to our Gallic cousins,' he added flicking his cigarette over the side into the night.

Chapter 4

Walking briskly through the centre of Leicester from the railway station, despite it being a Sunday evening, Lisa was conscious of the lack of people about. Even the lighted bar of the Standard in Charles Street as she passed appeared particularly subdued. It was she knew nothing to do with the cold night air or the thin dusting of snow covering the pavement and roadway – it was the flu epidemic.

Of recent days the newspapers had been full of doom and gloom concerning the sudden resurgence of the dreaded Spanish flu that was sweeping the country. It had first appeared amongst the troops in France during the previous summer before progressing across the Channel and into England. The seriousness of it was brought home to everyone by the number of deaths that it caused before petering out towards the end of the year. Now apparently it was back and in a much more virulent form, people were succumbing in the hundreds and an alarming number were dying from it.

According to the Kelsford Gazette the worst hit areas were the Midlands and the Northern counties, particularly around the coal mining districts of North Yorkshire and Durham where respiratory problems were endemic. She had picked up an edition of yesterday's Leicester Daily Mercury from the news stand on her arrival at the station, and scanning it, quickly saw that during the previous week ten people in the town had died from the virus as a result of which the Corporation had ordered all cinemas, theatres, and schools to close down in order to prevent the spread of infection.

Lisa decided that once she had spoken to Armstrong she would find a reason to return to Kelsford as soon as possible, hopefully later tonight. There was a train heading north soon after midnight which she could catch. At least things were not as bad in Kelsford, although she supposed that it would only be a matter of time.

The Irishman was not expecting her, they had not been in contact since she left to search out a premises two weeks ago, and she could not decide whether to go first to 42 Mansfield Street and check that everything was alright there before going across to the pub. Pausing at the corner of Belgrave Gate Lisa decided to go directly to the George first. Getting Armstrong's approval, and more importantly the money that she needed to complete the warehouse lease, was uppermost in her mind, settle that before she did anything else she decided.

As she turned into Abbey Street the young woman saw the hunched figure of Gimpy Todd emerging from Sadie Riley's. Slightly puzzled she watched as he turned to lock the front door before pocketing the key and hobbling awkwardly away on the slippery cobbles toward the lighted window of the public house.

Once he had disappeared into the George, Lisa continued down the road and ignoring the locked door peered through the grimy window pane. Inside she could see nothing other than a smoky oil lamp burning on the table next to where Sadie always sat drinking. Making her way down the entry at the side of the house Lisa went into the tiny yard and tried the back door. It was undone. Pushing it open she made her way into the darkened kitchen and along the hallway to the front room. As usual the house stunk, but there was an added odour which at first she could not identify. Going into the parlour she realised that it was the reek of sickness.

Sadie Riley was laying on the broken down settee in the middle of the room, a dirty blanket over her. Her crêpe bonnet was on the floor, and Lisa realised for the first time that the old crone was almost bald. A few strands of greasy grey hair spread over the arm of the settee which was supporting her head. The empty rum jar, it's stopper missing lay on the bare boards inches from her hand.

The woman's breathing was more laboured than usual and as she stirred slightly, a fit of thick chesty coughing racked her body. Lisa stood for a few seconds watching her. She understood now why the front door was locked. With the lodging house keeper down with the flu there was no one to deal with any itinerants who came seeking a bed for the night.

Picking up the oil lamp that Gimpy had left on the table for the old woman should she wake up, Lisa made her way quietly out of the room and up the narrow stairs to the first floor.

It was as she expected deserted, and like the rest of the house in darkness. Giving the usual tap on the connecting door she waited a moment and when there was no response, on turning the knob found that it was unlocked.

In the light cast by the lamp Lisa could see that Nobby Armstrong's office come sleeping quarters was even more untidy than usual. The overpowering smell of body odour and whiskey made her turn towards the double bed in the far corner. Covered in a thick layer of blankets against the cold of the unheated room was Armstrong. She could see immediately that he was very ill. Holding the lamp near to his face she saw that his cheeks bore the flaming colour of a high fever, and if confirmation were needed, despite the chill, lines of sweat running down his face made tiny rivulets in the grimy stubble covering his jaw.

The presence of the light seemed to register with him and without opening his eyes the Irishman stirred and mumbled something incoherent. The movement brought on a fit of coughing that lasted for several minutes before he subsided once more into the semi-coma that had overtaken him.

First locking both the door into the lodging house and then the one on the opposite side of the room that gave out onto the pub landing, Lisa put the lamp down carefully on Armstrong's desk before sitting down in the chair from which he normally conducted business.

Pushing to one side an half empty packet of *Fenning's Fever Cure Powders*, and a bottle of *Mother Seigler's Syrup* she took a bottle of Bushmill's and a clean glass from the desk drawer and poured herself a generous measure. The whiskey, for someone who rarely drank, was warming and helped to calm her nerves.

Armstrong's stertorous breathing was interrupted by another fit of coughing, he did not even know that she was there and was so weak that she doubted he would last the night. Her eyes fixed on the piece of cord around his neck that extended down under the sweat soaked blanket. On the end of it was she knew the key to the old fashioned Milner safe standing sombrely against the wall. She stared across at the Milner deep in thought. Four feet high it was probably two feet wide and the same depth – it had got to be where the cash was.

Sipping the whiskey she sat for a long while, studying the figure in the bed and thinking. The hubbub downstairs in the bar was muted and she heard the clock on the staircase strike ten. Closing time, give the staff half an hour to clear the place of customers and tidy round before someone was likely to come upstairs and check on Nobby's condition. Standing up she wiped the glass clean on the hem of her dress and replaced it along with the whiskey bottle in the drawer.

Leaning over the prone figure she lifted his left arm and gently placed it back beneath the covers from where it had strayed, before tucking the blankets under the worn mattress. Pulling the covers tightly down over him she repeated the process on the far side of the bed, then calmly picking up the cushion from the chair in which she had been sitting placed it over his face, and holding it firmly across his nose and mouth laid the weight of her body down onto it.

Despite his condition the Irishman's urge to survive immediately kicked in, but he was too feeble, and his arms were firmly pinioned under the tight blankets. After what seemed to Lisa an eternity the Dubliner's struggles diminished and finally ceased. She still kept the cushion pressed tightly down until she was absolutely certain that he was dead. Eventually, straightening up she stood back and looked at him. A thick stream of phlegm and mucous was trickling from his nose and mouth and the burst capillaries in his already bloodshot eyes gave the corpse a surreal appearance. Nothing she decided that would not be attributed to a final and fatal bout of coughing and fever.

Feeling around under his chin she located the cord and lifted the key from the recesses of the filthy vest which he was still wearing. As she had hoped the knot, which Armstrong undid each time that he went to the safe was easy to untie, and she had it free in seconds.

As the heavy steel door swung back her eyes widened, inside on three steel metal shelves was more money than she had ever seen in her life. The top two were packed with bundles of white five pound notes, the next contained stacks of coins, sovereigns and half sovereigns. On the floor of the safe were several bundles of papers and a cardboard box.

Searching around she found what she was looking for behind the desk – an old battered cardboard suitcase. Working quickly and not bothering to count she shovelled the bundles of notes into the case and was about to close it when out of curiosity she decided to open the box. It contained a revolver and a leather holster, with it was a smaller box bearing in faded blue letters the words 'War Dept: .38 calibre' which when she opened it held twenty rounds of shiny brass jacketed rounds of ammunition. For a reason that she could not explain, Lisa shoved the gun into the holster and dropped it into the case with the bundles of fivers before snapping down the two flimsy catches at each end of the lid. The coins she left where they were.

Satisfied that no trace had been left of her presence she re-locked the safe before carefully tying the key back onto the cord around the dead man's neck, and leaving it loose so that it would be easy to undo again. Picking up the oil lamp Lisa unlocked both of the doors then checking that the dormitory of the lodging house was still empty, slipped into the darkness, the suitcase in her free hand.

At the foot of the stairs a movement in the front room caught her ear and she froze at the sound of coughing coming from inside.

'…Was 'appening… oo's there?' from the slurred tones she realised that it was Sadie, and cursed her carelessness, the light from the lamp must have woken the old hag. There was a sound of further movement followed by a curse and a crash as losing her balance whilst attempting to get off of the settee, the old woman fell her length on the floor and passed out once more in a drunken stupor.

Without pausing any longer, Lisa moved quickly along the passage and into the kitchen, extinguished the lamp and left through the unlocked back door.

Once clear of the lodging house, Lisa paused to catch her breath in one of the alleyways that cut through to the town centre. The suitcase she knew contained ample money for her needs, and she was now free of any encumbrance. Edgar Armstrong was dead. She had little conscience about the fact that she had hurried his demise along, he would have been dead by morning anyway, all that she had done was to turn circumstances to her advantage. No one had seen her enter or leave the house and she had no intention now of going near her own place in Mansfield Street, she could think of nothing there that she would need or want.

For the first time Lisa had applied her own rules, in the knowledge that they would work.

If no one was aware that a crime had been committed, no one would come looking. To all intents and purposes, Nobby Armstrong was simply another victim of the Spanish flu epidemic. Whoever walked into that room tomorrow morning was by the very nature of Armstrong's associates going to be a criminal, and the first thing they would do, before summoning any undertaker, would be to untie the key from around his neck, open the safe, and remove the piles of sovereigns – of which she supposed there were several hundred pounds. Again, nobody was going to know that the bulk of the cash had already been removed, and thereafter that person was never going to be able to disclose what was, or was not in the safe when they opened it.

The one thing that she needed to do now was change her plans about returning immediately to Kelsford. First she had some business to conduct with Gilbert Manton, and it was not of the sort that they would normally be involved in.

It was almost eleven o'clock, but if she was lucky he would still be at the Sailor's Return. He went there most Sunday nights and often stayed back to play cards after the place closed.

There was still a light burning in the front room of the pub when Lisa tapped gently on the window. It was starting to snow and despite the warm coat she was wearing, Lisa began to shiver as the gas lamp at the back of the room was suddenly extinguished and the sound of a chair scraping on wooden floor boards was followed by a face staring out of the window.

'Come on Fred, the Coppers don't tap on the window,' she said irritably in a voice loud enough to be heard through the glass.

Fred Lineker the licensee, said something to someone unseen in the darkness and a second or two later the bolt on the front door was drawn to allow her into the bar.

'Bloody hell do you want Lisa?' he asked turning the pinpoint of light in the gas mantle back up to reveal three other men seated at a round card table next to the bar which was covered in empty glasses waiting to be washed by the pot boy in the morning.

Smiling disarmingly at him, she winked and looked across at one of the card players, a florid featured man in his mid forties with old fashioned pork chop whiskers and the beginnings of a beer belly.

'I've been away for a day or so, and I don't want Nobby to know – now I've missed my train, so I thought I would see if you were still here Gil.'

Gilbert Manton inclined his head and smiled back at her, his eyes on the suitcase. 'Always a pleasure to see you Lisa, I'm sure Fred can sort you out for the night.'

The other two men at the table smirked knowingly as, abandoning his cards he stood up and taking the case, fondled her bottom for the benefit of his cronies before following her and the landlord out of the room towards the living quarters.

In the upstairs room as she pulled the curtains he slipped his hand up the back of her skirt and began to kiss her neck. Turning to face him she gently pulled his hand away from it's explorations and said, 'that's not what this is about.'

An hour later Manton got up from the hard backed chair that he had been occupying and stretched his arms above his head before running them through his thinning hair.

'I knew that you were clever Lisa, but I didn't realise quite how clever.'

The young woman met his gaze and smiled. At forty five Gilbert Manton was purely and simply a businessman. The important factor being that like most businessmen he was always interested in a deal, and if the deal were slightly 'grubby,' that often added to it's attraction. Very few of his associates were aware that one in every five of the barges that left Gilbert Manton's wharf at Belgrave were carrying stolen military stores. Lisa only knew because in an unguarded moment of pillow talk he had let slip where the money had come from for his new house on the outskirts of the town. His wife certainly did not know – but then neither did she know about Lisa.

So far as Lisa was concerned, that phase of her life was now over, but there was no need for Gilbert to become aware of that just yet.

'I will be ready for the first cargo in four weeks time,' she told him.

They had arranged for a barge load of cigarettes which the manager at the army stores depot would write off as 'water damaged' to be unloaded from one of Manton's boats at Lisa's new warehouse in the basin at Kelsford. They would be stored there until arrangements were in place for their disposal to a dealer in Manchester.

So different from Nobby Armstrong and his strong-arm team of enforcers she thought. Smartly dressed, well spoken, no one would ever guess that the man sitting opposite to her who had made thousands of pounds legitimately during the last four years out of hauling government stores from one end of the country to the other, had made thousands more by illicit means.

'And my cut is twenty percent of the value of the load on collection from the warehouse,' she said.

'Deal.' He replied.

Manton's eyes strayed not for the first time to the battered suitcase beside the bed.

'I take it that you will be staying overnight?' he queried.

'Yes,' she replied. 'I came back to pick up one or two things from Mansfield Street, but I didn't stay long, as I said, I don't want Nobby to know.'

Leaning forward she touched a finger to his lips. 'To make this work I need to get clear of him. So you don't say a word to anyone, yes?'

Manton kissed the fingers and smiled, this could become a very cosy situation he decided - a business partner who he could sleep with.

For her part, Lisa was well aware that she now needed to get back to Kelsford as soon as possible. The premises were secured. She had already signed the lease, for which payment was now due, on the one remaining disused warehouse in the canal basin that could be made tenable again, but there was a lot to be done in the next four weeks if she was to be ready to start handling goods. First and foremost she needed to find a crew to work for her.

'One other thing Gil,' she said, 'I am going to need some legitimate goods to store as well. With each cargo of hooky, I need a cargo of legal. That way if the police come sniffing around, everything is safe.'

A frown creased his brow, 'That might not be so straight forward.'

'Of course it will,' she said decisively. 'It gives you the opportunity to double your trade. Also you can broker cargoes for other hauliers in the region – Derby, Nottingham, Chesterfield. Sheffield is isolated by the Pennines - goods from there have to go right the way over to the Trent, then back west to Chesterfield. We can make a fortune by piggy-backing them. Haulier delivers from Sheffield to me at Kelsford, your boat takes the load on and up to Manchester. That side is all above board and provides a perfect cover for our little enterprise.'

Manton lit a cigar and offered the packet to her, she shook her head. The woman had depth he had to admit. He decided to go along with the arrangement for the time being, after all she was taking most of the risks, once a cargo was in her warehouse it would be very difficult to prove where it came from. The basic proposition was a good one and it was sensible to remain in the background whilst the woman did all of the hard work setting things up. It would be a different matter once everything was up and running, then he could rethink his position and if it suited him, take her out of the equation.

'Alright,' he replied, 'two boats in four weeks time.'

Other than four men playing cards at a table in the corner of the room, the buffet at London Road Station was almost deserted. Lisa ordered a cup of coffee and sat down near to a window where she could watch the activities on the platform outside. The large station clock told her that she had twenty five minutes to wait before the Kelsford train arrived.

She was extremely pleased with the results of her weekend activities. Nobby Armstrong was now history, and her first two cargoes were secured. The money was safely stashed in the brand new carpet bag holdall that she had bought from the Bag Stores in the Market Place on her way to the station. She thought that Gilbert Manton was going to loose his patience with her and withdraw from the whole thing when she had demanded a handling fee of ten pounds for the storage of the legal load. As she pointed out to him, this was business and in the present climate, all the while his goods sat in her warehouse they were gaining in value. Manton eventually conceded that there was sense in this and the extra business that he could generate would compensate. Lisa wondered if he realised that she once established was quickly going to become the senior partner in this venture – she doubted it.

Sipping the coffee that the young waitress placed in front of her – it was the same blonde haired girl who was serving on the previous occasion she had been in the café – Lisa's eyes wandered across the room to where the card players were sitting.

The group was made up of two men in business suits and two army officers. One a middle aged, choleric looking man wore the insignia of a major, the other a Captain - who Lisa had seen purchasing a ticket to Sheffield whilst she was waiting her turn at the station booking office - was much younger, not more than about twenty five she judged. Finely chiselled features, set off by a pair of dark brown eyes and a strong heavy blue, close shaven jaw line made him, she decided an extremely attractive young man. They were playing Nap, an army card game similar to whist.

As she watched the young officer followed up some quip that she could not hear with a flashing grin which resulted in the other three subsiding into fits of laughter. Her eyes automatically flicked down to his hands and she saw that in the moment of distraction he had created, the Captain was gently running his thumb down the edge of the pack of cards in his hand. Following up his joke with another comment, he began to deal.

Lisa sat watching quietly for a few more minutes, the Captain lost the first hand, then won two of the next three. Satisfied that he was cheating, she finished her coffee, and leaving the buffet made her way back to the booking office where she bought two singles on the next train to Sheffield.

Half an hour later, having ignored the Kelsford train, Lisa stepped up behind the army officer into the third class compartment of the 10.42 to Sheffield and followed him into the compartment that he selected, which as she had expected was occupied by two men in cheap business suits who she instinctively identified as commercial travellers.

A momentary flash of annoyance passed across the soldier's face, as with a polite nod the young woman stored her holdall in the overhead net, and settled herself in a corner of the carriage next to him. Taking off his tunic he folded it carefully before placing it on the seat between them.

Ignoring her three fellow travellers, Lisa took a copy of the Daily Sketch from the voluminous woven handbag that she had also acquired earlier in the morning from the Market Place, and settled down to read it.

Behind the newspaper a quiet smile caught her lips as ten minutes into the journey she heard the officer say to the man opposite him, 'You going all of the way to Sheffield?'

He had, she noted a strange accent which she could not for the moment place.

The older of the two nodded, 'yes, we change there for York. We are going to a sales conference near to the Castle.'

Without looking, in her mind's eye she could see the charming, guileless smile as she heard him say, 'care to pass the time away with a game of cards?'

The accent was she decided American. What an American was doing in the British Army she could not imagine. There was a short burst of activity as coats were set to one side and the let-down table beneath the compartment window pulled out between them.

'Nap gentlemen, shilling a game?' He said, and Lisa politely eased her position to allow him to feel in the pouch pocket of the folded tunic for his deck of cards - the same pocket that she had seen him drop his rail ticket into as he walked through the barrier at the station.

Lowering the paper, Lisa smiled brightly at all three, and said, 'best of luck gentlemen, on your mettle now, he is a very good player.'

The two travellers, realising for the first time that the young woman was apparently travelling with the Captain, gave her self-conscious smiles and murmured polite responses, whilst the soldier stared at her in stunned disbelief.

Returning to her study of the middle pages of the Sketch, Lisa almost burst out laughing. At the Captain's suggestion, as there were only three of them playing, the lower cards were removed and using a deck of twenty four instead of fifty two, the game began.

For the next hour as the train chugged it's way north the three men played in earnest, and whilst the two travellers appeared to win a reasonable number of games, the Captain was according to Lisa's reckoning almost two pounds up. In the meantime, she had surreptitiously slipped her hand into the folded tunic pocket and removed his rail ticket. The tunic she noticed bore the 'Pip-Squeak-and-Wilfred' ribbons of the 1914-15 Star, the War Medal, and the Victory Medal. She wondered idly if as well as being a card sharp the man was also a total fraud.

The train began to slow down and the sound of the ticket collector moving along the carriage from compartment to compartment brought the session to an end.

'Sheffield,' said the younger of the commercial travellers, looking disinterestedly out of the window. Other than to make his bids during the play, it was the first time that he had spoken.

'Thank you for the game gentlemen, time to go, hopefully we will meet again.' The flat mid-west accent was barely noticeable as the cards were slid back into their box, and the men began gathering their belongings together.

'Tickets please!'

The train guard's thin face poked into the compartment, punch machine at the ready. The commercial travellers handed over their tickets in silence whilst the Captain first felt casually in his pocket, then with a look of consternation began to search his tunic and trouser pockets for his missing ticket.

'I think that I possibly have them my love.' Lisa smiled disarmingly and handed over her tickets to be punched.

On the station platform Lisa put down her bags and waited patiently as the officer strode purposefully towards her.

'What the hell is your game?' he demanded angrily.

'A much better one than yours,' she replied evenly, eying a railway policeman further along the platform who was deep in conversation with an elderly porter.

'Working the trains, playing mugs for a few shillings a time at Nap with a marked deck of cards is suicidal, especially as you are not very good at it. I picked you up at Leicester within the first couple of hands.'

Glancing along the platform she saw that the policeman was now eying them speculatively as if trying to make his mind up about something. She nodded at the small leather valise that constituted his luggage.

'Presumably you are also diving down the back stairs of hotels without paying, how long have you been working the trains?'

He glowered at her. 'Come on, I need to know,' she said urgently, 'that copper is too interested for my liking – and don't look at him!.'

'Couple of months.'

'Have you always worked alone?' she persisted.

He nodded, the policeman was making his way slowly along the platform towards them.

Reaching up Lisa gave him a peck on the cheek and handing her holdall to him linked arms and the pair started to stroll towards the staircase leading out into the street. As they passed the policeman the soldier gave him a polite nod whilst Lisa continued to stair straight ahead, it would not have been seemly for a lady to do anything other. The policeman paused for a moment and after giving the soldier a hard stare, turned down the steps into the gentlemen's toilets to check that there were no undesirables lurking down there.

Crossing to the opposite side of the tracks, Lisa bought two First Class tickets for Kelsford and they boarded the train that was preparing to steam out.

Safely ensconced in the non-corridor carriage, she took a long appraising look at her new acquaintance. Her first impression had she felt been correct. Medium height, slimly built, he had an air of authority that went with the Captain's insignia, and he was she decided, extremely good looking. The dark hair and almost black eyes, along with the smile that for the moment was missing would have charmed many a susceptible female. For his part the man now seemed to be intrigued with whatever it was that was going on, and returning her stare, waited for her to speak.

'It is very obvious to both of us,' she said, 'that the card sharking is going to get you locked up – and very soon for that matter. That copper had your description, he was only put off by the fact that you had a woman with you. What is your name by the way?'

The man returned her gaze for several more seconds before replying.

'Wade. Cole Wade.'

'Are you really a soldier or is that all part of the con?'

'Oh yes, indeed,' the accent was coming through again, she knew that without a doubt, that alone would identify him. If he was skipping hotel bills it was most likely that was what the police wanted him for rather than cheating at cards.

'What is an American doing in the British Army?' she asked.

He took a deep breath and settled back in the upholstered seat. 'I was over here working for the Great Central Railway Company as a civil engineer when the war broke out. In January 1915 I enlisted in the Royal Engineers and went to France with the British Expeditionary Force. From that point on it was the same story as for anyone else who was lucky enough not to get killed. By the middle of 1916 I was a warrant officer, and then after the Somme we had lost so many commissioned officers that I got promoted to Lieutenant then Captain.'

'Problems came after the peace. Officers do not get the year's insurance against unemployment that your government gives to the ordinary soldiers, and I doubt I would have qualified anyway being American. Great Central had too many Brits looking for jobs to be interested any longer in re-employing foreigners ... so that was how I came to be on the lam.'

Lisa nodded thoughtfully. 'I need an 'enterprising man,' to run a business for me. There might be one or two risks, but the money will make it worthwhile, are you interested?'

Chapter 5

'*Regent* is just pulling in Mrs Abbott, and there is a copper out on the loading bay.'

Lisa looked up sharply at the man in the doorway. 'What does he want Taff?' she demanded.

'Plain clothes, brought some flyers. Sniffing round – eyes like a shithouse rat.' The thick accent made the coarseness of the phrase almost lyrical.

'That's alright,' Lisa stared through the door, past the little Welshman into the morning sunshine. 'Alderton knows what he is doing, he won't start to move anything off the barge until we say so. Send the policeman in here.'

In the three months that had elapsed since she spotted Cole Wade dealing cards in the railway buffet things had moved on beyond Lisa's best expectations.

Wade, with his easy good looks and engaging American accent proved to have been a remarkable find, not merely for his ability to deal with men and charm the ladies, but because with little effort he proved to be an ideal front man for her operation at the basin warehouse. His prime qualification she soon discovered was that he was totally amoral. Having taken him into her confidence as to the true purpose of 'Abbott's Warehousing Facility,' he readily agreed to work with her. His perception of 'working with her,' was something about which Lisa chose not to disillusion him, so far as she was concerned Cole Wade was, and would always be, 'hired help.'

Within a week of his arrival at the basin Wade, having spent a few pounds of Lisa's money in the local public houses had recruited a team of four reliable men to work the boats that would be coming through the canal basin.

The employment criteria were simple – they had to be recently demobilised, and have a criminal record.

Wade had done well she thought. Tom Whiteman, a brick layer and Frank

Chesterton a labourer, were from Derby, and had served in the Sherwood Foresters. Before the war both had been before the Police Court on more than one occasion for shop breakings and other minor offences. Desmond 'Taff' Davis was a Welsh coal miner who had never actually been demobilised. Having come back to England in December 1918 on convalescent leave he was one of the many who - the war ended - refused to return to France, and was thus classed as a deserter. Not daring to go back to his home in the Welsh valleys he had settled in Kelsford. Moses Hawkins, had been discharged from the Royal Navy for assaulting an officer.

The partnership between Gilbert Manton and Lisa Abbott flourished from the outset. Once Manton was satisfied that Lisa was capable of successfully hiding cargoes at the Kelsford basin, goods began to pour in. Not just from his barges but, as she had suggested, from other haulage companies working similar scams to those that Manton was involved in. Lisa was amazed at how many other hauliers were involved in crime.

Manton's prime source of stolen goods was the Army Supply Depot at Leicester, however, this was only part of a much wider network of thieving that extended across the East Midlands and up as far as the military headquarters at York. Different boats, all in contact with each other, were handling thousands of pounds worth of stolen property every day. With 'Mrs Abbott's' as the warehouse quickly became known, open for business it gave them all the opportunity to channel several boatloads a week through one central point. At least one barge a day was docking at the canal basin from all over the region with some part of its cargo consisting of contraband.

The real discovery had come by accident. Taff Davis, whilst supping a Friday night pint in the New Inn, came into conversation with an old man who over thirty years previously had worked as a navvy during the construction of the basin.

In the late 1880's a spur had been cut from the main Erewash canal at Flixton into the artificial basin on the north side of Kelsford. In order for barge traffic to discharge their cargoes with a minimum of disruption, a narrow channel controlled by a lock gate at each end was constructed from the main waterway, around the rear of the warehouses and back into the Flixton Spur. The purpose of the lock gates was that every so often this channel, as it became silted up could be drained and cleared.

According to the old man, additionally three tunnels were dug out underneath the warehouses between the main basin and the channel at the back to facilitate an exchange of water between the canal and this secondary cutting. One of the tunnels he told Taff, ran directly under Abbott's Warehouse.

The significance of this information was immediately apparent to Cole Wade.

'In order to do that,' he explained to Lisa, 'there must be paddles at the main canal end of each tunnel which can be opened and closed to control the flow of water between the two. If we can find the paddles, it should be possible to close them, then by working the lock gates on the main cut it will be possible to drain the channel, and the tunnel!'

Lisa was already ahead of him. 'Once the tunnel is dry, we brick up each end, make a concealed access point from the warehouse, and we have got an undetectable vault!'

Locating the paddles in a disused outbuilding at the water's edge was an easy matter. The tunnel which was forty feet long, five feet wide and six feet high, having been submerged and untended for thirty years, was dank and slimy. With the paddles to the basin closed and the back channel drained, it took a week to dry it out sufficiently for them to clean it. During this time the men worked furiously at bricking up both ends to create a sealed store room before opening the locks again and allowing the water to conceal their handiwork.

'There is something I don't understand,' Wade said to Lisa on the morning that, the main part of the work completed, Moses Hawkins and Frank Chesterton, stripped to the waist began knocking a hole through the concrete floor of the main warehouse.

'The concept of the basin was quite clever. At the time it was constructed canal building was at its peak and the engineers really knew what they were doing.'

'Whilst the average depth of the water in the main canal is around five feet, the water in the basin and the back channel is twelve feet. It was done to create a reservoir for use in hot weather when the level in the canal could – and still does - drop to a point where boats can't navigate. Underground feeder pipes were laid out from here to the Flixton Spur where there are a series of sluices. Similarly, another set of pipes and sluices join the basin to the River Kell so that as water is fed from here out to the main channel a mile away, the reservoir, and the main canal can be replenished from the river.'

'The tunnels were built to give increased water storage and to speed up the flow. What puzzles me is that in a couple of places in this one that we have opened, some of the brickwork on the walls doesn't tie in with the rest – as if there were originally extra passages cut through to interconnect the main tunnels, similar to the communication trenches we used in France.'

'What are you getting at?' She asked.

He gave her an enigmatic smile. 'Well to do that would be unnecessary and possibly even detrimental because it could create a backflow. I get the distinct feeling that we are not the first to use this complex for a purpose other than the one it was intended.'

'I think that the original builders used the tunnels to hide something of their own - then when the job was completed, bricked up the communication links before flooding them and handing over the site to the owners.'

Lisa turned the idea over, then said, 'My mum used to talk about the Irishmen who cut the Flixton Spur. Apparently there was a lot of Fenian activity in this area at the time and a barge was caught running guns through the Town Locks. Perhaps they used this place to store them.'

Wade shrugged. 'We will never know Lisa, just count ourselves lucky we found them.'

A quick glance past the detective as he walked in through the arched double doors leading from the wharf , at the boat tying up behind him, confirmed that it was the *Regent*. Alf Alderton would have more sense than to begin unloading the spirits that were stowed in the special compartment beneath the cases of machine parts destined for the Raleigh cycle factory at Nottingham whilst there was a stranger on the site.

'Mrs Abbott?' the policeman enquired politely.

He was she saw an exceptionally big man in his early thirties, dark haired and clean shaven. Her initial impression as he walked in out of the sunlight was of a man not to be underestimated. It was a face she thought, old beyond his years, she had seen it before in men returned from the war. If the steel grey eyes were the mirror to the soul, then this man's was buried deeper than she cared to seek.

'What can I do for you?' she asked pleasantly.

'Detective Sergeant Rowell,' he replied. The deep softly spoken Scottish brogue belied the coldness of his eyes, 'I was out this way and thought that I would drop in the month's stolen property sheet.'

It was she decided, steering him away from the doors into her small office, a routine visit. Each month the police circulated to all traders and dealers a list of property recently stolen which was likely to be presented by the thief for sale. Usually the task was delegated to the local uniformed beat officer, but every so often if a detective was not overburdened with work, or more likely wanted to sniff around, he would deliver the sheets himself.

A new business opening on the disused waterfront was inevitably going to attract the attention of the local police, hence Detective Sergeant Joseph Rowell's decision to make an unannounced visit for a look around.

She briefly scanned the list of items on the first page. 'Five gentlemen's suits, forty pairs of ladies shoes, are these from shop breakings or warehouses?' she asked.

'They are from two shop breakings a couple of weeks ago,' he replied. 'The shoes are quite identifiable, a new style with laces, made in Northampton, they went from Lennard's in the Market Place.'

'None of these things are likely to turn up here,' Lisa told him. 'We handle bulk cargoes. Store the goods short term in transit for the carriers. One boat drops a cargo off, the next picks it up.'

'What is the one outside carrying?' he asked casually.

'Cycle parts. He is picking up some crates of pottery to complete his load, then heading on south.'

It was time to give the detective a tour of the premises, satisfy him that everything was above board, and get rid of him.

'Have a look round whilst you are here,' she said amiably.

As if on cue, Cole Wade put his head in through the office door. 'Is it alright to start loading *Regent* Mrs Abbott?' he asked innocently.

Framed in the doorway Lisa was once more reminded of the man's magnetism. Despite her good resolutions, since coming to Kelsford Lisa was beginning to feel slightly isolated. One of the reasons that the warehouse site was for her personally so attractive was the fact that the first floor storerooms lent themselves ideally for conversion into living quarters. Utilising Tom Whiteman's skills as a builder, she had converted the main store into a living room, and the two smaller ones into a bedroom and kitchen respectively. From the day that work on the apartment finished none of the men had set foot upstairs again.

The result was that, totally self sufficient Lisa did not need to leave the canal basin unless she wished to. The men filled her food shopping list each week when they went into the town to buy provisions, and very few people even knew of her existence. It also meant that she had no social contact with anyone other than her crew, and it was this that she was beginning to feel. During her previous existence there were clients with whom she had allowed herself in a detached way to enjoy having sex. Although she would never have admitted it to anyone, it was one of the ways in which she was able to keep some of her regular clients coming back on a regular basis - they knew that she was very good at what she did, but not why. She was a young woman with a healthy appetite, and of recent had started to come around to the old saying that '*man - or woman for that matter - cannot live by bread alone.*' For the time being she decided, Cole Wade could be put on the back burner, but perhaps not for too long.

The deep throaty growl of a large dog brought a momentary frown to Joe Rowell's face. Glancing around for the source of the sound, he did not have to look far. From behind the office desk emerged a tri-coloured black, brown and white Welsh border collie, ears back, head held down menacingly.

'Be quiet Gyp,' Lisa said sharply.

The growl subsided to a discontented rumble. Wade, obviously nervous of the animal remained in the doorway.

'Show Sergeant Rowell around the place will you Cole,' she said, 'and while you are at it, there were some samples from that consignment of gents outfits for Meynell's in Stoke, one of those silk ties would go very nicely with his waistcoat.'

On the loading bay Lisa was speaking quietly to Alf Alderton the skipper of the *Regent*.

Cole Wade stood a few yards away, near to where Tom and Frank, assisted by Alderton's eldest son were handing boxes from the hold of the barge for stacking on the quay.

'Twenty cases of whisky Mrs Abbott.' Alf Alderton told her.

'They are in the middle section, laid along the bottom between the ruck boards. Two layers of bike frames on top of them.' The boatman a short powerfully built man in his thirties spoke respectfully. Word travelled incredibly swiftly along the waterways, and the word was that 'Mrs Abbott,' was becoming an influential figure on this stretch of the cut. This was the third drop in six weeks that Alf Alderton had made at Abbott's Warehouse, and that meant his bonuses had doubled from the earlier days when he would probably take one load of hooky a month all the way to Manchester. It was always the same procedure. Pull in, un-harness the horse, and whilst his eldest lad walked him to the stable to be fed, he and the men shifted the illegal cargo into the holding bay at the waterside. He then unloaded some genuine items for storage in order that, should anyone question the purpose of his stop, everything was above board.

Lisa's gaze drifted across to the thin tired looking woman standing in the back of the boat wearing a grey headscarf and what had once been a white apron, now work soiled and grubby, one arm draped across the tiller, the other holding a small baby to her shoulder. Life Lisa had decided a long time ago, would never snare her as it did these unfortunates, worn out by the time they were thirty and trapped in a system over which they had no control.

'When the copper has gone shift both the legit cases and the Scotch into the warehouse Alf. Tom and Frank will give you a lift with them.'

She had two rules. First the boatmen never went further than the main loading bay, and never saw the goods transferred into the underground store. Second, no one other than her knew exactly how the boats were directed to the wharf. This she knew irritated Cole Wade intensely, several times he had queried with her about the contacts that she used to set up the drops and each time she stone-walled him. She knew the Cole Wade's of this world only too well. Let him find out how the system worked and before long he would be free-lancing, trying to cut his own deals and inevitably bring the whole thing crashing down around their ears.

As an added failsafe Lisa also insisted that every drop was arranged by Gilbert Manton. This she explained to her partner ensured that he controlled everything coming into the warehouse making the other hauliers dependent upon him.

She smiled inwardly, Gil had fallen for that one hook, line, and sinker. The truth was that if things went wrong he would carry the can. True the others involved – and at present there were three, Bill Grigson of Grigson & Grant at Chesterfield, John Capstock who owned Retford Haulage, and Sam Wooller, the manager of Don Navigation boats at Stainforth - knew that she managed the warehouse, but so far as they were aware she simply worked for Manton. Any disputes, and inevitably sooner or later 'thieves would fall out,' then it was to Gil that his partners in crime would look. later when it came time to wind up the scheme, she could slip anonymously away before any of the others realised her full involvement.

At the far end of the wharf Cole and the detective emerged from the warehouse and stood talking for a moment before briefly shaking hands the policeman turned and walked briskly off along the towing path in the direction of Kelsford.

'He's gone.' Wade's eyes searched around the loading bay for the dog.

Lisa nodded, whilst she was out here making sure that so as long as the policeman was on the premises, nothing was unloaded from the barge, Gyp was in the office curled up under the desk minding the shop.

She had bought the dog two months ago on a whim from a gipsy, who rumour had it lived about a mile away in the woods. It was Lisa soon decided, the best five shillings she had spent in a long while. At two years old the collie, typical of the breed was of a solitary nature, quickly becoming devoted to her new owner and singularly disinterested in other human beings. The fact that the dog had taken an intense dislike to her manager was probably not, mused Lisa a bad thing.

'Offload and let's get the stuff under cover,' she said, 'where is Moses?'

Tom Whiteman, Taff Davis, and Frank Chesterton, were already heaving crates onto the stone mooring in readiness to move them under cover.

'I sent him up to the overspill pool by the woods. With the hot weather the water should have dropped enough for me to have a look at the paddles. If we can get them working again, come winter we can use the pool to stop the cut flooding if the rains are bad.'

Lisa nodded again. Wade had in addition to his other attributes, proved to be a competent engineer. It was solely due to his skills that they had been able to drain the tunnel under the warehouse and create the hidden chamber. As an afterthought, having sealed both ends, using his military experience he had rigged explosive charges to the wall at the basin end connected to an electric switch in the warehouse that in an emergency could be blown to flood the tunnel.

As they were talking she spotted a figure hurrying down the towpath from the main canal end. It was Hawkins.

Older than the rest Moses Hawkins was in his mid-forties, and was one of the ugliest men she could ever remember seeing. Slightly over middle height he was of a stocky build with large powerful hands that as Taff Davis had once said, 'could strangle a cart horse.' It was his features that were striking. Tanned to a deep mahogany from years at sea his face was seamed with deep vertical lines running from the eyes down to the corners of his narrow thin lipped mouth. The little black pebble eyes were set each side of a nose that was large and straight but had no bridge. He was Lisa knew dangerous, which was not something that necessarily bothered her, it was in fact a quality that might well at some time in the future be used to her advantage.

Wade tugged at the bottom of his waistcoat to straighten it as they watched the man approach. Despite the warm summer's day he wore a collar and tie to denote his position as manager, his only concession to the weather being that his jacket lay neatly folded on a bollard nearby.

Hawkins was perspiring from his efforts Lisa noticed, but not out of breath. Pulling off the sweat stained bandana that he was wearing against the sun he paused to wipe his face before speaking.

'We've got a problem Mrs Abbott.' The Liverpool accent was a deep husky growl, the result of years of heavy smoking.

'There's a body in the pond. Water level has dropped and it's caught in the rushes at the far side.'

'What sort of a body?' asked Wade.

'Dead body, there is only one sort.'

Moses Hawkins had spent nearly twenty years in the Royal Navy before being sentenced to a year's imprisonment in the infamous naval prison at Bodmin for beating a Petty Officer senseless after a drinking spree whilst on leave in his home town of Liverpool, and he did not like officers - serving or otherwise.

Quickly Lisa stepped in, 'Is it a fresh one or has it been there some time?

Her mind was working quickly. A body on her property was the last thing that she needed. If it were someone who had only just died, then there was certain to be an enquiry, if on the other hand it had been there unnoticed for some time then the problem would be easier to deal with. Hawkins reply pre-empted her next question.

'Been there a long while Mrs Abbott. Can't even tell if it's a man or a woman.'

'It's in a mess,' he added.

'Get *Regent* unloaded and out of here, then we will sort this out,' she said in a low voice, 'and say nothing to anyone - either of you – until the Alderton's have gone.'

The overflow pond lay at the edge of Copinger's Wood, halfway between the basin and the point where the spur of the cut left the main canal, about a ten minute walk from the warehouse. It was intended as an overflow during bad weather, and although neglected for some years, had at one time been a favourite fishing spot. Accessed through a gap in the perimeter hedge leading from the towpath it was about a hundred yards long and fifty across. Surrounded by trees and bushes the stretch of water was secluded and on a day such as this, normally pleasant.

The morning sun was warm promising by lunchtime to provide another hot day. A brilliant iridescent blue dragon fly rose and dipped as it silently weaved through the mauve and white bell shaped flowers that adorned the weeds along the edge of the bank. Lisa wondered how many lovers over the years had slipped through the gap in the hedgerow, away from prying eyes into the seclusion of this well hidden spot with its soft springy banks and shady undergrowth.

With Hawkins in the lead, Lisa and Wade, accompanied by Tom Whiteman and Taff Davis picked their way through the tangled scrub. Gyp dropped back behind the group, ears back, tail down. It did not take long for them to pick up what it was that was disturbing her.

Now that the level had dropped by almost half, much of the silt along the bank was exposed and they could clearly see the object of their attention laying at the water's edge in some reeds. Distinct from the earthy smells of the rotting vegetation which now lay above water level, came a heavy unforgettable stench that invaded the nostrils as they approached closer, blotting out all other sensation.

The body was, as Hawkins had said, 'in a mess.' It had obviously been in the water for a long while, the flesh, what was left of it was clay white and looked as if it had been boiled. Fishes and canal creatures had taken the eyes and gnawed away the lips and ears. At some point the stomach cavity had been opened, probably since it had been exposed above the water level, by foxes and rats. It was naked and however the corpse had come to be in the water, the absence of clothing made it impossible to guess at whether they were looking at a man or a woman.

Whining deep in her throat, Gyp retreated further back from the group and lay down uneasily some distance away. Lisa wished that she could do the same, but knew that it was not an option.

'It can't stay here,' she said. 'Last thing that we want is a posse of coppers swarming all over the place.'

'How long do you think it has been in the water?' She looked around the group. It was important. Not long - and someone would be looking for whoever it was - a very long time and things just might just be alright.

No one spoke, they seemed to be mesmerised by the apparition. The men were back in France where bodies such as this were commonplace. Corpses, limbs torn away by shell blast or shredded by machine gun fire, laying for months in flooded shell holes or half buried in glutinous mud, rats gnawing greedily at the decayed flesh.

'Somebody make me a fucking offer!'

Her voice, harsh with the effort of trying to keep the bile rising in her throat from turning to vomit, brought them back to the present. None of the men had ever heard her swear before, and this as much as the tone focussed them.

'Several weeks, possibly months.' Cole Wade's face was regaining some of it's colour.

'I would think more likely months than weeks,' said Tom Whiteman, 'its been a hard winter so it could have gone in anytime after Christmas and been under the ice.'

'Even so, it should have come up before now though.' Moses Hawkins was moving in closer, the bandana now pulled across his lower face revealing a shiny bald pate.

Bending forward he looked carefully at something in the water before putting his hand under the surface and pulling.   The others saw that the corpse's ankles were tied together with what looked like baling wire which was attached to something beneath the surface.

It took the combined efforts of Moses and Frank Chesterton to dislodge the object sunk into the mud at the bottom of the pool. When they eventually drew it to the surface the group saw that having bound the feet together the wire had been attached to part of a heavy iron bollard that would normally have been let into the canal bank to secure the mooring rope of a barge.

The time taken to dislodge the metalwork had given Lisa the opportunity to gather her thoughts and decide on a course of action. It was now obvious that the corpse had not come to be in the pond by accident, which meant that it was even more imperative that the police did not become aware of it's existence.

She shot a look at Wade and said, 'Cole, get the hand cart and a tarpaulin from the stables, load this onto it and take it up to the old lime kiln. The top is open, drop it in and no one will ever see it again.'

'There's a couple of quid apiece when it's sorted - just don't be seen doing it!' she ordered giving the others a hard stare.

The three workmen returned her gaze steadily, a new respect in their eyes.

Moses Hawkins touched his right temple with a horny hand, 'It'll be sorted Mrs Abbott.'

'And a night's free beer,' she added with a quiet smile.

Removing the remains - it could hardly be called a body, a body has shape and dignity, what, or whoever the putrid amalgamation of bones and rotted flesh laying in the waterline had neither - was a long and unpleasant job. It took Frank Chesterton less than twenty minutes to make the round trip to the warehouse stables and back with the handcart. Whilst they were waiting Wade moved further along the bank upwind, and sat on an old tree stump. Moses and the Welshman were sitting on the grass smoking a few yards away from him. Not for the first time Wade reflected upon what an unprepossessing man the ex-sailor was. So narrow and tight was his mouth that the briar pipe sticking out of it looked as if it were lodged in a hole in his face.

Underscored by the harsh creases that ran down his deeply tanned cheeks like sets of parallel tramlines, the overall impression was of a pen and ink drawing. He reminded Wade of one of the trolls from the fairy stories that his mother used to read to him as a child.

Lighting a thin panatela, the American paused to review his present situation.

Actually he was not an American, but it suited his purposes for people to think that he was. The third of four children, he was born James Dinwoodie in Winnipeg, Canada, during the summer of 1887 to Samuel and Sarah Dinwoodie, and had in his thirty two years led an eventful if not particularly productive life.

When James was ten years old his father, a railway track laying ganger for the Alberta company of Sheen Engineering, moved the family seven hundred miles west to the small town of Frank in British Columbia to work on the spur line of the Canadian Pacific Railway that was being built between Lethbridge through the Crows Nest Pass to Nelson.

It was a hard life and the wages were poor, but there was a recession and men had to take employment where they could find it. To speed the work up the Canadian Pacific Railway Company divided the three hundred mile stretch of line into ten mile sections and sub-contracted the work out to companies such as Sheen. As a foreman Sam Dinwoodie was able to afford the rent on a small house in Frank whilst he and James's elder brother Tom lived in the ganger's camp at the diggings.

By the end of 1898 work on the main line of track was complete and Sam and Tom Dinwoodie were able to gain employment for the next year or two doing maintenance work on the trestle bridges that supported the line as it dropped three hundred foot across the deep coulees on its way to the valley floor of the Oldman River.

It was whilst they were engaged in this work that disaster struck. The town of Frank stood at the foot of the Turtle Mountain, known locally by the indigenous Indian population as 'the moving mountain,' and avoided by them because of its' instability. With the recklessness born of the 'pioneering spirit' a drift mine to hew coal was dug by the settlers deep into the mountain, and with almost inevitable predictability, in the early hours of Wednesday 29th April 1903 the face of the mountain collapsed burying a large section of the town and killing seventy people, amongst whom were James's mother and youngest brother. The only reason that James himself was not amongst the casualties was because he was away at the line camp taking food and laundry to his father and older brother.

Still too young to take on the demanding work at the railhead, Sam Dinwoodie decided to send his sixteen year old son to Winnipeg to learn a trade, and James found himself back in his home town living with his father's sister.

For the next three years he worked as an apprentice engineer for the firm of Gunn & Sons who specialised in civil engineering, until in the summer of 1906 he was sent by the company back to Lethbridge to work as a supervisor on one of the teams excavating the subsoil on a stretch of the viaduct that was being built across the Oldman River to replace the worn out wooden bridges.

Life on the Crows Nest was arduous. As an engineer, albeit hardly qualified he at least had the relative luxury of living under canvas. Track laying gangs such as the one his father and brother worked on were housed in box cars known as 'Jumbos.' Seventy feet long, and six to a gang, these converted box cars were a living hell. The interiors were divided into three tiers of bunks on each side, separated by a narrow alley down the middle just wide enough for a man to pass along. At the far end was a wood burning stove which at the end of the working day the men, filthy with mud and slurry, crowded around for warmth. With the most basic sanitation and men sleeping in wet clothes for days on end, the cars became rat infested hovels with the occupants suffering from horrendous skin infections, and infectious disease rampant. It was no surprise that the death rates from pneumonia and diphtheria were high.

Living in the tented encampments was only marginally preferable and James quickly came to a decision that he had no intention of spending the rest of his days living under these conditions. With winter approaching he sounded out two other young men, Seth Adkins and Jeremiah Corwell, two drifters who had taken work as labourers for the summer, and they formulated a plan to rob the company store which stood a mile away near to the Sheen camp.

Waiting until the end of September, when the cash office at the store was holding the most money in readiness to pay the trappers bringing in their supplies of meat and warm furs in readiness for the winter freeze, the three young men went in and held the staff up at gunpoint. Making good their escape the three divided the money between them and split up.

Unfortunately, his associates were not as bright as James and within a week had been arrested spending their ill gotten gains in a Lethbridge bar. Once under lock and key they were quick to implicate James, and it was only a matter of days before Sergeant MacDiarmid and Constable Leahy of the Northwest Mounted Police road up to the isolated cabin in the mountains at the back of Crows Nest where he was hiding out to arrest him.

It was here for the first time that the young James displayed a ruthlessness beyond his years. In the short gunfight that ensued, from the cover of the cabin he cut down both of the officers with a rifle before they had dismounted from their horses, killing MacDiarmid and seriously wounding Leahy.

Now a wanted and desperate man, Dinwoodie took off over the American border into Montana, where working alone, stealing cars and continually travelling, for the next six months he existed by robbing a series of isolated stores, before finding his way down into South Dakota. From here he moved on east to Chicago where having teamed up with a gang of bank robbers he was arrested when the stolen car that they were driving broke down. Incredibly, the false name that he gave to the Chicago police - Edward Roby - was not challenged, and he received a four year gaol sentence for his part in the Chicago robberies.

Released in 1912, he once more travelled eastwards, this time to New York where he became involved with a group of small time hoodlums who specialised in robbing clothing warehouses. In June 1914 they were disturbed during a break-in at a warehouse in Long Island by a night watchman. Now accustomed to reacting to adversity with violence, along with the others James fought his way out of the situation leaving two dead police officers on the sidewalk. This time however, his luck had run out. As in Lethbridge several years earlier, one of the gang was arrested and in a bid to buy his freedom identified his accomplices.

More thorough than the Chicago police had been, the New York detectives, working from Dinwoodie's prison photograph tied him in with the cross-border shooting eight years previously of the two mounties' and he became a widely circulated fugitive. Forced to lay low for a while, James used his connections and some of the money that he had accumulated to buy false papers in the name of Cole Wade, an engineer from New Jersey. As soon as the documents were ready he quietly boarded ship in New York harbour and slipped away to begin a new life in England.

For once fortune smiled upon him. Six weeks after his arrival in Liverpool war between England and Germany was declared and he found the perfect way to establish his identity by enlisting in the British Army. Four years later he emerged as Lieutenant Cole Wade with an unblemished war record, and what he considered to be, a bright future ahead of him.

What he needed to do now Wade decided, throwing away the half smoked cigar, was to work out how to transfer the running of this present enterprise from Lisa's hands into his own. He had noticed in the time that they had been operating out of the basin that a large proportion of the barges arriving at the quayside belonged to one 'Manton Boats,' of Leicester.

What he needed to do now Cole decided, was in the near future to take a trip to Leicester where all of his instincts told him he would find what he was looking for.

Chapter 6

'So who is doing what?'

Harry North looked enquiringly at the three men seated around the long table.

The meeting room on the first floor at Long Street had been Will Mardlin's idea and it was one that Harry approved of. Situated at the end of the corridor away from the other offices in the building, the meeting room, originally a store for old files and un-issued items of uniform and equipment, provided an excellent place to hold briefings and discuss current cases, away from inquisitive ears and the disruptions of the latest bane of Harry's life – the telephone.

Soon after the beginning of the war, Sydney Hall-Johnson had decided that it would be beneficial to have the outer stations linked to Long Street by means of a telephone system. Consequently in May of 1915 the Watch Committee was persuaded to set aside £225 from their budget, and a contractor was duly commissioned to install the necessary equipment. Initially this was, Harry had to admit a distinct advantage, as he along with other senior officers could keep track of what was happening far more efficiently. However with the passage of time and the expansion of the National Telephone Company's network, calls were now being received and made all over the town and even to other parts of the country, a situation which he felt would eventually lead to disaster as work slowed down to accommodate the demands of this latest imposition.

The daily conference at nine thirty each morning was an innovation of Harry's own since taking over as Superintendent. It served several purposes, not all of them so far as his three Detective Sergeants were concerned, totally beneficial.

Harry had for many years followed a set daily routine. Arriving at Long Street on the stroke of eight, his first stop was the charge office where he meticulously studied the details of each prisoner brought in overnight. Woe betide the Charge Sergeant who had released from custody someone who Harry wanted to speak to. Having looked through the charge book he next made a tour of the cell block, peering through the flap set at eye level in each door, checking on the occupants and exchanging a brief word with those of the many he knew.

Foxy North's morning visit to the cells was regarded by the duty Sergeant's as something of an ordeal. The problem was that North was an old hand who missed nothing, it was a regular occurrence for him to come back from the corridor, grim faced, a triumphant gleam in his eye, to inform the unfortunate Sergeant that the prisoner in one of the cells he had visited was booked in under a false name.

The visit to the charge office was followed by breakfast of coffee and cigarettes taken in his office whilst he went through the files of those overnight miscreants waiting to be charged, before finally making his way to the meeting room for 'morning conference.'

Usually lasting around a half an hour it provided the opportunity for him to allocate to the three Detective Sergeants, Bert Conway, Clarence Greasley, and Joseph Rowell, any new crime enquiries that had come in, and query with them the state of existing jobs that they were dealing with. It was this aspect that did not always sit well with the Sergeants, especially the two older men, Bert Conway and Clarrie 'Greasy' Greasley. The nature of their work led them to be secretive, closely guarding information until they could either resolve a crime or write it off. North's morning inquisition made this impossible – knowledge had to be 'declared and shared.' It also meant that the only person who could go about their daily activities undisturbed, was Harry. It was as Bert Conway on more than one occasion declared morosely, 'Foxy's Shudder Squad' - you should'er done this and you should'er done that.'

'Bert, have you and young Windram made any progress with the Lennard's job ?'

Bert Conway rubbed a meaty hand through his thinning hair, although in truth it was more an exercise in scratching his scalp. The heavy features twisted up in a scowl that gave him a remarkable resemblance to a bulldog chewing a razor blade.

'There is something wrong with this. Forty pairs of gents shoes out through the back window in the middle of the night. To get into the yard at the side, the gates had to be opened. They were padlocked when the manager left at half past six and were still padlocked when he opened up again at eight next morning. The presumption is that whoever broke in, climbed the gates, did the store room window, then chucked the shoes to an accomplice out in the street.'

'I don't think that was possible. The beat man patrols past there every twenty minutes, it doesn't leave sufficient time.'

North nodded, 'So if they didn't go out through the back they must have gone out through the front. Too many for a shop assistant to slip out with one at a time, so that leaves the manager – the person who locked up.'

This time it was Conway's turn to nod. 'I need a bit more before I put it to him. Need to see if he has got an account at the bookies, I will drop in at Freddy Goldman's during the morning.'

'*Early Doors* to beat '*Time gentlemen Please*' in the 3.30 at the Pack Horse is favourite,' chuckled Clarrie Greasley.

The others all grinned at the remark. Bert Conway was a regular at Goldman's Bookmakers in Ripley Street, and a legitimate excuse to visit the premises would not be lost on him.

'Clarrie, what about the five suits from Mansfield's?' Harry swung his attention to the portly figure of Clarrie Greasley.

'They went from the front window over the last weekend,' Greasley spread his hands in a gesture of surrender.

'Front door of the shop was forced between the beat man's visits along that stretch of property between two thirty and two forty five. Nothing to go on at all at present. Just got to wait until one of the suits turns up and then we can make a start.'

Harry tapped a pencil on the table top. 'Both jobs were done on the same night weren't they?'

It was as much a statement as a question. Conway and Greasley both knew what was coming next.

'So where were the beat men? Playing cards at Clara Beech's in the back of the Rat and Shafter? Getting their heads down in some nice warm privy? Get a grip on them for Christ's sake, if they can't see in the sodding dark then it's time they spent a bit more time on nights. Start shining their lamps on a few more villains and we might clear up some of this stuff.'

That the Superintendent was annoyed was patently obvious, it was also interesting thought Clarrie Greasley that Harry knew about the late night card sessions that took place in the back room of the beer house in Butt Close. Not that he was unduly surprised, he and Harry – Bert as well for that matter - had worked together in the detective department for the best part of twenty years, and Harry had been there a long while before that.

'Problem is, we are getting what we pay for.'

Harry allowed his gaze to settle balefully on the fourth member of the group, Joseph Rowell.

Joe worried him. He was a good copper – of that Harry was never in any doubt, it was the change in the man since he came back from the war that bothered him. Joe was a reserved and serious minded man, Harry had always put that down to his natural Celtic demeanour, but the three and a half years spent away, first in the Middle East, then later in France, had altered his outlook on life dramatically. At a time of national unrest, with the police forces across the country in a turmoil over pay and conditions, Joseph Rowell was now a man with strong political views - views which he was not frightened to voice. He was also Harry knew, a prime mover amongst the Kelsford officers in the present fight for the creation of a police union.

With the ending of the war, Sydney Hall-Johnson on the advice of Harry and Will Mardlin, increased the size of the Kelsford detective department in readiness for the inevitable crime wave that was to follow. The existing establishment of two Detective Sergeants – Bert Conway and Clarrie Greasley - was increased by the promotion of Conway's old partner on his return from the army in December 1918. With each of them partnered up by a Detective Constable this made a unit of six men, plus a Detective Inspector. Harry, when he replaced Will Mardlin, had declined the offer to appoint someone temporarily to his old position, preferring to keep hands on running of the department for himself.

He said nothing, waiting for Rowell to continue.

'If we are paying a man less than a factory hand, then we cannot expect more from him than a factory hand. Some of those men out there are tradesmen who could earn more money tomorrow back in their old jobs, and not be working nights and Sundays into the bargain.'

'That's being addressed Joe, meantime we can't let the villains walk all over us.' North did not want this line of conversation to continue, the others remained silent, Joe was a good man at his job, but he was walking a narrow line.

'What have you got on anyway? Harry wanted the meeting ended so that he could have a cigarette.

'Apart from doing some leg work for Bert on the shoe shop job, I'm tidying up the Alice Kitson enquiry, then I will be free, so let me have the next job that turns up.'

'Where are we with the Kitson woman?' Harry wondered if he should break his own rule and light up. He decided against it.

Joseph Rowell leaned back in his chair and putting his hands behind his head addressed himself to the other two sergeants.

'Alice Kitson, twenty six years of age, born 2 March 1893, her parents both died when she was a child and she was brought up in the Cottage Homes at Monckton until she was fifteen when she went to work for Oswald Kitson at his outfitters shop in the Market Place. In 1911 Kitson's wife Elizabeth died of a heart attack and six months later Alice and he were married.'

'No trace of any domestic problems – orphan girl makes good – everything normal until, on Friday 28th February this year she went out to the shops and never came back. Her clothing is all in her wardrobe. Jewellery, such as it is, still on her dressing table. No friends to speak of, nothing.'

'I have done all of the usual stuff, neighbours, railway booking office, hospitals. Missing from home posters sent out to surrounding forces. She simply vanished off the face of the earth.'

Turning to Harry he said, 'Loath as I am to give it up, I can't find a thing. There is nothing to suggest foul play, as yet I can find no trace of any third party being involved. She seems on the face of it to have exercised her right to leave home and disappear.'

'She got married to Kitson very soon after his wife's death, anything there?' Clarrie Greasley folded his hands across his ample waistcoat.

'Impossible to tell,' Rowell shook his head. 'There is no truly-truly girlfriend in whom she might have confided, and Kitson is not about to let me into his little secrets. I don't particularly like him so I would say that the answer has to be – very possibly.'

'And if there is no truly-truly friend to help us out, there is now a distinct possibility that at this very moment, someone else is shagging her, and she has moved on to pastures new.'

Bert Conway's voice was deep and gravely, in keeping with his large heavy frame, like Harry he wanted a smoke.

'Precisely, but until I can find 'something or someone,' I am going nowhere.'

'What do you want to do with it Joe?' North respected the Scotsman's judgement sufficiently to close the enquiry down if that was what he wanted. He sensed though, that was not what Rowell was looking for.

'She disappeared on Friday morning. On Saturday she was due to help out at a bring and buy sale in aid of the Monckton Cottage Homes. Thursday she went shopping and bought in flour and other stuff to do a load of baking for the bring and buy. That doesn't fit with her intending to disappear into the wind on Friday. She and Kitson lived quietly at 40 Lambert Close, no children, business is prospering, no real friends. I don't want to give it up, I just want some ideas.'

He looked around the room at the others.

'What's the age difference between her and Kitson?' asked Conway.

'He's fifty one, she is now twenty six. As I said I don't particularly like him, he is a little fat creepy sort of a bloke.'

'And the first wife?'

'Had a heart attack in the summer of 1911, nothing suspicious, I have looked at that Bert. The Doctor was Ducky Mallard, she had a previous history and just keeled over.'

Conway suppressed a burp. 'My bet is that having upgraded her status from Cottage Homes to Lambert Close, your blossoming young housewife has got fed up with being fumbled by this old fart and is off playing skin games somewhere with a new man who is more her own age.'

'Joe already knows that Bert, point is he needs some new ideas on how to prove it.' Clarence Greasley was studying the tip of a nicotine stained right index finger with which he had recently been exploring his nose.

Harry drummed his finger tips on the polished surface of the table, his need for a cigarette was becoming a deciding factor in the length of the discussion.

'Have we got a photograph of her Joe?'

Rowell fished in his inside pocket and produced a five by three postcard photograph of a tall dark haired woman wearing a wide brimmed straw hat trimmed with striped ribbon. She was dressed in a fashionable tailored dark suit, the long buttoned skirt of which ended a few inches above her ankles. A white blouse with a wide shawl collar reaching out across her shoulders completed the ensemble. At the open neck of the blouse a gold locket dangled from a thin chain.

'She's a big bugger,' exclaimed Greasley. 'You wouldn't miss her in the queue for the pictures.'

Rowell nodded, Alice Kitson was indeed a tall woman standing around five feet eleven inches in her shoes, and as his colleague said, the Station Master at Sheffield Road was hardly likely to have missed her boarding a train.

Harry North studied the picture. It was a standard studio portrait, along the bottom right hand edge of which was the name and address of the photographer – Alfred Saunt, 23 Ludgate Street, Kelsford. The back, sectioned on the left for a message to be written, and on the right for an address to which it could be sent, was blank.

'Alright,' he said finally, 'try going back and asking the man who took the picture about her.'

'It's a long shot, but we are struggling. This picture is fairly recent, it may just be possible that she didn't go to the studio on her own. It would be too much to hope that she was accompanied by a man, but she may have had a woman with her, or she may have said something to the photographer whilst he was doing the work.'

When the others had left Harry lit a Player's Navy Cut and inhaled luxuriously, releasing the smoke in a thin downwards stream away from his bushy moustache. Despite being a heavy smoker he took great pride in never having nicotine stains on his snow white whiskers or hands.

Quietly he sat and digested what had been said at the table and the feeling of disquiet which had begun earlier continued to gnaw away in his stomach. The missing woman was not a great problem, from experience he knew that it was something which would be resolved in time – there would be a break sooner or later, that was the way of things. It was the burglaries that worried him and he could not shake off the knowledge that if he was correct in what he was thinking, then he had a major problem on his hands.

Had he known it, the break in relation to the Alice Kitson case was to come much sooner than he expected.

Saunt's Photographers, in Ludgate Street was only a five minute walk from Long Street police station. Alfred Saunt the founder of the company had recently retired and sold the business on to a photographer from Chesterfield, Aldred Danson, who Joe Rowell had never met. For more years than Rowell cared to remember, Alf Saunt had worked as the photographer for Kelsford Police, appearing as if by magic at crime scenes, snapping pictures of bodies and locations, then disappearing as mystically as he had arrived. It was an accepted fact in the mess room that any forthcoming weddings, christenings, or other anniversaries could be preserved for posterity by Saunt's at particularly advantageous rates.

The entrance to number 23 was through a doorway between Bailey's Saddlers and Klein's pawn shop. Ascending the narrow stairway, Rowell was reminded of the house in which he was billeted in Boulogne whilst awaiting demobilisation from the army. After spending the greater part of the war in the Middle East, his unit had returned to Europe late in 1917 to spend the final year in northern France. Dark wall paper and an absence of carpet, footsteps ringing on polished wooden treads. It was the smells that were different. Madame Prèvost's house in Boulogne was redolent with the odours of cooking, garlic, and fresh herbs – here all that his senses picked up was the reek of furniture polish and disinfectant.

Aldred Danson answered Rowell's knock at the studio door himself. A small thin man dressed in a slightly old fashioned celluloid collar and waistcoat, Danson was in his early forties with thin sandy coloured hair cut very short and sharp pointed rodent like features. The detective introduced himself and briefly explained the purpose of his visit.

Inside, the studio was a large pleasantly furnished room with two comfortable armchairs and a settee at one end for clients to relax on whilst waiting. A cooling breeze drifted in through the open window. Arranged on a side table was an assortment of children's toys suitable for various ages to either play with whilst their parents were being photographed or for use as props when they themselves were being recorded for posterity. At the far end on a tripod stood a large cumbersome looking camera complete with a black dustsheet for the photographer to work under, in front of which were a formal set of drapes, a high backed chair and a writing desk. Dependent upon who was being pictured, one or other of these items would Rowell presumed be arranged accordingly.

Having just finished a family group, the photographer was about to begin processing the glass plates, and once the detective had explained the purpose of his visit appeared grateful for the opportunity to take a break.

'Would you like a cup of tea Sergeant?' He asked pleasantly.

Joe accepted the offer and followed the little man into a tiny side kitchen, marginally bigger than a broom cupboard. Filling a battered kettle from the tap over the sink he placed it on the single gas ring and applied a match. There was a pause for several seconds before, once the air cleared from the pipe, the gas ignited with a sharp bang.

It was the first time that he had been in the premises since before the war and the detective was surprised that so little had changed. He remembered clearly the layout of the studio from visits that he had made to collect pictures of crime scenes taken by the previous owner.

'How long have you been here Mr Danson,' he asked.

'I bought the place from Alf Saunt earlier this year,' the other man replied.

'The old boy was getting on and to be honest, the business was a bit run down. Most of the work was being done by his assistant, fellow by the name of Clifford Jarman. I need a bit of time to build it back up again, hopefully the summer will help things along – a few weddings, that sort of thing.'

Steam was jetting from the kettle in a steady stream that was causing the tiny sash window over the stone sink to cloud with condensation. The photographer tipped three large spoons full of black Maypole tea into a brown teapot from a caddy the motif on the sides of which celebrated Queen Victoria's Jubilee. Replacing the lid he returned the tin to the shelf, from where the late monarch stared down disdainfully at them.

Once the tea was mashed to his satisfaction Danson poured them each a cup, and returning to the studio they sat one at each end of a brocaded chaise longue which Rowell presumed was used as an alternative to the chair and escritoire.

The cup balanced precariously on his knee, Joe handed the photograph of Alice Kitson to Danson.

'This is the missing woman, as you can see the picture is one of yours, I was hoping that you could perhaps tell me something about her visit - was she alone, did you have any conversation with her that might shed some light on her disappearance.'

He paused, Aldred Danson was staring intently at the likeness. A trickle of excitement began to run through his body.

'Mr Danson, do you know this woman?'

Danson shook his head absently, 'No,' he replied, 'I have never met her.'

'You didn't you take this photograph then?'

Again a shake of the head, Danson's eyes were intense as he gazed at the picture of Alice Kitson.

'It was taken by my assistant, Clifford Jarman.'

Rowell sensed that he was on the brink of a discovery, the break that he needed to move his investigation forward.

'Where is Mr Jarman now?' he asked carefully, whatever was going on he needed to know what it was that Danson saw in the picture.

His tea forgotten, Aldred Danson shifted his position on the settee to face the detective. He did not appear to have heard the question.

'This photograph was taken by Cliff Jarman,' he repeated, easing a finger nervously inside the celluloid collar.

'I don't know when he took it, and I have never met the woman. Until now I hadn't the remotest idea who she was. Please, give me a minute, I have something that you need to see.'

Getting up from the settee he moved across to a door at the far side of the room and disappeared. Joe caught a fleeting glimpse of a small office, the window of which looked out onto Ludgate Street.

A minute or so later Danson returned with a large brown envelope. Sitting back down he took out a sheaf of photographs and handed them to Rowell.

The first was an enlargement of the carte postale that lay on the brocade between them. In the second, still wearing the broad brimmed hat trimmed with ribbon, Alice Kitson adopted the classic stance of a Greek goddess.

This time however, apart from the hat, she was naked.

Joe Rowell studied the picture carefully. The face staring out at him was entirely different to the serious looking woman in the dark suit and buttoned skirt.

Heavy eyebrows arched darkly over wide provocative eyes, what had previously been a severe straight mouth was half open, full lips raised in a sensuous, enigmatic smile.

In the second pose, hat gone, the hair was now unpinned and flowed in a dark cascade over her shoulders, this time leaning with an arm on the back of the chair, the left leg was lifted invitingly, her foot placed on the seat.

There were ten photographs in all, each becoming progressively more explicit.

Some were taken on the chaise longue upon which they were now seated. Alice laying recumbent, arm above her head to reveal a splash of dark underarm hair, Alice kneeling on the couch, smiling lewdly over her shoulder into the camera. In the last, which was obviously intended as a finale, she was straddling the studio chair, open legged, smoking a cigarette.

'So where is Clifford Jarman now ?' asked Rowell.

Danson exhaled a long deep breath. 'Gone I am afraid, he left soon after Christmas. At the time I was not that bothered. I inherited him with the business, and to be honest Mr Rowell, he was not that good.' He gave a small self-conscious smile and tapped the stack of photographs laying between them. 'Even these are technically speaking, not top quality.'

'Just after Christmas he told me that he had been offered a partnership with a man in Yarmouth. It's not unusual in this trade for photographers to move around to gain experience, and seaside trade is always good. In the winter, hotels want pictures taking so that they can have a stock of cards ready for the holidaymakers to send to their relatives, and in the summer months it is a case of setting up your camera on the sea front and happy snapping couples walking past. They pay you one and sixpence in return for a numbered ticket, then collect their holiday photo next day from the studio.'

'I just got a feeling that there was a bit more to it than that. Cliff was a single man who liked the ladies, and I wondered if he had got himself in somewhere a bit deeper than he intended.'

'Why did you think that?' Joe Rowell studied the man intently.

'He gave his notice in very quickly, said that he wanted to leave at the end of the week, it was just slightly strange.'

'And you think that he was involved with the woman in the pictures – Alice Kitson?' asked the detective.

Danson shrugged, picking up the prints, toying with them absently. 'That I don't know. These are primarily erotica – the sort of work that comes from Paris and Prague. The thing is, she is displaying to him – not to the camera – trust me Sergeant, I am a photographer, this woman is putting on a show for the man behind the camera, it is in her expression, in her eyes.'

'Then why,' asked Rowell, 'would he leave them behind when he left?'

Remembering his tea, Aldred Danson picked up the cup and saucer from where he had placed them on the floor, and took a sip of the now luke warm liquid.

'That is simple. It was mid-winter and the weather was freezing. On the Wednesday night we had a pipe burst in the loft and the ceiling over the stairs from the entrance collapsed. I came in about half past seven in the morning, and by half past eight I had got a plumber here sorting things out. In order to do that, Mr Norman - the plumber – blocked off the stairs so no one could go up or down.'

'When Cliff came in at nine o'clock, I told him that as we could not work, and as he only had one more day of his notice to serve, he could finish a day early, anything personal that he wanted from upstairs he could come back and collect the next week. He was very unhappy about that but had no choice. He went off back home and I never saw or heard from him again.'

'When did you find these?' Joe pointed to the pictures.

Danson raised his eyebrows and looked towards the ceiling. 'He left at the end of February, I cleared the cupboards out a couple of weeks after, so it would be the middle of March.'

'Mr Danson, can you tell me the exact date when you last saw Clifford Jarman,' Rowell was fairly certain that he already knew the answer.

'Yes,' replied the photographer, 'It was Thursday, 27th February.'

'Jarman left Danson's employment the day before Alice Kitson disappeared.'

Joseph Rowell waited for a reaction. Harry North steepled his fingers under his chin and continued to examine the photographs spread out on the desk in front of him. Whatever the significance of the pictures he had to concede that Alice Kitson was an attractive woman.

Dark wavy hair framing thick sculpted eyebrows leading down through a long straight nose to a heavy square chin, gave her a strong face which was unexpectedly softened by the almost coquettish smile playing around her lips. Although tall for a woman she was he thought well proportioned. The heavy breasts were firm with large darkly circled nipples, her waist narrow, giving onto ample hips and long straight legs. She was he noticed, still wearing the gold locket.

'Why did he take the pictures?' It was almost a rhetorical question, as if Harry was talking to himself.

Rowell's face took on a thoughtful expression, it was he knew a very relevant question.

Harry waved him to take the easy chair that faced his desk. Reaching in his top drawer he pulled out a new packet of Players, and taking one proffered them.

Rowell shook his head and Harry remembered that having been gassed in the latter months of the war the big man no longer smoked.

Replacing the cigarettes, North picked up a box of Salmon & Glückstein's Vestas. Dragging a match along the side of the box, he wondered not for the first time why such a simple commodity should have such a pretentious name.

'Let's think about this,' he continued.

'Clifford Jarman is having an affair with Alice Kitson. He persuades her to take her clothes off and do a few nifty poses in front of the camera. The thing is, did he do it for his own, or their mutual gratification - or had he something else in mind.'

'Jarman was intending to go to Yarmouth for the summer season. These,' he waved a hand at the pasteboards laid out on the desk, 'are all 'naughty nineties' stuff... and 'naughty nineties' were intended for sale. Usually came in from the Continent, but not always. Were there any plates?'

Rowell shook his head, Aldred Danson had already made a thorough search of the cupboards and there were none. 'No, and if the ceiling hadn't collapsed the day before he was due to leave, these would not have been there either.'

Harry stroked his moustache with a finger.

'It would be interesting to see if any more married ladies have been playing 'Dolly Dimple,' for our 'Mr Flash.' Perhaps this is just the tip of the iceberg. Perhaps he has been shagging one or two more of the town's best, and making a collection of bedtime jollies to take to the seaside with him and sell on the front to selected clients.'

Rowell made a gesture with his hand, indicating that he had not finished.

'More important though, Alice Kitson had become a nuisance – I spoke to a mate of Jarman's.'

North took a deep draw on his cigarette and waited for him to continue.

Secure in the knowledge that he now had a positive new lead, Rowell questioned Aldred Danson about his assistant's associates. It seemed that his closest friend was a young man by the name of Peter Jennings who worked at Mason's grocery store further down the road.

A two minute walk from the studio brought him to the shop. It was a large old fashioned double fronted establishment, the windows stacked with hams, and tins of cooked meats. On entering he was struck by the heavy atmosphere inside, redolent with a mixture of bacon, and cheeses. Several young men in ankle length white aprons were engaged in stacking shelves or serving one or other of the half dozen middle aged women who were stocking up with their week's provisions.

Five minutes later, after a brief conversation with the manager he found himself in a small upstairs room marginally bigger than the one at Danson's studio, which served as a meal room for the staff.

Seating himself down on one of the four kitchen chairs set at a plain deal table, he took out a stiff backed notebook and laying a pencil alongside it on the smooth surface sat back.

Rowell did not have to wait long before the sound of slow uneven footsteps mounting the stair boards caught his ear.

Peter Jennings was a thin young man barely turned twenty, with a pasty complexion and a bad case of acne. Joe Rowell's first question – why Jennings had not been conscripted into the army - was immediately answered, the young man wore a heavy black surgical boot on his right foot. Aldred Danson had told him that the reason Cliff Jarman was not in the army was because had been discharged in April 1915 after being wounded in France.

Jennings was very obviously nervous about being questioned by the policeman, and stood rubbing his hands along the edges of his apron. Rowell noticed that there were dark stains on the armpits of his shirt above the long green cotton grocer's over-sleeves held at the elbows by elastic.

'Sit down Peter,' he said indicating the chair opposite him.

Jennings pulled out the chair and did as he was instructed, perching on the edge of the seat, his body stiff.

'I want to talk to you about your friend Cliff Jarman.' Rowell watched the youth's reaction. He remained tense, eyes wary.

Good, very good, thought Rowell. He knows something. His reaction should have been one of relief that this visit was not about him, and that he was not in trouble, instead it was still one of apprehension.

'Where is Cliff now Peter.' The tone was calm, no emotion, neither friendly nor hostile.

'I don't know Sir,' the words tumbled out. 'I haven't heard from him since he left Mr Danson.'

'Cliff is in a lot of trouble,' the detective scratched his pencil on the notepad as if making a note of the denial.

Beads of sweat broke out on Jennings' forehead, the patch on his shirt deepened and spread.

'Perhaps you don't know where he is now – we will see about that later. However, you were his friend, so you can tell me one or two other things that I need to know.'

Licking his lips the youth stared at him like a rabbit cornered by a fox.

'Did Cliff have a lady friend?' Joe held Jennings eyes.

'I don't know Sir,' despite his desire to break contact with the big man's gaze, Peter Jennings was physically unable to look away.

'Yes you do Peter.' Joseph Rowell gave his quarry a quiet smile, the deep Scottish burr became softer, 'I will tell you why you do.'

'I told you that Cliff is in a lot of trouble, and you haven't asked me what sort of trouble, which means that you already know. So before you also get into a lot of trouble yourself, I think that you had better tell me exactly what you know about Cliff and about his lady friends.'

The sweat was running into the young man's collar, tears of fear began to trickle down his cheeks.

'I want to know about the pictures Peter.'

Perfect timing. For a moment he thought the lad was going to be sick, then his shoulders convulsed as the tears burst into a flood.

Rowell waited face impassive, until the sobbing eventually slowed to a halt, and Peter Jennings wiped his eyes on his apron and composed himself.

'The pictures Peter.'

Jennings nodded. 'Cliff had a spare key to the studio. He used to take them on a Thursday afternoon when the shop was closed for half day.'

'How many girls did he take pictures of?'

Jennings swallowed hard, 'about four or five,' he said miserably, voice little more than a whisper.

'Which is it - four or five?' The tone was clipped now, pointed.

'Five Sir,' the answer was almost inaudible.

'Were you there hiding, watching whilst he took them?'

'No,' I was never there Sir, it was nothing to do with me. Cliff showed me them later round at my digs. He used to bring them round for me to have a look.'

Rowell pondered a moment. Jennings was not lying, he did not have the nerve for that. Jarman took the photographs, then ever the voyeur, he could not resist showing them to his mate, it was a form of bragging.

'What do you know about this woman?' He laid the first picture of Alice Kitson on the table and turned it round to face Jennings.

The young man barely glanced at the nude figure, as if the act of looking at her would be sufficient to tip him over the edge of the abyss on which he was teetering .

'Alice ... that's Alice,' the words were barely audible, throat so dry that his tongue was glued into the roof of his mouth, face the colour of the fat on the bacon that he served downstairs.

Rowell remained silent, gazing into his eyes, allowing the tension to build. After almost half a minute, looking as if he were about to pass out, Peter Jennings filled the silence.

'It was because of her that Cliff left. He used to take the pictures, then they would have sex, but she got very serious and wouldn't leave him alone. She started to turn up at the studio when he wasn't expecting her. Then she said she was in love with him and was going to leave her husband. Cliff wasn't having any of that. He was going to go to Yarmouth at the beginning of the summer anyway, but he decided that he needed to get away from her before her husband found out, so he gave in his notice and went just after Christmas. He told her that he would get somewhere for them to live in Yarmouth and send for her, but he wasn't going to, he just wanted to get away.'

'Where did he go to in Yarmouth?'

The tongue flicked over dry lips. 'I think he was going to work at a studio on the front, but I am not sure where, I never knew the name of the place.'

'Where are your copies Peter?' the voice was soft.

The change of tack caught Jennings unaware, 'I haven't got …'

'Don't piss me about sonny!' The young man physically started back in his chair as if he had been struck. Anger flared across Joseph Rowell's face.

'Jarman gave you copies of the photographs - didn't he?'

Frightened at the detective's sudden change of mood, Peter Jennings glanced to left and right, once more the rabbit and the fox, before nodding his head, a look of desperation on his face.

'Where are they?' This had been easier than Rowell could have hoped, and he wanted to close the interview now.

'At my digs Sir.'

'Bring them to me at Long Street police station within the next hour. I will then decide whether or not you, as well as Cliff Jarman are 'in a lot of trouble,' and what I intend to do about it.'

Rowell reached into his other pocket and laid down a second set of photographs, these unlike the large prints of Alice Kitson were the standard postcard size.

Harry picked them up and examined each one carefully. There ten, two each of four different women and two of the Kitson pictures. They were all a variation on a theme, erotic poses, the furniture and back cloth the same in each – Aldred Danson's studio.

The women had one thing in common, they were all young and had voluptuous bodies. It was the faces that Harry was primarily interested in. Three of the four he knew, two were local prostitutes and the third the barmaid at the Golden Eagle in Lenton Street.

Arranging them in order alongside the larger prints he tapped the three he knew with his finger, 'Lottie Sharpe - bangs for a shilling, Susan Myers – works the railway station on Sheffield Road, and Maria Daley from the Eagle. Two pros' and a barmaid who does a bit when she is short of the rent. Not much in the way of a challenge there, they would all have paid him to take their pics for advertising purposes.'

Joe Rowell gave a grin, he only knew Myers and Daley by sight. Trust Foxy to be able to add to the list.

'Any guesses on the last one?' asked North.

Joe shook his head, 'no, looks as if she might be halfway respectable though.'

He indicated the image of a slim well proportioned woman in her late twenties who was standing by the studio escritoire beckoning seductively with one hand whilst the fingers of the other were splayed across her crutch.

Harry gave him a sceptical look before returning to his study of the photograph. 'Half way respectable' did not he thought cover what the young woman was obviously offering, however he had to agree her face was less coarse than the others, and despite the nature of the picture, her demeanour did have something different about it. Taking a magnifying glass from his desk draw he examined the picture more closely.

'Difficult to tell,' he murmured, 'she could be a redhead, other than that nothing, no rings no jewellery, but if you look closely, she has got a mole near her left eye.'

Taking the glass from him, Rowell studied the photograph closely. The mole was about an inch below the corner of the woman's eye and barely detectable without the aid of the magnifier.

He handed the glass back to Harry who, returning it to the drawer sat back in his chair, marshalling his thoughts.

'Go and see the girls - usual thing, put the frighteners on them then get statements about their involvement. Send a telegram to Yarmouth - we locate Jarman and we find Alice Kitson – or at least find out what happened to her.'

Rowell nodded in agreement. 'I will telephone the local police, get them to do all of the photographic studios along the front.' He hoped that North had not picked up his amendment to the telegram suggestion.

Harry glared at him. 'Whatever. And Joe, keep those photos under lock and key, I don't want word of this getting around the station – you know what coppers are, they will be like flies round a privy.'

As Rowell was about to leave, Harry said suddenly, 'whilst I think about it, you said this morning that you have done some leg work for Clarrie on his burglary, what was that?

Joe paused in the doorway and turned to reply.

'I took some stolen property leaflets out to the dealers. Went over to that new warehouse on the canal.'

'Who is running it?' asked the Superintendent.

'Woman named Abbott,' he replied, 'I think she's a widow, got some blokes working for her and a manager, a Yank. All seems straight enough.'

Harry nodded thoughtfully, his eyes on the plum coloured silk tie tucked neatly into the Sergeant's waistcoat.

Chapter 7

The room was becoming perceptibly lighter. Harry turned over restively and looked at the woman laying on her side next to him. He and Laura had been together for over twenty years now. At first, after her husband was killed it had been simply as landlady and lodger, then with the progression of time they became first lovers then later in love. Harry acknowledged that over the years he had strayed. He had always liked women, not just for their bodies – he appreciated their minds as well, and accepted the fact that a clever woman was almost without exception cleverer than a man. Laura was clever, although she chose not to display the fact. Her Scottish upbringing led her to be retiring, appearing shy when in fact she was not. After her husband Frank was killed nineteen years ago in the railway accident, Laura Percival reconciled herself to spending the rest of her days quietly as a widow and had taken Harry as a lodger purely to eek out her meagre funds. For his part North had never set out to take advantage of his landlady - he did not need to - seven years older than the young widow, one thing the debonair Harry was rarely short of was female company.

They had slipped into a more intimate relationship almost by accident. It was the second anniversary of Frank's death and in an attempt to take her mind off of the day, North booked a table for two at the Marlborough Hotel on Derby road. Never one to stint on a lady, the evening's meal of duck à l'orange accompanied as befitted by good French wine, was a quiet success. Despite her lodger's reputation, Laura seemed to appreciate the true sentiment behind his gesture, and as the food and wine achieved what Harry had hoped it would, she talked quietly of her feelings of loss and loneliness, and her desolation at what the future held.

When they returned soon after midnight to the house at 5 Tennyson Street, Harry knew instinctively that if he made an advance it would not be rejected.

That was not what he wanted, it would have rendered the entire evening pointless. He wanted to ease the pain at the loss of her husband, not complicate matters in a way that they both would later regret. At the top of the stairway he gave her a quiet kiss on the cheek, and turned into his own bedroom, closing the door behind him.

The following night, about twenty minutes after he turned down the gas light and settled into his bed, the door opened quietly, and without a word Laura slipped beneath the covers beside him.

Since that night they had lived together as man and wife without the formal ties of marriage to bind them together. Both were easy in the relationship and it had never really occurred to them to marry. Speculation, especially at Long Street, had for nearly twenty years been rife as to what their true relationship was, but Laura had no close female friends who might enquire, and it was a brave man who would have dared broach the subject with Harry.

Absently he laid his hand on her thigh, the light summer night dress had ridden up above her waist and he slid his hand into the curve of her back. She moved restively then turning began to snore gently. Harry removed his hand and turning restlessly towards the window resumed his study of the light that was creeping across the night sky through the gap in the bedroom curtain.

It must he thought be around four o'clock, he had been awake for about an hour. Not without reason was this called the dead of night. It was the time that the body was at it's lowest ebb, the time when, working nights it was difficult to stay awake, and when at home in bed almost impossible to sleep. The time when death visited the weak and vulnerable, more people passed quietly from one world to another during this hour of the night than at any other.

His mind returned to the disquieting thoughts that had woken him in the first place and prevented him from sleeping since. However he tried to avoid the conclusion, there was only one solution to the recent burglaries at Lennard's shoe shop and Mansfield's outfitters. The gates to the yard at Lennard's were padlocked and secure. The front door of Mansfield's had been forced and the shop window emptied. It was not just a matter of the theft, the goods, once stolen had afterwards to be removed from the scene. In both cases a vehicle would have been required – a motor van at least. There was not time for the break-ins to have taken place and for the goods to be spirited away before the policeman working the beat made his rounds. A vehicle driving through the deserted streets – two vehicles if they were separate robberies, in the dead of night could not have passed through the town unnoticed - yet no one saw anything. The only logical conclusion was that the crimes had been committed with the connivance of the night duty police officers.

He thought about Joe Rowell's assertion that you only got what you paid for. The Constables were on subsistence wages – 26/- a week, and as Rowell pointed out, a man could earn more than that driving a tramcar. Men such as Joseph Rowell, fresh back from the war were no longer prepared to work for such a pittance. The moves for the formation of a Police and Prison Officers Union were becoming a serious impedance to the functioning of police forces all over the country. The question that Harry was asking himself was, had things come to such a state that policemen were now participating in crime. Here in Kelsford, were the men who he had worked with over the years become so desperate as to become corrupt.

A faint shaft of light was now visible through the curtain. The sleepy voice next to him broke his train of thought.

'What are you thinking about?'

'Nothin love, I just can't sleep.'

Laura was not put off, fully awake now she snuggled closer to him. She knew that when Harry lay awake at night it was rarely so simple as the fact that he could not get to sleep. 'Do you want me to go down and get us a drink?' she asked.

'No,' he replied, 'I think that I will get up, make an early start.'

Slipping into the main building at Long Street through the stable yard Harry made his way up the back stairs and let himself into his office. Glancing at the clock on the wall he saw that it was five thirty. He decided against going down to the charge office and making an unexpected visit to the cells, that could wait until later, no point in advertising the fact that he could not sleep.

Picking through the pile of papers on his desk the first thing that caught his eye was a neatly penned message on a half sheet of buff coloured paper. The writing was Eric Broughton's.

The note immediately sent Harry's train of thought off on a tangent. Until earlier in the year Eric had been the station office boy, however on his seventeenth birthday in March, he was elevated to the position of assistant to the administration manager - a man to whom, despite the fact that he had only been with the force some three and a half months, Harry North had taken an instant and abiding dislike.

Precedent demanded that the position of force administration manager should always be held by a serving Inspector, usually one who was in the latter days of his service and had earned a well deserved break from the stresses of street duties. Consequently when Caldwell Frazer retired in February of that year and left to tend his roses, the expectation was that the job would go to

Alfred Tedder, who after twenty two years with the force was Frazer's natural successor.

However Sydney Hall-Johnson had other ideas and persuaded the Watch Committee to appoint an old army crony, Captain Montagu Parfitt to the position, making Eric his assistant. To say that Harry did not like the Chief Constable's choice of candidate was an understatement. Totally ignoring his situation as a civilian, Parfitt had from the outset considered himself to be of equal standing to the Inspectors in the force, and having discovered that Harry held his position of Superintendent on a temporary basis, placed him in the same category. His attitude to the rank and file Constables and Sergeants was much that which he would have adopted to other ranks in an army barracks – total disdain.

He would, Harry had already decided, have to go. How and when, he had not as yet worked out, but sooner rather than later, Montagu Parfitt would be departing, courtesy of Harry North.

Picking up the note he glanced at the neatly penned message.

'Supt., Mardlin telephoned. He is arriving Kelsford on Thursday and would like to speak with you. Could you meet him at his house at 2.pm please. E. Broughton.

What, wondered Harry was bringing Will up from London? Thursday was tomorrow, so he would soon find out. Meantime there were one or two things he needed to do today once the sun was up and the streets aired.

The towpath was dry underfoot and easy to follow, later in the year when the weather changed and it was soaked with rain or worse still snow, the heavy towing horses that tramped along dragging the barges through the muddy brown waters, would churn it into a quagmire making it difficult to maintain a safe footing.

It was one of the hottest summers for a long while. There had to be some compensation North reflected for the horrendous winter that they had endured along with the killer flu epidemic that had ravaged not only England but the entire Continent. In a newspaper report he had read it was estimated that worldwide in excess of twenty million people had died, which he seriously doubted. Kelsford however had been lucky insomuch that the death toll had been relatively low at around fifty.

He paused to light a cigarette and take stock of his surroundings. At present there were no barges in sight, and none had passed him since he got onto the towpath at Bridge 64.

It was years since he had been down here, and he was surprised how little the waterway had changed. Taking a draw on the cigarette Harry spent a long while gazing at the old bridge, lost in thought. Over thirty years ago a man named Eddie Donnelly had been murdered under the bridge by one of his accomplices in a payroll robbery. It was the start of Harry's career as a detective. A young beat man he was taken out of uniform to help with the enquiries into the activities of the Fenian gang responsible for the robbery. Faces, long forgotten flashed through his mind. Joseph Langley, the Detective Inspector whose job North now had. Joe Langley had been an absolute bastard, but he knew his trade. Ruefully Harry wondered if he was thought of in the same terms. You had to do the job to understand it he thought.

Tom Norton who succeeded Langley, Jesse Squires, the Detective Sergeant who he had worked with until Jesse took over as Detective Inspector when Norton retired. Henry Farmer and Joel Dexter, both killed by the Irish brotherhood, the one dumped in a ditch to be found by two passing schoolboys, the other gunned down at the Town Locks less than a mile from where he was standing.

Throwing the cigarette stub into the water, North turned to continue along the narrow pathway towards the bend that concealed the canal basin warehouses from view. Joe Rowell thought that the new occupants of the renovated main building were alright. What was it he had said, '... *a woman named Abbott - got some blokes working for her and a manager - a Yank. All seems straight enough....*' Harry was not so certain, it was a matter of instinct, but he had decided to have a look for himself.

Approaching the bend he was surprised to be confronted by a tri-coloured collie dog standing in the middle of the path eyeing him. The dog, ears back and head down stood four square, front legs wide apart defying him to attempt to pass.

Harry stopped a few feet from the animal and dropped down onto his haunches.

'Hello dog,' he said quietly, holding out his hand palm downwards for inspection. The dog did not move, tail down it continued to study him warily.

North locked his eyes onto the animal's and held it's gaze steadily. It was he saw in very good condition with bright eyes and a sleek well brushed coat, her tri-coloured markings – he knew instinctively that it was a bitch – were particularly attractive, a black body with snow white ruff and blaze down the front of her face set off by tan coloured legs and white paws.

Very slowly he sat down on the hard ground, the hand still held out, his eyes were now on a level with her's. 'So what's the problem,' he asked in the same soft voice.

The ears were no longer laid flat and a quizzical look had come into the brown eyes, the detective knew that he was winning. Although he had spent the last thirty years in Kelsford town, Harry was a country lad by birth, born and brought up in the nearby village of Somerton where his father had owned the one and only general store. If there was one thing, other than police work that Harry knew about, it was dogs.

Still maintaining eye contact, North slowly withdrew his hand and reached into his jacket pocket. When he pulled it out again he was holding a peppermint humbug. This time when the hand reached out the palm was upturned with the sweet in it.

Slowly the bitch moved towards him and cautiously sniffed his fingers, he remained stock still hardly breathing, the wet muzzle pressed against his palm as the humbug was accepted. Putting his other hand out now, he gently touched her head just behind the right ear and caressed the silky fur, the dog did not protest as he ran his hand across the top of her head.

'Very good,' the woman's voice was cold and flat. 'She doesn't like strangers, I was hoping she would bite you.'

Harry continued to stroke the dog's head whilst she noisily crunched the candy into fragments.

'Hello Lisa,' he said without looking up, 'I heard Nobby Armstrong was dead and the light of his life had gone missing.'

'Things move on,' she retorted, 'another twenty yards and you are on private property – and you aren't welcome, so turn around and piss off, come on Gyp!' The dog immediately turned and went to stand by her.

Harry eased his position as if he were going to stand up, but instead put himself into a kneeling position, looking at Lisa Abbott.

It was the first time that he had seen her since the morning of Frank Kempin's arrest. She was he thought, still a very attractive young woman and had obviously come on somewhat since her days in Mansfield Street.

'If I do that Lisa I won't be able to sort your dog's tics out for her, and chances are she will finish up with blood poisoning.'

It was not the response the woman was expecting and for a moment she was at a loss for words.

'What are you on about?' she demanded suspiciously. Lisa knew Harry North and did not trust him an inch.

Harry made a small thin whistling sound between his teeth, and the dog's had came up sharply. 'Gyp, come here love,' he said in the same soft voice that he had used previously when speaking to her, inwardly gleeful that he now knew the bitches name.

Obediently the collie trotted back to him.

Ignoring Lisa's look of annoyance, he put his face close to the dog's and spoke to her very quietly in a reassuring voice, the woman could not make out he was saying but it was obvious to her that this was a different man to the one who she remembered from their last meeting.

Parting the hair on the top of the animals head with the fingers of one hand he displayed a dark red protrusion sticking about half an inch out of the dog's skull.

'They are a parasite that dogs pick up from sheep and deer. They burrow their head into the flesh, bloat themselves with the animal's blood and after a day or so drop off. Problem is they can give the animal blood poisoning – especially if you don't get them out properly.'

Feeling around inside her thick ruff he grunted, 'As I thought, there are a couple more in here.

Lisa peered closely at the torpedo like parasite embedded in Gyp's head.

'You say that you can get it out?' there was concern in her voice, the animosity towards the policeman temporarily set aside.

'Oh yes,' he replied. 'I need some gin and a pair of thin nosed pliers.'

Half an hour later, on the loading bay outside of the warehouse he stood smoking a cigarette and gazing speculatively at the two hundred yards of water running down to the main stretch of canal just out of sight around the bend. It was here in one of the feeder tunnels under the waterline that had been dug to provide an interchange of water between the basin and the main canal system, that Henry Farmer had been murdered by Connor Devlin.

Farmer was a Detective Sergeant, and in truth he and North never got on, but reflected Harry he was good at what he did, and certainly did not deserve to have his brains blown out by that bastard and then dumped in a ditch out at Spilsby. And now something else was going on at the basin - there had to be if Lisa Abbott was involved - just what it was he did not know, but he was certainly going to find out.

'The fact that you have sorted my dog doesn't mean that you are welcome here.'

Lisa was standing next to him and he was once again aware that whatever her history, she was a desirable young woman.

Flicking the cigarette end into the muddy brown water Harry ignored the remark and said, 'you know what to do next time?'

She nodded following his gaze along the canal. 'Pour gin onto the bug, leave it for about ten minutes until it releases its grip, then twist and pull with the pliers – and you are still not welcome.'

Harry gave her one of his most charming smiles and touched the fingers of his right hand first to his lips, then to her forehead.

'I'll see you again soon Lisa,' he said, then turned and strolled off back along the towing path towards Kelsford.

Lisa Abbott watched the slim figure, looking somewhat out of place in his elegant light grey summer suit, as he turned the bend and was lost to sight in the overhanging trees.

From experience she knew that the detective was ruthless and clever – a dangerous combination. When Frank Kempin was arrested by the local police in Leicester, North was one of the detectives who came from Kelsford to collect him and to search her house in Mansfield Street. One of the other policeman at the house was Nathan Cleaver who was responsible for having her falsely charged with the theft of some money from a previous employer. The man in charge of the raid, Superintendent Mardlin made a deal with her that in return for her showing him where Frank was hiding some postal orders, he would give to her a letter exonerating her from the charges. It was this that had enabled her to come back to Kelsford with a clean pair of heels.

Mardlin and North for their own reasons wanted to get rid of Cleaver and later that morning North had returned to Mansfield Street to make her a proposition. If she gave him a statement alleging that when Cleaver arrested her over the money, he had raped her in the police station, then she could get her own back on the detective and North could put him out of a job.

That statement she reflected was North's mistake. She knew from the minute that she gave it to him that if Inspector North was prepared to bend the rules one way, then she could persuade him to bend them the other. Sooner or later he would be useful to her.

A movement caused her to look down, Gyp was standing next to her brushing her leg.

'Come on you bloody traitor,' she said running her hand along the dog's back affectionately, 'let's take a walk.'

Back in town, North consulted his pocket watch – he flatly refused to wear one of the new style wristwatches – and saw that it was almost twelve o'clock. During the twenty minute walk back to Bridge 64 his mind had been busy. According to Palmer Osborne, the Detective Inspector at Leicester, prior to Nobby Armstrong's death in the flu epidemic, Lisa Abbott had not been seen in the town for sometime. There were various rumours, the favourite being that with a turf war impending, Nobby had entrusted Lisa to be his banker and at the time of his death she was away setting something up.

Harry thought this was a distinct possibility and one which would account for Lisa having access to the funds that were now being fed into the warehouse.

Logically with the location of the premises, combined with the cargoes that were passing by on a daily basis, whatever she was involved in must be related to the movement of goods. Therefore the probability was that she was fencing stolen property passing along the canal. The fact that electric lighting had been installed on the outside of the main building to enable loading and unloading after dark had not escaped his notice.

It all fitted in. He would run checks on the men working for her and would be surprised if they came up bright and shiny. The American who was working as her manager definitely answered the description of a man posing as an army officer, circulated by both Leeds and Bradford forces as being wanted for hotel frauds.

North's thoughtful demeanour deepened. The American – if in fact he was American, he could he supposed be a Canadian – had appeared at the office door with a query whilst Harry was removing one of the tics from Gyp's neck. He was North noted, wearing a dark blue silk tie with a narrow black design running through it, identical to that on the red one that Joe Rowell had taken to wearing.

Turning off of the High Street he made his way through a series of back streets and twisting lanes until he was in a small suburb on the opposite edge of the town. Turning into a tiny pub on the corner of Watt Street he immediately spotted, seated in a corner reading a copy of the Daily Mirror, the man he was looking for.

Lewis Arthur was a slightly built man for a policeman, his hair had over the years turned from light blond to silver grey, which parted precisely down the centre, had not in the process lost any of its thickness. The pale watery blue eyes peering at Harry through the half rimmed spectacles that he wore when off duty, were the only clue to his addiction to drink. It never ceased to amaze Harry that despite the copious amounts of beer Lew consumed, he never gained a pound in weight.

Twenty years ago when detectives were all Sergeants, they had worked together out of the first floor office at Long Street. He was one of the few men Harry trusted implicitly. There were those who maintained that Sergeant Arthur was an alcoholic, others that he was simply a character. Whichever was true, his capacity for drink was legendary, he could find beer at any hour of the night or day, and it rarely impaired his working ability. Harry now needed his help.

Purchasing two pints of Starbright, North took a seat at the table opposite to Arthur.

'Morning Harry,' the eyes held an enquiring look. 'What are you after?'

North smiled, 'Morning Lew, I was passing and thought it would be nice to drop in at the Trooper and have a pint with you.'

94

Lew Arthur returned the smile and drained the pint pot in front of him before picking up the one that North had brought to the table.

'In that case, nice to see you, cheers. Now, what are you after.'

Harry sighed and leaned forward confidentially. 'I need a bit of advice.'

Arthur removed his spectacles and touched the end of one of the arms to his lower lip, 'Last time you asked me for advice, you were knocking off that barmaid from the Black Horse and wondered if I thought you should go and have a word with Ducky Mallard.'

Harry glared at him. It was twenty years since he had been involved with Sarah Day and after certain details of her previous history came to light, Lew Arthur had found Harry's concern for his personal wellbeing extremely amusing.

'I'm buying the beer – stop pissing about.' He noticed that the Starbright glass was already half empty.

'Alright, I'm listening.' Folding the newspaper Arthur set it to one side.

Harry talked for the next ten minutes, then signalled to the middle aged landlady behind the bar for two more pints.

Lew Arthur stared steadily into his beer for a few moments, then transferred his gaze to a point somewhere on the wall behind Harry's head before returning to look once more at his old colleague.

' There is talk,' he said quietly.

'Two burglaries on the same night. Must have been a vehicle used at both of them. Time it must have taken for each job to be pulled, plus noise and coming and going, it should have been impossible for the beat man to miss either never mind both.'

'Trouble is Harry, there is so much dissension and unrest at present it is almost impossible to say who might be at it. The two men on the beats when Lennard's and Mansfield's were done were Ben Gunn and Bradley Green. Both twenty year men, both of them essentially uniform carriers. Idle bastards who are now serving their time out. Night Sergeant was Charlie O'Keefe, again twenty years service, waiting to see his time out. If Ben Gunn and Brad Green were involved then he had to be as well.'

North nodded and lit a Player he did not bother offering them to the other man, Arthur had never smoked.

He knew the three men well. Fred Gunn, better known as 'Ben' from Robert Louis Stevenson's character in the novel Treasure Island, and Brad Green were both at the end of their service and devoted most of their energies to avoiding any suggestion of work. Charlie O'Keefe, prior to being promoted to Sergeant ten years previously had been a detective. North, like Lew Arthur did not rate him highly.

'I know the men Lew, I know what I think. I want to know whether I am right or not.'

An hour and two more pints later, Harry North took his leave of Arthur to make his way back to his office. After he had gone, the newspaper forgotten, Lew Arthur sat for some time in deep thought. Should he have told Harry what he suspected was going on, or should he wait until he had proof? He would wait he decided, check something out first and then talk to Harry again.

Cole Wade tidied up the papers on Lisa's desk and took a quick look around to ensure that he had left no trace of his search of the office.

Lisa was out walking Gyp and could be back at any moment. Although Cole was not averse to dogs in general, the collie had taken a distinct dislike to him, and the almost permanent presence of the irascible canine meant that opportunities to have a look around were rare. Although she was careful never to leave her desk drawers or the filing cabinet next to the back wall unlocked, he had still been able to glean bits of information from overheard telephone conversations, and the invoices that accompanied the legitimate cargoes that came in. Since dumping the body in the lime kiln, Wade had redoubled his efforts to discover exactly how Lisa was sourcing the cargoes that were being brought to the warehouse. Without that knowledge he had no means of achieving his prime objective - to supplant Lisa in what was obviously a highly lucrative enterprise.

He was he felt, almost there. A couple of days previously he had overheard her on the telephone discussing a forthcoming drop. She used the name 'Gil' several times during the conversation which confirmed his suspicions about Gilbert Manton's involvement. A chat with Mr Manton was he felt, becoming more and more pressing. That the setup was being run reasonably well by Lisa he had no doubt, but it was not a job for a woman. If he convinced Manton that it was in his best interest to replace her, Cole was convinced that he could double the amount of stolen property being handled and cut a much larger slice of the cake for himself.

He was on the point of leaving when the strident jangling of the telephone bell startled him. Hesitating a moment before lifting the earpiece from it's cradle, he picked up the speaking trumpet of the candlestick telephone. There was silence at the other end for several seconds before a man's voice said quietly, 'Good morning Mr Wade'.

'Who's calling?' the response was far from automatic. Whoever was ringing had expected him not Lisa, to pick up the telephone, so they must know that she was out with the dog.

'At the present, it doesn't matter who is calling Mr Wade, there are certain things that you and I need to discuss'.

The voice, deep and muffled, was difficult for Wade to place, he waited in silence for the caller to continue.

'Excellent, no silly questions or protests'. I have a job for you to do – one for which you are eminently qualified'.

'And if I am not interested in your *job*?' Wade was trying hard to find something about the voice that he could identify.

'Oh you will be interested, and even if you are not you will do it. Let us say that your personal situation is very much in question at the present time. A telephone call to, say the police in Leeds or Bradford, would solve one or two small matters that they are investigating concerning some unpaid hotel bills… the railway police would love to identify the 'American Captain' who has been taking money from passengers in bent card games… and then of course there are the activities that brought you to this country in the first place…'

The voice trailed off leaving a pregnant silence.

'Alright, you have my attention, what is it you want'.

Wade was off balance, whoever the caller was, he may or may not know as much as he was inferring. He had been fairly specific about recent matters, but the important thing was, did he know about Cole's reasons for leaving the States or was he making educated guesses?

'In town, near to the bomb site of the Albert pub is a deserted church – St Edward the Confessor. The two were both hit by a Zeppelin. Tonight at ten o'clock you will go there. Go into the confession box and wait. Be alone, and please do not be so stupid as to bring a firearm with you – this is after all consecrated ground.'

The phone went dead and Wade realised that he was sweating. How did the caller know that Lisa was not here. It meant that he was being watched. Was the voice guessing, or did he really know something. Cole knew that he would have to keep the rendezvous.

The atmosphere in the street was still and oppressive. Storm clouds made the summer's evening unusually dark and menacing and there were very few people about. The ruins of the Albert pub in the High Street, demolished by a bomb just prior to Christmas 1915 were on his left, a hundred yards further along on the opposite side, set back from the roadway, was the façade of what appeared to be an undamaged but closed church.

On closer inspection Wade saw that this was not the case. Although the pub had taken a direct hit and absorbed a large amount of the blast, the church of St

Edward the Confessor had also taken its share of the impact. The windows were devoid of glass and the heavy front door was splintered and swinging loosely on one hinge. Roof slates, split and shattered lay haphazardly around the base of the wall.

Making his way up the short pathway from the road that led to the doors, he noticed that the once carefully tended grass edges were now overgrown and covered with weeds. Although not a particularly religious man Wade was still conscious of the air of menace now pervading this desecrated house of God, as if it were waiting for those responsible to return to the scene of their crime in order to punish them.

Pushing the heavy timber door open far enough to allow him to slip through it, he found himself in pitch darkness. He could feel the cold stonework of the nave under his feet and as his eyes became accustomed to the darkness began to orientate himself.

A shiver ran down his spine, the air in the church was cool after the heat of the summer evening, but it was no less oppressive, and a feeling of claustrophobia was enveloping him. Over to his right the blackness was not quite so impenetrable and feeling his way cautiously he walked a few paces in that direction. Outside a rumble of thunder heralded the onset of a summer storm. Never a nervous man, Wade began to feel distinctly uncomfortable and realised that he was succumbing to the overall atmosphere of the deserted building. He wondered if he were alone, or was the man he was to meet already here – watching him.

Slipping a hand into his belt he felt the reassuring warmth of the butt of his three eight service revolver. Moving forward a pace or two he felt the polished wood of a pew under his outstretched hand. He continued to move forward slowly running his fingers along the woodwork, if he was correct, the confessional should be near to the side wall of the church, away from the congregation.

Concentrating on what he was doing, he was totally unprepared for what happened next. His trailing hand guiding him along the inside of the pew, suddenly encountered a human body. His fingers ran first into the thick matted hair of a beard, then the greasy flesh of a face, an open mouth and jagged uneven teeth.

'Jesus Christ!' he jumped back, slipping on the smooth stone floor and losing his balance fell to the ground. Stunned and now completely unnerved he got unsteadily back onto his feet, the revolver cocked and held out in front of him.

A flash of sheet lightning followed by a massive thunderclap for a split second illuminated the scene along the chancel. Through the empty holes of the massive windows above the sanctuary the lightning silhouetted the cross, still standing in its place on the altar, and showed him the snoring figure of an old vagrant, clad in a filthy overcoat tied at the waist with string, unconscious in an alcohol induced stupor.

Wade had hardly recovered his breath when without warning a sack was thrust abruptly over his head and two pairs of strong arms grabbed him from behind, the Webley was snatched from his hand and before he knew what was happening a tight leather belt, looped around his waist, pinioned his arms to his sides.

Seconds later he felt himself being thrust into a narrow cubicle and the belt loosening. His movements still restricted he was turned around and pushed down onto a hard wooden seat. As he struggled to release himself from the sack he heard the sound of the flimsy wooden door through which he had been pushed, being closed.

Pulling off the sack Wade saw that he was in what he presumed to be the penitent's side of the confessional. A stub of candle guttered in a small alcove near to his head giving some illumination. The box – for it was little more than that – was just large enough for him to sit on the hard wooden seat. Pushing the door with his feet he found that it was wedged tightly from the outside, his gun was nowhere to be seen.

There was a metal grill next to his head and as he watched, a wooden panel at the rear of it slid back. The priest's compartment on the other side was in total darkness.

'Had you not chosen to ignore my instructions about coming unarmed, you would not have been manhandled Mr Wade'. The voice was that of the telephone caller, still muffled, impossible to detect any defining feature.

'Please do not resort to any further stupidity, if you attempt to leave without my permission, you will not I can assure you make it to the church door'.

Cole considered his position. There had been three assailants, two to grab him, and a third to throw the sack over his head and disarm him. For the time being, compliance was going to be the best policy he decided.

'What is your interest in me?'

'Ah, now that is a sensible question, and hopefully the starting point for a working business arrangement'. The voice sounded almost affable, the threatening undertone no longer present. Cole was not prepared for what came next.

'As I told you on the telephone, I know sufficient about you to guarantee a short stay in a British gaol and probably a much longer one in America. However that is not presently to my advantage, but I did need to get your attention – hence this little charade'.

'I want you to obtain some keys for me. This will involve you and your associates, Messrs Whiteman, Chesterton, Hawkins and Davis, in a small larceny, something which of course is nothing new to any of you, it might also involve a degree of minor violence. For this service you will be well paid. One hundred pounds in advance, and a further one hundred pounds when the job has been completed'.

Wade frowned into the darkness, it was impossible to make out the features of the man in the other box, all that he could see in the dim candle light was that he was wearing a broad brimmed soft hat deliberately pulled down over his face. He suddenly had a feeling that he might possibly be on the brink of something bigger than the canal venture. If he could run the two together the possibilities might be very rewarding.

'That shouldn't be too much of a problem', he said quietly.

For the next twenty minutes Cole Wade listened intently as he was given a series of very specific instructions before he heard the door to the priest's box being opened as the man prepared to leave.

As instructed he waited a further five minutes before attempting to leave the confessional. He utilised the time by going over and assessing the recent conversation. Two things were immediately apparent. First the man, whoever he was, knew a lot about Cole's present activities. Second, he had referred to the possibility of a prison sentence awaiting him in America. He had not mentioned Wade's real name, nor the fact that it was Canada rather than America where he was wanted. Cole nodded to himself in satisfaction, whoever it was that he was dealing with, was not as well informed as he would like to be, and that gave him a considerable amount of room to manoeuvre.

Pushing the door Wade found that it now opened freely, and stretching his aching limbs he stepped back out into the darkness of the church.

The rain had bated to a steady downpour and he could see that it was coming in through a hole in the roof and pooling in the middle of the nave, splashing noisily off of the wooden pews. The drunk was where he had left him, now snoring noisily, oblivious to the rain coursing in and soaking him. On the stone font at the back of the church near to the entrance door was an envelope containing one hundred pounds in five pound notes, and his revolver.

Chapter 8

23 Lyndon Terrace was a large pleasant detached house overlooking Cranley Park on the outskirts of Kelsford. It would, Harry reflected be described as situated in one of the most desirable suburbs of the town. Since Will Mardlin had moved down to London the house had been occupied by his housekeeper, Mrs Lynam and the young maid Edith, both of whom had been with him since before his wife Susan was killed in the second big air raid of the war. The thought occurred to North that now that he was Detective Superintendent, perhaps he and Laura should think about moving. He dismissed the idea out of hand, they were happy where they were, and anyway Laura had just had the back bedroom at Tennyson Street converted into a bathroom with running hot water.

He walked past the shiny maroon coloured Morris Cowley Bullnose parked outside the house and rang the door bell, which within seconds was answered by the housemaid.

'Good afternoon Edith', he said politely, handing her his hat as she showed him into the hallway.

'Good afternoon Mr North Sir', the young woman liked Inspector North, or Superintendent as he was now that Mr Mardlin was in London. Even when she was a young fifteen year old school leaver new to her first job, he had always shown her courtesy whenever he visited Mr and Mrs Mardlin.

'When you have taken Mr North's coat Edith, would you ask Mrs Lynam if she could provide some refreshment for us please'. Will Mardlin appeared in the hallway, and after briefly shaking hands with his old colleague, showed him through into the front drawing room.

Ralph Gresham rose from the chair that he was occupying near to the bay window overlooking the Park to greet the detective.

'Harry, nice to see you again'. Harry remembered the charming smile that

Gresham could flash - sometimes genuinely pleased, at others to deflect someone or something.

Pleasantries exchanged the men waited until Edith reappeared pushing a trolley laden with sandwiches and an assortment of cooked meats. Even if it was the middle of the afternoon, Elsie Lynam knew better than to serve cucumber slices and fairy cakes to three healthy men.

Once they were alone Mardlin went to the sideboard and produced a bottle of Dewar's Scotch Whisky along with three crystal tumblers. He spent the next half an hour filling Harry in on recent developments, including the murder of André Tessier.

When he had finished, Will put down his now empty glass and moving to the trolley began filling a plate from the selection of ham sandwiches and pork pie.

'Help yourselves', he told the other two, returning to his seat. 'I didn't realize how hungry I was, we haven't eaten since we left London this morning'. Turning to Harry he added, 'train up to Chesterfield, then drove straight here after we picked up the car'.

Harry nodded absently, his eyes on Ralph Gresham. 'Two questions', he said thoughtfully.

Gresham smiled and waited. Harry North and Will Mardlin had made a formidable team together in Kelsford, which was why he had chosen Mardlin for his new partner. Harry alone was one of the most capable policemen he had ever encountered.

'There is a perfectly good train service from London to Kelsford, why do you need to collect a car - from I presume - the army depot at Chesterfield?'

'I think Harry, the answer to that lies in your second question', replied Gresham.

Pursing his lips North continued. 'Which is - why have you told me any of this? You are both working on a high security intelligence job. Russian activists organising strikes, a man is killed in Boulogne, a counter espionage agent who you have lost …'

He let the words hang, turning his gaze from Gresham to Will Mardlin then back again.

'… But you haven't lost him though have you? That is what this is all about isn't it?'

Gresham smiled again, this time to himself, they had made the correct decision including Harry North in the events that were unfolding. If things continued to develop, the present head of the Kelsford detective department would prove to be an invaluable asset.

'As ever Harry you are quite right. Fedir Yurkovich made contact with us at the beginning of March. Because his controller Tessier was dead and the French were struggling to re-establish a cover for him – no one really seemed to know what André had set up – we offered to take over looking after him, and the Sûreté Générale jumped at it'.

'In truth it appears that Yurkovich has lost some of his usefulness to the French – always a dangerous thing for an agent. Vasily Petrov, who intriguingly seems to be paranoid about becoming invisible, apparently never was in Boulogne, nor was he en route to England. That was a ploy to enable them to remove one of the few people who could identify him – André Tessier. Petrov it would appear has much bigger fish to fry in Weimar Germany, following the deaths of Rosa Luxemburg and Karl Liebknecht he is apparently in Berlin busy reorganising the Spartakusbund'.

'With Petrov currently out of the equation the French are much more intent on resolving their own domestic problems and are happy for Yurkovich to work with us for the time being'.

Feeling in his jacket pocket he produced a packet of Passing Cloud. Lighting one for himself he offered them to North.

'We have established Yurkovich – obviously with a new name - in a house on the outskirts of Manchester, his cover being that he is a Polish refugee who works as a clerk for the War Office Pensions Department. Because of his activities in Boulogne, the local Bolshevik group in Manchester, or the 'communists' as they now term themselves, have accepted him without question and he is feeding us valuable information on their intentions concerning the planned police strike in Liverpool that they are orchestrating'.

Ralph paused to gather his thoughts before continuing. His mind went back to another meeting earlier in the week with Sir Percy Leigh-Hunt.

The old man was starting to look his age he thought as he took his place in the armchair opposite to him in the Carlton Club. It was unusual for Leigh-Hunt to venture outside of Whitehall these days, and it was a mark of the discretion he wished to exercise, that he had taken the walk along Pall Mall to brief Gresham.

Toying with the black ribbon of the pince-nez dangling from his waistcoat, the politician's expression was even graver than usual.

'I want this handling correctly Ralph', he said - apparently confident that the cloistered environs of the Carlton were safer than those of Whitehall.

'We want this police strike to take place sometime in August. That will be down to your man. You have done well by the way to poach him from the

French - try to sort it out so that when this is over, it is advantageous for him to remain with us.'

Gresham nodded, he would he knew be able to find some way to compromise Yurkovich with the French, but that could wait for the time being.

Leigh-Hunt steepled his fingers in front of him, the pince-nez hanging loosely from them.

'The army we can deal with. Push Haig up into the Lords, bring in a new and popular commander who can be the 'soldiers friend', and in a month it will be under control'.

'The police are a different matter. Allow them to succeed with industrial action resulting in the establishment of a police union and we will have lost control of the most vital organ in society. It is unthinkable'.

He paused and gave Gresham a knowing look, for a fleeting second Ralph thought that the old man was going to wink at him.

'However, if we handle things properly, we will I can assure you come out of this rather well. Winston is extremely nervous, he has very little faith in Vernon Kell's public school amateurs at MI5, and is relying on us to resolve matters, as he puts it *'in a decisive manner'*.

'Are we satisfied that the unions will not support the police Sir Rowland?' asked Gresham. A slight twitch caught at the side of his mouth.

'Absolutely', the diplomat replaced the pince-nez in his waistcoat pocket.

'That is where the entire police strategy will collapse. They are being very naïve, which is to our advantage. Part of their expectation is that when they call their strike the industrial unions will immediately throw down with them and bring the country to a halt. They are wrong. That will not happen, there is too much bad blood between the established unions and the police - for goodness sake, the police have always been the government's strike breakers! No, despite any promises that have been made, they will definitely find themselves isolated'.

'Our contingency plans are in place. Reliable units of the army are on standby. Immediately the strike is declared, infantry and tanks move straight in and the troops will take over. Every man-jack of a policeman who strikes - ring leaders down to rank and file - will be dismissed from the force the same day and never reinstated. That way, in one fell swoop the organisation will be cleansed of all militant elements'.

'Once the strike is broken – which should be no more than a few days, we bring the iron fist out of the velvet glove – the committee chaired at Lloyd George's instigation by Lord Desborough to examine the demands of the police nationally, has already recommended proposals for better pay and conditions to be arrived at. That has had the immediate effect of eroding the support for strike action amongst the more liberal faction. Meantime, an Act of Parliament is about to be passed, hopefully next month proscribing membership by police officers of a union, and directing them to form a Federation'. A vague flicker, which was the closest thing to a smile that Leigh-Hunt allowed himself, passed over his thin lips, '…which will be tied to government negotiations for bargaining, and prohibited by law from striking'. 'It is for that reason that we don't want the strike to take place until August – not until after the Act becomes law. By the end of August the police will have hung themselves by their own petard and be committed for ever more to the government's bidding'.

'We Colonel Gresham, will have gained the gratitude of both a present Prime Minister and a future government, because believe me David Lloyd George's Liberals will not serve another term in office for a long time to come'.

'…And the car, let me guess - you are going to meet him… but where do I come in?' Harry touched a match to his cigarette.

The other two exchanged quick glances. 'Harry we need to know if the men in Kelsford will join the strike'. Will Mardlin's face showed concern.

North's mouth twisted in a noncommittal gesture.

'I don't honestly know Will,' he replied carefully. 'There is a meeting of the pro-union faction planned to take place in the back room of the Rufford on Wednesday night. Hall-Johnson has sent a letter to every man on the force to the effect that within the next week or so an Act of Parliament is to be passed that will make membership of the police union a disciplinary offence punishable by dismissal'.

'I have got a couple of people on the inside who will be at the meeting, so we will know what has been decided as soon as it finishes. Until then … how long is a piece of string?'

Joseph Rowell's face stood out clearly his mind. The Scotsman would he knew be speaking at the meeting, along with someone from the soon to be proscribed National Union of Police and Prison Officers, who was coming up from London. How persuasive would Rowell be in his arguments – how strongly would he support the pressure from the London and Liverpool branches for the proposed strike. The men in Manchester, and Sheffield had already voted against militant action, opting to negotiate – everything was he knew in the balance so far as the Kelsford men were concerned.

'It would help if I was put in the picture as to what is going on', he said pointedly.

North was annoyed at the prospect of being used. If Will was now tied in to Ralph Gresham's secret world of intrigue so be it, but they had been partners and if that relationship no longer existed, then Harry was wasting his time being here, he already had enough on his mind without playing games with the secret squirrels.

Realising the older man's growing antagonism Ralph Gresham stepped in smoothly.

'The strike in Liverpool will definitely go on', he said decisively. 'The unionist cause in the city has been infiltrated and the police leaders worked on'.

He glanced at Mardlin to take over.

'Abraham Hyam and Michael Donlevy', said Will.

'Hyam has been in the force for about ten years, he has a Jewish background and lost a brother during the war. He has been a supporter of the anarchist movement for years. Donlevy is an Irish activist, who with the failure of the Rebellion in 1916, came over here and joined the Liverpool police. He signed up to the Bolshevik cause following the revolution'.

'The cell that Yurkovich has infiltrated is based in Manchester, nicely distanced from whatever is going to happen in Liverpool. They are using a house in Barlow's Croft, backing onto the Eagle Foundry, near to the Exchange Railway Station so that if necessary they can slip away quickly.'

'Hyam has persuaded the two Liverpool unionist leaders, Holliday and Smithwick, that if the police go ahead with the strike, the so-called Triple Alliance – the Miners, Rail Workers, and Transport Unions – will all come out in support. When that happens the troops who have been drafted in will lay down their guns in sympathy and join them'.

'Just like the workers Soviets and the military in Russia,' put in Gresham.

North turned the proposition over. 'And if that happens the strike will spread like wild fire across the country'.

'We need them to keep thinking that is what is going to happen', continued Mardlin.

'That is Yurkovich's job. We have got here a copy of a letter purporting to be from the Head Constable of Liverpool, Francis Caldwell, to the Home Secretary saying that he has information that the army units standing by to establish martial law in the city are unreliable'.

'It is of course a forgery but it's exactly what Hyam and Donlevy want to hear. Once Yurkovich has given it to them they will use it to fan the flames all the way down Lime Street'.

Harry had a slightly perplexed expression as he asked, 'do I take it that you actually want this strike to go ahead?'

Mardlin nodded slowly. He and Ralph had discussed on the journey up from London the political ramifications of the forthcoming confrontation between the government and the police. Although he did not realize it, his next words could have come directly from Rowland Leigh-Hunt.

'The strike will fail Harry because the other unions, the miners and the dock workers won't lift a finger to help the police – it is anathema for them to come to the aid of the very people who have consistently been the anvil on which their own strikes have been broken!'

'Half of the police demands for better pay have already been met, so the vast majority of coppers won't risk their livelihoods now. The union has been banned, every striker will be sacked and lose everything. The axe will fall and the government will cut out every militant and communist sympathiser in one clean manoeuvre. As soon as that is done, we step in and round up the Manchester cell'.

'What about Petrov?' North asked.

'Our information is that Vasily Sergeyovich is in Berlin'.

Gresham took over once more. 'The political situation there is to say the least, delicate. With the deaths of two of its leaders, Karl Liebknecht and a woman by the name of Rosa Luxemburg the left wing Spartakus movement which is opposing the new régime, is in danger of collapsing. Petrov, according to our intelligence has been dispatched there by Lenin with orders to destabilise the Weimar government'.

'Petrov is without a doubt one the most dangerous men in Europe. He has connections linking him directly to Lenin and Stalin, and is clever as a fox. The entire Boulogne charade was to lull Tessier into a sense of false security and then eliminate him – one less person who could identify Petrov'.

Mardlin sat watching his old friend. He sensed that Harry had something on his mind that he was not telling them. His answer to Will's question as to the state of the Kelsford police had been evasive. Something was going on that he was keeping to himself. Will sighed inwardly, the fact that they could not be entirely open with North concerning the French agent was the root of the problem.

On the journey from London Gresham had laid down the ground rules for this meeting. Harry could not be told everything that was going on with Fedir Yurkovich, the agent was too valuable to risk compromising his cover, however North needed to be made aware of his existence because if things went wrong in Manchester, Yurkovich's instructions were to come to Kelsford and seek out the Detective Superintendent. Mardlin had argued that Harry needed to know that, and also exactly how Yurkovich would make the contact with him. Gresham was adamant – North was only to be given that information if it became absolutely necessary.

The main business dealt with, after another whisky and some desultory chat, the meeting broke up and North deep, in thought made his way back to his office at Long Street.

Holding an unlit cigarette between his fingers, he sat for some time deep in thought, absently tapping the Players packet on his desk whilst turning over the events of the afternoon.

His mood was interrupted by the new office boy, Thomas Bowler cautiously tapping on the door to announce that he had a visitor.

Although he and Arthur Mallard had been friends for over thirty years, other than on official business Mallard was an infrequent visitor to his office.

'I want to talk to you about something Harry', the doctor sat down in the armchair opposite North's desk and regarded him seriously.

'We are none of us getting any younger, and like yourself I have never married, so I have no one to carry on in my place.'

The Yorkshire accent, so strong when they were young men, had Harry noticed with the passage of years lost its emphasis, to be replaced by a flatter Midlands tone. For the first time he saw that his old friend's face, always thin and angular was now becoming pinched with the lines of age. A tiny note of apprehension sounded in his mind.

'Arthur you are not ill are you?' Concern, not a familiar emotion to Harry North, filled his voice.

'Good heavens no!' Mallard's face broke into a grin. 'I'm as fit as a mule. No, I am taking an assistant!'

Having first experienced a wave of relief, North's mood again took a downturn, he did not like change – not where it might affect him personally.

'An assistant, are you thinking of retiring?'

'Not immediately'. Mallard had known the detective for too many years not to see where his thinking was going.

'Don't worry, I will be around for as long as you and Laura will need advice'. He was probably the only person apart from Will Mardlin who could safely get away with linking Harry and Laura together.

'No, I want to scale down my workload a little and at the same time give someone worthwhile a chance'.

'The fellow I have chosen has one particular qualification that attracts me'. Mallard eased his position in the chair. 'During the war he was with the Red Cross - worked first in the Balkans, then as things progressed, alongside the RAMC in France. From the work he did at the Front - treating trauma injuries - he developed a particular interest in forensic, medicine which he now wants to pursue. Consequently he has been looking for a position with a practice that has an involvement in police work, which suits me nicely'.

'And you want to know if I can arrange for him to be taken on by the Force as a police surgeon…' Harry raised his eyebrows. 'If you are vouchsafing him I don't see any problem. I will simply put it to the next meeting of the Watch Committee, and it will take effect from the time that he becomes part of your practice'.

Mallard eased his position once more in the chair, and for the first time began to look uncomfortable.

'He is here already, arrived this morning'. The doctor cleared his throat before continuing. 'There is something that you need to be aware of Harry', he said.

'Jonathan Dilkes spent most of 1915 in the Balkans at the Red Cross Military Hospital in Skopje, which is in Serbia. The patients there were predominantly Austrian – as is his wife Heidi, who was a nursing sister there'.

North's face remained impassive, his expression giving nothing away as he turned over this latest piece of information.

A new doctor in town would not go down well with the older community. A new doctor with an Austrian wife was not going to go down well with anyone. Arthur Mallard had made a brave decision in engaging his new assistant, a decision Harry was being asked to endorse, certainly so far as the police were concerned.

'Let me have a short letter Arthur for the benefit of the Watch Committee and I will have Dr Dilkes engaged at a similar - if not quite so beneficial - retainer as yourself as second police surgeon. I look forward to meeting him and his wife'.

The look of relief on Mallard's face was palpable.

'Thank you Harry, you won't regret this', he said as shaking hands he took his leave.

Next morning, after another broken night's sleep, Harry North sat glowering at the sheet of clean white blotting paper on his desk.

It was Friday and over breakfast Laura had reminded him of an earlier arrangement to take the day off and go into town with her to the showroom of the Corporation Gas Department to look at a new cooker that she had seen. With absolutely no intentions of going to look at gas cookers, promising to return later in the morning Harry had escaped to the sanctuary of his office.

Continuing to glare at the blotting paper he resisted the urge to light a cigarette, he was smoking far too much recently. Nothing about the meeting the previous afternoon made sense.

If Yurkovich was in Manchester, why had Will and Gresham really come to Kelsford? It was certainly not to enquire of him if the Kelsford police were likely to go on strike. There was, as he had pointed out, a perfectly good direct train service from London to Manchester, so why had they stopped off to pick up a car?

Most importantly, why had they told him about Yurkovich being in Manchester? He did not need to know that, so why compromise security by involving him?

There was he decided only one answer - Yurkovich must have a safe house in or near to Kelsford. They needed the car in order to make a rendezvous with the agent, probably later last night. Harry had to be briefed about his existence, because if something went wrong at the Manchester end they had formulated a fallback plan for the man to contact him.

North's mouth set in a tight line.

'Cheers Will', he said softly. The tone did not echo the sentiments.

His mood was interrupted by a gentle tap, followed by Thomas Bowler's face peering timidly around the door.

'What is it this time?' he demanded irritably.

'P…p…please sir, m…m… message from S…S…Sergeant Rowell Sir.'

Harry immediately regretted his churlishness. The new office lad he realised, had a bad stammer, and he was not helping him.

'Come in', he said beckoning to the boy with his finger. 'You are new are you not?'

'Y…yes, s.. sir.' The lad was Harry supposed about fourteen, with fair straight hair cut short and parted at the side. He wore a pair of steel rimmed spectacles from behind which a pair of clear blue eyes peered nervously at him.

North leaned back in his chair and picking up his own spectacles put them on, then pushing them down his nose peered over them.

'What is your name?' he asked.

'T…T…Thomas sir'

'Are you usually called Thomas or Tommy?

'Tommy sir'. The boy was appearing less frightened, calming down slightly, his speech was becoming clearer.

'What have you got to tell me Tommy', Harry asked almost conversationally.

Tommy Bowler took a deep breath. He was very apprehensive of the white haired man with the sweeping moustache who occupied the office at the end of the corridor. Superintendent North was he knew one of the most powerful men in the building.

'Sar... Sar... Sergeant Rowell said to tell you that a b...b... body has been found in the old Lime Kiln, sir, and he has gone over there'.

'Did he say if he was taking anyone with him?' asked Harry quietly.

The boy nodded. 'S... said to tell you, S... Sir, that he was taking, a uniform man with the p...p... prisoner van, and Detective Scofield Sir'.

North looked thoughtful. Good, if the death was suspicious Joe could leave the uniform officer at the scene whilst he and Dan Scofield made a start on dealing with things. He avoided the impulse to be annoyed that the Sergeant had gone on ahead of him, he would have done the same thing. Have a look before the brass arrived and started tramping around.

'Right, come with me young man', he said standing up and pushing his cigarettes into his pocket.

The administration office was at the end of the passage, next to the large library type room that was used by the Watch Committee for their fortnightly meetings. Montagu Parfitt was seated at a desk facing the window, studying a sheet of figures. Eric Broughton was busy re-jigging a duty roster.

Wasting no time on pleasantries North said, 'Montagu, I have a body out at the Old Lime Kiln, I shall need to borrow Eric'. The word '*borrow*', sounded as if, stuck deep in his throat it had been dredged up by some supreme effort.

'Sorry, impossible. Eric is busy on some work for the Chief Constable'. Parfitt's eyes did not leave the accounts that he was studying.

'This is *police* business, and I have need of an experienced clerk', growled North, the colour rising in his neck would have been adequate warning for most of those who knew him.

Unperturbed, Montagu Parfitt lifted his gaze to meet Harry's.

'Eric is now the admin assistant, not the station office boy, I think you have your answer standing next to you'. There was a smugness in the admin manager's tone that infuriated North.

Laying a hand on the office boy's shoulder Harry said calmly, 'put your coat on, bring a notepad and pencil, and meet me in the yard in five minutes'.

Without a further word he turned and walked out of the door.

Down in the yard Harry, standing by the Ford model T which Sidney Hall-Johnson had bought the previous year along with the closed sided prisoner van, realised that he had a problem. He could not drive and there was no one else in the yard. He would wait a few minutes he decided until a Constable who could drive appeared, and commandeer his services. Meantime his annoyance at Parfitt's arrogance subsiding, he watched as Tommy Bowler, wearing a large cloth cap and clutching a spiral notepad, appeared through the doorway that gave out into the archway over the yard.

'We just need a driver and we will be on our way Tommy', he said to the lad.

'Please Sir, I can drive Sir'.

Harry looked sharply at him. 'Can you indeed?', he said, a slow smile breaking out across his face, '… can you indeed'.

'Yes Sir, my father has a farm, I sometimes drive his van'.

With interest, Harry registered that the stammer was gone. The fact that the boy was too young to hold a drivers licence was, given the circumstances in his opinion irrelevant and it would be a brave Constable who would challenge the Detective Superintendent.

'Well come along then, what are you waiting for', he replied.

Twenty minutes later the Model T pulled off of the road next to a gate with a dilapidated sign nailed to it. The faded writing bore the legend 'T.E. Dawlish & Co. Strictly No Entry'

Tommy Bowler switched off the engine and looked nervously at North, neither had spoken since setting off from Long Street.

Harry grinned, and gave him a mischievous wink, 'Well done lad, don't tell anyone you are not old enough to drive'.

The boy smiled back shyly, almost glowing with pride. 'Th… th… thank you sir'.

'Come on, work to be done', Harry muttered gruffly, climbing down from the passenger seat and striding off towards a tall stone edifice half hidden by a rise in the ground a hundred yards away.

Disused for over twenty years, 'Dawlish's Crypt' as the huge granite block was commonly known, had for years prior to the turn of the century been used by the firm of T.E. Dawlish & Co., to produce lime for sale as both an ingredient in mortar and as a fertiliser.

Twenty feet high and fifteen wide it was built of massive granite blocks let into a small hill that rose against its back wall. When it was a working plant, pulverised limestone from the quarry ten miles away on the far side of Flixton was brought over daily by cart, then layered with a mixture of kindling from Rooks Woods and slow burning peat imported from Ireland, carefully reduced with fires that brought the stone to melting point, into a caustic quicklime that was drawn off through the four foot square arched doorway let into the front of the stone blocks. The reason that the kiln was built into the hillside was to enable the carters bringing the limestone shale to drive their horses up a narrow pathway cut into the slope to the top of the structure, and discharge their load through the open circular loading aperture at the top.

Before the newly produced quicklime could be used by either the building trade, or local farmers, it had first to be slaked with water from the nearby stream which was diverted to flow through the now disused sluices a short distance away.

It was a desolate and inhospitable place, shunned by the locals, and often used - along with the threat of a visitation by 'the midnight horses' - to frighten local children. Since the continuous fires that had burned there for over fifty years were allowed to peter out around the same time as peace was declared following the South African War, the place had acquired a reputation for being haunted.

The reason for this last was quite simple. Theophilus Dawlish, a widower and the final member of the Dawlish dynasty to engage in the back breaking occupation of tipping stone into one end the kiln and clearing lime out of the other, had in his last will and testament decreed that, 'upon his death his remains were to be loaded into the fires of the kiln for cremation, whereafter, said fires should be allowed to die down, never to be re-kindled, and his mortal remains spread upon the hillside that had for some fifty years provided his living'.

A uniformed Constable who Harry had never seen before saluted smartly as he picked his way along the overgrown path from the gate. North touched the brim of his hat politely in return. The man he saw was wearing the three standard medal ribbons denoting recent war service. The number on his collar, '82', was that of Gussie Packer who had been killed at Cambrai in 1917.

Climbing the steep slope that wound up to the top of the kiln, North spotted Detective Constable Daniel Scofield leaning over the stone parapet talking to someone out of sight inside. On seeing the Superintendent stomping towards him Scofield straightened up.

'Morning Sir', he said, 'Sergeant Rowell is down in the bottom, I think he is about done'.

Harry nodded, 'What have we got then Dan?' he asked.

'Couple of local lads came up here earlier for a dare – usual thing, who has got the nerve to climb down into the crypt – when they got to the bottom, they found a body. Absolutely terrified them, they didn't need any hand holds to get out, just clawed the brickwork. Ran to Sam Drew's farm down the road, and he sent for us'.

Scofield was interrupted by the dishevelled figure of Joseph Rowell pulling himself up over the stonework. The Sergeant's shirt was grimy from clinging to the handholds let into the wall to allow Dawlish's men in the old days to climb down twice a year in order to clean out the great stone bowl.

Wiping an equally grubby hand across his face he straightened up and came across to the other two. Harry North noted the grim expression on his face.

'Anybody we know?' he demanded.

Rowell nodded slowly, and reaching in his trouser pocket produced a heavy oval shaped gold locket on a thin closely linked chain.

North took the trinket from him and weighed it carefully in his hand, immediately recognising it from the photographs.

'Alice Kitson'. It was a statement rather than a question.

Rowell nodded. 'Problem is – she's not on her own. There are two bodies down there'.

Harry's head came up sharply, 'go on'.

Rowell ran his fingers through his hair as if trying to make sense of what he had seen in the bottom of the fire pit.

He held up a finger. 'Body one. A woman – presumably Alice Kitson - fully dressed, well knocked about, which one would expect if she has dived or been thrown in from the top here.'

'Body two', a second digit was extended, 'is all over the place. Bones and things as if it was already in bits before it was chucked in. If I had to guess, the second one has been dead a lot longer than the Kitson woman'.

Harry lit a cigarette. 'Bones and stuff all over the place… what about clothing?'

Rowell shook his head, 'no, the second one must have been stripped first'.

Taking a pull at his cigarette Harry studied his shoes for a moment. He needed to have a look at what was in the kiln, but he had no intention of climbing down a brick wall.

'If we break through from the bottom, can we get a better look?'

Again Joe Rowell shook his head. 'Not until later Sir. There is at least three feet of clinker and ash built up. If we try to clear it, we will totally lose the crime scene'.

'Ladder?'

Again the Sergeant shook his head, 'too deep'.

North felt his frustration building. How was he to investigate a murder if he could not get to look at the bodies. Five years ago he would have shinned down the stone work without a second thought, now he could already feel his rheumatics sending warnings.

'Right', he said sourly turning to the diminutive figure of Tommy Bowler.

'You get back to Kelsford. First go to Dr Mallard's house and ask him if he will attend here as soon as possible, after that go on to Mr Danson's photograph studio and ask him to come over right now and take some pictures. Then come back here to me – and be quick about it'.

It was almost lunchtime before Aldred Danson had completed the job of taking pictures in the bowels of the excavation, leaving the ground clear for

Arthur Mallard and his new assistant to begin their preliminary examination of the two bodies.

A tall slim man, Jonathan Dilkes was, Harry supposed around thirty five years of age. Unruly dark brown hair framed a long pleasant face with a large generous mouth which was given to breaking into a smile when he spoke. Like North, Dr Mallard opted not to make the arduous climb down the stone wall, allowing his younger assistant the privilege.

Forewarned of the location of the bodies, the two medical men had taken the precaution of bringing along protective clothing, and having donned a set of brown engineer's overalls, Dilkes, accompanied once more by Joseph Rowell, disappeared over the ledge.

It was almost half an hour before the sound of scrabbling hands and feet announced the return of the two men. Once back on the top, they first made their way down the slope to the sluices at the bottom in order to wash away the grime and sweat of their exertions.

Harry and Mallard, accompanied by Daniel Scofield followed them.

Stripping off his overalls Dilkes recovered the collar, tie, and jacket that he had placed on the passenger seat of Arthur Mallard's tiny Austin saloon.

'So what have you got doctor?' asked North impatiently.

Lifting his chin, Dilkes slid a flat gold tie bar through the ends of his collar and deftly secured it behind the knot in his tie. Joe Rowell suppressed a grin. The old man was becoming more and more annoyed by the minute at being excluded from a first hand view of the crime scene.

The young doctor eased his jacket on, then resting his hips against the wing of the car gave them a broad smile. 'Interesting gentlemen, don't you think so Joe?'

North almost exploded, not only was he excluded from his own crime scene, the new doctor and his detective sergeant were now obviously on first name terms.

Rowell, seeing the colour rising in the Superintendent's face replied quickly, 'yes doctor, perhaps you would like to explain'.

Dilkes, apparently oblivious to the policeman's growing irritation began to pack an old briar pipe with tobacco from a leather pouch.

'Two bodies. First is a woman, mid to late twenties I would guess, been down there some time. Tall, well made, fully dressed. She may have died as the result of falling into the pit, or she may have been dead prior to going in'.

Addressing himself to Arthur Mallard he said, 'until the post mortem we won't know of course'.

Mallard nodded and waved a hand for him to continue. Although concealing it better than Harry, he was equally frustrated at not having first hand access to the bodies.

'The second is going to be more complicated'. Dilkes succeeded in getting his pipe going, and a cloud of thick blue smoke began to obscure his face. Taking the briar from between his teeth he waved his free hand to clear the air.

'Whoever or whatever it is will be difficult to identify'.

He again addressed himself directly to Mallard. 'Flesh is almost totally gone from the limbs. Legs are still attached to the torso – despite deterioration the ligaments have held - as is the right arm and what is left of the head, the left arm has become detached and appears to have been thrown down separate to the body'.

Harry interrupted, 'Why are you are sure the second body was thrown down?'

Again the grin, 'Because I would put money on it, that it has been immersed in water for some length of time before being chucked down there'.

North thrust his hands deep into his trouser pockets and stared down at his shoes for a few moments thinking.

'Joe', he said decisively. 'I am going back to Long Street. I will get a builder out here and have that bottom door broken open. We have got all of the pictures of the evidence that we need. Get everything raked out and the remains removed, let's see if there is a weapon in there.

'I will send either Clarrie or Bert to give you a hand. We should be able to clear things before dark if we get a move on'.

'Arthur', he continued, 'could I ask you to supervise the safe removal of the remains'.

'Certainly', Mallard had worked with Harry North years enough to know exactly what the detective would want.

'I will leave Jonathan here and sort out with Sharpe's to have the bodies taken to the mortuary. Shall I give you a lift back?'

Harry was about to refuse when he realised that the Ford motorcar with Thomas Bowler was nowhere to be seen. He frowned, having done the errands that he had been given the boy was supposed to have returned to the kiln with the car some time ago.

Had he not been so engrossed in his own thoughts, he might have spotted the thick set figure of Moses Hawkins watching quietly what was happening from a stand of trees a few hundred yards back from the hillock into which the disused kiln was built. As the detective turned to join Arthur Mallard at his car, Hawkins slipped silently away into the shadows of the wood.

Back once more at Long Street the first thing that North spotted, parked in a corner of the yard was the Model T. About to go into the building he saw the burly figure of Sergeant Cedric Lyner emerging from the charge office. Harry paused, then turning called over to him, 'Cedric do you know where young Bowler is?'

Lynam came over to where Harry was standing, they had known each other for too many years to stand on ceremony.

'As a matter of fact I do Harry', he said. ' That jumped up bugger Parfitt caught him driving yon car around the yard. Gave him a right good clip across the ear, did a lot of shouting, then kicked his arse into the building'.

Climbing the stone stairs up to the first floor, Harry North felt a cold anger sweeping through him. Eric Broughton seated at his desk, looked up at the figure standing in the doorway to the administration office and knew instinctively what was going to happen. Tommy Bowler was standing in front of the filing cabinets, a frightened look on his face, a livid wheal mark across his cheek. Behind the large polished desk at the back of the room, reading a letter sat Montagu Parfitt.

'Eric, go and make some tea, and take the boy with you'. North spoke quietly, the anger controlled.

Broughton got up and signalling to the lad moved silently past Harry.

'…and close the door'.

'What is going on?' Captain Parfitt, put the letter down and stared enquiringly at North.

Harry moved across the room to the desk and leaning forward rested his hands on its polished surface, his face inches from the other man's.

'What have you done to that boy?' the words were barely audible.

'If you mean Bowler, he was playing around in the station car, I caught him actually trying to drive it'. The office manager seemed strangely unaware of the danger that he was in.

'He was working for me, he can drive a motorcar!' Harry felt the rage building with every word.

'You have given him a beating – and he was working for me!'

'Then he should have explained that to me', the words were clipped, Parfitt annoyed at his actions being questioned.

'The boy can hardly speak – you terrified him shitless!'

The roar could be heard out in the parade yard. Outside the office door Thomas Bowler grabbed hold of Eric Broughton in fright. Broughton putting his arm around the lad remained stock still.

Parfitt began to rise out of his chair, which was a mistake. Harry's fist hit him in the solar plexus with the force of a steam hammer. All of the day's frustrations combined with his pent up anger went into the blow, the office manager crashed backwards into the filing cabinet behind the desk before slumping in a half sitting position against the wall fighting for breath, the recently vacated chair overturned beside him.

North moved around the desk and set the swivel chair back upright before, grasping the half conscious man by the lapels of his jacket, he dragged him back up and dumped him in the seat. Parfitt his face blue with lack of oxygen was barely conscious.

Putting his hand under the man's jaw Harry pulled his head up sharply. Leaning forward he said softly, 'if you ever lay a finger on that boy again, Captain *fucking* Parfitt, I will take you out in the yard and beat you senseless … do you understand?'

Parfitt was beginning to function again, his eyes were less glazed and his breathing coming back to normal.

Removing his hand from under Parfitt's jaw, Harry slid two fingers into his collar and twisted viciously. The office manager, eyes bulging began to turn an unhealthy shade of blue.

'I said, do you understand?' Choking, Parfitt made a gurgling sound.

North released his grip and stepped back, 'I will take that as *yes*' he said coldly.

'If you should think of running to your guardian angel, the Chief Constable about this little matter, think first that I am now going to take a statement from Sergeant Lyner that he saw you hitting the boy out in the yard, and believe me, young Broughton will be only too happy to do the same as to anything that happened in here before I came in'.

Turning he walked out into the now deserted passage. From behind him came a steady dripping sound as the contents of the overturned bottle of Swan permanent blue ink that was obliterating the paperwork on Montagu Parfitt's desk made its way in a steady stream onto the floor.

Chapter 9

Laura Percival was excited, it was Saturday morning and she had finally persuaded Harry to accompany her to the Gas Department showroom where they had bought a brand new cooker with four rings on the top and an oven. With fitting included in the price of £27. 19s the salesman had promised her that it would be installed next Wednesday, and that the job could be completed during the morning.

'Do you think that we should have the old black range taken out Harry?' she asked as they strolled along the High Street in the summer sunshine, away from the town centre towards the Pack Horse Hotel where he had promised to finish the morning off with lunch.

He was she thought proudly, with his snow white hair and rakish straw boater hat, the most handsome man she had ever seen. Laura knew that because of who he was and what he did, many people were apprehensive of Harry and uncomfortable in his presence but the man she knew was different. Naturally, generous, he was kind and in her case, totally indulgent, she had never known him to refuse her any reasonable request in all of the years that they had been together. They had talked recently about the prospect of moving from the little terraced house in Tennyson Street to somewhere bigger now that Harry was a Superintendent. To her relief he was not keen on the idea. After almost twenty years together the house in Tennyson Street meant a great deal to both of them. Apart from anything else, she was inordinately proud of the fact that they were the only couple in the road who owned the property they lived in.

Although neither of them were particularly demonstrative, she loved Harry deeply and knew that he felt the same about her. Despite the reputation that he had gained in his early years, Laura knew that Harry was as committed to their relationship as she was. At forty eight she was still a very presentable woman. Short and slim her deep red hair - a legacy of her Scottish ancestry - was worn long and tied at the back in a slightly old fashioned chignon which suited her bold features. She sometimes wondered if they would ever marry but then quickly dismissed the prospect, she was a widow and he was not the marrying sort.

Realising that he had not responded to her question, she stopped and turned around. Harry was several yards back up the road looking in the window of Wilberforce's second hand shop.

North stood perfectly still, staring intently at the black Malacca cane propped up in the side of the window between an ornate water jug - a washbowl from some unidentified night stand - and an ancient Hidalgo Moya typewriter.

It was exactly as he remembered it.

Heavy, not the elegant item carried by some gentleman as a fashion accessory. A substantial stick which in a case of necessity would serve as an admirable weapon of defence. The silver head, plain but unmistakable, still as brightly polished as it had ever been. Joe Langley's stick!

Joseph Langley had been the Head of the Kelsford Detective Department when Harry first came to the force as a young man in 1884. A formidable and feared figure, the old man ended his life a hopeless alcoholic, to be replaced by Harry's mentor Tom Norton.

The stick had been Langley's 'badge of office', he was never seen without it. After Tom took over as the Detective Inspector, by default he inherited the cane, and Harry had always assumed that when he ended his days with the Force it had gone to France with him - but he was wrong, it was here in Stan Wilberforce's shop piled up amongst the stack of bartered household goods littering the window.

'What are you looking at love?' asked Laura.

'The stick', he replied almost reverently. 'It was Joe Langley's, I always thought that Tom took it to France when he and Ruth went there to live'.

Laura's face immediately clouded over. She remembered Joseph Langley only too well. A drunken brute of a man who died years ago in a fit of DTs after being carted off to the asylum on the outskirts of the town. Looking at Harry's face she realised that it meant something entirely different to him.

'Would you like me to buy it for you?' she asked.

Back at home Harry examined the stick carefully...

According to Stan Wilberforce the shop owner, it had been found in a cupboard at an unoccupied house in Victoria Road when it was cleared by removal men about a month ago. Harry knew exactly what had happened. It was Ruth Samuels house, he remembered it well. She had moved Tom Norton in with her after he had been shot, in order that she could nurse him. They left England to be married, and the stick, overlooked in the move had lain unnoticed in the cupboard ever since.

Although it was thirty years since the cane had been used Harry resolved immediately that it would be restored to its original purpose - the Head of the Detective Department's stick of office.

Laura put a hand on his shoulder, touched that her gift was so obviously giving him such pleasure. 'Alright love?' she asked.

'The best thirty shillings you have ever spent,' he replied slipping his arm around her waist.

Just before noon on Sunday, a telephone call from Clarrie Greasley interrupted North's weekend, bringing him sharply back to reality.

'Need to talk to you Harry,' the Detective Sergeant's usually lugubrious voice had an edge of urgency.

Having agreed to meet in the Pack Horse, with a promise to be back by half past one, Harry put on his jacket and hurried off out.

'I don't know what Joe is doing but he is courting disaster!'

Greasley picked up his pint of bitter and stared anxiously into it before taking a swallow.

'He's going to get himself the fucking sack.' Bert Conway drummed his fingers anxiously on a beer mat.

Both Bert and Clarrie had attended the mid-week meeting of the Union of Police and Prison Officers in the Rufford Arms on Wednesday evening. The upstairs room was packed with off duty rank and file police officers. On the makeshift platform sat Joseph Rowell flanked on one side by Simeon Greenwood, a Constable with over twenty years experience on the Kelsford Force, and on the other by Thomas Scott a metropolitan officer who had travelled up for the gathering.

'The government are lying to us with their promises.' Scott was getting into his stride. 'This Desborough Committee is making proposals that will not be met. Now is the time to strike - we have the solemn word of all of the trades union leaders that a police strike will be actively supported by the workers of this country!'

'Regrettably, I am in agreement,' contrasting with the Londoner's harsh clipped vowels, Joe Rowell's soft Scottish burr seemed to spread across the assembly like a gently moderating hand.

'If we do not take action now, the moment will pass and our opportunity will be lost forever. Throughout the last four years we have all served in one way or another. Some of us went to the Colours, we fought and many died, for our country. Others served here, long shifts with insufficient pay to even begin to meet the massive rises in the cost of living that the war brought. A few war bonuses and promises made by the government of a better future after the armistice. That time has now come, but the promises have not been fulfilled. If we go along with the Desborough Committee's proposals - a few bob in our pay packets and some extra days off, short term things will improve slightly, but the trade off is that we will be tied forever to the government's will. We must take action now or we are lost for all time!'

Rowell's words met with a mixed reaction. Some of those present were in agreement, others, more cautious advocated a 'wait and see' policy. The arguments flowed back and forth for another hour before the meeting broke up in disarray.

'And now Joe has had a letter printed to be sent out to every member of the force outlining why they should go on strike.'

Greasley's doom laden tones lay heavily on the group.

'Who is printing it?' asked Harry.

Bert Conway cleared his throat, his voice troubled. 'Manfred Escher at Weatherstone Press in Arden Street.'

North stared into his beer, his face set in stone. 'You go together and see Escher. Tell him that the night before the printing is to be collected, he is to hand every single copy over to you. Tell him that if he does not do that, I will close him down as an undesirable alien and have him and his family deported back to Poland, or wherever it is he came from, within a week. You pass the word amongst every other printer in the town that if they accept so much as an envelope from the strikers I will close them down as well.'

Both of the sergeants nodded in agreement, it was what they had counted on.

The new week was to be an eventful one. At three thirty on Monday morning, Harry was awakened for a deep sleep by the insistent ringing of the telephone bell downstairs in the hall. It was Lewis Arthur who was the duty Station Sergeant.

'Sorry to wake you Harry, but Byram's jewellers has been robbed. David Byram and his wife were attacked at their house late last night and the shop keys taken. They were tied up and the shop cleared out. Byram has only just got free and raised the alarm.'

Harry shook off the remnants of sleep and having been told that Clarrie Greasley was already at the scene, dressed hurriedly and set off for the shop.

Situated between Stamford Gate and the Market Place, number 3 Albert Parade was the town's most prestigious jewellery shop, outside a uniform Constable standing on the pavement touched the rim of his helmet respectfully to the Superintendent. Harry returned the gesture with a brief nod and made for the portly figure of Clarrie Greasley framed in the doorway, deep in conversation with a diminutive little man of around forty years of age.

With a brief acknowledgement to Greasley, Harry turned immediately to the second man.

'What happened David?'

The small man ran a hand through his thick wavy hair. David Byram's father, Israel had been the town's leading jeweller since before the Boer War, a tradition that the younger Byram had continued in the ten years since his death.

'Miriam and I were at home last night, it was about half past ten, we were ready to go to bed and I was just locking up when there was a knock at the front door. I opened the door and three men burst in. They were wearing long riding coats, big wide brimmed hats pulled down over their faces and black bandana style scarves over their lower faces. They all three had revolvers. Only one of them spoke, he told us to go into the drawing room and while he held me at gunpoint, the other two grabbed Miriam and tied her to a dining chair. The one who was doing the talking said that if I didn't hand over the keys to the shop and to the main safe they would kill her. Believe me Mr North, I am certain that he would have done it. I gave him the keys and they sat me in another chair, back to back with Miriam and tied us together. Then they gagged us and left. It took us hours to get free, when we first tried, we tipped the chairs over and couldn't move. Eventually we managed to work our way across the floor to the china cabinet and knock it over. It made a tremendous crash which woke Mr and Mrs Marks the housekeeper and butler. They came downstairs and set us free. We had to go next door to telephone because the robbers had ripped out our telephone connection in the hall.'

Harry peered into the interior of the premises. The lights were on and he could see at the back of the shop Clarrie's partner Detective Constable Robert 'Bill' Sykes, notebook in hand talking to a tall spare young man with a pronounced stoop.

Following his gaze Clarrie said, 'Richard Pohlman, Mr Byram's assistant, we turned him out as soon as we arrived. He's going through what is missing with Bill.'

'Any rough estimate David?' North asked the jeweller.

'It is going to be several thousand pounds worth of gem set rings and other jewellery, plus the gold items. The main safe has been cleared of all of the good stuff, so we are probably looking at ten thousand pounds or more.'

North grimaced, this was the last thing that he needed. Two unsolved deaths and now a major jewel robbery. Together with David Byram and Clarence Greasley he went into the shop to examine the crime scene. It was quickly apparent that other than the empty display shelves and a similarly bare walk in safe vault, there was very little to see. No signs of any forced entry or traces of their visit had been left by the perpetrators.

North checked the time, it was a quarter to six and daylight. 'Finish up what you are doing here Clarrie, and leave them to tidy up. I doubt if either David Byram or his assistant will be going home. Get that uniform man to go round to Bert's house and then Joe Rowell's and wake them up. I want a meeting with all three of you at seven in my office.'

Without waiting for an answer he turned and walked off in the direction of Long Street.

Watching the Superintendent stomping purposefully off through the Market Place, Clarence Greasley frowned, where he asked himself, had the old man acquired that walking stick from?

That Harry North was in a foul mood was apparent to everyone seated around the table in the conference room. Joe Rowell and Bert Conway looked up expectantly at a tired Clarence Greasley as he slumped down in the fourth chair.

'Alright Clarrie, go over the story', said North as soon as the Sergeant was seated, 'and smoke if you want to,' he added glancing briefly at the others. The concession was more for his own benefit than for theirs, Harry had spent most of the last hour pacing up and down in his office gathering his thoughts and working out how to deal with what was fast becoming a major problem.

Greasley rubbed a hand over a meaty unshaven jowl. He had been up for most of the night and was exhausted. Having been summoned from his bed soon after 2 a.m., he and Bill Sykes had gone first to the Byram's large town house in Leaminster Gardens, and then accompanied by a very frightened David Byram to the shop in the Parade.

The large plate glass door whilst closed was unlocked, as if those responsible for the break-in were leaving a calling card saying, 'we were here -where were you? Inside other than the fact that the display cabinets and the vault had been cleared of almost everything of value there were no signs of the disruption, everything seemed to have been done with meticulous care. Having finished at the shop, he and Sykes next returned briefly to Leaminster Gardens to check on Mrs Byram, who they were told, having been sedated by Dr Dilkes, was now asleep.

'So, suggestions… Harry threw the discussion open. No one responded, too many things had happened recently for any of the three sergeants to be the first to open the can of worms.

'Alright, let's start with the basics.' North glared around the table.

'Inside job? If it is, then the shop assistant Pohlman, from what I have seen is not up to putting the frighteners on Byram and his wife at the house - he would have very much been the middle man who supplied the information for someone else to do the job.'

'Joe, you take that angle. Usual enquiries, has he got domestic problems, is he involved with another woman and got money troubles, has he got any previous form.'

Rowell raised his hand a few inches from the table top in acknowledgement and gave a brief nod.

'David Byram, do we know anything about him that might be useful?'

'Wealthy jeweller, model of society, happily married …' volunteered Conway glumly.

'For fucks sake Bert I said something useful, not his Masonic pedigree,' snapped North.

Bert Conway made a similar gesture to the one that Rowell had just made, except that this indicated his acceptance of the rebuff.

'What I am saying,' he continued unruffled, 'is as yet, that is the extent of what we know. I will do some digging. Actually, its rumoured that my faithful assistant young Windram is one of the chosen few, taking his place each Thursday evening on the square. I'll bone him about it, as you pointed out Byram is bound to be a Mason, so Laurence can share a few of the secrets of the society with me.'

North frowned. He had not previously been aware that Bert's partner Detective Constable Laurence Windram was a member of the Kelsford lodge. Thinking about it though, Windram's father owned a large building company in the town, which young Laurence had declined to join, so it should have occurred to him that he would on his coming of age, have proposed his son for membership.

'Yes, do that. And get round to see Mrs Byram as soon as she has recovered from the vapours, and go over this story about the masked men. Lean on her, if this is bollocks then it ends right there.'

Bert Conway pushed open a new packet of twenty Players with his thumb, took one out and threw the packet into the middle of the table. Foxy was edgy he thought, and not without reason. They were all entertaining the same unspoken fear. If this were part of the recent pattern of shop breakings, and it was somehow connected to the massive discontent amongst the men of the police force, then the implications were unthinkable - and certainly could not be uttered by any of those present.

North and Greasley pulled a cigarette each from the packet and the Superintendent offered Conway a light, a conciliatory gesture for his previous sharpness.

'About these masked men Clarrie, what has Byram got to say? Let's have some details.'

Greasley stretched his arms to ease his aching shoulders. 'Three men, identically dressed. Long, ankle length riding coats, large wide brimmed hats, bandanas over the lower half of the face, all armed with pistols -revolvers to be exact. They were working to a pre-arranged plan, only one spoke, and he had a local accent, so we have the absolute minimum to work on.'

'Which means,' put in Joe Rowell, 'that the other two either were not locals, or at least had distinctive accents.

'Tall, short, fat thin?' Harry was exasperated, it was obvious that the whole thing was carefully planned and they were grasping at straws.

Clarrie Greasley shook his head. 'No, I did that bit. Although both of the Byram's were traumatised, they gave identical descriptions of the men, who were average height and so cloaked up it was impossible to tell what they looked like, so we have essentially got nothing.'

'Alright, there is no point in going around in circles.' North said decisively.

'Clarrie, you go home and get some sleep, tell Bill to do the same. Joe and Bert can do the ground work this morning along with Lol and Vince. We four will meet again at one o'clock in the Lamb and Pheasant to see where we are going.'

Clarrie got to his feet and nodded, 'one o'clock it is,' he said.

'Joe, you and Bert hold on,' North told the other two who were also preparing to leave, 'there are other things cracking off that we need to talk about.'

Harry consulted his pocket watch, it was a quarter to eight. Opening the door of the conference room he bellowed down the passage in the direction of the administration office. Within seconds Tommy Bowler appeared. 'Go and get us three mugs of coffee and some bacon sandwiches from Phipp's,' Harry gave him two shillings, 'You can keep the change,' he added.

'Joe where are we with Alice Kitson?' Harry pushed the paper wrapper that had contained his bacon sandwich out of the way into the middle of the conference table. The atmosphere was more relaxed now that the three had consumed the food that Tommy Flowers brought in along with a steaming jug of coffee which Joseph Rowell was now pouring into three thick pot mugs.

Rowell took a sip from his mug. Awakened soon after six o'clock he had only had sufficient time to quickly shave and dress, before whispering to his sleepy wife Ailma that he had been called out. He was grateful for the break and some impromptu breakfast. Foxy could be an old bastard he thought, but he was a knowing old bastard. He and Bert had tumbled into work direct from their beds whilst Harry North and Clarence Greasley had been up most of the night. The early morning meeting was fraught with tension - there was a serious crime to be worked on, and it was accompanied by background apprehensions that none of them wanted to countenance.

The old man had broken the tension, drawn a temporary line under the events of the night, and was now moving them on.

'The post mortem report and the photographs of the body are here,' Joe said taking a sheet of paper out of the thick folder that he had fetched from his desk whilst they were waiting for the boy to return from Phipp's coffee house.

'Ducky Mallard and the new man - Jon Dilkes - are in agreement, she was strangled with a scarf that was still tight around her neck when we found her. The body was in an advanced state of decomposition, it was mostly the clothing that was keeping her together, they estimate that she had been there for about four months, which puts her as being murdered around the time that she disappeared.'

North already knew as well as the Sergeants what the findings of the post mortem were. Joe and Bert had gone over all of the evidence, including her association with Clifford Jarman, both together and with Clarence Greasley. This was an exercise to review everything, discuss ideas, see if anything had been missed.

'No signs of any bruising other than where the scarf went around the neck?'

'No, it was a straightforward strangling, the doctors are of the opinion that the assailant was behind her. All of the medical terms are in the report, but it comes down to whoever murdered her coming up behind, whipping the scarf around her neck and choking her.'

'What about signs of any sexual activity?' asked North, again he knew the answer, the body had been in the kiln too long for Mallard or his assistant to be able to conduct any constructive examination.

'Not a clue,' Rowell toyed for a moment with one of the photographs on the table. As was standard procedure he had been present at the autopsy.

'There was a lot of decomposition, rats had been at most of the face and extremities - hands and feet. Then when we cut her clothes off for the p.m the body was heavily maggot infested, especially round the crutch and anal areas. They had got inside her chasing the body fluids, absolutely no chance of finding out if there was any recent sexual activity before she died.'

He paused a moment, fingers still resting on the photograph of the bundle of clothing that was a body lying at the bottom of the kiln. In his mind he was comparing it with those in his desk drawer, the erotic poses of an alluring young woman staring provocatively into the lens of the pornographer's camera.

Harry drummed lightly on the polished wooden surface with his fingertips, he knew exactly what was going through the Scotsman's mind. 'Might be an idea in future to have photographs taken of a body at the time of the post mortem,' he said thoughtfully.

The other two looked at him enquiringly. 'Doesn't make any difference here,' he continued, the fingers were now steepled under his chin. 'But there are times when it might. If say the victim had taken a beating and there were marks and bruises, or there were other circumstances that were relevant.' He did not need to add the impact that they would have when shown to a jury.

'Danson will love that,' grunted Bert Conway. 'Put a few of those in his window, he will be well away.'

Both Harry and Joe Rowell grinned at the suggestion.

'Alright,' said Harry. 'If either of you, or Clarrie are working a case where you think that it will be of benefit, then do it and tell me afterwards.'

The other two nodded in agreement.

'Was she wearing an overcoat?'

Harry and Joe looked at Bert Conway sharply. Bert might be the basic down to earth member of the team, but he was a good detective and nobody's fool.

'Yes she was,' replied Rowell, 'it was a winter's day when she disappeared, presumably the same day she was killed - what are you thinking Bert?'

'The scarf that was used to kill her is a light cotton one.' The others both nodded. The cream and red paisley scarf that Jonathan Dilkes had cut away from the dead woman's neck was with the rest of her clothes, stored away as evidence in the property cupboard at the back of the charge office.

'Now that was definitely identified as her's wasn't it?' Again nods of assent.

Joe Rowell gave him a puzzled look, 'Oswald Kitson confirmed it along with her other clothing and the cross she was wearing.

'Right!' Conway helped himself to one of his cigarettes, and tapped it on the table without lighting it. Holding it like a pointer he waved it in Rowell's direction.

'Think about it Joe, that is a light summer scarf, and it is a winter's day. If she was wearing a scarf when she went out it should have been something heavy, most likely wool. But that wouldn't do the job - a woollen scarf would stretch and never get tight enough! Plus the fact that whoever killed her could hardly say, 'excuse me, would you take your scarf off please, I want to strangle you with it.'

'No, she wasn't wearing a scarf at all, because if she had been, it would have gone a long way to preventing her killer her from getting sufficient purchase to strangle her.'

Looks of comprehension were dawning on North and Rowell's faces.

'So, whoever killed her took the scarf with them!' It was unusual for Bert Conway to become animated, and his heavy features had taken on a remarkable resemblance to a startled bulldog.

'Not just any scarf, but her own scarf, chosen deliberately for the purpose.'

Conway sat back and scraping a match into life applied it to the cigarette. The craggy face relaxed back into its customary dour folds.

'Which means that it was definitely premeditated and had to be someone who had access to her personal belongings,' North picked up the trail, 'either Cliff Jarman or her husband.'

Joe Rowell frowned, 'yes,' he said cautiously, 'that is the obvious conclusion. However, we know that she was promiscuous, so there is always the possibility that there could be a third person who as yet we know nothing about.'

'We have got to find Jarman,' Harry was once again in control, bringing the meeting to a close.

'Anything come back as yet from Yarmouth?'

Rowell shook his head, 'Yes and no. 'Yes,' we have had every photographer in the town checked by the local police, and 'no,' he never turned up there. He was supposed to go to work for a small one man firm run by a man called Cecil Greet just off of the sea front, but he didn't show up. I think that whatever happened here, whether he killed Alice or simply decided to disappear to get away from her - in which case he may not even know that she is dead - at the last minute he changed his plans. Hopefully he is not all that bright, and went to another seaside resort on the East Coast. I am at present having all of the photographers in Cromer, Skegness, and Hunstanton seen. It is a waiting game, with the holiday season in full swing it might take a while.'

'What about the husband, is he making any noises?' asked Conway.

Rowell paused to consider the question. He and Vincent Porter had gone directly to Kitson's shop in the Market Place after leaving the lime kiln as Joe wanted to inform him before the Gazette got hold of the story.

Kitson was in his opinion a very cold man. Not overly tall he was inclined to corpulence with a round pudgy face and bulbous fish like eyes. A thinning head of hair was compensated for by a closely trimmed, old fashioned beard. He took the news of his wife's death quite calmly. Sitting down on a dining chair in the little room at the back of the shop, he seemed to absorb the shock of the news as if it was something that he had been waiting some time for.

'Thank you Mr Rowell,' he said quietly. 'I knew that something like this had happened, Alice would never have gone away of her own free will. Please find the person who did this - for both of us.'

'He was fairly calm when we broke the news, almost philosophical,' he replied. 'We got him to do the identification from her clothing, there was no point putting him through the trauma of seeing what was left of the body. Obviously he still hasn't got a clue about the photos or Cliff Jarman.'

'And what about before we found the body - when she was simply missing?'

Rowell thought again before answering. 'He was concerned, but accepted that we were doing our best to find her,' he replied.

'You see,' mused Conway, 'If I was married to a big handsome woman like that, twenty odd years of age, who had got - as we well know from Clifford's collection of party time pics - a definite taste for being shagged on a regular basis - I would have been on your doorstep everyday until I got her back…'

Alone in his office Harry North sat gazing distantly out of the picture window at the street scene below. The window was, along with a couple of others on the façade of the building, arched. The others being the main window in the administration office, and the middle window of the Chief Constables rooms. Briefly his mind flicked to the admin office and his bête noir, Montagu Parfitt. The subject of many long early morning hours of reflection, when sleep eluded him and he could allow his mind the luxury of wandering over the multitude of things that he needed to put into their correct places, he now knew exactly how to deal with the good Captain, and would thoroughly enjoy the process. It was simply a matter of 'when'.

Swinging his chair back round to the desk he looked at the large folder made out of plywood laying on his desk. The folder - it could be described as nothing other - was made of two identical sheets of ply, twenty four inches high by eighteen inches wide, separated by an inch square length of wooden baton and held together by sturdy brass hinges. Inside screwed firmly to the woodwork was a large brass 'alligator clip' which retained securely inside the covers a sheaf of papers. The papers themselves were specially printed and cut to size. This was 'the roll'.

The roll was in itself a work of art. The sheets, neatly ruled and sectioned by the printer in light red ink, contained the details of the duties apportioned each day to every man on the force . One double sided sheet for each day, containing the warrant numbers and ranks of two hundred and thirty five men and officers gave the duty state of the entire force at a glance.

Fingering the battered timber, Harry wondered who had made the roll. Continually locked into the problems of the present, he was seldom troubled by retrospective analysis of the past. For the first time he realised that when he joined the force thirty five years previously, the roll had been something that he saw on a daily basis, and it was old and battered then. Officers paraded for duty each day and night in the parade room in front of the muster desk. Spread out in two lines, a Sergeant at the right hand end, fifteen minutes before the start of their shift, awaiting the arrival of the duty Inspector with 'the Roll' to brief them. He thought of the muster desk itself, still out there at this minute in the parade room. An old teacher's desk acquired from some forgotten schoolroom, it had also been there long before his time.

Putting aside nostalgia, Harry opened the folder and began a detailed examination of the duty state over the weekend. The sheet for today was on top, at the back were those for the previous weekend, waiting to be filed.

Harry pulled out the sheets for Saturday and Sunday. Studying them he was not certain if he should be thankful or frustrated by what he found.

Each working shift of officers was made up of six men and a Sergeant. Three of the men formed the nucleus, working together all of the time whilst the remaining three floated about between shifts, allowing for flexibility in re-arranging manpower when it was necessary.

The duty rosters showed that all of the previous week, Sergeant 31 O'Keefe was on night duty along with Constables 84 Gunn, 179 Green, and 101 Wales, they were the regular men, the ones that Harry was interested in. The three 'floating officers' were relatively new recruits, 205 McClintock, 208 Holder, and 82 Boston. Of the three, the only one to whom Harry could put a face to was Boston, who he recollected as being the uniform officer with the medal ribbons at the lime kiln. The shift's last tour of night duty was Saturday. His speculation that the night police might be a part of the setup was based on a need to ensure that there were no interruptions whilst the criminals were doing their work. So logically, O'Keefe and his men could not have been involved in the burglary at Byram's on the Sunday night, because it was a different shift that was on duty.

North sat studying the sheet of paper for a long while, lost in his own thoughts. On the one hand he was relieved at what he saw, on the other there was still a doubt in his mind that somehow he was missing something. Checking along the top line of numbers he saw that Lewis Arthur had been the night Charge Sergeant all week. He would have a word with Lew when he came back on duty tomorrow.

Chapter 10

Checking the wiring from the vault to the mains switch in Lisa Abbott's office, Cole Wade's mind was busy turning over the events of the recent weekend. The robbery at the Byram's house had been simplicity itself. Leaving Moses Hawkins outside on watch, he and the others, muffled from head to toe to prevent identification, had found no difficulty in forcing the terrified jeweller to allow them into his house. His specific instruction that Frank Chesterton, and no one else, was to speak meant that the Byram's only heard a man with a local accent. Similarly they were presented with a three man group of attackers. The police were not fools and a four man team would lead them straight to the basin. Once they left the house, the keys were deposited as instructed behind the first milestone out of town on the Derby Road and the package with the remaining hundred pounds picked up from the same place.

He frowned at the length of cable in his hand. Whoever the man in the church was, he had made a killing, there would Wade estimated have been well over ten thousand pounds worth of gold and jewellery in a shop the size of Byram's. His part had been bought cheaply and Cole resolved that if the situation occurred again he would hold out for more cash - a lot more cash.

'What are you doing?' The question broke his train of thought and looking over his shoulder he saw that Lisa had come into the office. The dog he noticed, taking up its usual place under the desk, head on paws was watching him intently.

'Altering the wiring into the vault charges,' he replied.

'I have built in a failsafe, don't want us switching the lights on and blowing the joint up,' he grinned.

Pulling himself to his feet he pointed to the two mains switches on the wall. The metal lever on the one on the left was in the down position. The lever of the newly installed one next to it was up.

'Previously to set off the charges, all you had to do was hit the button under the desk. That was okay, but if you caught it by accident - ba-bam - everything down there has gone all the way to Dixie!'

She smiled at the American twang in his voice and the unusual manner of speech. One day she decided she would go to America, perhaps when this particular scheme had run its course.

Mistaking the smile for something more personal, Wade moved a little closer. Dressed in a man's cavalry twill breeches and a working shirt, the top buttons undone sufficiently to reveal an inch or two of cleavage, he was beginning to find the lovely Mrs Abbott more attractive by the day.

A subtle whiff of eau-de-cologne caught his nostrils as turning away slightly she dropped her hips onto the edge of the desk, readjusting the distance between them.

He is certainly keen she thought, but now was neither the time nor the place. Lisa was somewhat surprised at her own reaction, the American was definitely attractive, and she would enjoy making love to him -but later.

'There was a robbery last night,' she said, 'three men broke into the house of a jeweller in town, stole his keys and ransacked the shop.'

Wade returned her stare without flinching. 'I heard about it,' he replied. 'Be a good job to have pulled off.'

'If I find out it was you Cole, with Pip, Squeak, and Wilfred out there, it won't be the only thing that gets pulled off. Do you understand what I am saying? I have got some pretty heavy people backing me. They don't like cowboys, and you are from cowboy country aren't you?'

The menace was not lost on Wade, and he wondered what exactly the woman had been involved in before he met her.

'There is absolutely no problem Lisa,' he said smiling easily, 'I wouldn't even know where to begin with a job like that. As I say, it would be interesting but for a start I don't have the contacts.'

She nodded slowly. Time would tell she thought, and if he were involved, then rest assured, some of the spoils would be coming her way - that she could guarantee.

'I may have to go to Leicester for a day or two,' she said casually.

'Business?' asked Wade equally casually.

'Yes I need to see a man about a dog.'

Why was she telling him this he wondered. Had they finally moved into a situation where she was beginning to trust him, or was she expecting trouble and needed his help.

'Is this the same man who arranges the cargoes?' he asked picking up a pair of pliers and twisting the cable ready to connect it.

'He has a certain involvement,' she was watching him intently. A phone call earlier in the morning from Gil Manton had disturbed her. He wanted, he said, to talk to her about bringing in some more help and enlarging the number of cargoes going through the basin. She did not believe him. He was up to something. Here she was secure with backup if anything went wrong, in Leicester she would be alone and vulnerable.

Lisa had no intention of going to Leicester, but she was streetwise enough to be able to sniff trouble in the air and had decided that it was time to bring Cole Wade a bit closer to her. Sitting on the edge of the desk she actually reconsidered her earlier decision. Perhaps now was not a bad time to seduce him. Take him up to the flat on the pretext of explaining a few things in private, the rest would be a simple matter for someone of her experience. With some small reluctance she dismissed the idea, Cole was also very streetwise he would know in a flash what was going on and she would lose the advantage.

'You were explaining about the electricity,' she needed to change the subject.

'Its quite simple. If something goes badly wrong and we need to get out, you still blow the charges by pushing the button under the desk, but now you also need to have the second mains switch down. So you can't accidentally …' He stopped realising that she was no longer listening to him.

Gyp had got up from under the desk, and having shook herself purposefully was now standing looking at the door out onto the quay, her tail wagging slowly from side to side.

Seconds later a shadow fell across the entrance followed by the dapper figure of Harry North.

Touching the brim of his hat he gave them a broad smile, 'Good day to you both, I do hope that I am not interrupting anything,' he said breezily.

'What do you want, this is private property and I have told you before you are not welcome,' Lisa's voice was as cold and uninviting as her words.

Harry put his hand down and quietly stroked the dog's head before slipping a humbug into her mouth. She dropped to the ground, chewing it noisily.

'Actually, you are not totally right about the private property bit,' he continued unabashed.

'I had a word with the Town Clerk. Apparently all of the towpaths and quayside areas are public rights of way. In here, '*and within the curtilage of your buildings and office*' you are quite right. However, I come with the best intentions, to warn you that there are those about at the moment who would do you harm.'

'A local jeweller, David Byram, and his wife were attacked in their home last night and within hours his shop was robbed. You are isolated and a touch vulnerable out here Lisa. I thought that you might appreciate a friendly warning.'

'I am not vulnerable and you are not a friend, nor am I likely with four strong men on site day and night to be a target for robbers,' she retorted.

'Ah yes, that's right, you employ *four* men - if we include Mr Wade - I was thinking that it was three, but I was mistaken.' The smile had been replaced by a quizzical look, not once did his gaze drift across to Wade. 'But can you be sure that they are all here night and day? Exactly where they should be when you want them? Men have to have some free time, they like to 'nip off for a drink'. What if three of them 'nipped off' without your knowing, leaving just Mr Wade here?'

The sweet gone, the dog was back on its feet, sniffing at North's trouser pocket.

'Come her Gyp and settle down!' Lisa could hardly control the anger bubbling up. The policeman was sniffing round, bating her, telling her that her team was directly under suspicion. What was really worrying her was how long had North been outside listening to their conversation before Gyp gave him away.

'I said, come here and settle!' The collie gave Harry a resigned look, and slumped back under the desk.

'I'll be on my way now,' he said, inwardly rejoicing at the affect that his visit had made, and wondering which of the two mains switches on the wall it was that Cole Wade was referring to which needed to be in the 'on' position before the charges could be blown. Most likely the one on the right hand side - with the brick dust beneath it on the stone floor, where someone had been drilling to put up fixings.

'Good day to you both.'

'Have you got any idea what time you will be finished tonight?'

Connie Armitage put down the dish towel that she had been using to wipe dry the frying pan in which she had just cooked a hurried meal of eggs and bacon for Bert Conway.

The detective shook his head and putting his half empty tea cup down on the table, glanced at the large Smith's' kitchen clock over the pantry door. It was almost half past twelve. 'Not a clue Con. Harry is coming round any time now and we are going down to the Lamb and Pheasant for a meeting with Joe and Clarrie. After that, it is a matter of what wants doing, and how long it takes, so don't worry about an evening meal, I will eat on the hoof.'

Connie nodded cheerfully and said, 'If you are not in before I go to bed, I'll leave something cold out for you.'

Other than her son Ashleigh, she could think of no one in the world she loved more than Bert. Three years ago during the summer of 1916 her world had been torn apart when Bernard Ashe, the man she was going to marry, was murdered by a demented killer in Whitby. She and Bernard had been lovers for some time and had sneaked off to the seaside resort for a bank holiday weekend of sunshine and romance that went terribly wrong.

Bernard was a detective on the Kelsford Police Force, his partner the irascible Sergeant Conway. Bert Conway had a reputation around the town as a man not to be meddled with, and in truth the only times that she ever came into contact with him were when she served him across the counter of the Pack Horse where she worked. A big man with a florid face and deep voice, Bernard had always told her that 'Bert was alright - you had to know him', something which during her time with Bernard she had studiously avoided. The Pack Horse was a favourite meeting place for the detectives headed by Inspector North, to gather in a smoky corner to discuss cases in private away from Long Street police station. Stealing glance across at them between serving customers she would see the two older men, the big coarse Sergeant Conway and the equally big but fatter Sergeant Greasley nodding across in her direction and laughing together before sending an embarrassed Bernard over to get a fresh round of beers. Inspector North, who Connie knew was nicknamed named 'Foxy', seemed to stay out of these humorous sallies on Bernard about his relationship with her.

She would never forget the sunny August morning two months after Bernard was killed, that Bert Conway walked into the bar five minutes after Josh Littleton, the landlord unlocked the front door, and disappeared back upstairs, leaving her to open up. She was behind the bar, stacking bottles of beer on the shelf ready for the lunch time trade to begin when he came in.

'What can I get you Mr Conway?' she asked politely, it was the first time that she had ever been alone with Bernard's old partner and she felt distinctly nervous.

'Pint of bitter please,' he said, pulling a tall stool up to the bar, and sitting down on it. Opening a copy of the Daily Sketch that he had just bought from Boughton's newsagents, he spread it on the counter and turning to the back became absorbed in a study of the racing page.

Unsure of whether or not to engage him in conversation Connie decided against it and returned to stacking the bottles. After a few minutes she heard him say from behind her in a quiet voice, 'You are pregnant aren't you?'

She froze almost dropping the bottle of Mackeson that she was placing on the shelf.

Turning to face him she saw an expression on his face of concern. He waited, saying nothing. Wiping her hands down the sides of her skirt, she stared at him for a long moment.

Bert Conway sat perfectly still, the slim figure of the tall blonde haired barmaid seemed to have shrunk before his eyes. He knew that he was right, he had sensed it on a couple of occasions when he had been in recently, there was nothing tangible, just an instinct, now the terror on her face confirmed it.

There was sadness in his eyes. Sadness for this young girl, in her mid-twenties, young enough to be the daughter he never had; her life about to collapse in ruins around her. Sadness for Thelma, the woman who he had loved unstintingly and who after five short years of marriage had been taken away from him in the typhus epidemic of 1897. She was four months pregnant, their unborn child dying with her.

'How did you know?' she asked, finally finding her voice.

'I have been around a long while,' he said quietly. 'Thing is, what are you going to do?'

Connie shook her head. It was the question that she had been asking herself every waking minute of every day, and most of the nights that she had lain awake in bed, looking at the ceiling of her bleak lodgings, crying herself to sleep.

'I'll manage.'

'What do you mean you will manage?' The question was asked softly, there was a concern in his voice that very few people had heard in the last twenty years.

'I will manage,' the words sounded hollow and unsure.

'No you will not manage,' he said gently. 'I will tell you what will happen. When, in a couple of months you begin to show, people will start to talk. Then as you get bigger, and can't work, Josh will dispense with your services - he will have no choice, a pregnant barmaid in a busy pub is a liability.'

'When your time comes, your landlady will kick you out of your lodgings, and you will finish up on the doorstep at the workhouse. Then three days after your child is born you will be discharged under a 'Workhouse Master's Order', onto the streets. From there, your guess is as good as mine.'

Tears streaming down her face, Connie gave him a look of desperation.

'Don't you think I know all this, but what can I do?' she asked. 'The baby is Bernard's, we were going to get married. It happened whilst we were in Whitby, then he was killed. I just don't know what to do Mr Conway!'

Conway folded his newspaper carefully and pushed it into his jacket pocket.

Placing a piece of paper on the bar with an address neatly written in pencil on it he said, 'I need a housekeeper. Two pounds a week and keep. Give Josh your notice on Friday, pack your bags, and start work a week on Monday.'

Speechless, Connie looked at him for several seconds as she took in what he was saying. Overwhelmed with gratitude she could not believe what was happening.

'People will still talk,' she said, her mind in a whirl.

Conway shook his head, 'Oh no they won't,' he replied.

Watching the bulky figure disappear through the doorway back into the summer's morning, Connie stared, mesmerised at the paper clutched in her hand with the address written on it. She suddenly noticed that Bert had not touched the beer that he had ordered.

Ashleigh Bertram Armitage was born at Kelsford Cottage Hospital on 3rd March 1917. Named after his father Bernard Ashe, he was christened four months later at the Church of St Mary Magdalene, in Rosemary Street, his godfathers' being Harry North and Bert Conway, with Laura Percival his godmother. Clarence Greasley, by common consent was made an honorary godfather at the celebration held that same Sunday afternoon in the function room of the Pack Horse, funded by Harry and Laura.

Connie smiled fondly at Bert Conway. The last three years been a revelation to her. The man that the outside world saw as a dour, recalcitrant and solitary figure, was in reality she had found, an intelligent and kindly person who had spent the larger part of his life deliberately creating a shield against the hurt that he had experienced when he lost his wife. As Bernard had told her, you needed to know Bert, and very few people did, not even she thought his friend Harry North. Although he did not talk very much about his life with Thelma, he did on occasions allow her glimpses into the time that they spent together. She understood from the way that he treated Ashleigh his deep sense of loss at having no children of his own.

When he said that no one would talk about her having an illegitimate child, he was she knew deluding himself. Certainly no one would dare to say anything in his hearing, however she knew that behind their backs there was gossip. Some people even surmised that Bert was Ash's father. If Bert was aware of the chatter he certainly did not discuss it with her. The 'two pounds a week and keep' was also something of a myth. Since Ash was born Bert had paid for everything, baby clothes, food, a perambulator; even her clothing, of which she bought very little, was on an account that he settled as and when it was necessary. Most of the wages that he paid her went into her Post Office savings account at the end of each week for a rainy day, which she suspected had been his intention all along, and over the three years, Connie had come to love him like a father.

A knock at the front door interrupted their conversation, it was North.

'Did you sort those printers out Bert?' he asked as Conway pulled on his jacket.

'Yes. Clarrie and I frightened the shit out of Manny Escher,' he chuckled, 'and everyone else in town - except Joe - knows that to do any printing for the union is to invite disaster.'

North nodded, he was reconciled to the fact that his actions would result in a confrontation with Joe Rowell when he found out, but is was necessary, both for the Force and for Rowell's own good.

For the detectives to meet in the Lamb and Pheasant at this time in the week was something of a deviation from tradition. Usually it was Friday lunchtime when Harry and the three detective sergeants adjourned to the back room of the little pub in Crich Lane. During the week any 'business' was conducted in the bar of the Pack Horse, the reason being that it was the usual watering hole for solicitors taking a lunchtime drink after a morning in court, businessmen sealing deals over a gin and tonic, and on market days thirsty farmers bemoaning their losses and counting their money. In general it was the place where information could be quietly exchanged and understandings arrived at. The Friday lunchtime meeting in the 'Lamb' was different, it was the end of the week and gave the detectives an opportunity, away from prying eyes and unwanted interruptions, to unwind and discuss informally things that would go no further.

'I decided to meet here,' he explained to the others, 'because that fat bugger Bathurst will be sniffing around the Pack Horse by now and I want to deal with him on my own terms when I am ready.'

The others nodded in agreement. Gilmour Bathurst, the editor of the Kelsford Gazette was a thorn in the side of the detective department. Ever since the discovery of the two bodies in the lime kiln he had been running what he claimed were 'daily updates of the situation.' In fact his column was a source of constant sniping at the lack of progress, and perceived misuse of the Kelsford ratepayers money by the police.

'He was having a meeting with our leader this morning, which I managed to sidestep, but I don't want to be where he can find me.' When Eric Broughton had poked his head around the office door to summon him to the meeting with the Chief Constable, the Superintendent told him to report back that 'Mr North was out on urgent enquiries', Harry had then left the building by the back stairs and disappeared into the town.

The present meeting however produced little new information on the Byram robbery. The story that the couple told of the events of the previous night did not change, and they had to accept that it was genuine. Now, the consensus was that they would have to wait until something, such as items from the burglary turning up gave them a much needed lead.

Joe Rowell was edgy and Harry wondered whether he suspected that his union activities were under close scrutiny, or if it were simply the lack of progress on the Kitson murder.

'How did you get on at the Cottage Homes?' he asked. Over the weekend, Rowell had been to see the Master and Matron, a man and wife couple who were in charge of the institution where Alice had been brought up.

'Dan and I went over yesterday morning. Nice old couple - Mr and Mrs Pearson - been running the home since it opened in 1884. They have an encyclopaedic knowledge of the kids who have been through their hands over the last thirty odd years. They remember Alice as a youngster, and of course she stayed in touch after she left. She was going to be helping them with the bring and buy that was taking place the day after she disappeared.'

Rowell paused, gathering his thoughts. 'According to Mrs Pearson, Alice was twelve when she was admitted to the home. Her mother died and her father who was a farrier, buggered off leaving her on her own - only child, no brothers or sisters. He dumped her at the workhouse door and simply disappeared. They transferred her to the Cottage Homes at Monckton and she stayed there until she was fifteen when Oswald Kitson showed up looking for a shop assistant and the rest we know.'

'Apparently she was a quiet girl, mature for her age, kept herself to herself and did whatever she was asked to do - classic attitude for coping in any institution.'

North nodded in agreement. 'Any friends, was she close to anyone?'

'Just one. A girl called Celia Rutherford. She had been in the home since she was quite young, about nine or ten, and was about six or seven months older than Alice. Took her under her wing so to speak, and looked after her until she was settled in. The Pearson's say that the two girls became very close.'

'What happened to the Rutherford girl?'

'Same as happens to all of them,' Joe replied. 'She left the home around the same time as Alice. Again, shopkeeper from Chesterfield turned up looking for labour, she suited the bill and went off to take a live-in job working for him.'

Harry pulled a face. It was common practice for such institutions, having checked out a prospective employer, to release the youngsters in their care to be taken off to work. By 'checking out' he knew that provided the person looked respectable and was well dressed, they would pass muster. The homes, however caring - and he was under no illusion that they offered a far better start for a child than the old workhouses were under constant pressure once their charges reached working age to make space for newcomers.

'It would be worth our while trying to have a word with this girl. Alice had no friends here and she might well have stayed in touch with her.'

Rowell shook his head resignedly. 'I thought about that. I telephoned Chesterfield police with the name and address for her employer that Mr Pearson gave me last night. Because it was urgent, Chesterfield went round first thing this morning and rang me back. He is still there, name of Howitt, owns quite a large store in the centre of the town, employs about twenty staff. Celia Rutherford stayed with them for about six months then gave in her notice and left. He has no idea where she went to. Its eleven years ago, absolutely no chance of finding her now.'

'Any news about Jarman?' Harry asked him.

Again the Scotsman shook his head, 'No, not a bloody thing!'

Clarrie Greasley swirled the beer around in the bottom of his glass before replacing it carefully on the table. 'That is not really surprising,' he said, 'its middle of the holiday season and the east coast forces will all be stretched dealing with the holiday makers - usual thing, pick pocketing, stolen luggage, drunks…'

'People screwing other people's wives for the week whilst every body thinks they are visiting a sick aunt,' Bert interposed.

Harry glared at him, 'what are you thinking Clarrie? he asked.

'What I am thinking is,' continued Greasley, 'this is a murder enquiry, so why don't we just bite the bullet and do it ourselves. We have got a full description of Jarman, let young Dan Scofield and Bill Sykes get on a train to Cromer and walk the front for a morning looking at the beach photographers, if our man is there they will spot him. If they draw a blank, then they move on, to Skegness and Hunstanton. No need to bother with Yarmouth because we know he's not there. They could do all three resorts in four days, and hopefully come back with a body.'

North stared at him in stunned amazement. 'What the bloody hell are you thinking of!' he exclaimed. 'Do you think I am going to authorise sending two detectives paddling at the seaside, pissing it up and shagging housemaids who are off the leash for a week - you can forget that !'

'It would work,' Rowell said tentatively, 'and it is a murder Harry.'

North glowered, the suggestion made sense, but he knew what policemen were like when they were left to their own devices. After a minute's thought he said slowly, 'Alright, but not Bill and Dan. I want a Sergeant. Joseph, you go with young Scofield. Check the times of the trains, get travel warrants from Parfitt, and I want an expenditure sheet for every penny that you spend.'

For the first time since they sat down Rowell grinned at the Superintendent.

'Do I get an ice cream allowance?'

'What you do, is you go and get some beer in before I change my mind,' retorted North sourly.

Clarrie looked at Harry approvingly as Joe Rowell went to the bar to bring a second round of drinks.

'So, we keep Joe occupied and out of the way for a few days,' he raised his eyebrows enquiringly.

North grunted non-commitally. 'He had better come back with a body.'

'Speaking of getting travel warrants from your mate Parfitt, how much would you reckon to pay for a good piece of information Harry?'

Clarrie Greasley gazed speculatively at the Superintendent over the rim of the glass of bitter that Joe Rowell had just set in front of him.

Harry North studied the glowing end of his cigarette before replying. 'Let us say', he replied meaningfully, 'that not telling me whatever it is that you think you know, could result Clarence, even at this late stage of your auspicious and successful career, in a return to the refreshing experience of walking the streets of this fair town during the dead of night, in the pissing rain locking up drunks'.

Bert Conway's bulldog features crumpled into huge grin, 'have you ever seen him in uniform', he growled, 'he looks like a fucking Toby jug!'

Joe Rowell and Harry, both joining in with the joke burst out laughing.

'I repeat', said Greasley undeterred, 'good information comes at a cost and I have laid out my own money to avail us of this little gem'.

'Ah', he's been chatting in the bookies !' exclaimed Rowell. 'We are not subsidising your expenditure at Fred Goldman's'.

'So be it. Perhaps better if I keep things to myself', said Greasley reaching for his pint pot.

'What have you got?' asked Harry seriously.

Greasley took a pull at his beer before replying. 'Fred Goldman had a chat with me yesterday when I was in there. He is somewhat concerned that our man Parfitt is having a bit of a bad streak at the moment … and owes him forty pounds…'

Clarrie let the others take in the information.

Slowly North drew a circle with the tip of his finger in a damp patch where some beer had spilled on the table. 'What did you tell Fred?' He continued to study the table top.

'To let Parfitt run, and we would see to it that at the end of the day he wasn't out of pocket'.

Harry nodded, the finger erased the circle to replace it with a cross.

'Good. Very, very good. As yet our administration manager has no idea what a bad run looks like - but he will do soon.'

Pulling two half crowns out of his pocket he handed them to the sergeant.

'Four pints and whisky chasers.'

Chapter 11

'Who else knows about this document?'

The man they simply knew as 'Fedir' studied the thin faced individual without replying. He did not like Albert Wales, nor for that matter his companion, who everyone referred to as Ben. He had noticed them earlier in the day as he boarded the train from Kelsford to Liverpool at Manchester. Avoiding contact with them he had slipped quickly away when the train arrived in Liverpool and sat in the station buffet for half an hour ensuring that he had not been followed.

The two Kelsford policemen talked a lot about revolution and seizing power, but instinctively he knew that they were not committed to the cause. Behind their rhetoric he was certain that they were simply laying in wait for the chaos which would follow the imminent police strike, before lining their pockets with some of the spoils that would come their way during the subsequent period of disorder and looting.

Albert Wales shifted uncomfortably on the kitchen chair pulled up to the old fashioned dining table in the parlour of the tiny terraced house at the back of Vauxhall Road. The foreigner unnerved him. It was nothing he said or did, it was just the menacing atmosphere surrounding him. All that Wales knew was that since coming to England during the war he had been given a post in Manchester working for the War Office Pensions Department. It was a convenient day job which allowed the military and the Manchester Police to use him as an interpreter during interviews with foreigners who wanted to live in the district.

'What I mean is,' Wales licked his lips nervously wishing that he had not spoken. There were five other men present, he should have left it to one of them, 'what I mean is, how sure are we that the letter is genuine?'

'Oh I think its genuine alright.' Michael Donlevy's soft Irish accent contrasted significantly with Albert Wales's flat Midlands vowels.

'I've seen Caldwell's' signature hundreds of times. Every piece of paper that floats around the Liverpool nicks is signed by the bastard. He wrote that alright.'

Spreading his hands on the green velour table covering, Yurkovich held the gaze of the man sitting opposite. 'All I can tell you is that my contact intercepted this two days ago, he confirms that it is the original letter from Francis Caldwell, the Chief Constable of Liverpool to Edward Shortt, the Home Secretary. What I do know is that if it does not go in the despatch bag to London tonight, someone is going to smell a rat.'

Wales nodded briefly. He might not like the man, but he certainly had access to some very sensitive material.

'Do you agree with me Abe?' Donlevy put the question to the broad shouldered man seated on his right, smoking a pipe.

Abraham Hyam took the briar from his mouth and also nodded. 'Yes, that's Caldwell's signature. Looks to me as if we are on a winner. They reckon that when we strike, the government will throw an iron circle round the 'pool' and then bring in the tanks. This definitely tells a different story. If the troops, led by the Guards, refuse to obey orders, then Caldwell is fucked. Two days and nights of looting and they will be begging us to come to terms. But we won't, because it will just be the start of the revolution.'

'Think about it,' he pointed the stem of his pipe at Jeb Lyle from Birmingham, and the Sheffield man, Peter Warner, seated across the table from him, his outstretched hand swung around to encompass the Kelsford men. 'Every policeman across the country on strike! The alliance unions out with us - no coal being mined, not a bus, railway carriage, or truck moving - a general strike led by the police!'

Fedir watched the group's reactions from behind quiet eyes. A big man, his size belied an intelligent and calculating mind. He was a survivor, and upon the success of his present mission rested his future. He had travelled the breadth of Europe to the furthest point possible in order to escape the consequences of the Bolshevik revolution, and if nothing else, for the time being desperately needed the protection that men such as Ralph Gresham could afford him.

Quietly he suppressed at smile at the childishly naïve way in which these amateurs had accepted the letter. He had no idea as to the identity of the forger who had painstakingly created the document, and cared less. The ease with which he had been able to pass it off as genuine was incredible. It was he knew made so much easier by the fact that the contents were exactly what the men gathered around the table wanted to hear. That it contained a promise that soldiers detailed to put down the strike, would simply lay aside their arms and join with the insurgents, totally mesmerised them. It had to be genuine, it was their passport to success.

Lyle, the Birmingham man, sat back in his chair and folded his arms across his chest. 'What exactly do you get out of this Fedir?' he asked.

'Me personally - nothing.' The thick accent was heavier than ever.

'What does the cause get out of this - everything!' The words carried a deep conviction. 'In Russia we have shown the world what the people can do. We overthrew a repressive régime and replaced it with the workers soviets.. Everyone is now equal, no wealthy *kulak* landowners, no corrupt politicians - that is what we can offer you here. Even in the British government there are those dedicated to the cause.' He indicated the sheet of paper laying on the table between them.

'Look at this letter from your Head Constable to one of your leaders. Look at the fear in it! Our agents are making this available to you in order that you can move forward in the knowledge that you cannot fail!'

Jeb Lyle's mouth twisted slightly. 'And do we also take our King into a cellar and shoot him?'

Fedir flashed him an engaging smile. 'That comrade is a decision for you to make - after you have taken away his power, and that of his minions.'

Outside an hour later, the two Kelsford policemen turned up their jacket collars against an unseasonal flurry of rain as they made their way towards the railway station.

'What do you think Albert?' asked Ben Gunn.

'What do I think about what?' grunted Wales. Taller by half a head than Gunn, he stood just over six feet, but was not particularly heavy. Years of pounding a beat around the streets of Kelsford had kept him slim and fit for his age.

'Will the Kelsford lads go on strike?'

Wales considered the question, it was the very thing he had been asking himself. He and Ben Gunn, along with Charlie O'Keefe and Brad Green had put a lot of time and effort into keeping the pot boiling, quietly agreeing with the discontent pervading the mess room, feeding the complaints, prodding away at men's disgruntlement over their pay and lack of rest days, the money owed to them for overtime for which they had received empty promises of payment.

'We need it to work. A couple of days and nights without a copper on the streets - think about it - there will be mayhem. Christ, think what we can clean up! What we have had up to now is small time. Although...' he added as an afterthought, 'Byram's was worthwhile in anybody's money.'

Ben Gunn took the pipe from his mouth and spat a stream of yellow tobacco juice into the gutter. 'And we can't touch it can we? Not a fucking penny. Charlie has got it all stowed away somewhere that only he knows about. Security - yes that's fair enough, but whilst we aren't in a hurry I am not waiting for ever for my share.'

'Don't be stupid Ben, we agreed, the shoe shop and the suits, that is one thing - a few quid in Nottingham and no one any the wiser. This one was big though. Charlie is right, it goes away on ice, probably a couple of years until we retire, then one big divvy-up and we are away for ever, out of sight.'

Wales paused a moment and looked over his shoulder to ensure that they were not being overheard. 'Plus, Charlie has got something else lined up. He mentioned to me last week that if Byram's worked out alright, he had one more big one in mind to be pulled on the night of the strike, then we pack in before someone gets too nosey.'

Gunn replaced the pipe in his mouth and gave a lopsided grin. 'Yes, that sounds good to me, we will screw Foxy fucking North into a hole in the ground. The lads are listening to Big Joe Rowell, so all things being equal - a strike it is!'

'He's late.' Will Mardlin allowed the net curtain to fall back into place. The view from the tiny bedroom over the pawnbroker's shop at the back of the Eagle foundry was restricted, but it had he acknowledged the advantage that it was almost impossible to be overlooked. The cul-de-sac below was shrouded in darkness, Percy Longman having extinguished the only gas light an hour ago.

'He will be here,' responded Gresham in a low voice. 'He is a professional. Just what sort of a professional we will find out very soon.'

Mardlin nodded in the darkness. They had spent a lot of time in the last couple of days discussing the Russian and the meeting with him tonight should he thought, be very interesting. Raising his hand he made a gesture towards a movement in the street below which was quickly swallowed up by the darkness.

A minute later there was a creak on the stairs behind them as a cautious footfall encountered the deliberately loosened board half way up. Moonlight shining through an uncovered store room window at the opposite end of the landing silhouetted the bulky form which appeared in the doorway.

'Good choice,' he said approvingly. 'Only one approach, which I presume is covered by your man in the car at the end of the road. Escape route into the next street over the back garden wall, and if necessary, a nice target coming in through the door. What happens if there is no moonlight?' Other than the deep baritone, Albert Wales and his companions would have been hard pressed to identify the well modulated tones of the now almost accent free voice.

'It is irrelevant,' Gresham said. 'There is a man with a shotgun behind you in the storeroom. He can cut you down from ten feet away, and in the doorway your body will absorb the blast so we are quite safe.'

Unperturbed by this revelation, the newcomer moved into the centre of the room and sat down at the wooden table. Gresham pulled up a chair opposite -

Will Mardlin remained to one side, studying the street through the net. There was no need for the man to ask why these precautions needed to be taken for such a simple meeting between people who were on the same side. In Russia and the surrounding states it was not sensible to trust anyone, friend or enemy. When dealing with men like Josef Stalin and Felix Dzerzhinsky, you went nowhere unarmed, and never knew what the outcome of the simplest conversation would be.

'So Fedir, did the letter pass inspection?'

The heavy features split into a huge grin showing square white teeth with the exception of one on the upper left of his mouth which was of a flat gunmetal colour.

'They are like children,' he said contemptuously. 'Show them what they want to see and they believe it unquestioningly.'

'We all do that from time to time Fedir,' murmured Gresham absently. 'What I am wondering is, where is Petrov?'

Fedir shrugged his shoulders. 'Good question. He certainly never left France after André was killed - if in fact he was ever there in the first place. The word is that he became involved in dealing with Liebknecht and the Luxemburg woman, which would put him in Berlin. There is such chaos there now that your guess is as good as mine as to where he is. The devious bastard could be back in Petersburg for all that I know. In fact, that is not such a bad supposition, with the city under siege at the moment by Yudenich's Whites they will be needing every able bodied man they can get hold of.'

'But what if he did come here after you?' Gresham persisted.

'He went to a lot of trouble to have André Tessier taken out in order to prevent Tessier from being able to identify him. What if there is another reason for him to be here, following you? Something that we know nothing about.'

The man's eyes became inscrutable slits, the heavy brows and wide mouth giving him the appearance in the shadowy room of some medieval Tartar warlord.

Making up his mind about something he said, 'yes, you are right, he is not in Berlin, he followed me here. I don't know why, but after removing Tessier he came here after me. I have dealt with the matter.'

'The body in the lime kiln?'

'Yes, he followed me to Kelsford. You know the arrangement, I was to check out the safe house near to the canal, then move on here to Manchester. I realised that he was on to me, so I led him out past the canal basin to a secluded part of the towpath, hid until he passed and then it was easy. He was not a very big man, I broke his neck and hid the body in a deep overflow pool at the back of the canal.'

'So how did the body get into the kiln?'

147

The question produced another enigmatic shrug. 'That is interesting. I do not know the answer, I read in a newspaper that two bodies had been found, and from the description of the more decomposed I knew what it was.'

Gresham leaned back in his chair.

'You see, this does not add up,' he said, almost talking to himself.

'Why would Petrov go to all that trouble to kill André Tessier - simply because he might one day recognise him on a street somewhere in Europe - and then, alone and without backup, follow a middle grade operative, who is on a relatively low key mission, to England, and - God forbid for a man of his experience - allow the operative to kill him?'

Gresham leaned forward in the chair, his elbows resting on the table, in his right hand was an automatic pistol.

The man opposite continued to eye him implacably before turning his head slowly towards the window. Like Gresham, Will Mardlin held a Browning pointed at his head.

'No,' continued Gresham, 'that body, however it got to where it was eventually found, is Fedir Yurkovich. Which means that you are Vasily Petrov.'

The oriental features remained expressionless.

'Now it is time for you to tell us what this is really all about Colonel Petrov - that was your Okhrana rank was it not? Or, we can shoot you here and carry on with our business as if nothing has happened, because as you yourself have been at great pains to establish, you are at this very minute officially in Berlin.'

'It took you long enough to work it out Colonel Gresham - that is your rank in the Guards is it not? We may or may not have things to discuss, time will tell.' The Russian gave him a bleak smile.

A flash of headlights lit up the small room as a large six seater touring car which had reversed down the street halted beneath the window.

Will nodded briefly to Gresham as Percy Longman appeared from the landing, a wicked looking sawn off shotgun held casually in his right hand. In the other was a set of handcuffs which he passed to Mardlin, who moving behind the Russian, secured his wrists.

Standing in the shop doorway five minutes later, they watched as Petrov was loaded into the spacious back seat of the Crossley limousine between two of Gresham's agents under the watchful eye of Percy Longman.

'This has the makings of something big Will,' murmured Gresham.

'He has come far too easily,' responded Mardlin. 'He expected to be caught, I think that he has set us up.'

The twitch caught at the edge of Gresham's mouth. 'Oh yes, he intended to make contact all along. The question is, why? He will be in London by tomorrow morning, then we will see what this is all about. I quite fancy spending a bit of time at the Clarence after roughing it up here for so long.'

Ralph put aside the breakfast plate, and producing his cigarette case from an inside pocket of the jacket carefully hung over the back of his chair waved it enquiringly across the table at his companion. Will made a small gesture for him to go ahead, and taking one out he lit it before snapping the case closed.

It had been a long night. Whilst Vasily Petrov was being driven down to London with his escorts, Will and Ralph took the night train from Manchester to the metropolis. On the way they talked little, either dozing or lost in their own thoughts.

Both were experienced enough interviewers to know better than to attempt to plan out what they were going to say to the Russian. To do so would be folly - although sadly within Will's experience it was an error that policemen commonly made. Have a broad idea of the direction in which the interview should be going and leave it at that.

So many detectives, concentrating on their own preconceived plans, missed what the prisoner was actually telling them. There was also another stumbling block with planning an interview. When he was a young man serving in the Leicester Force, an old detective Sergeant by the name of Ted Kendall had asked him a simple question - what is the purpose of an interview? The young Mardlin had unhesitatingly answered that it was to substantiate the evidence that you had gathered, and prove the offence with which the prisoner was charged. Smiling sadly Kendal informed him that he was completely wrong. The purpose of an interview was to establish the truth!

Will had never forgotten this adage, and it was he hoped, that which had steered him up through the ranks. He was trusted by those who worked with him and also in a perverse way, by those with whom he dealt. It was an established fact amongst the criminal classes of both Leicester and Kelsford that, 'Mr Mardlin was a man who did not take liberties'.

He was pleased that Ralph had indicated, because of Will's long experience, he wanted him to take the lead in interviewing Petrov.

'Do you know what I think Will?' Gresham exhaled a thin stream of smoke as he spoke. 'I think that our man is on the run.'

Will speared a piece of bacon from the oval platter before him and took a bite before replying. After the night's journey he was famished and was inordinately pleased that on their arrival at the hotel at the back of Wellington barracks, despite the fact that it was almost 11.a.m., they were immediately offered a full English breakfast.

'That is very likely, but let's see what he has to say. I think that whether or not you are right, he will have something to offer us. There is something else that I am not happy about, and the answer to that might go a long way to shedding some light on this.'

Gresham raised an eyebrow, however before he could pursue the question a uniformed waiter appeared at his side with an envelope on a silver salver.

Taking it, Ralph split the cover with the bone handled paper knife laid precisely along the side of the dish. Reading through the note that it contained he quickly told the waiter that there was no reply.

Watching the man disappear as discretely as he had arrived, Ralph gave Mardlin a quizzical smile. 'It is remarkable how well informed certain people are. This is a 'request' for me to *ensure that all relevant details of our discussions with Colonel Petrov are communicated to interested parties without delay.*' The facial muscle flicked as Ralph stubbed out his cigarette in the cut glass ashtray on the table.

'I think that when we have covered things here, it is probably time for you to meet the man who we are working for.'

'You intrigue me Colonel Petrov, and I have a problem. I think that you are so steeped in your own mysteries that it is your intention to unnecessarily prolong the issue concerning what you are really doing here - and we both know that eventually you do intend to tell us exactly that.'

It was not only Petrov that intrigued Will. The whole setup at the hotel interested him. He was used to dealing with people taken into custody from the street, locked up in a cell, interviewed, and then either charged with an offence or released.

This was different. It was Ralph had explained, one of the reasons for the existence of the Clarence Hotel. Will thought back to his first visit, what was it Ralph said when he raised the question of the purpose of the premises? '*It is owned by the government. The man who we work for 'acquired' it during the war as a place where certain highly secret meetings could be held, and rather sensitive guests accommodated.*' A system had been developed during the war Ralph explained over breakfast for 'softening up' defectors from the service of the Kaiser. There was, in the cellars of the hotel a secure holding cell, somewhat better appointed than a police cell, but still a cell, where an inmate or defector could be held for such time as it took to make decisions concerning his or her future. The inmate was then moved into one of the upstairs rooms where security - still strict - was less obvious. A decent bathroom, clean clothes and a good meal, could he assured Will produce startling results.

Petrov, freshly bathed and fed, wearing a pair of twill trousers and a clean collarless shirt, both of which Will noticed were deliberately too large for him - a not unremarkable feat considering the man's size - gave him an interested stare.

'We have not really been introduced,' The Russian replied evenly.

'Colonel Gresham I know from his file. Born 1877; joined the British Army - 5th Dragoon Guards - in 1892 and served in your South African War. Rapid promotion, and in 1904 was sent to observe our war with Japan as a Lieutenant. Then served in Turkey and various other places across Western Europe until the recent war when he was promoted to full Colonel.'

'But you I know nothing about, and that I think we should remedy.'

Will knew that Ralph was seething at the revelation of the extent of the pre-revolution Okhrana file which must have existed on him. Without moving his eyes he was aware of his partner's jaw locking and unlocking as he clenched and unclenched his teeth.

He also knew that he had the advantage. Petrov was fishing and it was Will who interested him. He did not know who Will was, or if he were senior to Ralph Gresham.

'We will come to who I am in good time.' He pushed the packet of Abdullah cigarettes that had been left on his night stand, across the table.

Petrov took one and accepted the light which Will offered. Through the haze of blue smoke that drifted momentarily between them, the slanted eyes and Slavonic features gave him once more the appearance of a Mongol warlord.

'Where did you learn to speak English?' Will asked suddenly.

The Russian was momentarily phased by the change of direction. 'Not all of the old Tsarist staff, or for that matter the present leaders are ignorant peasants. I was educated in Paris, my father was with the Russian embassy. I also speak excellent French and German.'

Will released his gaze and looked briefly at the ceiling. The man's moment of confusion told him the one thing that he needed to know. Petrov was a 'doer', a field man, he was not an interviewer, something which might make his present task easier.

'You came here to find Fedir Yurkovich, am I right?'

'Yes.'

'Why'

'Because he was a traitor. He betrayed our cause to the French and through them to you. He had no intention of organising this police strike. He was going to give you information that would bring the strikers down.'

'So you killed him.'

'Da.' Petrov dropped back into Russian, not certain of where Will was going.

'It does not make sense. You kill André Tessier to *prevent* him from identifying you, then readily admit to us who you are ... I will tell you what I am going to do shall I ..?'

Will rested his elbows on the table and steepled his hands under his chin.

'I don't know who you really are, but I don't think that you are Vasily Sergeyevich Petrov. This is another Bolshevik bluff, and not a very subtle one. Petrov is where he has been for most of this year - in Berlin. It was convenient to set up an imposter to trail a red herring half way across Europe. Felix Dzerzhinsky appears to be brighter than we had given him credit for. Yurkovich - as you say a traitor to the communist cause - is taken out by you. After killing him you take his place and push the strike through. If you were arrested neither we nor the French could put you on trial because it would show that we were running our own espionage missions.'

'So we would be forced to do exactly what we are going to do - release you from custody, and slip you quietly back into Russia.'

He sat back, a satisfied smile on his face. He sincerely hoped that the Russian would not spot the fatal flaw in his logic. The thing that had been bothering him for so long - the shooting of André Tessier.

Nothing changed on the prisoner's face. Not a flicker of emotion showed behind the slitted brown eyes. Mardlin got to his feet and addressed himself to Ralph Gresham.

'We fly him across to le Touquet this afternoon, no need to tell the French at this stage. Military train to Vienna, once he is there hand him over to a British unit going back to the Dnieper and let the Cossack's have him.'

Gresham also got to his feet. 'Agreed.' He said coldly. 'I will telephone and make the arrangements.'

'The single most dangerous man in Russia is Josef Stalin. I have something which will bring him down.' The tone of the man at the table was flat and emphatic. Gresham and Mardlin both sat back down again.

'Rest assured, I am Vasily Petrov. I have a document which if made public will destroy Stalin. Lenin knows nothing about it, he is an idealist and will not be allowed to live long enough to influence what is to come. Dzerzhinsky is simply an opportunist thug. Stalin now suspects that I have the document, which is sufficient to have signed my death warrant. That is why I am here. Believe me, if I had not wanted you to discover my identity you would never have even suspected that I was in your country.'

'Josef Vissarionovich Dzhugashvilli was born in the village of Gori, in Georgia

152

just before Christmas 1879. I was born in the same village three months earlier. His father was a boot maker, mine was the village farrier, both of our mothers took in washing to make ends meet. He didn't change his name to Stalin - man of steel - until years later'

The Russian pulled the packet of Abdullah's toward him and accepted a light from Gresham, he longed for the flavour hitting the back of his throat of the harsh black Russian tobacco that he usually smoked.

'At school Josef was clever but unlucky. When we were seven there was a smallpox epidemic, he caught it badly and it left him quite scarred.' Petrov paused and took a deep draw on the cigarette whilst gathering his thoughts.

'He isn't very big and has a bit of a squeaky voice, also he has got a withered hand, so one way or another the village kids used to make fun of him a lot. In those circumstances you either go under or toughen up. His way of toughening up was to become involved in politics. As I said, he was a clever kid and he won a scholarship to the Tiflis Theology Seminary. Well he certainly wasn't interested in religion but he joined a group that was dedicated to achieving independence for Georgia, and at the same time started reading Karl Marx.'

'Because of his political activities the Okhrana put together a file on him, he was arrested several times and also got sent to Siberia for a spell. I lost sight of him quite early, when I was twenty I was recruited by the Okhrana and moved out of the Tiflis district.'

'Years later, just before the war, I was stationed in Paris when a routine arrest file on Stalin came through from a Captain Zhelezniakov in Yenisiesk province. Stalin had escaped from a term of exile that he was serving in the province and it was thought that he was trying to make his way from Russia into France.'

'Attached to the file was a letter written to Zhelezniakov by a Colonel Alexander Yeremin who was head of the Okhrana station in Tiflis, stating that from 1906 until 1912 Josef Stalin had worked as an informant for the St Petersburg Okhrana. The letter was no doubt intended to mitigate for Stalin when he was recaptured, but it was also a damning indictment against him. At the time Joseph was simply one of hundreds of revolutionaries in Russia, and I filed the document with his arrest dossier until such time as we might need it.'

'A few weeks after this when the Rue Grenelle station was closed down I moved back to Petersburg. By early 1917 with the revolution just around the corner, everyone in the Okhrana was running round in circles trying to buy themselves a safe passage through the revolution. It was obvious that anyone who could be linked to the police was going to meet with short shrift. Stalin had already become a central figure and I remembered the Yeremin letter. I caught a train to Paris and went to the offices of the *Agence Bint et Sambain where the*

Paris station had been moved to. Sure enough, there in the files was the letter. It took me a matter of minutes to slip it out of the folder, burn the arrest file, and be on a train back home. In the chaos no one in Petersburg even realised that I had been away for a day or so.'

Petrov paused and looked carefully at his inquisitors, Mardlin returned his gaze steadily. 'Go on,' he said quietly, 'you have our full attention.'

Once more the enigmatic smile, 'but you want to know about now, yes.'

'At the moment we have a fairy story, the only way that you will keep our attention is to show us this letter,' replied Mardlin.

In fact both he and Ralph Gresham were strung out as taut as bowstrings. If the man before them was telling the truth, then the implications were monumental. The potential that one of the two men controlling the Russian empire might be a traitor to the cause which had carried him to a position of unlimited power presented undreamed of opportunities.

Petrov drew a deep breath before continuing. 'Since achieving a degree of power, Josef Stalin has become without question, the most ruthless man I have ever encountered. Old scores have been settled and anyone who crosses him disappears out of hand.'

'With the knowledge that a file existed in the Tiflis district concerning his activities as an agent, one of the first things that he did was have Alexander Yeremin - who had been promoted to Major General and posted as head of the Okhrana in Finland - arrested and brought back to Russia. He and his family were taken to the Lubyanka and never came out.'

He caught the quick glance that passed between the other two men.

'Ah, you do not know about the Lubyanka,' he said enigmatically. 'When Stalin and Dzerzhinsky set up their own secret police - the Cheka - they took over the old All-Russia Insurance Company building in Lubyanka Square in Moscow as their headquarters. It also houses some of the deepest prison cells in Russia.'

A light glinted in the slanted eyes. 'There is a joke in the Cheka, which says that Lubyanka is the highest building in Russia, because you can see Siberia from its basement.'

'Yeremin told his interrogators that he had sent the arrest file along with the letter *to* Zhelezniakov in Paris. I know for a fact that both Yeremin and the two Cheka men who interviewed him were taken out and shot in the Lubyanka execution yard within minutes of them reporting back to Stalin.'

'That was where I came in. At an early stage of the revolution I had been able to present *Dzerzhinsky with sufficient Okhrana material to convince him that I would be an asset to the Cheka, and consequently I was working in Moscow when this happened. Because of our childhood association,* Josef Vissarionovich saw me alone and gave me the job of tracking down Captain Zhelezniakov and recovering the letter. It was he said, a forgery, and all part of an Imperialist plan to discredit him. Bring it back to him personally and I would immediately be given command of a Cheka district, along with all of the perks that went with it'

Again the smile, rueful this time. 'It was of course a death sentence. To even know of the existence of the letter was to drink from the poisoned chalice - he had already had the investigators who had talked to Yeremin shot. What he could not know of course was that Captain Zhelezniakov did not have the original letter - I had it.'

'*What neither of us knew was that Vladimir* Zhelezniakov had kept a duplicate of the file which he sent to Paris in 1913. By late 1917 he was fighting with the Cossacks against the Red Army. I soon found out that he had recently been captured in an ambush on the Don and was being held prisoner in a camp near the river. When I saw him he couldn't talk fast enough to save his skin. He told me that he had destroyed the duplicate arrest file, but in order to buy himself some insurance, had sent the copy of the letter which it contained to Karl Liebknecht in Germany. Also he had told Fedir Yurkovich what he had done. Yurkovich was a little shit who had worked as an Okhrana informant for Zhelezniakov before the revolution, and had ingratiated himself with the Cheka when it was formed. I knew that the Pole - *Dzerzhinsky - thought that he could be trusted, and had sent him to organize the police strike in England, which shows what dumb bastards the Poles are!'*

'*So, in one way a problem, in another a blessing. Liebknecht was organizing the Spartakist Movement for the communists in Berlin, which I have to say was not going well. That he had a copy of the letter was very bad. On the other hand, it provided me with an opportunity to leave Russia and travel west to Germany without arousing Stalin's suspicions. Also, I knew without doubt that Fedir Yurkovich would be on the trail of the letter as well.'*

'*Did you know at this point that Yurkovich was working for the French?'* asked Gresham.

'*Da'.* The huge head nodded once. '*I had known for months that the bastard was working for the Sûreté. I was waiting for him to lead us somewhere, then denounce him.'*

Petrov's mouth twisted in a gesture of contempt. 'And of course, he thought that he was chasing the original - not a copy.'

'So it was relatively easy. Because I had priority travel documents authorised by Stalin himself, I actually arrived in Berlin before Yurkovich. When I got there the Spartakists were besieging the offices of the Social Democrat newspaper Vorwärts. One of the Freikorps units that was based on the outskirts of Berlin stepped in to deal with them. The communists had absolutely no chance against the Freikorps men, couple of days fighting and the majority of the Spartakists were laying dead on the street. *Liebknecht along with his mistress, Rosa Luxemburg were taken prisoner on the day that I arrived and handed over to a unit of the regular Guards.'*

'*Whilst they were being held at a Berlin hotel waiting to be taken to Moabit Prison, I simply went to where they were living in Mannheimer Strasse and searched the place. The copy of Yeremin's letter was under the bedroom carpet.'*

'*Again at the hotel where they were being held it was easy. You have no idea how short money is in Germany, everyone even the Guards officer in charge of the escort party is living at subsistence level. When I got there the crowd outside was baying for their blood, I spoke to the officer in the lobby, convinced him that they would not get either him or Luxemburg out alive and that it was worth the wad of marks that went into his tunic pocket to resolve the matter early. Liebknecht was shot later that night trying to escape. The woman finished up being found dead down by the canal. It was all over before that arsehole Yurkovich got off the train.'*

Mardlin stood up and stretched his arms above his head, he needed time to digest the raft of information that the Russian was giving to them. His brain was teaming with questions. This was just the beginning, it would take days to sift through what Petrov was telling them, then go back and tease out all of the details. That he was telling them the truth, Will was satisfied, but there was one more issue he needed to resolve.

'*And this is where we come into the story isn't it,*' he said, sitting back down.

'Yurkovich knew that you had got there ahead of him, which told him that Stalin knew about the letter and had set the dogs onto him. Yurkovich was also aware that you would be after him personally, because knowing of the existence of the letter was sufficient to have him killed.'

The Russian gazed at Mardlin stone faced, waiting for him to continue.

'You said you already knew that Yurkovich was working for the Sûreté.'

A hand halfway to the cigarette packet paused for a second to make a small acknowledgement.

'Fedir Yurkovich didn't know that it was a copy letter in Liebknecht's apartment, he thought that it was the original. He had to get you off of his back before you caught up with him, so he deliberately tried to lead you to France where Tessier could deal with you.'

For the first time a genuine rumble of approval came from somewhere deep in the Russian's chest. The cigarette remained unlit held in mid-air.

'We were set up by the French.' *Although Will's comment was addressed to Gresham his eyes never left the Russian's.*

'Yurkovich was working for Tessier, who knew that he was going after the letter in Berlin. That is why Yurkovich was delayed, he had to wait for instructions from the Sûreté. When he thought that you had got the letter he contacted Tessier again and was instructed to make a run for it to Boulogne. You would follow him, the Sûreté would ambush you and take possession of the letter. We were brought in as insurance. If it all went wrong and there was a shoot-out, then the French would disappear and leave us - British Intelligence - on the scene, holding the bag.'

'André Tessier miscalculated though. He didn't realize that the copy letter was not important - I would think that you had already destroyed it. What was important, was to maintain the value of the original letter by eliminating everyone who knew of its existence, which included him. You simply set up an execution team to take care of André and continued after Fedir Yurkovich. André was killed purely to keep things tidy. But if what you say is true, you are also now in great danger, which is why you have come to us. Once you didn't return from Berlin, Stalin immediately knew that you had recovered whatever it was that Liebknecht had received from Zhelezniakov, making you priority target number one.'

'So, where is the letter now comrade?' asked Ralph.

Chapter 12

It was cold in the tiny storeroom and Lewis Arthur shivered as he struck a match to light the single gas mantle mounted on the wall. Although electricity had been installed throughout most of the offices at Long Street, there were still a number of small areas, storerooms such as this one, and outbuildings that relied on gas lighting. Even on a summer's night the dead hours between 2 a.m., and four were cold and unwelcoming.

Quickly he ran his eyes along the rows of small brass hooks on the wall opposite the door, as he expected, the item he was looking for was no longer there. Next he opened the tall thin ledger on the desk. Turning to the last page of entries, Lew reached up absently and adjusted the gas mantle to give a brighter light. The writing was neat and orderly - the last entry staring up at him from the page was as he knew it would be, in his own handwriting. He stood for a long minute, far from any flush of exhilaration at the confirmation of his suspicions, it was a wave of depression that swept over him as his eyes returned to the line of hooks.

Closing the book he extinguished the light, allowing the darkness to envelope him whilst he gathered his thoughts. There was he knew no way around it. Tomorrow morning it would have to be dealt with.

Locking the storeroom door he made his way along the darkened corridor towards the stairs leading back down to the ground floor. His footsteps echoed hollowly on the marble surface of the deserted passage, at this time of night all of the lights in unused parts of the building were extinguished to save electricity, but it did not matter, he had spent the last twenty five years of his life in daylight and darkness, walking these corridors. Without checking his watch he knew that it was almost two thirty and the night patrol Sergeant, Joe Mason, who was relieving him in the charge office whilst he was supposedly taking his meal, would be expecting his return.

At the head of the stairs he paused and stopped to listen, something, he was not sure what, had caught his attention. Motionless he focused his senses. There was nothing other than the sound of his own breathing. He was he told himself, unnecessarily jumpy and letting his nerves get the better of him.

About to descend the stone staircase he suddenly knew that he was not alone, although soft, the footfall behind him was unmistakable. Before he could turn around the impact of a crashing blow to the side of his head knocked him off balance into the wall. Barely conscious, Lew struggled to prevent himself from falling headlong down the stairs. His efforts were in vain, with the second blow everything went black as he pitched forward into the void.

'Unfortunately Harry, there has been a fatal accident during the night.' Harry North had been to say the least, surprised to find the Chief Constable waiting for him at the door of his office when he arrived just before eight o'clock on Wednesday morning.

Unlocking the door Harry ushered Hall-Johnson in, and offering him a seat waited for the Chief Constable to continue.

'Most unfortunate I am afraid,' looking up from the armchair at North who was now standing expectantly by his desk, with his scraggy neck and thin features, Sidney Hall-Johnson resembled more than ever a bird of prey. From the angle that he was looking across at him, Harry noticed for the first time that he had started to comb his hair over a bald spot.

'Sergeant Arthur fell down the back stairs during the early hours. It looks as if he hit his head on the way down and must have fractured his skull. When he didn't return to the charge office from his meal break his relief, Sergeant Mason, went to see where he was and found him at the foot of the stairs.'

Harry felt as if he had been hit in the stomach, he and Lew Arthur had been friends for more years than he cared to remember. His mouth twisted as he lifted his head to stare up at the ceiling whilst he got his emotions under control. Sooner or later everyone had known that something like this would happen. Lew's capacity for drink was legendary. At any given time whatever duty he was on, Lew could find himself a drink, and this was particularly so when he was on nights. As senior Sergeant, on night shift he invariably drew charge office duty. Although usually busy, the charge Sergeant was at least guaranteed to be in a warm office out of the weather. It was also a known fact that two or three times during his tour of duty, Sergeant Arthur would slip out through the back gate of the station into the yard of one or other of the hostelries within a five minute walking distance of Long Street and return with a sealed quart bottle that had been left out for him by the licensee.

A known fact to everyone that was, except Sidney Hall-Johnson. North pulled himself together and addressed himself to the Chief Constable.

'Do we know exactly what happened Sir?' he asked.

Hall-Johnson shook his head slowly. 'Not at present. Dr Mallard will perform an autopsy during the morning, but I doubt that it will be of any assistance. Inspector Wilson, who was the night Inspector thinks that having had his meal, Sergeant Arthur decided to make a security check of the building before returning to his duties in the charge office and missed his footing in the dark.'

'I think that from now on,' he added, a worried frown creasing his brow, 'we will cease the practice of dousing the lights along the first floor.'

Harry's mind was elsewhere. Good, he thought. As soon as Joe Mason found Lew, he would have known what had happened. Lew must have stashed some beer upstairs and gone up for a drink. Somehow or other on the way back down he misjudged the stairs and went down them head first. Joe got hold of Tug Wilson the night Inspector, and between them they would have got rid of whatever it was that Lew had hidden, agreed the story about the security check, and then sent for the doctor and the Chief Constable.

'Yes,' he said, 'that is about it. The charge Sergeant is responsible for the building during the night. It would be normal for Sergeant Arthur to take a walk around the building before going back to the charge office.'

'There has been concern for some time about the building being in total darkness at night,' he added for good measure, 'I was going to bring it up, but it slipped my mind.'

Hall-Johnson's frown deepened, how would this reflect on him with the Watch Committee he wondered. 'Perhaps you should do a report to the Watch Committee', he said, 'outlining your concerns and the fact that you were about to bring them to my attention.'

Harry gave a brief nod. Bastard he thought, abdicate responsibility by pretending that he didn't know that the lights were switched off, but at least he was not questioning the story, and consequently, neither would the Watch Committee when it was put to them.

'I will give you the report at conference this morning', he replied smoothly.

At 10.30 a.m., on the last Wednesday of each month, a senior officers conference was held in the Chief Constable's office. Present usually, were the Chief Constable, Sidney Hall-Johnson; the Detective Superintendent; the uniform Superintendent, Webster Pemberton; and Montagu Parfitt as the Administration Officer. Each was required to give a breakdown of his department's workload during the previous four weeks, and any proposals for the immediate future which might require discussion.

Hall-Johnson opened the meeting by going over the known details of Lewis Arthur's fatal accident, before beginning the business of the day.

North sat for fifteen minutes, patiently listening to Webster Pemberton outline the problems that he was having in controlling the unlicensed beer houses that were springing up all over the town, and the unprecedented readiness of drunks and other miscreants to offer violence to uniformed police officers attending incidents. He passed twenty minutes shuffling pointedly with ill concealed irritation in his seat, whilst Montagu Parfitt went into detail concerning his difficulties in working out accurately the amount of overtime that was due for payment to officers, and rising sickness levels within the force.

For his contribution the Chief Constable then spent further time going over a proposed contract with a local hack master for the supply of horses should an emergency occur. To Harry, the emergency for which he was making contingency plans was clearly the possibility of civil disorder in the event of a police strike. Montagu Parfitt engaged energetically with him as a fellow military man in debating the small print of the proposed arrangements. What the fools have not taken into consideration mused Harry, with a certain degree of amusement, is that if there is a police strike, there will be no one to ride the horses.

Eventually it was Harry's turn. Briefly he outlined the situation in relation to crimes committed during the period since the last meeting before turning to the Byram robbery.

'At present there are no substantial leads to follow,' he said with an air of finality. There was no point lying. 'We have simply got to wait it out until some of the items that were stolen surface - and that will I am certain happen. We will then be able to go after the people responsible.

He felt his colour begin to rise at the supercilious smile that had appeared on Montagu Parfitt's face.

'And the Kitson murder, where are you with that?' Hall-Johnson's face had taken on a look of concerned interest.

Harry had anticipated the question. 'I am in the process of sending two officers, Detective Sergeant Rowell and Constable Scofield to the East Coast to follow up a very promising lead in respect of a photographer who we think may be involved.'

Out of the corner of his eye he caught Webster Pemberton attempting to suppress a grin. Obviously the amusement pervading the station over the 'detective department seaside holidays fund', had reached the first floor.

'The other ongoing matter that is occupying our time is the identity of the second body that was found with the Kitson woman.' Harry paused, this could be tricky he thought.

'From the little that could be discerned from the doctors examination, it is the body of a male, five feet eight inches tall, probably around early middle age, say forty to fifty. No one fitting the description has been reported missing in the district, nor for that matter the in surrounding counties. From the level of decomposition, and the fact that the corpse had been stripped of clothing identity is virtually impossible.'

He took a deep breath before continuing. 'At present we feel that the likelihood is that this may be the result of a dispute between two vagrants, and the perpetrator is now tramping the roads somewhere else in the country'.

Harry looked around the table. Hall-Johnson and Montagu Parfitt merely nodded an acceptance. The death of some unknown tramp in a fight on a canal bank was of little interest to them. Pemberton shot Harry a quick look from under his eyebrows. Webster is not buying it Harry thought. The only two professional policemen present, they both knew that having killed someone in a dispute, a tramp might drop the victim in a pool and make his getaway as quickly as possible, what he would not do was strip the body, weight it down, and then take the clothes away with him. They exchanged meaningful glances, Pemberton remained silent.

'What is the present situation Harry amongst the men?' asked the Chief Constable.

Parfitt gave the detective a look that was laden with malice, which in turn initiated in Harry a feeling of deep satisfaction. This was the first time that they had come into contact since the incident in the administration office, and North wondered if he was able yet to do his collar stud up without wincing.

'There was a meeting last week at the Rufford which was well attended. A union representative from the Metropolitan police spoke to them about forming a branch of the union here and there was a lot of interest.'

'What about strike action?' It was the first time that Parfitt had spoken directly to North since the meeting began.

Ignoring him, Harry continued speaking to the Chief Constable.

'So far as strike action is concerned, the men are very much split down the middle. There are some agitators who we have identified, their spokesmen are a couple of uniform Constables.' He made a show of consulting a slim file of papers that he had brought with him in anticipation. 'PCs 84 Gunn and 101 Wales. Both of them are long serving officers with a lot to lose if this goes wrong. At the same time they are very small fish in a rather large pond. I am letting them run for the time being.'

He had no intention of mentioning Joseph Rowell's involvement with the union. That was something that he would deal with himself at the appropriate time.

The Chief Constable cleared his throat before speaking. 'In line with government policy I have prepared a letter to be sent to every officer as soon as the new legislation proscribing membership of any union becomes law. It is a direct notice that anyone who even joins a union will be dismissed from the force.'

Harry wondered if Hall-Johnson had completely missed the fact that information concerning the meeting at the Rufford must have been obtained clandestinely, or whether he was simply avoiding any such knowledge.

'Is there anything else that anyone else wishes to bring up before we adjourn?' he asked.

Parfitt, eager to be out of Harry North's company shook his head and began to rise to his feet.

'Yes, I have. In the present unstable climate there is something which I feel needs addressing,' said Harry easily, looking for the first time directly at his adversary, then enquiringly at the Chief Constable.

Hall-Johnson signalled Parfitt to sit back down, then indicated for Harry to continue.

'I am bothered about the level of firearms that are floating about around the town'.

Hall-Johnson peered at him over the rim of his spectacles, 'in what respect'.

A frown creased North's brow as he continued. 'Over the last couple of weeks there have been two instances where firearms have been produced at incidents. First there was a fight in the Wheatsheaf where one of the men involved started waving a revolver around - it came to nothing and the landlord quietened him down. Second, PC Tyler on nights last week approached a man in Bonsall Lane at 3. a.m, he again pulled a revolver out and threatened the officer before running away'.

'The truth is that a lot of men brought weapons home from the war with them in their kitbags. Some are officers and military police with the side arms that they were issued with, others are souvenirs that rank and file soldiers picked up on the battlefield from dead or captured Germans. The point is we need to take them out of circulation'.

'How do you propose to do that?', asked the Chief Constable.

Harry sighed inwardly, this was the problem in dealing with people who had limited practical police experience.

'An amnesty for one week'. He replied patiently. 'We talk to Bathurst at the Gazette and get him to run a piece about the number of illegal firearms that are in unsafe hands – left in dressing table drawers for children to find, ammunition deteriorating and becoming unstable, the usual stuff – then we take out a full page advertisement in the Gazette offering an amnesty. Anyone in possession of an unlicensed firearm can walk into Long Street and hand the weapon in at the front desk. No questions asked. What is the military term, *'no questions, no pack drill'*.

'And what do we do with them?'

Again Harry sighed, this time audibly. Webster Pemberton eased his position in his chair and shook his head imperceptibly.

'At the end of the amnesty a local gunsmith collects them, renders them useless and then destroys them', he explained patiently.

'I think that I am best qualified to undertake this'.

Up to this point Montagu Parfitt had remained silent, now leaning forward in his chair he continued.

'This is an administrative undertaking and as an army officer I am highly cognisant of most types of firearms. I will deal with this'.

A thunderous expression clouded North's face, 'You are an *ex-army officer*, you have no powers to receive anything into your custody, and this is a police matter', the words were charged with suppressed anger.

'I think that Montagu has a point Harry', intervened Hall-Johnson smoothly. He was well aware of the antipathy between the two men.

'Yes I think that this could be treated as an administrative issue. That way we will not be taking you, or your detectives away from the more pressing matters that you are dealing with. Montagu, speak to Mr Bathurst if you would please, and we will schedule the amnesty to begin tomorrow'.

North glared malevolently across the table at Parfitt who returned his gaze evenly, a glint of satisfaction in his eyes.

Walking down the passage from the Watch Committee room towards his own office, Harry paused to look out of the window down into the parade yard. Absently he watched as Elfred Warner, a retired policeman who now occupied the position of horse master, led Jenny the brown mare that pulled the prison van across to the stables. Montagu Parfitt would have been justifiably puzzled had he seen the smile playing around North's lips and the look of satisfaction on his face.

Back behind his desk, Harry picked up the telephone from its cradle and jiggled the arm to attract the attention of the switchboard operator. A minute later his call was answered by a familiar voice.

'Arthur', as ever North was brief and to the point when speaking on the telephone, 'if you are not busy at lunchtime, could we meet in the Pack Horse, I have a favour to ask of you'.

Passing the office door on his way to deliver some papers to the Chief Constable, Eric Broughton paused for a moment to listen. It occurred to him that he had never before heard Superintendent North whistling.

Harry's apparent light heartedness was short lived. In less than an hour the telephone on his desk broke out into an urgent clamour and on answering it he was told by the officer on the switchboard that Dr Mallard wished to speak to him. North frowned, he hoped that the doctor was not going to cancel their lunchtime rendezvous.

'Can you come down to the mortuary Harry, there is something I would like you to see.' Mallard's voice was unusually edgy.

'About fifteen minutes,' he replied, and replaced the speaking trumpet on its cradle. There could only be one reason that Mallard wanted him to go to the mortuary - the autopsy on Lewis Arthur was being conducted that morning.

North sat in thought for a few minutes, his fingers drumming on the desk top. He regretted that he had not taken the opportunity to speak to Lew before his death. What was it he wondered that Arthur had found in the post mortem?

Five minutes later he was seated in the model T next to Tommy Bowler, pulling onto the forecourt of the Kelsford Infirmary. Two years ago, following intense pressure from the police surgeon, the old mortuary at the back of the Long Street stables had been abandoned in favour of a purpose built one at the Infirmary. Harry hated the place. It was not just the mortuary, he hated post mortems, and this time it was going to be the mutilated body of a man who he had known for a large part of his adult life that he was going to view.

Giving Tommy sixpence he told him to go to across to the cab driver's stand opposite and get himself a cup of coffee, then tapping his walking stick on the ground purposefully, set off in the direction of the hospital entrance.

It was as he knew it would be - as it always was, and as every mortuary he had ever been in was. A small airless room in the basement of the hospital with a bench along one side for the practitioner to lay out his tools, and a large cupboard screwed to the wall above it for the storage of the mysterious bottles and compounds that seemed to be essential to the mortician's art. In the centre of the cramped space was a steel trolley on which was laid out the naked body of Lewis Arthur.

The stomach cavity was spilt open from the pubic bone up to the sternum and the corpse's various organs - Harry had to focus on the fact that he was no longer looking at an old friend, this was simply an anonymous cadaver - laid out neatly beside it, ready for the final indignity of being dissected further and searched through.

The head was turned to the left exposing a shaved area that was black and discoloured in comparison to the rest of the skull which was an unhealthy white colour. To his infinite relief he saw that the butcher's saw laid neatly beside the body had not as yet been used to remove the skull cap.

Gathered around the table were Arthur Mallard, Jonathan Dilkes, and a small slim blonde woman in her early thirties wearing a crisp nurses uniform and starched cap. The two men in their shirt sleeves wore heavy leather aprons that were stained dark with blood and an assortment of other material that North chose not to even begin to identify. He crunched down heavily on the humbug that he had slipped into his mouth as he entered what he considered to be the charnel house.

'Harry, thank you for coming over,' Mallard proffered him a hand that North saw had been washed clean of its owner's recent activities. Having telephoned, the doctors must have ceased the post-mortem and washed up to await his arrival. He was beginning to like this less and less.

'Jonathan you already know, this is his wife Heidi.'

'*Wie gehts gnädige frau,*' he said making a small bow and extending his hand to the woman.

'Thank you Superintendent North,' she replied in heavily accented English, 'I am most pleased to meet you also.'

Arthur Mallard had already told her that Harry North had a reputation for charming the ladies, and she immediately understood why. He was she could see, even in middle age a very attractive man, certainly not handsome, but he exuded charm and had done nothing more than make the effort to speak to her in her native language, however she was captivated by his magnetism.

'I didn't know you spoke German Harry,' grinned Mallard. The exchange had not been lost on him. This was simply 'Harry', effortlessly switching on the charm at the first sight of a new woman. It was not a conscious thing, he didn't thought the doctor, even know that he was doing it.

'I had a German housemaid once,' North replied smoothly. Mallard almost burst out laughing, he had known Harry North for over thirty years, and Harry's background most certainly did not include the employment of domestic staff, which left only one other inference.

The woman was probably around thirty and not unattractive Harry thought. Her hair was a dark blonde, not the pale ash colour that German and Austrian women so often carried and she had large dark brown eyes. There was a small scar just beneath her left eye, he was not certain whether this added to or slightly marred her attraction.

'We have stopped the PM Harry because there is something that we - or rather Jonathan - would like you to have a look at.' Mallard stepped to one side to allow his assistant to take the floor.

'Would you come and take a look at the skull please Mr North,' said Dilkes turning towards the table.

'I have found certain irregularities in the injuries that worry me somewhat.'

Harry peered down at the area of skull that the young doctor was indicating.

'The subject appears, in my opinion to have received two blows to the head prior to death that are not consistent with his having fallen down the stairs.'

'This one here,' he indicated an indentation in the skull at the right hand side, is I think the result of the first blow to be administered, and this,' he touched a soft darkened area at the back, 'is the second.'

'How do you know which came first?' asked Harry.

'I dealt with a lot of head wounds during the war,' Dilkes explained, 'and there is a pattern to the sequence.'

'When a skull is fractured, cracks are created which run away from the site of the blow in different directions. We encountered this a lot in shrapnel wounds to the head,' he added by way of explanation. 'However, where a second injury is sustained the cracks to the bone which it creates, stop when they reach those created by the first blow. How can I explain it?' He searched for a moment.

'Its like the tributaries of a river - they don't cross it, they simply flow into the existing river.'

'And this has happened here?' Harry's voice was grim.

'Yes definitely. Also, they were administered before death, the darkening around the wounds are the result of momentary bleeding and bruising, neither of which occur after death.'

North stepped back from the table.

'How do we know that these didn't happen as he fell down the stair?' He already knew the answer.

'Because,' Dilkes replied, 'all of the other injuries are to the face, sustained as he went head first down the stone steps.'

'Also,' he added, 'there are very few injuries to the hands and arms.'

'If a person falls headlong down a flight of stairs, one expects them to throw their hands forward to protect themselves. This has not occurred here. I am almost certain that this man was stunned by two blows on the head, and pitched semiconscious down the stairs.'

Harry paused to think, he longed for a cigarette but knew that it was not possible until he got outside.

'Would these two blows have killed him?'

Dilkes nodded carefully. 'I think so. If he were not dead when he hit the bottom, he would have quickly died afterwards.'

'How certain are you of your findings?' Harry waited whilst the young doctor considered the question. This was his first official autopsy and he did not want to make assertions that might be later challenged in a court of law.

'In my own mind I am certain. However I understand your question, and in a judicial hearing I could be challenged. My assessment is made purely on my own experiences gained in the field of military medicine.'

North nodded. 'Can I make a suggestion?' he asked.

'At present I am in the middle of a very complicated and delicate enquiry. I do not doubt Dr Dilkes that your assessment is correct. However it would be distinctly to my advantage if the person who committed this murder, because without a doubt, that is what we are looking at, were to be allowed to think that he had got away with making it look like an accident.'

'For the time being, it would help me if you could prepare a post-mortem report outlining all of your findings but not drawing your present conclusions. I will take that to the coroner, privately discuss what you have told me, and ask him if for the time being he can bring in an open verdict on the death and adjourn the hearing *sine die*. That way, he is aware of the facts, the body can be released for burial, and once I have caught the killer we can use your evidence to bring him to justice and adjust the verdict to one of wilful murder.'

Jonathan Dilkes exchanged a long hard look with Arthur Mallard. After a few moments, Mallard gave him a perfunctory nod, and turning back to North, Dilkes also nodded in acquiescence.

Back at Long Street Harry strolled seemingly aimlessly along the first floor corridor. A brief and confidential conversation with the two officers who had dealt with the apparent accident, Sergeant Mason and Inspector Wilson, had confirmed that although as North had surmised, they made an immediate search for any telltale evidence of Lew Arthur's drinking, they had found nothing.

Harry ran his hand absently along the surface of the corridor wall as he walked slowly down the corridor. He had already decided to tell no one of the doctor's discovery. Someone wanted Lew Arthur's death to look like an accident, and that was the way he would for the time being allow things to play out.

He stopped in front of the storeroom door and stepped back, deep in thought. Whilst there were offices on this floor - including his own - this was the only one to which the keys were kept in the charge office. If Lew were on this floor in the dead of night for his own purposes, then it would be to here that he had come.

Harry spent a full ten minutes silently studying the solid oak panelling before turning away to retrace his steps. He needed time to work out what it was that Lew had uncovered, but in the meantime he intended to keep the knowledge that his death was a murder to himself.

Back in his office North looked out of the window at the busy street below. The favourable summer weather had given way to a slow drizzle. He picked up his top coat and closing the door behind him made his way off towards the Pack Horse, he still had a lunchtime appointment with Arthur Mallard to keep.

Chapter 13

'Oh I do like to be beside the seaside, oh I do like to be beside the sea,' Dan Scofield was thoroughly enjoying this interlude at the coast. Strolling along Lumley Road he and Joe Rowell turned left at the clock tower onto the seafront. Out of the shady tree lined main street, the summer sunshine carried a heat that was only slightly mitigated by the soft breeze coming in off of the sea.

To the young detective it had been a blissful three days away from the humdrum life of Kelsford. Dan had never been to the east coast before, and to make a tour of three resorts in as many days was an unimagined treat. Not that as yet the trip had been in any way productive. The first day spent on Cromer's West Cliff promenade watching the comings and goings along the pier below, had after the first couple of hours begun to pall.

The only sign they had of a photographer was a stout unprepossessing looking man in excess of sixty with a large red nose, who at regular intervals left his equipment in the care of a well made dark haired man in his thirties, who was encouraging passing holiday makers to sample 'Enzo's Italian Ice cream', whilst he disappeared into the bar of the nearby Dolphin public house.

At four o'clock Dan and Joe Rowell abandoned their observation point in favour of a seat for themselves in the taproom of the Dolphin, where they had booked a night's bed and breakfast, and enjoyed a well earned pint of bitter.

The following day, as instructed by Superintendent North, the two detectives got off of the mid morning train further along the coast at Hunstanton. A quick look around told them that this was definitely not going to be a place that Clifford Jarman would be making for. The small town could hardly be called a thriving holiday resort, and of the few holiday makers that were in evidence, all were elderly couples. One look at the prices of the solitary hotel overlooking sea, told Joe Rowell that if he wanted to induce his already unhappy boss into a state of apoplexy, then a bill for a night's accommodation at 'The Sandringham' would do it. Without wasting any further time, he and Dan caught the next train to their final destination - Skegness.

It was three o'clock Wednesday afternoon when they booked in at a small bed and breakfast just off of Drummond Road. Having arrived ahead of schedule they now had until Friday morning to see if their quarry was here. A late afternoon stroll quickly told them that this was the best prospect yet. Skegness was bustling with activity. Shops, small and large selling seaside rock, nic-nacks and souvenirs proliferated. The pubs - seemingly there was no restriction on opening times - were full of couples bent on spending their hard earned savings on a week of enjoyment and inebriation. Along the front they spotted two photographers taking pictures of couples and families. Each followed the established practice of handing to the customer a ticket inviting them to call the next morning at the office of the cameraman's employer to purchase the snapshot commemorating their annual holiday.

By mutual agreement the two detectives avoided approaching the photographers. Neither of the men they saw resembled the description given by Aldred Danson of Cliff Jarman, one was too old, and the other too tall. Jarman was they knew in his late twenties, of middle height, slim, with a heavy black moustache which Rowell sincerely hoped he had not shaved off. To have approached either of the men who were on the esplanade might well have elicited the information that a photographer of Jarman's description was in fact working the circuit, but it would equally have risked tipping him off.

The plan was that Joe and Dan would make an early start next morning and spend the day watching. If Jarman was working the sea front they knew that they could expect to see him by mid-morning at the latest, and it was this that brought them onto the sea front at half past nine on Thursday morning.

For his part Joe Rowell was immersed deep in his own thoughts. The coming conflict with authority was going to be a momentous one. The strike was planned to take place in early August, which left just a few more weeks for negotiations with the government. After the weekend he would collect the flyers from Weatherstone Press and have them distributed around the Force in readiness for the meeting on Wednesday night. The information sheets were important. They explained for the benefit of those who were wavering exactly what the government and local authority shortcomings were, and why their only redress was to withdraw their labour in a coordinated strike with the men in Liverpool, London, and other parts of the country.

Born in the small Scottish village of Killin, just north of Stirling, Joe Rowell had witnessed first hand the poverty suffered by the small crofters in the neighbourhood under the iron hand of the Highland landlords, many of whom had never ventured out of England. His father ran a general store in the centre of the village next to the river bridge. Joe well remembered as a child waking every morning to the thunder of the Falls of Dochart, as the great black river crashed under the road bridge just yards from his bedroom window. He also remembered the housewives, eking out their meagre stipend in his father's shop, relying on the humanity of Angus Rowell to allow them until the end of the week to settle up for their goods.

A big strong lad, accustomed to earning his living as a casual labourer working for the local farmers on a day basis, in August 1909 at the age of twenty two, Joseph Rowell married the girl he had grown up and gone to school with, Ailma Campbell. By mutual agreement, the young couple decided to move to England and set up home, in the town of Kelsford, where Ailma's aunt, Laura Percival assured the young bride that a well paid job as a policeman awaited her husband. The next time that Joe returned to his native Scotland was six years later in April 1915, his destination Stirling Castle, the home of the Argyll and Sutherland Highlanders. Standing in front of a wooden trestle table, on the parade square of the barracks overlooking the town below them, he swore the oath of fealty before a grey haired, moustachioed recruiting sergeant, himself recalled from retirement to serve the colours, and became Private 20876 Rowell of the 1/5 Argyll's.

An intelligent man, Joe Rowell quickly began to question the army philosophy of dumb obedience that required soldiers such as himself to do and die without question. The mentality of senior officers who, their thinking firmly rooted in the concepts of Wellington and Cardigan, dreaming of cavalry charges and sabre duels that were - and in reality always had been - a total myth, chose to ignore the realities of machine guns and aircraft. Men like Douglas Haig who having replaced the choleric and incompetent Field Marshal French as commander of the British Expeditionary Force, refused to acknowledge the simple innovation of aerial information secured by Royal Flying Corps officers, on the grounds that his cavalry patrols on the ground had not sighted any enemy.

The hot sunshine and perfect morning light gave the calm sea between the gently lapping rollers a pale pink tinge which took him back to another very different beach far away in the Ægean.

On 6th August 1915 Joseph Rowell's unit landed at Suvla bay on the west coast of the Gallipoli Peninsular. For the next four months they were pinned to the narrow strip of beach by the constant accurate fire of the Turks on the headlands above them. The Turks they had been assured prior to the landing, were sparse in numbers, little better trained than armed native infantry. Rowell and his comrades immediately discovered that this was a total fallacy. Six divisions; 84,000 well trained men, fighting on their own territory for the security of their homeland, were positioned on high ground above the invading infidels, and had no intention of allowing them to ever get off of the beaches.

The Argyll's, along with the other allied troops who had waded ashore from the navy ships through the barbed wire strewn shallows, spent days and nights of pure hell trying to stay alive, unable to move further inland, awaiting a decision by their commanding officers to accept the situation and order a withdrawal. Weeks that stretched out into months, living in slit trenches dug in the sand, cold and wet, every crevice of their bodies infected by lice. God Almighty Rowell reflected, the lice … often the only way that you knew a wounded man had died was when the lice crawled away from the cooling body. Life, day after day, viewed through the sights of a Maxim machine gun, under constant fire from the Turks on the cliffs above.

What these simple troops, trapped and dying on the beaches, failed to understand was that the decision to withdraw did not lay with Ian Hamilton the General officer in overall command. Back in London, careers were at stake, primarily that of Winston Churchill who had jurisdiction over the naval operations in the Dardenelles. To admit that the risky Turkish venture, taken against heavy political opposition, was a gamble that had not paid off, was to the egotistical Churchill, simply not an option.

It was not just Suvla Bay. Suvla was only one part of a three pronged offensive that incorporated a landing further along the coastline by the Australian and New Zealand Contingent of the British Mediterranean Expeditionary Force, famously known as ANZAC Cove, and finally an offensive at the southernmost point of the landmass at Cape Helles. Each of the contingents were blocked in their offensives and pinned down. Thousands of troops, helpless and being picked off at will by the Turkish snipers.

Not until November was an evacuation finally authorised. Meantime to add to the miseries of the ill equipped men trapped on the beaches, the interminable summer heat had given way to bleak winter conditions. It took a personal tour of inspection by Field Marshal Herbert Kitchener to bring about the withdrawal. With a howling snow blizzard cutting across the disputed sands, the decision was finally taken. The stealthy evacuation of the Suvla beaches began on the night of 6th December and continued until the night of the tenth. Private Joseph Rowell was one of the last to climb into a small boat and be rowed out to the safety of a British Navy destroyer.

The campaign cost over two hundred thousand casualties, of which the dead totalled 43,000. Of the thirty three and a half thousand ANCAZ casualties, over a third of the men were killed. The action resulted in a massive rift between Britain and her southern hemisphere dominions which was to last for almost the next twenty years, and it brought about a change in Joe Rowell that would scar him for life.

Clifford Jarman adjusted his bow tie in front of the hall mirror of his lodgings in Edinburgh Avenue, tipped his straw boater slightly forward to a more rakish angle, and studied his image. The striped blazer, he felt was absolutely ideal for the warm summer's day and definitely set him on a level with the 'better class' holiday makers. Stroking the heavy, dark brown moustache, for the hundredth time in the last few days he wondered if he dared to risk waxing it into needle points. The problem was that, elegant though it would look, the style had fallen into total disrepute since the war. A waxed moustache such as that favoured by the Kaiser Wilhelm was perceived to be highly un-British, and as such 'not the thing to do'. Locking the front door of his basement room, he climbed the stone steps up to road level and paused to look lovingly at his newly acquired Clement Talbot motorcar. The soft top four seater was the first luxury item that his burgeoning - if illegal - latest enterprise had afforded him. Running a hand along the polished midnight blue front wing, he allowed himself a self satisfied smile before making his way up the short roadway to the seafront.

Jarman liked Skegness, coming here was the best move he had made for years. Kelsford was not bad, better than his native Birmingham, but things had become too complicated, plus the fact that the town could not begin to compete with the East Coast for opportunities. His big mistake he conceded, had been his involvement with Alice.

He first met Alice Kitson in late October 1918 when she came into the studio at 23 Ludgate Street to enquire about having a family portrait taken. Always an eye for the ladies, Cliff immediately decided that this big, good looking, full figured woman, was well worth cultivating. He could he knew have taken the necessary portrait studies there and then, and asked her to collect them in a couple of days time. Instead he arranged with her a series of sittings beginning the following week. On the second visit he spent time arranging her in various poses which he told her, 'brought out to the best her personality'.

On this second visit he became certain of something in his own mind. Alice Kitson liked posing, and liked being photographed. In apparently innocent conversation he discovered that she was married to a local shopkeeper who was much older than her. He also became convinced that she knew that he was playing a game, and was participating.

For some time Cliff had been involved with three local women, Lottie Sharpe,

Maria Daley and Sukie Myers, taking nude photographs of them, which he later sold on to a contact in Nottingham. On the third visit he took a chance, and casually, left a photograph of each of the women on the side table in the studio.

As he expected, it was not long before Alice spotted them, and picking them up began to study them carefully. He knew that it would go one of two ways. Either she would be outraged, and he would be proven wrong, or she would be interested. As he hoped it was the latter.

'I didn't know that you did modelling photographs,' she said, holding the picture of Sukie Myers at arms length, as if to obtain a better perspective.

'Occasionally Mrs Kitson,' he murmured smoothly. 'Purely for the lady's own interest you understand. They never leave the studio.' He did not however offer to put the pictures away, and left them on the table.

Cliff deliberately made Alice's next appointment for the afternoon of Thursday the following week when the shop being closed, Aldred Danson at home reading his newspaper, would not be aware of his assistant's extra-curricular activities. The date was 14th November, three days after the announcement of the armistice - and the town was still celebrating.

He knew when she came to the studio that there was something different about her. She was fashionably dressed in a dark suit topped off with a wide brimmed straw hat trimmed with a broad ribbon. Having taken some formal full length pictures of her, he was about to suggest that she might like a cup of tea whilst he processed the plates when she said, 'are you not celebrating the armistice Cliff?' They were by now on first name terms.

Carefully he put down the photographic plates, and replied, 'there is a bottle of gin in the office Alice, we could take a glass to the demise of the Kaiser and the return of our boys.'

From there on, he could not believe how easy it was. With hindsight he now knew that with little forthcoming at home, she was desperate for sex. After two large glasses of Booth's gin she asked to see the photographs once more of Suky Myers and Lottie Sharpe.

'Will you do one of me?' she asked, 'purely for my own interest.'

Within minutes she was naked, posing for the camera as if she had done it a thousand times before, whatever position he asked her to take up she did with relish. At the end of the session it was a foregone conclusion that they would have sex. It happened first on the studio divan, then on the sheepskin rug that was used to photograph babies, and the third time on Aldred Danson's office desk.

The problem was that Alice became a problem. Her appetite for sex was Olympian. For a while, the Thursday afternoon sessions were the highlight of Cliff Jarman's week, however, it was not long before she wanted more. She was she told him unhappy with her husband. Cliff had made a point of visiting his shop, and understood why. Oswald Kitson was a small, balding man, with a slightly old fashioned beard and a pasty face. Cliff could see the reason Alice was seeking to fulfil her needs elsewhere. To his dismay though, she announced just after Christmas that she was contemplating leaving Oswald and wanted to set up home with him. Jarman very definitely had other plans which did not involve settling down with one of his models, skilled as she was at sex. It had been for some time Cliff's intention that once the weather began to improve and winter moved into spring, he would quietly slip away from Kelsford to the East Coast where he was certain that he could expand his nascent pornography activities. Alice suddenly made matters pressing by announcing that she had made a definite decision to leave Oswald. With the obvious consequences to both of them she was hardly likely to expose his little sideline, but he needed to be rid of the woman. Telling her that he was going to Yarmouth to set up a love nest for them, he packed his bags and at the end of February gave in his notice to Aldred Danson and quietly disappeared - not to Yarmouth, but to Skegness.

The fact that he arrived some two months before the season started in the resort in fact worked to his advantage. Having first secured a lodging in the basement apartment of the old three storey house fifty yards from the seafront, he set out to find a premises nearby to use as a studio. During his time in Kelsford Cliff had, through the discreet sale of his under the counter pictures, accumulated a tidy sum of money - over two hundred pounds - and made several useful if dubious contacts, something which he now intended to put to good use. It took less than a week of diligent searching to locate a house, ten minutes walk from his lodgings. The small villa at number 24 Brunswick Drive was ideal for his purposes, a quiet, residential side street just off the beaten track, but near enough to the town centre so as not to draw attention to the odd holiday maker wandering off of the beaten track and possibly visiting one of the houses.

A trawl through the local newspapers resulted in him spotting an advert in the Louth & North Lincolnshire Advertiser for an auction in the nearby town of Louth of farm equipment and miscellaneous military surplus items. The twenty five mile journey proved to be time well spent. For an outlay of seven pounds he returned to Bismark Drive with an elderly Eastman Kodak roll film and plate camera complete with tripod, that had lain unused in an army depot somewhere in the North of England since before the war, along with a hand-held 1913 Leica 35 millimetre, to which the auctioneer attributed the hazy provenance of having 'been confiscated from a German officer'.

He now simply needed to find some girls willing for a suitable fee, to pose for him. Armed with a knowledge of human nature and an undeniable charm,

Cliff spent the next week dropping into the less reputable pubs around the town enquiring of barmaids who he considered to be worthwhile candidates, if they would care to do some fashion modelling for a company that was making corsetry products. Applying what he termed, 'friends of the bride' rule, he shrewdly did not necessarily approach the best looking candidates. His targets were women who looked to be of easy virtue and were 'resting' until the holiday season began. His philosophy being that once hooked, the 'bride' although probably not particularly photogenic herself would have one or two friends who would be both amenable and better looking.

Using this simple process, and by virtue of the fact that in being photographed initially wearing nothing but a skimpy corset the woman was already in such a state of undress that it was a small step to negotiate for an increase in fee from two and sixpence to ten bob, the removal of the solitary garment and a change of tempo to erotic poses.

Clifford Jarman quickly became known amongst the shadier denizens of the seaside town, and the small but trusted circle of contacts that he had built up in Kelsford was expanded at a remarkable rate. By the time Harry North agreed to Joseph Rowell turning his attentions to the seaside resorts, Jarman had enlisted the additional services of two very well proportioned young men who spent part of their time working on the small seafront fairground, and the remainder behind the closed curtains of his back room studio pleasuring the half dozen young ladies who now were the stars of his rapidly growing photographic venture.

Giving the gleaming bodywork of the Clement Talbot a last appreciative stroke, Cliff turned away and strode purposefully along the road towards the Parade.

'Joe, hold on a minute.' Dan Scofield's tone was quiet, just loud enough for his companion to hear.

Rowell, his mind brought back to the present, halted and glanced at his partner who had also stopped and was busy filling the pipe that he had brought out of his pocket.

'Other side of the road,' Scofield said apparently engrossed in opening up his tobacco pouch.

Joe stole a glance down the side street. 'Oh yes,' he murmured. The small dark blue tourer was the only vehicle in the roadway, and whilst the man gazing admiringly at it, was not carrying a camera, he was dressed in the striped blazer and straw boater of a beach photographer, and had a luxurious dark cavalry moustache twitched up in military style at the ends.

They stood still, two holiday makers chatting, until the man had crossed the road and walked past them along the parade. Dropping in a hundred yards behind they watched as he approached a street photographer dressed in similar attire to himself. The man leaned casually on his camera as they chatted for a short while before, clapping the photographer on the shoulder their man took his leave. Both the detectives saw the hand that came away from the shoulder slip a slim packet inside his jacket.

They were almost caught out as their target turning abruptly walked back past them, and they had to wait until the cameraman busied himself taking a snapshot of a young couple walking arm in arm towards him, in order to spin around and walk quickly back toward the Clock Tower at the end of the parade which was where their man appeared to be heading. He was they realised heading towards a second street photographer, this time a tall, cadaverous individual who acknowledged him casually whilst lining up the camera on a small child in a sailor suit trotting a few yards ahead of its parents. Almost without stopping, the man with the moustache touched the photographer on the shoulder in friendly acknowledgement, at the same time dropping a second package on the small tray containing numbered photo tickets attached to the tripod.

'Where is he going now?' Dan Scofield's question was rhetorical. Having left the seafront and turned right off of the busy main street into Lumley Avenue, Jarman was walking briskly in the direction of a large church around which the road formed a circle before diverging in different directions.

Before Rowell could offer an opinion, the man turned left at the church and disappeared out of sight. Quickening their pace they were just in time to catch him turning right into a side street and then left into quiet avenue of terraced villas. Dropping back out of sight at the corner they watched with interest as half way down on the right Jarman turned to check around before going in through a garden gate and disappearing into one of the houses.

'Well, well, things are looking up,' murmured Rowell. 'Two addresses, one he is going to be living at, and the other is where his studio will be. Which is which, remains to be seen.'

'I would say that this is the studio Joe,' said Scofield, peering through the privet hedge which surmounted the wooden picket fence behind which they were standing.

'Off the beaten track, access from both ends of the road. He could even put a 'B and B' sign in the window to cover the fact that different people come in and out. Do you want to pull him now or let him run a bit longer?'

'We'll take him when he comes out,' decided Rowell. 'I'll go down the road towards the other end then we have got him whichever way he moves.'

It was at this point that things started to go wrong. Sauntering casually down the road Rowell was only a few yards past number twenty four, when their suspect came out again.

The two drops safely made with Fred Merton and Harold Steerforth, Cliff Jarman only needed to collect a package of photographs that was waiting, sealed and addressed in the false back of the Welsh dresser in the kitchen at Brunswick Street. It was a two minute job to retrieve the parcel and slip it into his jacket pocket. All he had to do now was take it into the post office for onward despatch to his contact in Amsterdam. Holland was where the big money was made - it was the Dutch connection that had funded the brand new Clement Talbot.

As he opened the garden gate and stepped back into the street, out of the corner of his eye he spotted a big man in his thirties about twenty yards down the road to his right. The man seemed to stop suddenly and pause as if taken by surprise. In a split second Jarman recognised him as having been on the front with a companion earlier, when he slipped the pictures of Maude Goodson and Evelyn McIntyre into Harold Steerforth's tray.

All of his instincts told him that wherever the man's partner was, they were police. As quickly as he dare he turned left away from the man and began walking towards the corner of the road. His suspicions were confirmed when with less than five yards to go to the corner, a second figure stepped out from the bushes and began to move towards him.

The fact that the policemen did not know that he had identified them gave Jarman an advantage, and the younger of the two, the one who had been hiding around the corner was not prepared as they drew close to each other for Jarman suddenly lashing out with his right hand and knocking the detective off balance, before breaking into a run.

Joe Rowell was still looking for a suitable place to take cover when Jarman reappeared. Pausing a second, he allowed him time to close the garden gate and head off up the road to where Dan was waiting before he set off to follow him.

Neither he nor Dan were prepared for the fact that Jarman had realised that they were police, and when he broke away from Dan they were both caught off balance. Dan reeled backwards into the hedge behind which he had been hiding, the low wooden picket fence in front of it giving way with a splintering crash, deposited him on his back in the front garden of number three.

Ignoring his partner struggling to extricate himself from the wreckage, Rowell charged into the adjoining side street in time to see his quarry disappearing out of sight further up the road. Taking off after him Rowell came to the place where the roads split into different directions with the church in the middle.

Pausing to recover his breath he stared around angrily. There was no sign of any fugitive.

A minute later he was joined by a dishevelled Dan Scofield.

'Sorry Joe, he caught me by surprise,' gasped Scofield.

Rowell shook his head impatiently, he was concentrating on the open doors of the church. Touching his partner lightly on the arm he pointed, and made his way across the road.

At the end of the short pathway leading up to the doors stood a notice board on a wrought iron mounting proclaiming this to be the Church of Saint Matthew.

Stepping inside he saw that the main body of the building was to his right. Rows of pews separated by a central aisle ran down to a wide chancel surmounted by three stained glass windows. The church was surprisingly light and airy with a row of high vaulted arches on both sides. In front of the altar was a large arrangement of fresh flowers in tall vases standing almost three feet high, laden with heavily perfumed lilies.

Moving across to the left hand side of the church he signalled Scofield to take the right. Slowly they moved in tandem down the length of the church checking each row of pews, one by one. Halfway along Rowell paused for a long minute to listen. There was total silence. Perhaps he was wrong, and his man had not come into the church. Glancing to his left he saw that he was standing beneath a tall stained glass window depicting a bearded figure wearing brilliantly coloured medieval robes, his hand on the shoulder of a sad faced youth in a hooded brown jerkin. At another time the irony of the small pane of glass beneath the figures bearing the legend '*AND HE WAS ANGRY & WOULD NOT GO ON*', would not have been lost on him. Instead he resumed his slow walk to the front pew and stopped to glare across at Dan Scofield.

Joe knew that his annoyance with Dan was unreasonable. These things happened, caught unawares their man had managed for the time being to elude them. It was an inconvenience that could quickly be remedied. Walking forward a few paces he placed his hand on the cool woodwork of the raised pulpit before moving to the left and checking the short stairway that led up into it. As he had expected, it was empty. The adjacent door into the vestry was closed and locked. Unless the vicar or verger had been careless enough to leave the key in the lock, then that was not going to provide a hiding place.

Dan Scofield was on the far side by the baptismal, giving him a quick shake of the head, a frustrated Rowell made his way back out into the sunshine.

Chapter 14

Had Joe Rowell not been so angry with himself at losing the suspect, he might have noticed that the flower display at the front of the church chancel was not quite right. There were three large vases of lilies on the right hand side, but only two on the left. Whereas a single vase stood immediately in front of the raised pulpit obscuring the space beneath it.

Hidden behind the three feet tall vase which he had dragged over to mask the well beneath the pulpit, Cliff Jarman hardly dared to breath as the detective paused less than a hand's breadth from him before moving away to check the vestry door.

After the two men left the church Cliff waited for what seemed a half an hour, although it was in fact less than ten minutes, before cautiously emerging from his hiding place. He spent the time crouched under the pulpit frantically trying to assess what was happening. To his knowledge, unlike in Holland where his contact was part of a much wider network of organised crime, there was no criminal element or local gang of villains here that his activities might have upset. That left his original and obvious conclusion that these were Skegness detectives, and that they were on to him. Somehow the police had uncovered the location of the Brunswick Drive studio – probably one of the girls had either been careless, or more likely been bragging about her activities in the wrong place, and blown things. What he needed to do now he decided was to get back to Edinburgh Avenue, throw his few possessions into the car and head off into the sunset. He would write off his assets at Brunswick Drive – to return there was out of the question. The seaside resorts were a gold mine, he would move inland somewhere, take a break for a week or so until things cooled off, then drive down to the south, Brighton possibly, and try his hand there.

Finding a small door at the rear of the church insecure he let himself out, and having ensured that the coast was clear, headed off up the road.

Approaching Edinburgh Avenue from the direction of the North Parade, Jarman bought a copy of the Daily Express from a nearby paper stand and took up a position in one of the seafront shelters favoured by elderly holiday makers seeking respite from the sun or sheltering from the sea breezes. He spent a quarter of an hour pretending to read the paper , whilst watching the approach to Edinburgh Avenue. Cliff had deliberately chosen to lodge in the basement of the end house because it was ideally situated for his purposes.

Built in the mid-Victorian years before the township ever entertained any pretentions as a holiday resort, the three storey houses with their bay windows and below ground level basements were now becoming decidedly shabby. Built up on one side only, the roadway was narrow with an area of wasteland opposite the houses which, obscured by some trees and bushes at the bottom gave onto a small park with a bandstand. The cul-de-sac was short – only seven houses – and number seven was at the end. In case of necessity Cliff could come and go across the park, through the bushes and into his basement flat undetected.

Without doubt, this was a case of necessity. After satisfying himself that there was absolutely no police activity, Cliff folded his newspaper, straightened his blazer, and made his way off past the end of the road along the Grand Parade. It took less than ten minutes for him to work his way cautiously along the side streets, and into the park. Peering through the bushes at the bottom end of Edinburgh Avenue he smiled with relief. They might have found the studio, but he had been careful to ensure that none of the girls knew where he lived. It was a precaution that had paid off, in less than half an hour he would have the car loaded up and be away from Skegness without a trace. Cliff's only regret was that there was a small fortune in pictures at Brunswick Drive that he could not now get his hands on. It had to a lesser extent been the same when he left Kelsford. The presence of the workmen at Ludgate Street had prevented him from clearing everything away there – he had often thought that old Danson must have had a right turn when he came across those 'artistic studies.'

Crossing the ten feet of open ground Jarman slipped through the gap in the low pavement level wall and down the narrow stone steps to his front door. He reached the bottom before he saw the man standing in the corner of the basement area next to the dustbin.

On leaving the church of Saint Matthew, Joe Rowell and Dan Scofield made their way quickly to Edinburgh Avenue, and it was to their intense relief that they found the blue motorcar still parked outside. A swift examination of the basement flat confirmed that the door was locked and on looking through the window that no one was in. After a short conference they agreed that this was where Jarman would eventually have to make for. Dan settled himself down in a corner of the small area below street level whilst Joe crossed the road and found a spot on the wasteland amongst some trees.

They had been in place just under an hour when Cliff Jarman appeared from amongst the bushes and cautiously climbed over the low wall next to the end house.

Jarman froze, then turned to run back up to the street. His escape was blocked by the bigger man who was coming down the steps after him. In desperation he spun around towards the younger policeman, the gap between them had closed.

Dan hit him hard in the midriff. Doubling over Jarman fell to his knees retching, hands outstretched on the concrete surface.

'I'll teach you to fucking run you bastard.' The quietly spoken words were full of malice, venting the policeman's frustrations at what had gone before. Grabbing Jarman by the hair Dan hauled him to his feet and threw him up against the wall.

'Alright Dan, leave it for now.' The Sergeant's even tone carried an authority not to be ignored.

A quick search of the prisoner produced the keys to 24 Brunswick Drive, plus those to the basement flat. The car they learned did not have a key, the ignition was activated by a hidden switch under the dashboard. Once inside the two roomed flat Rowell carefully opened the package that Jarman was still carrying in his jacket pocket, and smiled with satisfaction at the contents. The Skegness police would be over the moon.

With the evidence laid out in front of him Cliff Jarman knew better than to protest, electing to remain silent, although extremely wary of the younger detective.

Whilst Dan went to find a telephone in a nearby business premises and speak to the Skegness police, Rowell sat down at the tiny kitchen table opposite the photographer who was now securely handcuffed to the chair on which he was sitting.

'You are in big trouble Clifford,' he said almost conversationally.

Jarman remained silent, glowering at the Scotsman.

'Taking and distributing pornographic pictures, and smuggling them out of the country,' he tapped the label on the brown wrapping paper hat lay open on the table, 'you are going away for a long while – with, I suspect hard labour.'

'Before anything happens here though, you are going back to Kelsford with me to answer a lot of questions about a lot of things that have gone on there.'

He paused, waiting for a reaction, Harry North had been specific. If Jarman were arrested he was to be brought back to Kelsford, ostensibly to answer charges of producing obscene pictures there. Nothing was to be said to him about Alice Kitson's murder until he was safely in custody ay Long Street.

'I want a solicitor,' Jarman said truculently, 'I have my rights.'

Rowell's voice hardened, he wanted to get this man back onto his own territory. 'At present, I will decide what rights you might or might not have. You have already deeply upset my partner, if you continue to be silly, you might just do the same with me.'

'When we get back to Kelsford, we are gong to talk about Maria Daley, Lottie Sharpe, and Susan Myers, just for starters. Then we are going to talk about your little friend Peter Jennings, what his part in your enterprise is, and what he can still tell us ...'

A silence ensued, once again Joe had deliberately not mentioned Alice's name.

For the first time Cliff Jarman began to look uncomfortable. They were interrupted by a rapping on the front door. Rowell got up and without turning his back on the prisoner let in Dan Scofield and two other men who he introduced as Detective Sergeant Slingsby and Constable Durham. Before setting off on their expedition, Joe Rowell had contacted the police offices at each of the places that they were going to, including Skegness, to make them aware of what they were doing.

Cyril Slingsby was perfectly aware that the two Kelsford officers were looking for a potential murderer who was probably committing other offences in the Skegness area. A quick conversation with Dan Scofield in the street outside had put him in full possession of all of the available information, along with the fact that Jarman was going back to Kelsford before anything at Skegness was put to him.

'Right, let's get off down to your little shop then, see what you got down there,' Slingsby's heavy Lincolnshire accent was far from friendly, neither was the bleak smile which he gave him.

The train journey from Skegness to Kelsford was conducted in almost total silence. For their part the two policemen did not want to start questioning the prisoner until he had sweated for a night in the cells at Kelsford, whilst Clifford Jarman was completely preoccupied with what was happening to him. At nine o'clock that morning life had never been better. A couple of drops to local contacts, send off the valuable package to Holland, and then a photograph session after lunch with Maude and Julia, the new girl she had brought along last week with the incredible bust. For the benefit of the camera the girls would have had sex together, then for a ten bob bonus he would have had sex with both of them. Instead he was sitting in a draughty railway carriage handcuffed to a detective who had already displayed a distinct, and in his opinion, unreasonable dislike to him.

At Kelsford station they were met by Eric Broughton driving the Force's one and only motor car and taken to Long Street Police Station where after being once more searched and documented he was locked away in an uncomfortable cell with a wooden plank bed to sleep on and a bucket in the corner in which to relieve himself. On Superintendent North's instructions, during the night he was woken by the gaoler every hour on the hour to the polite enquiry as to whether he was alright, or needed anything.

The following morning, worn out and unshaven, Cliff was given a cup of tea and slice of toast and margarine by the early morning cells officer. Half an hour later he found himself sitting in an interview room at the end of the cell block on the opposite side of a wooden table to the big Scottish Detective Sergeant who had arrested him. He still did not know the man's name, a second chair was unoccupied.

Silence reigned for a full five minutes before the door opened and a dapper middle aged man with white hair and a moustache that rivaled his own, except for the fact that it was the colour of burnished silver, walked in and sat down at the second chair.

The man brought nothing in with him, no file of papers or notes. Both men sat in silence watching him, unnerved, Cliff eventually broke the moment.

'Alright, you've got me cold,' he had been rehearsing all night how he would play the interview. Admit to what they could prove, offer the names of a couple of contacts, and try to negotiate a way out of his predicament. 'I have been taking a few happy snaps to sell on and make a few bob. If we can talk about this sensibly, I can give you the names of the people who are really making some money out of it. There are people here in Kelsford very high up who you would be amazed at, people who would be very upset to think that I am going to tell you about them.'

He sat back in the chair. There were, at least to his knowledge, no 'influential people' who could bail him out on his mailing list, but these detectives did not know that, perhaps he could play along and see how things panned out. Nervously he licked his lips and looked from one to the other of the men opposite him.

The cold stare of the newcomer was glacial, the hostility in the pale blue eyes palpable. When he spoke Jarman felt as if a bucket of icy water had been poured over him.

'Clifford Jarman, I am arresting you on suspicion of the murder of Alice Kitson on or around the 28th February this year.'

Jarman's jaw dropped open, the words that he was trying to say would not come out, all that he could do was emit a strangled gasp.

'I am Detective Superintendent North, Detective Sergeant Rowell you already know. Before we go any further, I will ask you formally – do you admit to killing Mrs Kitson?'

'Alice is dead?' Jarman's vocal chords began to function once more. 'How, when? I don't know anything about this, what is going on here?'

'Prior to leaving Kelsford earlier this year you were involved with Mrs Kitson were you not?'

Jarman shook his head, 'how, I mean how is she dead, she was alive when I left.'

North's jaw tightened, 'answer the question – you were involved with Alice Kitson were you not?'

Still mentally reeling Jarman nodded his head, 'yes we had a thing going, but I haven't killed her.'

Harry made a brief movement with his hand, and Joe Rowell laid the photographs of Alice on the desk.

'You took these pictures didn't you?'

Again Jarman nodded. 'Yes, yes I did, but she came to me for them, she was the hottest woman I have ever met. She loved being photographed.'

'And afterwards, did she love what happened afterwards?' It was almost as if North were talking to the wall behind the man.

'Yes, we had sex, but I didn't kill her, please tell me what happened.'

'I will tell you what happened Jarman.' Again the hand movement, and the silver haired man was passed a sheet of paper containing closely written script with what appeared to be a signature at the bottom of the page.

'According to your good friend Peter Jennings, over a period of time since before Christmas last year, you were taking obscene pictures of Alice Kitson at your place of work, Aldred Danson's studio at 23 Ludgate Street, and having sex with her on a regular basis. She became obsessed with you and began putting pressure on you by saying that she was going to leave her husband.'

'That, according to Jennings did not accord with your plans – you told him that you needed to rid yourself of her. You were last seen at your place of work on Thursday 27th February this year. The following day Alice Kitson disappeared and was never seen alive again. On Friday 13th June her body was discovered in a lime kiln on the outskirts of Kelsford. She had been dead for just over three months, or to be more precise, since exactly the date that you disappeared.'

The full import of his situation was beginning to dawn on Jarman. That he had to convince them that he was not Alice's killer was obvious, and he made a swift decision that to be successful in doing so he would have to be honest about his other activities.

Taking a deep breath he said, 'I know this looks bad for me, but I have not killed anyone. Yes I had a little thing going here taking few naughty nineties on the side. Yes Alice was involved, and yes she had become a liability. She was obsessed with sex, and she wasn't getting any at home – have you met her husband? She was going to leave him and move in with me – which I did not want.'

'I decided to pull out and get away from her. I told her that I would go to Yarmouth and get us a place. She believed me, she was actually quite a clever woman, and she had come up the hard way living in the home, we agreed that she would do nothing until I contacted her. Last time I saw her was at lunchtime on the Thursday, she came to see me off at the station. I had got to change trains at Peterborough, she still thought that I was going to Yarmouth, but my ticket was actually for Skeggy.'

'In Skegness it was easy to put together another, and better pictures business,' he paused, need to be cautious now he thought, no point in giving them more than necessary. The Lincolnshire police had recovered about a hundred photos at Brunswick Drive and would over a period of time doubtless identify the people in them, they were after all locals, and most of the girls would be well known. He would deal with that aspect of his problems later.

'I had no idea she was dead. How did she die, you haven't said.'

'She was strangled with a scarf,' Joe Rowell spoke for the first time, 'and you have got to do a lot better than this to convince us it wasn't you that did it.'

Joe glanced at Harry North who nodded to him, then sat back in his chair and lit a cigarette.

'Tell me about these,' Rowell tapped the photographs laying on the table.

Jarman leaned forward and turned the images to face him although he knew each one without having to look at them.

'Lottie Sharpe. As you can see not a natural blonde, nice features, very slim, good on camera.'

He pushed the pasteboard to one side and examined the second. 'Sukie Myers. Well past her best, carries too much weight, but there are a lot of clients who she appealed to. Just had to be a bit creative in what you did with her. Maria Daley, very good on camera, almost as good as Alice.'

The detectives were intrigued by the man's sudden absorption in the photographs, he was they realised quite proud of his work.

With a long sigh his attention returned to the picture of the dead woman. 'Jesus,' he breathed, 'I never realised ...' his voice trailed off.

'What about this one, who is she?' Joe dropped the image of the fifth and as yet unidentified woman on the top of the pile.

Jarman shook his head and appeared to study the likeness.

'I don't know.' He said. 'She was a friend of Alice's, that is all I know. Alice arrived for a Thursday afternoon session just before Christmas, and she brought this other woman along with her.' He tapped the photograph with his forefinger.

'This is the God's truth. I had never seen the woman before. It was only the third or fourth session that I had done with Alice – I just thought that she had found another girl for me.'

Harry North leaned forward in his chair interested. The man was not lying, of that he was certain, and this could be crucial.

'Did she have a name - this woman?'

Jarman glanced at him nervously. 'Alice called her Sarah, that was all, just Sarah. It was a bit weird though. She was good looking enough, big tits and dark red hair – what we call 'Titian' in the trade. But she was, I don't know, ill at ease, as if she had never done it before. Alice kept telling her how good she looked, and helping her arrange herself. At the end of the day though, she didn't come over very well, the camera didn't really like her, so I wasn't too bothered when she never showed up again.'

'She just came the once, then you never saw her after that?' Rowell sounded suspicious.

'No, that was it.'

'Did you and Alice have sex whilst she was there?' asked North.

'No, Alice said to me, very quiet like, that she was due to start her period and we would have to leave it until the next week.'

Harry lit another cigarette and looked thoughtful, Rowell caught a small change in the Superintendent's demeanor and was puzzled, what had Foxy seen that he had missed?

The interview continued for another hour without anything new emerging, and it was almost eleven o'clock before Joe Rowell tapped on the door of North's office.

'Sit down Joe,' North indicated the armchair in front of his desk, 'is he sorted?'

'Yes. Dan Scofield has charged him with taking obscene photographs with intent to publish them here in Kelsford, and he is in the cells waiting for an escort to arrive from Skegness to take him back there. The Lincolnshire Poachers are overjoyed with what they found at Brunswick Drive, they have got a whole string of things to talk to him about. What was it that DS said, '*we got this ole boy cold, he could be goin'away till after I be gone on pension ...*' Joe's impersonation of Cyril Slingsby's lilting Fenland accent brought a broad smile to Harry's face. In the back of his mind he hoped that he would be able to protect Joe from the consequences of his rash political activities, irrespective of his wife being related to Laura, Harry liked the Scotsman and respected his abilities.

'I take it that we are agreed that he didn't kill Alice ...' Joe looked quizzically at North.

Harry shook his head. 'No he was a good candidate until we spoke to him, but he's not our man.' He got up and went to look out of the picture window down into Long Street below. The prison van was pulling through the main gates into the station yard.

'No, Cliff Jarman is a dirty Ernie, but he's not our killer. We get him locked away on our charges and whatever Skegness want to put to him, and carry on looking. Have that lad at Mason's seen again – best do it yourself, he's frightened of you – make sure that he is telling the truth when he says that this woman Alice called 'Sarah' only went to the studio that once. He will know. Jarman was his mate. It's important.'

Joe looked at him quizzically, 'I knew in the interview room I had missed something, but I still don't know what.'

Before replying, Harry went to the office door and bellowed down the passage, within seconds the bespectacled figure of Tommy Bowler appeared. Since the incident with Captain Parfitt Tommy's life had improved immeasurably, and his admiration for the white haired Superintendent now amounted to something approaching hero worship.

'Go down to Phipps' and get us some coffee please Tommy,' he gave the lad a shilling, and waited until he had departed before returning to his place by the window.

'Alice started doing jollies for Cliff Jarman, so far as we can make out around the middle of November. Right from session number one they were having sex. That was what, for her was the turn on. Aldred Danson said to you that she was posing for the man not the camera. Jarman says that she turned up for the third or fourth session with this woman who she called 'Sarah'- which is obviously not her real name. Now that wants some thinking about.'

He paused to watch as a motorised taxicab halted in the roadway to allow the prison van to pull out of the yard, this time on its way across to the Police Court at the Town Hall.

Time he decided absently to get rid of his beloved motorcycle combination and invest in a car.

'We have looked at the photos of 'Sarah', and are agreed that, Alice excepted, she is a cut above the other girls that Jarman was happy snapping. Now Alice didn't just say to one of her coffee morning acquaintances, '*by the way, if you want an afternoon out, come down to this photographer I know, you take all of your clothes off, and he takes pictures of you bollock naked in every position you can think of – it really is good fun.*'

Rowell nodded, he was beginning to see where North was going.

'No,' Harry continued, 'the clue is that Alice got turned on by having her picture taken, and she wanted to include 'Sarah' in that experience. Alice wanted 'Sarah' on camera, and she wanted some pictures of 'Sarah' for herself.'

'I think you are right,' Joe stretched his legs out in front of him and looked up at the ceiling.

'We know that Alice was sexually very active, there is no reason at all why she should not have been bisexual. We know that when she was in the Cottage Homes she had a very close friend – Celia Rutherford. It is possible that, two young girls with no other emotional outlets, they could have formed a relationship, Alice could well have developed a taste for women as well as men. That's why you asked Jarman if they had sex that afternoon isn't it?'

Harry nodded approvingly, 'it confirms it. Alice convinces 'Sarah' to come along for some pictures, but she and 'Sarah' are having an affair, so at the end of the session she really can't say to her, 'excuse me for a few minutes, at this point in the proceedings we usually have a shag.' No, she makes an excuse to Jarman and beats a retreat.'

'But 'Sarah' didn't particularly like having her picture taken,' Rowell looked speculative. 'She was not comfortable and as Jarman said, it showed and she never went back.'

'Which is why,' said Harry, 'we are extremely fortunate to have that batch of photos. I think that if we can find 'Sarah' we will crack this case wide open.'

'And I would like,' added Rowell, 'to see if I can go back and find Celia Rutherford. If we are right, she might be able to tell us a lot of things.'

'It all started to go wrong when Alice became infatuated with Cliff Jarman,' commented Harry, 'from that point onwards, someone decided she had to go.'

Further conversation was interrupted by Tommy Bowler with a jug of coffee and two mugs.

'Mr Phipps says to tell you good morning Mr North Sir,' said the lad brightly. Joe Rowell looked sharply, first at him, then with interest at Harry North. He had never before heard the boy utter more than three words consecutively, and never without stammering.

The conference over, Joe Rowell set his coffee mug to one side and stood up to leave, now with a new direction to follow, he had work to do.

'One thing before you go Joe,' the Scotsman paused wondering what the old man's agile brain had now lighted upon.

'Jarman. You said that he has got a brand new motorcar standing in the street outside his digs.'

'Yes,' Rowell replied. 'Very nice actually. Clement Talbot, dark blue, four seater tourer. I presume it has been taken into safe keeping by the Skegness police.'

'Where he is going he will have absolutely no need of a car for the next five years. Offer him a hundred quid for it and get him to authorise the locals to sign it over to you.'

Joseph Rowell gave a deep sigh as he made his way down the stairs to the cell block. He never ceased to be amazed at the labyrinthine workings of Harry North's mind.

Chapter 15

Monday morning, Harry stared down at the street below. He watched as the Model T Ford turned in through the gates from Long Street with Montagu Parfitt behind the wheel. Parfitt he knew had taken the motorcar home with him on Friday evening in order to collect a consignment of stationery from Elwood's on his way in to work this morning. It also Harry reflected, gave him the use of the vehicle over the weekend, a perk which the Administration manager seemed to think accorded with his position.

He looked at his pocket watch, it was two minutes to nine, Sidney Hall-Johnson's Morris saloon had passed under the archway ten minutes previously. He would by now be safely ensconced in his office.

Turning his back to the window, Harry regarded the other two occupants of the room.

'Lock the door after I leave Eric, and don't open it to anyone other than me - and don't answer the telephone - you understand?'

Eric Broughton gave a brief nod of acknowledgement, 'yes Mr North, I understand perfectly.' If Tommy Bowler, seated next to him, regarded Superintendent North as some sort of special being, the truth was that although he was at pains to conceal the fact, Eric

Broughton was also in complete awe of this man. During the time that he had spent working at Long Street as an office boy, the stories of 'Foxy North's' escapades were legendary, and now he was a part of his latest, and he would most certainly never let him down.

Eric's heart was thumping in his chest, this was probably the most important day in his life. Glancing sideways at Tommy, he saw that the lad was totally bemused. Not to worry Eric thought. The lad did not need to understand what was happening, in fact it was essential that he did not.

North picked up the cardboard shoe box and the two notebooks on the desk. Handing the key to Eric he left.

'This is I have to say, most unfortunate, but it is something which requires your urgent attention.'

Sidney Hall-Johnson stared unbelievingly at the contents of the cardboard box.

'Are you certain about this Harry?' he asked quietly. Hall-Johnson's Monday morning routine had been shattered by the untimely arrival of his Detective Superintendent.

'I am sorry, there can be absolutely no doubt,' reaching into the box he drew out the automatic pistol and laid it carefully on the Head Constable's desk.

'Since the incident with David Byram, Arthur Mallard has become very nervous in relation to his own safety. Apparently last Thursday evening at lodge, he asked Montagu Parfitt for advice as to where he might be able to buy a pistol, and what sort he would suggest. He expected Parfitt to recommend a local gunsmith, instead he told him that he could get one for him, and he would be in touch over the weekend. The next day, at the end of surgery, he arrived at Dr Mallard' practice with this.' He tapped the box lightly, an unnecessary gesture as the Chief Constable's eyes had not left it or its contents, whilst Harry had been speaking.

'Mallard paid him the fifteen pounds that he asked. It is a Mauser …'

'I know what it is,' Hall-Johnson interrupted grimly. ' Nine millimeter Mauser Parabellum, with a ten round magazine.'

What a joy Harry reflected, to be working with men of a military background.

'What about ammunition?'

'Fifty rounds in a box,' Harry replied blandly.

'… And you say that this was delivered by Montagu to Dr Mallard last Friday. That would be the second day of the amnesty …?'

North nodded. 'Mallard telephoned me later on Friday. He was worried that some impropriety had occurred. Over the weekend I have made one or two discreet enquiries. It appears that Parfitt owes quite a lot of money - in excess of forty pounds - to a local bookmaker. Plus, and I don't know if you are possibly already aware, I spoke to the adjutant of his old regiment, the King's Own Yorkshire Light Infantry - which I understand was also your regiment, although you pre-date him by some years. When he left the army, it was not totally straight forward. There was some sort of an involvement with a married woman to whom he threatened violence. It was all hushed up, but it was a contributory factor in his resignation.'

Hall-Johnson lifted his eyes for the first time from the box and stared hard at Harry.

'No', he said, 'no I certainly did not know anything about that. 'Had I known, I would possibly have been more circumspect.'

For a fleeting moment, Harry was almost sorry for the man in front of him. An essentially honorable man, Hall-Johnson had offered a position to an ex-member of his old regiment who was down on his luck. Now, not only was he discovering the man's duplicity, but also the fact that he had left the regiment under less than pristine circumstances.

'So, what you are saying Harry, is that Montagu Parfitt, in the knowledge that he was in financial difficulties, waited for a suitable firearm to be handed in under the amnesty, failed to book it into the system, and sold it on to Doctor Mallard.'

Harry nodded. 'I am afraid so.'

Hall-Johnson picked up the automatic, and almost without thinking, checked that the breech was clear and released the action, before replacing it on his desk. 'Can we be certain that this is what happened,' he asked resignedly.

'Actually, yes we can.' Time to deliver the coup-de-grace.

'Eric Broughton, the office assistant is a particularly bright young man. When the amnesty began, purely as a matter of interest he decided to record the serial numbers of weapons that were handed in so that later on he could try to trace their history. He kept a list.'

Harry dropped the first of the two notebooks on the desk.

'You will see that there are to date, twenty one different firearms handed in. Each time Eric was sent down to the front desk to collect a gun, he made a note of the make, model, and serial number in his book before taking them up to the office. Here, on Friday 27th June, is this particular gun.'

'This,' he said laying the second notebook alongside the first, 'is the admin log of weapons handed in. Twenty entries - but not this one.'

'Where is Broughton now?'

'He is in my office,' replied Harry. 'In view of the fact that I have taken possession of the admin office log, I thought it prudent not to keep him away from Parfitt until you and I had spoken.'

'There is something else that you might wish to consider,' he added quietly.

'Gilmour Bathurst. The man doesn't like us, and I am reliably informed that he is about to run a series of articles focusing on the local authority employing ex- officers in various positions exploiting the old boy network and masonry. I am informed that he is a member of the Kelsford Lodge.'

'Can we keep the lid on this Harry?'

North breathed a sigh of relief. He had not been sure that playing the Masonic card might be a step too far. Not a mason himself, he was aware that the Chief Constable was.

'I think so, but not so long as Parfitt is still around. If he were to be removed from the equation, I could probably placate Arthur Mallard and find something to persuade Bathurst, to focus elsewhere'.

Rowland Leigh-Hunt cast an appraising eye over the stocky policeman seated across the table from him. It was not that he did not trust Ralph Gresham's judgement in including his new partner in the present discussion so much as the fact that Ralph had chosen to step outside of the accepted bounds of the intelligence world and involve someone who was not strictly 'military'.

'So that Sir Rowland, is basically what we have got with Vasily Petrov,' concluded Gresham.

'Interesting.' The old man closed his eyes for a moment whilst he ordered his thoughts.

'We have two issues. Firstly where is the original letter? We need to recover, and authenticate it. Until that has been done, make it clear to Petrov that he is expendable. We are not playing games Secondly, presuming that the document is genuine, how are we going to handle it?'

Gresham and Mardlin remained silent. It was obvious that the questions were rhetorical.

'He would be less than sensible to give us the letter without being shown some form of personal security, so we need to deal with that aspect as a priority, and at the same time ensure that he irrevocably ties himself to us - 'burns his boats' so to speak.'

He gave Gresham a quizzical look. 'I am sure my dear Colonel that you have already been exercising your mind on the matter.'

Leaning forward slightly Ralph folded his hands on the table. He and Will had discussed the subject in great depth and come to what seemed the only sensible, if extremely hazardous conclusion.

'Both Petrov and the letter need to re-appear exactly where they are supposed to be - in Germany.' Ralph spoke decisively. 'Petrov should then meet with a 'fatal accident resulting in the destruction of the letter'. That way, Stalin stops looking for both of them. We then bring our man back to England where we provide him with a new identity and utilise his undoubted talents within our own organisation.'

'You are proposing a somewhat risky venture,' Leigh-Hunt murmured absently. 'At present Germany, and particularly Berlin is in a state of complete anarchy. Ebert's government is holding on by a thread and since this Spartakist thing, it is becoming apparent that it is the Freikorps and the army, not the government, who are running the country. On the other hand, that very situation could be made to work for us. There is open warfare on the streets between the communists and the Social Democrats. It would present a perfect backdrop to resolve our own situation.'

Leigh-Hunt gazed over the shoulders of the two men at the painting on the wall behind them of Count Otto von Bismark. The picture of the Iron Chancellor had over the years come to serve him as something of an inanimate counselor. The old German would he decided, approve such a bold scheme, not least of all because the dangers involved in its implementation would, for himself be minimal. Given the state of civil war in Germany, if Gresham's plan succeeded then they would be in a very strong position, and if it failed then it was most likely that those involved on the ground would be killed out of hand by one side or the other - 'if at first you fail, remove all traces that you ever tried'. It was an adage that over the years had served him well.

'... And long term Sir Rowland ?' Gresham was curious as to how the old man was going to eventually use the letter.

'Nothing for the present,' Sir Rowland's eyes were once more engaged with those of Count Bismark. 'For the present Russia, in common with Germany is a land in turmoil, ruled by brigands. I have no doubt that in a year or so, when things have settled down, either Lenin or Josef Stalin will establish himself as a dictator. Lenin I think you will find aligned himself with the Germans at a time when his fellow countrymen were fighting against them - something which we should be able to exploit. If on the other hand it is Stalin who gains supremacy, then the Yeremin letter will give us the necessary purchase in that direction.'

'There is something else - Kell's people are becoming a nuisance.' Leigh-Hunt took the pince-nez from his waistcoat pocket and began toying with it.

Gresham raised an enquiring eyebrow.

'They have picked up on the Tessier thing, and are showing some curiosity.' The politician studied the glasses dangling from his fingers. 'Rattling around Europe, and France in particular, are rumours that something is in the wind, although thankfully, exactly what it is seems to be eluding everyone. Except us that is,' he added, allowing the corners of his mouth to twitch momentarily in the nearest thing that he allowed himself to a vestige of a smile.

'Do Kell's people at MI5 know of our specific involvement?' asked Gresham carefully.

'No,' the old man shook his head emphatically. 'The Sûreté don't like MI5 any more than we do, they have kept their mouths tightly closed. Kell's people are still 'evaluating their sources'. However, its not beyond the bounds of possibility that they could uncover a link to us, and I would like to be prepared for all eventualities'.

It was now his turn to raise an enquiring eyebrow this time in Gresham's direction. Ralph remained thoughtful for a short while before replying.

'I think that is eminently possible - and may become a necessity' he said slowly.

'Will and I have been discussing this. Petrov had to hide the letter somewhere safe but accessible after he came to England. We think that it is distinctly possible that it is somewhere in the Kelsford area.'

'We have a contact in Kelsford, there is a nurse - an Austrian woman - who is married to a doctor...'

'I don't like involving women in these matters, they are unreliable,' Leigh-Hunt interrupted him.

Gresham held up his hand. 'No, not the woman - her husband.'

He sighed inwardly at his controller's irrational dismissal of fifty percent of the potential intellect at their disposal. Over the years some of the most efficient intelligence agents that Ralph had encountered had been women. They seemed to possess an ability to focus which eluded most men. Who was it he wondered, once made the observation that, 'the only true adults are women.' He smiled deprecatingly.

'Allow me to explain. The husband Jonathan Dilkes was, during the war a Red Cross Doctor. During 1915 he was the head physician at the Red Cross military hospital at Skopje in Serbia. By the nature of that organization's work cutting across the boundaries of nationality, the vast majority of the patients in that particular hospital were Austrians - the enemy. Amongst the nurses was a young woman by the name of Heidi Siegfeld, herself an Austrian. In the way of these things the young couple fell in love and were married during the late summer of 1915 by a local pastor. Things were naturally somewhat fluid in the Balkans at that time, and by the end of the year the unit had been forced to withdraw. For the remainder of the war the couple then worked in various hospitals across the Western Front. At the beginning of this year, wishing to return home, Jonathan Dilkes found that his wife being an Austrian national now presented certain, to put it mildly, 'difficulties'. He approached his brother - an officer in the Royal Flying Corps, or the Royal Air Force as it is now - who I know slightly, and who in turn, asked if I could help out.'

Leigh-Hunt nodded sagely, the frown creasing his brow was lifting.

'Arranging papers for Mrs Dilkes was obviously a mere bagatelle, however I did put him under an obligation that should we ever need to call upon his services, he would not refuse. As yet of course she cannot even think of obtaining British citizenship, and consequently her terms of tenure continue to be rather fragile.'

Again the nod, Leigh-Hunt knew that Gresham would not be explaining this unless there was a good reason.

'Jonathan Dilkes is now a partner in a practice in Kelsford, and he tells me that there has been a slightly unusual development which could work to our advantage.'

'Recently the local police organised a firearms amnesty - usual thing - hand in any war souvenirs and no questions will be asked. However the administration manager at the police station, one Captain Montagu Parfitt, late King's Own, having some financial difficulties, hived off one of the weapons and sold it to Dilkes's partner a Dr Mallard. Mallard realizing that something illegal had occurred, has approached Superintendent North and turned him in. As a consequence I have no doubt that he will be dismissed from his position.'

'Ahh,' Leigh-Hunt sat back in his chair and steepled his fingers across his waistcoat. 'And now the good Captain is without a job, and still in financial difficulties. What have you in mind Ralph?'

'I thought,' continued Gresham, 'military background, troubled times, if we could find him another low key job, and you could quietly feed him across to one of Kell's talent scouts, then we have the makings of a rather nice fall back position. If we are right about the location of the letter and Petrov's activities lead Lady Luck to point her blazing finger at Kelsford, we can ensure that it is on Captain Parfitt and MI5 that the spotlight falls...'

Walking down the steps of Whitehall Ralph paused to light a Passing Cloud. It was not necessary he decided to complicate matters by mentioning Jonathan Dilkes' concern that something had 'gone on' over the pistol incident that he did not quite understand.

What was it the young doctor said? *Mallard rang Harry North about it, but it was as if North already knew, all that Arthur said on the phone was, 'I've got the gun ...'*

'He is a bastard, but he's a clever bastard, you have got to admire him.'

Joe Rowell placed three pints of bitter on the table before sitting down himself. Clarrie Greasley and Bert Conway exchanged uneasy glances, the unspoken message that when Joe became aware of Harry's intervention in his own plans, he might change his opinion, did not rest well with them.

'Harry set him up from word one,' Clarrie took a sip of his beer. 'He let him take over the amnesty, then primed Ducky Mallard to ask him where he could get a gun. After that it was all downhill.'

'Where would he get the idea though?' mused Joe thoughtfully.

Clarrie and Bert once more exchanged glances.

'Lew Archer did it in 1910,' said Bert quietly.

Joe stared from one to the other. 'Jesus Christ,' he said sadly.

'The South African war was long over, but the Irish problems were all in the mix, and there were a load of Mausers and all sorts of shit floating about that had been grabbed off of the Boers and brought home by the troops.' Bert took a deep draw on his cigarette. 'Foxy had just taken over as Detective Inspector when Jesse Squires retired, and decided 'new broom' he would sweep the cupboard. So, he instigated an amnesty.'

'He gave his old partner, Lew the job of firearms officer - nice and simple, record any shooters handed in, and arrange disposal with a gunsmith. Lew was short, and he sold off a couple of revolvers. He should have had more sense, especially with Harry around. Harry found out, there was one hell of a row, but he kept it in the family. Lew put the money in the widows fund and nothing more was said.'

'Alright, but even then Harry couldn't have known that Eric would keep his own private list ...' Even as the words came out, Rowell saw the flaw in what he was saying.

'Yes he could Joe', grinned Clarrie, 'and I bet you the next round of drinks that within a week young Eric will be the new admin manager - which I have to say will make life a lot easier for all of us!'

Chapter 16

'Hello Joe, we've not seen you for a while,' Laura Percival was both surprised and pleased at the sight of the bulky figure of her niece's husband at the front door, although the fact that it was the middle of the morning on a working day told her that his visit was more likely to be about police work than social.

'Is Harry in Laura?' The peremptory tone of his voice took her somewhat by surprise. By mutual agreement he had not called her 'aunt', since the day that he came to live in Kelsford, but neither was he ever discourteous. 'Come through, he's in the kitchen,' she replied turning to lead him down the hallway.

As soon as he heard the sound of Rowell's voice at the front door Harry knew what the purpose of his visit was. From the time that he briefed Bert Conway and Clarrie Greasley to deal with the printers he had known that this moment would come.

'You bastard Harry, you had no right!' Joseph Rowell's anger bubbled over at the sight of the older man, collarless in front of the square shaving mirror hanging from its hook next to the sink, a Gillette safety razor in his hand.

Putting down the razor Harry swilled his face in the washing up bowl full of hot water and dried his face on the towel beside it before answering.

'We need to talk Joe - sensibly. I did what I had to do.'

Perplexed, Laura looked from one to the other. She had absolutely no idea what this was about.

'Laura, would you excuse us for a few minutes,' Harry said, and waited whilst she went back into the sitting room.

As she closed the door behind her Rowell, burst out once more.

'This has nothing to do with you Harry. You with your gui'd pay packet every Friday, and your comfortable house, things that the men I represent will nai'r be able to afford.' Anger thickened the Scottish accent to a point where Harry could barely understand what the Sergeant was saying.

Turning to face the other man, Harry rested his back against the sink and folded his arms.

'I repeat Joe. I did what I had to do, now are you prepared to listen to me?'

Rowell glared at him in silence, the muscles along his jaw clenching and unclenching.

'You have a good case, and everything that you are trying to achieve is reasonable, but the timing is wrong. The government will never let you form a union, and they will never let you get away with calling for industrial action. When the Met men went out on strike last year it frightened the government shitless. They set up the Desborough Committee, and back peddled on sacking men who went on strike - but that won't happen again, they are ready this time.'

'You had no right to stop those leaflets being printed. You are doing exactly what we are fighting against - blocking the democratic process for representation to better our rights.'

'For fuck sake Joe, listen to yourself, 'blocking the democratic process for representation ..!' Phrases like that alone put you on the losing side. Lloyd George and his merry men at Whitehall have already got massive problems with the army and the navy, without even considering any other industrial unrest. They are terrified of a political movement that will succeed in bringing the country to its knees. Believe me they will not allow that to happen.'

'They can't stop it,' Rowell retorted emphatically. 'On the day that the police withhold their labour, all of the other unions across the country will do likewise. Yes, the country will come to a halt, but it will be temporary, just long enough for us to achieve our goals.'

North shook his head sadly. 'Joe, you are not being realistic. Since last year's strike, the government have learned a lot. Desborough has already started to deal with issues of pay and conditions. That fact alone has been sufficient to placate a huge number of men who twelve months ago might have considered strike action. As yet you haven't even got a union, and I can tell you that within less than a month from now there will be legislation passed that will make it illegal for police officers to belong to a union - any union.'

'You are wrong Harry, this strike will succeed, and from now on, you stay out of my business.' The Scotsman's tone was flat, the message final.

Harry regarded him implacably. 'I know beyond a shadow of doubt Joe that if you take part in any strike action, you will be dismissed from the Force, and steps will be taken to ensure that you never work again. You are too good a man for me to let that happen. I will do everything in my power to stop you.'

The two men stood looking at each other for another long moment before Rowell turned on his heel and left.

'Are you going to tell me what that was all about Harry?' asked Laura quietly from the doorway.

North sighed and rested his hands on the edge of the stone kitchen sink. 'Joe is deeply involved in the setting up of a police union, which in itself is not a bad thing, but it looks like ending up in them taking strike action. The powers that be are dedicated to crushing any such a movement, and are looking to sack anyone and everyone who becomes involved. I am simply trying to stop Joe from ending up in the workhouse.'

Laura remained silent a moment, then said, 'Ailma is pregnant, she has just found out, she only told me last week.'

North's head sank forward, his chin resting on his chest, 'Christ, what a mess,' he muttered.

In an attempt to bring things back to normality Laura handed him his collar and tie from the back of the chair. 'You're late going out this morning, did you expect him?'

Harry nodded, 'It was on the cards, and Clarrie is coming round shortly, we have got a job to do which is nearer here than Long Street, so I decided to go direct. Its only a security visit to Pierpoint's warehouse.'

'When is this consignment expected in Clarrie?' Harry North and Clarence Greasley were strolling along Chalfont Street toward the turn into the old coal wharf, enjoying the morning sunshine. The wharf, long gone, was now the site of a complex of single storey buildings enclosed by a high barbed wire fence and double gates.

'Between two and two and a half weeks. Coming up by rail from Players at Nottingham. Unload and shift them from Sheffield Road Station into store here at Pierpoint's by lorry, then from here the following week by barge to Liverpool on the west, and Newcastle on the east.'

Harry grunted. In the present climate a major consignment of cigarettes sitting for the best part of a week in a warehouse on the outskirts of town was not something that filled him with enthusiasm. The notification that the shipment would be passing through Kelsford had arrived on his desk yesterday morning. Absently running his hand over the packet of Players in his pocket, he went through the figures again in his mind.

A packet of twenty cigarettes cost a shilling. The train that would be coming in direct from the John Players factory at Nottingham would be bringing in five hundred cases. A thousand packets to a case, meant a retail value of fifty pounds per case. The cigarettes would be brought from the station to the warehouse, and then from the warehouse to the awaiting canal boats by three lorries. With each vehicle fully loaded, according to his calculations the value of the consignment would be a total value of £25,000.

'Wonderful,' he muttered half to himself, half to the Sergeant, 'absolutely wonderful.'

Turning in through the steel gates of the compound they were met by the sparse figure of an elderly man in a dark blue jacket and peaked cap.

'Hello Clem, how are you keeping,' Harry held out his hand to the gatekeeper.

'Not badly thank you Harry, yourself?'

'I keep going,' replied Harry. Clement Waldron was an old police pensioner, who since his retirement some years previously had worked on the gate at Pierpoint's.

'You young Clarence? You're not getting any slimmer,' the old man chuckled.

'I have had to work hard over the years to maintain an imposing presence,' replied Greasley with a grin.

'I suppose', said the gateman, 'that you've come to see if you can scrounge some free fags, wait here I'll see if there's any fallen off a lorry.'

A minute later he reappeared from his hut with two packets of Black Cat cigarettes.

'A load split open last week, the boss wrote them off. One of the perks of the job. Mr Haddow knows you are here he'll be over in a minute.'

Taking their leave, the two policemen sauntered across the compound to await the arrival of the site manager, Stephen Haddow. 'How long do you reckon Clem has been finished now Clarrie?' asked Harry idly.

Greasley's pudgy features screwed up in concentration. 'Well he took me out when I joined,' he said pensively, 'that was in '92 and he was an old sweat then. He went well before the war, so if he did his twenty five, I reckon he's been gone about eight years, say 1911. He was a good old copper though, I remember ...'

Clarrie's reminiscence was interrupted by the sight of a portly man in his late forties hurrying towards them from the door of the office block.

By the nature of the goods that moved in and out of the warehouses, Stephen Haddow knew most of the Kelsford detectives, along with a number of uniform officers who made a regular practice of calling in to check that the watchman was alright and avail themselves of a cup of coffee and a welcome warm at his coke brazier of a winter night.

Pleasantries exchanged Harry came to the point of their visit. 'Stephen, we are a bit worried about the consignment of cigarettes that you are expecting from Players in the next couple of weeks.' Harry paused to light a Black Cat from the packet that Clem Waldron had given him, having first offered them to Haddow and Greasley.

Haddow shrugged non-commitally. 'It is a large shipment Harry, but I have to say we have had bigger. I don't anticipate it being here more than a couple of days. Abbott's Warehousing will take delivery of a single lorry load each day over three consecutive days. They won't be holding the goods. Mrs Abbot will telephone here when the barge arrives at the basin and we will transport the cigs., over there for immediate loading. After that we are finished.'

Harry was not convinced. 'Even so, we are talking about twenty five thousand pounds worth of goods Stephen, its dutiable - are customs or the army sending any escorts?'

The answer was little better than he had expected.

'Four soldiers and an NCO are travelling up from Nottingham on the train. They will mount a guard at the station on the two quarante-huits, then stay here until we have offloaded to the canal stage.'

Harry grunted non-committaly. The term 'quarante-huit' meaning literally 'forty-eight', had been coined early in the war by soldiers on the Western Front, for the bleak French railway boxcars in which they found themselves being carried across the country between railheads, and which bore on the sides a stencil indicating a maximum loading capacity of either forty men or eight horses.

'In all honesty,' continued the yard manager, 'in terms of some of their shipments, Players would not consider this to be particularly large shipment.'

'Perhaps not,' conceded North, 'but the reality is that with a black market value of around £10,000, it is going to be very attractive target.'

'Let's hope that we can keep it a secret,' Clarrie's gaze drifted around the yard. It was deserted except for two covered wagons at the far side that were being loaded with anonymous cartons by a team of men.

'Yes', said Harry resignedly, 'let's hope we can keep it a secret.'

Lisa Abbott paused on the pavement to allow the two men to pass by on the opposite side of Ludgate Street. Deep in conversation neither Harry North nor Clarence Greasley noticed the smartly dressed young woman in the doorway across the road from them.

Allowing them to disappear around the corner into the High Street she crossed over to look at the display in the ground floor window of Saunt's photographer's.

'Hello Lisa, long time no see.'

The words stopped Lisa in her tracks. She did not need to turn around to know who the woman was. Lilian Barstow. The flat Birmingham accent was unmistakable. Lilian was a barmaid at Gilbert Manton's favourite pub, The Sailor's Return.

'What do you want Lil.' Lisa continued to stare into Saunt's window, she had been considering for some time having a portrait taken of herself, but that was now the last thing on her mind.

'Looking up old friends - what else?' The voice was mocking and Lisa turned to face the woman.

'And why would you want to do that?' she asked.

Lil Barstow had changed little since they had last met. In her mid forties she was a thin pasty faced woman with a slight squint that gave her an air of permanent short sightedness. She would never Lisa thought, even as a young woman have been particularly attractive . Her watery eyes, the result of years of surreptitious dipping into the various spirits jars when Fred Lineker's back was turned, gazed coldly at her a sly smile twisted up one corner of her mouth.

'Still Mrs fucking-high-and-mighty aren't you.' The voice had now developed a definite edge. 'Let's talk about that shall we Lisa, because you see there are one or two people who would like to know where you are.'

Lisa moved casually into the recessed doorway at the bottom of Saunt's stairs, as if looking at the prints of the happy smiling couples on display. It was Thursday afternoon, half day closing, and her quick glance up and down the deserted street confirmed that, other than an old lady walking along the opposite side of the road they were not observed.

The woman continued, talking quickly, unable now that she had tracked down her quarry to contain her excitement. 'When Gimpy went up the stair to see how Nobby was and found him dead, there wasn't a sou in his safe, but you know that don't you Lisa.'

'I had heard Nobby was dead,' Lisa replied evenly, 'I was away and there was no point in coming back after that.'

Barstow allowed herself a thin smile revealing crooked and uneven teeth. 'But you weren't away were you dearie? That's the whole point. You weren't away, you were slipping in through the back door of the Sailor's!'

'Now while they were all a-wondering where Nobby had stashed his readies, I began to think about where you might have been going that night with your suitcase - never to be seen again. Then I heard a couple of the lads down at the wharf talking about this safe drop off in Kelsford, run by one 'Mrs Abbott' and I thought, I know someone called Abbott who comes from Kelsford, I think I ought to pop over and see her.'

So, thought Lisa, the only way in which Lilian Barstow could know of her late night visit to the Sailor's on the night that Nobby died was if either Gilbert Manton, or Fred Lineker had told her. Fred would know better than to discuss such things, so it had to be Gil. Gilbert Manton had sent the woman to keep an eye on her.

Her mind was working fast, deciding what to do about the woman. One thing was certain she had no intention of allowing Manton to install his spy at the basin.

'So what do you want Lil?' Her tone was resigned, appeasing.

'I want my cut dearie, that's what I want. You went up to that room on the Sunday night and found Nobby dead. You cleaned out the safe and legged it with the money. Now, I want half. Simple enough for you?'

Lisa regarded her evenly, turning things over.

'I'll tell you what I will do Lilian,' she said quietly.

'I will cut you in. I have got a good thing running here and I might be able to use a hand. Any money that I have got is tied up, but the scheme is big, and very safe.'

The older woman appeared indecisive.

'Take it or leave it Lil,' Lisa's voice was hard now. 'There is no cash on offer because I haven't got any - understand that. But I can find a way to cut you in.'

She was certain that the proposition would fit in with whatever brief Manton had given the woman.

Barstow blew out her pasty jowls in a sour gesture of indecision, then gave a quick nod. 'Alright. But you try to work a switch on me, and believe me you'll regret it,' she said menacingly.

Lisa relaxed slightly, feeling the tension easing out of her body. 'Meet me tonight, nine o'clock at the railway station, and don't be late, we have got a train to catch and it's important.' Moving out of the doorway she flicked a glance once more up and down the street and was relieved to find that it was still deserted. Without any further conversation she walked briskly off down the road toward the town centre.

At five minutes to nine, Lisa walked through one of the arched brick porticos of Sheffield Road railway station and checked the chalk board in the main booking hall that was constantly being updated by a young lad of about fourteen wearing the livery of the London Midland Railway Company. As she already knew, the next train due in was the nine o'two for Sheffield. Standing at the far side of the concourse was the sparse figure of Lilian Barstow, from the jaunty angle of the broad brimmed had that she was wearing and the slightly unsteady gate as she approached, Lisa knew that the woman had spent at least part of the time since their conversation, celebrating her success in one or other of the town centre pubs. She just hoped that she had kept her mouth shut.

'So, where are we going then?' The steadiness of her speech belied the alcohol that Barstow had undoubtedly consumed.

'All in good time,' Lisa murmured. 'Take this ticket and get in one of the middle carriages of the Sheffield train when it arrives. You have got just over five minutes. I will come down and join you on the train.'

'And where will you be?' Barstow demanded.

'I have to collect a parcel from that man standing over there,' she indicated a short well rounded figure in an old fashioned bowler hat, smoking a cigar and reading an evening newspaper near to the booking clerk's office.

'He isn't expecting you, and if we both go over he will think something is wrong and be away like a jack rabbit.'

The woman gave one of her sharp nods, well versed in the ways of petty crime, the precaution made sense to her. Taking the proffered ticket, she watched as Lisa went over and spoke to the man, before turning away and marching off towards the steps leading down to the platform, her shabby grey skirt swirling out behind her.

The gentleman, concentrating on an article on the back page of his paper concerning the recent victory of the Kelsford Cricket XI over a local Derby team, gave a start at the attractive young woman's polite enquiry as to whether he could tell her time.

Pulling out an ornate silver pocket watch he confirmed for her that it was one minute to nine o'clock. With a charming smile, a polite 'thank you,' and a further enquiry as to whether or not Kelsford had won the cricket match referred to in the paper, Lisa watched the portly figure disappear out of sight.

It was dark by the time the train began its final run in towards Sheffield and the blinds in their carriage were pulled to prevent anyone walking along the corridor from looking in. Lisa had done the trip several times since moving back to Kelsford and knew the run well, there was she estimated about twenty minutes left before their arrival. During the journey she had passed the time away explaining as much of the 'enterprise' that she was engaged in as she felt would keep Lilian Barstow interested.

Not that she did not already know exactly the nature of the business being conducted at the basin - Gilbert Manton would have ensured that. Lilian's assumptions as to what had taken place in the upstairs room of the George on the night Nobby Armstrong died were exactly that - assumptions and gossip.

So she reflected, it was the faithful Gimpy who had opened the safe. In her mind's eye she could see him, standing by the side of the bed, first confused, then with the full realisation that Armstrong was dead, tearing frantically at the cord to release the key. Lisa could imagine his fury on opening the safe to discover that it contained a fraction of what he expected. He would have cleared away such cash as was left, taking it through the door into the lodging house and stashing it away somewhere secure - possibly enlisting the help of Sadie Riley if she had not also succumbed during the night to the flu. Gossip would have been rife, and as she well knew would have centred on her own whereabouts.

Lilian had let herself down though. She should not have mentioned Lisa's visit to the Sailor's Return - or the suitcase. Gilbert Manton had sent Lil Barstow to Kelsford, and it was not difficult to figure out why. Now that the activities at the basin were up and running he was planning either to supplant Lisa altogether, or at least to put a leash on her by installing his spy in the camp. Lisa looked at the woman seated opposite with renewed interest. For Manton to entrust her with this job, he must either now, or at some time in the past have been in some sort of a relationship with her. Looking at her, the latter seemed to be the far more likely answer.

'So what did Gimpy say about you coming over here to see me?' she asked casually.

Lilian grunted and gave one of her sly lopsided grins. 'Do you think I'm stupid. No, I had you worked out from word one. You nicked Nobby's stash. If I put the word out, half of Leicester would be over here, then where would we be lovey - neither of us would get to keep anything. No there's just you and me know about this one.'

Lisa nodded slowly. Only the man who had sent her knew that Lil was here, and he now needed to be sent a message.

'Pity for me you were a bit shrewd, but there you go, I can possibly do with a bit of a hand, so let's seal the deal.'

Digging down into her bag she brought out a half bottle of Jamieson's Whiskey and pulling the stopper out with her teeth, offered it to the other woman.

'Thought you didn't drink.' It was a statement rather than a question.

'I do occasionally, just a drop once in a while,' Lisa replied. 'Take a pull and I'll have mine in a minute, I need some air first.'

Without waiting for a reply she got up and slid the carriage door open, behind her Lilian Barstow took a long pull at the Irish whiskey.

In the corridor she moved to the carriage door and pulling the leather fastening strap, dropped the window down. The train was slowing up for a slight gradient on the approach to Sheffield station, and the air that came in was cool and refreshing. Leaning out Lisa reached down the outside of the door until she felt the cold brass of the recessed handle. Bracing herself against the solid door frame she pushed the latch downwards and felt the door swing outwards slightly. Holding it tightly against the slipstream so that it did not open more than an inch or so, with her free hand she pulled a piece of thick card from the folds of her skirt and trapping it in the frame where the tongue of the lock fitted, pulled the door back into the closed position, wedging it tight.

Back in the compartment, her companion was looking distinctly unwell. Her normally unhealthy pallor was now the colour of day old pastry dough, and she had difficulty in forming her words.

'Jesus, do'n feel very well,' she mumbled, 'gonna be sick.'

'It's the train, you're not used to them lovey, come on lets get you some fresh air,' said Lisa in a concerned voice. 'Here we go.' Hauling the rapidly deteriorating woman to her feet she steered her through the door into the corridor where the draught of cool night air was coming in through the open window.

Lisa shot a quick glance up and down the carriage to ensure that they were alone before withdrawing into the shadows of the compartment.

She watched through the doorway as staggering drunkenly, Barstow stumbled to where the fresh air streaming in through the open window was becoming an icy blast as the train gathered speed once more on the straight stretch of rail through the drab soot stained houses on the outskirts of Sheffield. Putting her head out into the night, her entire weight was thrust against the door as she began to retch out of the window.

It was, Lisa estimated less than two seconds, before the door swung outwards propelling Lilian Barstow with a shrill scream into the dark oblivion.

Ensuring that the corridor was still deserted Lisa stepped quickly forward and pulled the door back into place, locking it securely. If anyone had witnessed the incident, all they would have seen was a drunken woman stepping out of a compartment and falling through the door.

With a deafening clatter and flashing of carriage lights as it hurtled past on the adjacent line, the late night London express, gathering speed as it left Sheffield flew by in the opposite direction.

Resuming her seat, Lisa replaced the laudanum laced whiskey bottle in her travelling bag. In her mind she ran swiftly over the evening's events. Other than for a brief minute in the booking hall at Kelsford they had not been seen together. Lilian had boarded the train on her own and with the carriage blinds down, no one had seen them together in the compartment.

She smiled to herself quietly. A simple accident, if the fall from the train did not kill her, the express hurtling up the outbound track would certainly do so. Fishing about in her bag she brought out her train ticket which she held in readiness for the collector who had entered the carriage from the far end.

Chapter 17

Vasily Petrov was uneasy. Bavaria, and Munich in particular, was without a doubt the most dangerous place in Europe for him to be at the present time. He eased the Luger from the holster at the back of his belt, and placed it on the bedside table before laying back to gaze at the peeling plaster of the hotel room ceiling. The Adler, a tiny dilapidated bierkeller was hidden away at the end of a narrow alley five minutes walk away from Herrnstrasse. At the rear, a second alley or *Gasse* led into a dismal cobbled market square where, he presumed once a week the locals gathered to buy whatever was on offer from the farmers who brought their scanty wares into the town. Accustomed as he was to the hardships of life in Russia, Petrov was relatively unperturbed by the obvious shortages being experienced in post-war Germany. Bavaria was, he reflected better off than the capital and towns further north where the staple diet consisted mainly of boiled potatoes supplemented with rabbit and the occasional scrawny chicken. Here at least, it was possible to order a proper meal in one of the few restaurants that were still open, even if such relative luxury was reflected in the prices.

What particularly bothered him was the atmosphere of frenetic political activity that pervaded the town. Everyone seemed to be consumed by an intense nationalism which focussed on the activities of the right wing Social Democrat party and hung like an all encompassing cloud over the town. On his arrival earlier in the day, as he left the railway station, a group of uniformed soldiers - part of the infamous Ehrhardt Freikorps Brigade - ambled past him in full uniform all carrying either rifles or side arms. It was rumoured that General Ludendorff, secretly returned from hiding in Sweden, was currently living openly in one of the hotels near to the town centre. To be identified as a communist agent here in this place - which was exactly what he was intending to have to do - would be tantamount to committing suicide.

The plan worked out by himself and Ralph Gresham during the previous week in London was simple, but hazardous. Petrov sent word back to Russia through a Cheka contact in Paris, that having been working undercover in England since the elimination of Tessier, he was now in possession of 'certain sensitive material', and was returning to Moscow. In order to avoid Berlin, he would travel south into Bavaria, then via Vienna to Budapest where he could safely make contact with the local communists. He would they presumed, be safe until Stalin had his hands on the Yeremin letter, after which he was a dead man. In disclosing the route that he had chosen, Petrov was giving Felix Dzerzhinsky the opportunity to monitor his progress, which was precisely what was needed for the plan to succeed - the Russians needed to know when he arrived in Munich.

For their part, Ralph Gresham and Mardlin, posing as members of the Allied Control Commission with their driver - Percy Longman - would follow the Russian through France into Bavaria, giving to the Cheka the impression that they were bent on catching the escaping agent.

Petrov lit a cigarette and watched the smoke drifting lazily towards the ceiling. For the time being it remained a double bluff. As yet Gresham and Mardlin did not know where he had hidden the real Yeremin letter. Something that he would not reveal until this mission was over and having shaken off his communist masters he was safely back in England.

If nothing went wrong, the three Englishmen should arrive close on his heels sometime tomorrow. The arrangement was that he would be contacted here at the bierkeller sometime this evening with details of the arrangements to collect a car. Tomorrow he would take the road out of Munich followed by Gresham and his two companions, in a remote part of the countryside he would drive his vehicle into a ditch and make it look as if he had been attacked. The contact who had supplied the car would pick him up in a second vehicle and drive them over the border into Austria, from where he would be smuggled back to England.

Minutes after he dumped the car, Gresham and Mardlin would arrive at the scene, fire a few shots into the bodywork, which with any luck would be heard by a farm worker nearby, then turn around and drive as fast as possible back to Mulhouse. To all intents and purposes, Vasily Petrov had been shot by the British, his body disposed of, and the continued existence of the Yeremin letter would remain a mystery to haunt the Russian leadership for a long while to come.

Petrov stubbed out the cigarette in the bedside ashtray. Simple plans were always the best, the fewer things to go wrong, the better.

A soft knock at the door brought him off of the bed, pistol in his hand. Moving to the side of the doorframe, he demanded, 'Ja, wer ist?'

'I am from the garage Mein Herr, with the keys to your car.'

The words were spoken quietly in a well educated voice carrying a Viennese lilt.

Reaching across Petrov turned the key in the lock and waited, back pressed against the wall. The door swung open to admit a man of medium height wearing the dress of an Austrian army officer. Without turning his head he said, 'there is no need for the pistol Mein Herr, this is not a trap'.

Moving in behind the officer, Petrov swapped the Luger to his left hand and pressed the barrel gently against the back of the man's head whilst with his right he flipped the gun from his belt holster onto the bed out of reach.

The Russian stepped to one side and moved round to face his visitor.

'The car keys bitte,' he said.

Reaching into the side pocket of his tunic, the officer produced a ring with a single small key attached. He was Petrov saw, in his early thirties, of slight build with a pleasant if rather pale face. A small dark moustache, neatly trimmed and at odds with the usual heavy waxed appendages commonly sported by Austrian and German officers, seemed slightly out of place.

Holding the key out, the younger man nodded an acknowledgement and said, 'Leutnant Klaus Siegfeld, Imperial Austrian Army.'

'Late of the Imperial Austrian Army,' corrected Petrov wryly. 'Does everyone here think that the war is still going on?'

'Be careful Herr Petrov,' replied the man seriously, 'in this part of the world, the war truly is still very much, 'going on', as you put it.'

Petrov nodded slowly, he had booked in at reception as Jules Beke, a Belgian engineer. 'How do you know my name?'

Siegfeld ignored the question. 'I can be trusted Mein Herr, and if we are to accomplish what you are here for, you need to accept that - and put the gun away if you please.' The dark slanted eyes and Mongol features gave the Russian a menacing appearance which the officer found slightly unnerving.

'And what is our purpose?' Petrov asked, dropping the gun back onto the night stand. Despite the lateness of the afternoon, the sunshine was still warm and bright, and he noticed that the pike grey tunic and breeches were worn and had seen better days, the red collar flashes told him that the Leutnant was an artillery man.

'Precisely? That I don't know. My instructions are that tomorrow I am to take you to a garage near here. I shall vouch for you to the proprietor and you will collect the motorcar which these keys fit.'

'By the way,' he added, 'your associates have been delayed, they will not leave Mulhouse until tomorrow, I was asked to tell you, that you should look at making the trip out of town the following day.'

A dark scowl spread across Petrov's face. A further twenty four hours doubled the risks involved.

'The arrangement is,' continued the Austrian, 'that early on Saturday morning, around 7 a.m., you will drive out along the road to Schäftlarn, after about ten kilometres there is a secluded stretch with woodland either side. There I will be waiting for you in another car. We put your vehicle into the ditch at the side of the road, and I drive you across the border into Austria where you will be met by a contact who will take you on to your destination.'

'Why?' Demanded Petrov, 'why are you doing this?'

Siegfeld sighed, 'before the war my family was comfortably off. That quickly changed after Sarajevo. The old Emperor made some misjudgements, and we were plunged into a war that we could not possibly win. I joined the army before the war, in 1914 with everyone else, I went away to fight - I came back in 1918 to find that my parents were dead, everything I had was gone, and I needed to fend for myself. I came here a month or so ago and joined the Ehrhardt Brigade. It is not I have to say, to my taste. First and foremost, despite the fact that we are hundreds of miles from the sea, it is primarily a naval unit - I am a soldier. The men are German, and mainly *arschloken* - I am an Austrian, and a gentleman.'

'...And I need the money,' he concluded, picking up Petrov's cigarettes from the bedside table and lighting one.

The following morning just before eleven o'clock, dressed in a suitably shabby suit and soft grey hat, Petrov stood in the almost deserted market place at the rear of the Adler smoking a cigarette. He did not have to wait long, as a nearby church clock chimed eleven the trim figure of Klaus Siegfeld emerged from a turning on the opposite side of the square and without speaking walked past him.

Grinding the half smoked cigarette under his heel the Russian followed at a discreet distance. After about five minutes they turned into a mean little side street, the eaves of the old buildings leaning out so far across the cobbles as to almost touch each other. Suddenly he unexpectedly lost sight of the Austrian as he disappeared into a gateway on his right. Reaching the entrance Petrov saw that the open gates gave access to a cobbled courtyard in which two ex-army lorries stood. On the far side was a Mercedes touring car. The sign on the gates declared this to be the premises of 'Armand Seckler Automobile Engineer & Purveyor of Benzin Fuel.

Petrov checked around him, everything appeared to be in order, they had not been followed. The Austrian disappeared into what appeared to be the main workshop, in the doorway of which a short thin man in greasy overalls stood wiping his hands on a piece of rag.

Inside, the workshop was surprisingly well lit by a series of electric light bulbs hanging from the rafters. Another lorry minus front wheels was propped up on axle stands to one side, and on the other was a work bench with what appeared to be a dismantled gearbox laid out. Siegfeld was standing next to the bench watching the yard through the doorway.

Vasily Petrov paused, instinct told him that something was not right. Why had they come in here if the car was outside in the yard? Why bother to bring the keys to his hotel room the night before, but leave the car at the garage? As he turned to look back into the yard, the man in overalls slid the heavy workshop door behind him closed on well oiled runners. Petrov's hand was closing around the butt of his gun when a guttural Bavarian accent behind him said, 'don't even think about it comrade.'

Glancing over his shoulder he saw a thickset man wearing military breeches, and a dark brown shirt with a broad leather belt and should strap, pointing a revolver at him. From behind the jacked up lorry two more brown shirted figures emerged, both were armed with stubby Bergmann MP 18 submachine guns.

'Regrettably Comrade, times - as I explained to you yesterday are hard,' said Siegfeld smoothly. He was, Petrov noted the only one not pointing a gun.

The Russian ignored him, if he got out of this safely, he would make a point of killing the Austrian. Turning he gave the man behind him, who from his insignia was obviously the officer in charge, a hard stare. He was short, with a square clean shaven brutish face, like the other two he was wearing a soft military kepi.

'What is this all about?' demanded Petrov. He was he knew in trouble, the Austrian had sold him out to one of the right wing nationalist groups. From the uniforms, he suspected that he had fallen into the hands of the infamous *sturmabteilung*, who working with the Freikorps had virtually established a military dictatorship throughout Germany.

'That is what we intend to find out Comrade,' a thin smile flitted across the officer's face. Turning to the two troopers he spoke in rapid German, Petrov was unable to follow the local dialect, but the intention was obvious. The taller of the two, having relieved him of the Luger prodded him unceremoniously, indicating the workshop door, which at some unseen signal had been slid open once more.

In silence, the officer leading, Petrov was escorted through the now busy streets at gunpoint. It was he thought, a sign of the times in this part of the world that the cavalcade drew little attention, the Austrian Leutnant had disappeared. After a few minutes they turned into Herrnstrasse, and arrived at the door of a dilapidated bierkeller over which hung a sign proclaiming it to be the Alte Rosenbad.

Barely lunchtime, inside it was deserted other than for a girl of about eighteen polishing glasses behind the bar. Petrov was led to the rear of the premises and into a dingy room with a single table set at the back near to a rickety staircase.

Incongruously the unplastered brick work was painted a dark red which served only to make the room gloomier. He speculated from the size of it that this had at some time been an outhouse which had been knocked through into the main building.

Seated at the table was a thin pale faced man wearing steel rimmed spectacles. 'Any problems Jakob?' he demanded.

'Nein Herr Drexler, everything went as planned,' the officer replied smugly. 'Our master spy walked into the trap like a schoolchild.'

The man called Drexler regarded Petrov speculatively for a moment. 'Much as I dislike communists, you Herr Petrov appear to be something of a valuable commodity.'

Again, the use of his real name. It was apparent to Petrov that having traced him once more, Joseph Stalin had openly issued instructions that he was to be intercepted en route and, however metaphorically, 'returned to him in chains.' To choose to travel through Southern Germany had been a risk too many, he could only hope that when he failed to make the rendezvous with Gresham and Mardlin they would be able to come to his aid.

He returned the man's gaze steadily. The officer had called the him 'Herr Drexler', he searched his memory banks in vain, then it came to him. Just before he had set off after Yurkovich he had read a short report on a German by the name of Anton Drexler, a locksmith by trade who worked for the Munich Railroad Company. He and another nationalist by the name of Karl Harrer had established a minor political group in Bavaria entitled the German Workers Party.

'So Herr Drexler,' he said quietly, 'so much for political idealism. Whatever you have been promised to betray me, it will not, I can assure you be paid. You would be better served by allowing me to contact certain people who will reimburse you and your organisation handsomely for my safe return.'

The German continued to regard him straight faced. 'No, you are wrong, Comrade,' the title was spat out, 'we are not looking for money, we unlike yourself are serving an ideology which will in itself reward us.

To the officer he said, 'take him up to the storeroom. Tomorrow morning when Armand brings the car, we will take him to Freiburg and hand him over to Kapitän Röhm. He has made arrangements for the Russians to pick him up.

Late that same afternoon Percy Longman parked the Renault car, which they had picked up in Mulhouse, at the rear of the hotel Leipzig in Bismarckallee and stretched his aching limbs. It had been a long hard drive to Freiburg over poor quality roads, and he was ready for a stein of the local beer and something hot to eat.

Climbing down from the back of the car, Will Mardlin looked around him at his new surroundings with interest. He was still coming to terms with the world of espionage into which he had so recently stepped, there was a degree of surrealism attached to it that he was finding difficult to come to terms with.

A short time ago at the Clarence Hotel, watching the interplay between Vasily Petrov and Ralph Gresham, Will had begun to realise something of the nebulous world that he had entered when he had agreed to partner Gresham. The one thing that was clear to him was that unlike police work, where although they might on occasions touch and part, there was a clearly defined line drawn between police officers and criminals, here there were no such rules. Everything was fluid with no discernable boundaries. A matter of days previously, Petrov had sat in a dingy upstairs room opposite Gresham, looking down the barrel of a gun, now the two of them were involved in a joint operation in southern Germany.

The discussion had been a lengthy one centring around how the fake Yeremin letter could be made to appear to be in the process of being returned, and then disappear along with the agent. For once there were no elegant waiters gliding in and out of the suite that the company were occupying on the ground floor of the Clarence. Sandwiches and coffee were left at regular intervals in the passageway to be brought in and placed on a side table by Percy Longman.

Initially Ralph had favoured Berlin. 'It is the best place for us to operate from,' he asserted lighting a Passing Cloud from the stub of the one in his hand.

'We are going in as members of the International Allied Control Commission which is based in Berlin. It is the one place that we can set up some backup and a communications system.'

'Ralph, I have been in Berlin much more recently than you have. The situation there is impossible. The city is like you have never seen it,' Petrov objected, stubbing out a cigarette. 'And you know what, much of that is down to you stupid idiots. You have won the war, but you are going to lose the peace.'

'Your Versailles Treaty has hamstrung Ebert and his government. You have restricted the Reichswehr to one hundred thousand men. That gives two massive problems. You have created a country in turmoil but have not allowed sufficient men to control that situation. Then you have refused to acknowledge that there are thousands of men coming back from the war to a bankrupt economy with no work, men who you could have legitimately allowed to remain in uniform and under control.'

'No - you didn't do that! You allowed the commanders coming back from the front to bring with them their old fighting units and reform them in Germany itself as Freikorps! They are still in their old uniforms and are carrying all of their weapons, and they have one purpose - literally, to kill anyone who gets in their way. They are being funded by the regular army generals! A lot of the Freikorps even have artillery pieces and tanks for Christ's sake! Munich is the place to do it,' he insisted emphatically.

'From Mulhouse in Alsace we can slip across the border to Freiburg - it is less than fifty kilometres, then east to Munich. There are so many dissident groups in Munich that we can take our pick.'

Gresham looked thoughtful, a quick spasm flicked across his jaw.

'Tell me about Munich,' he said.

The Russian lit an Abdullah. The strong Turkish tobacco was he had decided the next best thing to the black Georgian mix that he was used to.

'It would not be my first choice, but then none of this would be. Munich, situated where it is, deep in Bavaria is remote and steeped in Germanic lore. For some reason it doesn't seem to have sunk in to them that they have actually lost the war. They still think that they were betrayed by the politicians - *dolchstoss* - the stab in the back. In reality they would like an independent Bavaria, but if that is not possible then they will settle for whatever they can get. Munich is a political hotbed of little right wing groups, which means that any of Dzerzhinsky's agents would be spotted straight away - which should make it easy for me,' he added in a resigned tone.

'If I were to take a train from Paris, south to Alsace, then across the border. The east bound express from Freiburg, would get me to Munich in about three hours. You follow me leaving a trail a mile wide. Two days, and we can be out again. You head back into France, I get over the border into Austria and make a loop back to England under an assumed name.'

'How would our cover as members of the Inter-Allied Control Commission stand up?' asked Mardlin.

Petrov shook his head. 'The English and French Commission Inspectors in reality have no authority at all, not just in the south but anywhere in Germany. They are hated, but it doesn't matter because we want the Cheka to know that you are on my heels.'

Refreshed after a hot bath and a meal, the three sat in a quiet corner of the hotel lounge. Gresham and Longman each smoked one of the aromatic local cigars, whilst Will sipped appreciatively at a large brandy balloon. Irrespective of their cover story the fact that they were English isolated them from the other guests. Will was glad that they were only going to be in Freiburg for a very short time. The place was oppressive, and he was aware that to venture into the wrong place was actually dangerous. Easing his position in the leather armchair he was grateful for the reassuring weight of the Browning under his jacket in its shoulder holster.

It was approaching ten o'clock and the summer evening had, in the last few minutes finally drifted into darkness. Looking out of the window into the deserted square Ralph stubbed out his cigarette and said, 'if you will excuse me for a moment, there is something that I need to check on.' Without further explanation he stood up, straightened the crease in his trousers, and left.

'How did you get into this business Percy?' Will asked casually. He knew absolutely nothing about the quiet self effacing third member of the team.

Longman leaned back in his chair and stared up at the ceiling before replying. 'I often ask myself that Will,' he replied.

'I was a soldier before the war - Sergeant. I speak good German, and French - my mother is from northern France - the Colonel was going to France on an undercover reccy of the French defenses and needed a driver. We sort of hit it off. Got into a couple of scrapes which confirmed that we could work together, so he arranged for me to be seconded onto special duties and I stayed with him.'

Will took a sip of the brandy, 'I was brought up in an army family,' he said. 'Spent all of my early life in India, didn't see Blighty until I was in my teens. My father was posted to Kelsford as a Recruiting Sergeant, I didn't fancy the army so I worked on the railway for a start, then joined the police at Leicester.'

He paused, 'What rank are you Percy?' The question had intrigued him for some time.

'W.O.1- Regimental Sergeant Major. Although I have rarely worn the uniform, it is one of the perks of these 'secret squirrel' jobs, no medals, but you get some decent promotions ...'

Their conversation was halted by the sight of Ralph Gresham striding towards them across the dining room, a look of deep concern on his face.

'Problem.' He announced.

'Vasily's contact was an Austrian artillery officer. His job was to see him over to the rendezvous where we could dump the car as planned. I had a backup contact of my own who I have just spoken to. It seems that the Austrian sold Vasily out to the locals, who are now planning to hand him on to the Cheka. Fake letter and all!'

'What are we going to do about it?' asked Will.

'My man says that they are proposing tomorrow to bring him to Freiburg. Ernst Röhm, the commander of the Brown Shirts, the *S. A,* is here. He has arranged - for a finder's fee - to hand him over to the Russians. I think we need to arrange an intervention along the way.'

Despite the warm summer morning the drive along the pot holed road from Munich to Freiburg was chilly in the open touring car. It was, Petrov noted when he was pushed roughly into the back seat outside the Alte Rosenbad, the car that was in the garage courtyard the day before. The brown shirts deliberately drove with the top down in order to impress the local inhabitants with their uniforms and overt show of weaponry. The two guards in the rear, between whom he was wedged were armed with carbines whilst the square face officer seated in the front passenger seat carried a Bergmann.

The night had been spent in an uncomfortable store room with nothing more than a straw paliasse to sleep on and a bucket in the corner for his ablutions. Petrov had quickly discovered that escape, certainly at this stage, was not an option. The tiny window in the room was barred and from the sounds that permeated through the solid timber door it was apparent that there was a guard permanently posted in the corridor outside.

Petrov flexed his shoulders against the bulk of the troopers each side of him. It amused him that they were as cramped as he, and it also told him that given an opportunity he was in a more manoeuvrable position than they were. Also, the fact that they were armed with carbines was a mistake. Although considerably shorter than a rifle, the weapons were still too unwieldy for use in such a confined space. Had he been in charge of the escort, they would have each carried a revolver, unholstered and pressed firmly into his sides.

Because of the condition of the road, laid down in the previous century for use by farm vehicles and carriages, the large car could not utilise its power to make swift progress, and was limited to the driver picking his way over the uneven surface.

Petrov saw that they were passing through an area of woodland, the thickly growing trees would he thought provide excellent cover if he could only reach them.

As if sensing his train of thought, the guard on his right shifted the carbine from between his legs and laid it across his knees.

Minutes later, rounding a bend in the road, the driver slammed on his brakes at the sight of two army lorries parked broadside on across the road to form a roadblock. Flanked by a group of soldiers standing in front of the lorries, a heavy Maxim machine gun had been set up in the middle of the road to cover traffic approaching around the bend. An officer wearing the uniform of a Captain stepped forward and held up his arm in a signal to stop.

It was now that the Brown shirt officer made a fatal mistake. Leaping to his feet he laid the barrel of his Bergman across the windshield of the Mercedes with the obvious intention of creating a stand-off. Instead, the machine gunner, a veteran of four years in the trenches reacted on pure instinct and opened fire, hosing a spray of bullets back and forth across the front of the car at windshield level. The S.A., man had just sufficient time to fire a short burst from his sub machinegun, which took the officer commanding the roadblock off of his feet, before he and the driver were reduced to bloodstained rag dolls by the Maxim.

In the ensuing seconds of confusion, shielded by the men in the front of the car, Vasily Petrov grabbed the carbine laid across the trooper's legs next to him, and swung it upwards in an arc, the butt hitting the man in the mouth, reduced his face to a bloody mask. Reversing his action he brought the weapon down on the side of the other guard's head before throwing himself out over the back of the car.

Lost in the gunfire, rolling sideways Petrov dropped into the ditch at the side of the road to be grabbed by Will Mardlin who, pistol in hand was laying concealed under the bank.

'Grenades' Ralph Gresham's voice was perfectly calm.

Coming up onto their knees, out of sight behind the cover of the ditch, in one smooth movement, he and Percy Longman drew the pins from the grenades in their hands and threw them unerringly into the carnage in the back of the Mercedes. Dropping flat again, the firing by the patrol into the now inert vehicle continued during the four seconds that elapsed before the air was rent by two simultaneous explosions followed by a further blast and a sheet of flame as the fuel tank exploded.

Before the débris had finished falling to the ground, the four men were crawling silently along the ditch unseen by the soldiers, who were now tending to their mortally wounded officer, and away from the scene.

It took them twenty minutes to reach the Renault that was parked in some bushes off of the road half a mile behind where the roadblock had been set up. Five minutes later they were making good time back towards Freiburg.

'How did you manage to lay that on Ralph,' asked Petrov as steadying his hands he lit a Passing Cloud from the glowing end of the one Gresham held out to him.

Lighting a third, Gresham passed it over to Percy in the driving seat.

'Once we realised that little Austrian bastard had double crossed you, I made an anonymous phone call to the Reichswehr Intelligence Headquarters in

Freiburg. The commanding officer there is a Captain Karl Mayr. The message I left was that a group of S.A. Brown shirts would be travelling along this road this morning in a car loaded with explosives with the intention of blowing up his offices. We simply followed the patrol out and parked up. You did your bit by jumping ship, and after that everything went rather well'

Petrov nodded in agreement, Gresham he decided definitely knew what he was doing. 'Nobody saw you throw the grenades, so the patrol will say that the car simply exploded, and so far as my comrades in Moscow are concerned, there is no way now of identifying who died in the car. Excellent!'

'Yes,' murmured Gresham, 'excellent'. Vasily Petrov settling himself back in his seat failed to notice the quick spasm which jerked at the side of the other man's mouth

'I am not sure Colonel, that you didn't take an unacceptable risk.'

It was a rare thing for Leigh-Hunt to criticise his best operative, and Ralph raised his eyebrows at the note of censure.

'Deliberately handing our man over to the German nationalists was an extremely risky strategy.' The pince-nez on the black ribbon swung backwards and forwards between the old man's fingers in an irritated movement.

'Not really Sir Rowland,' replied Ralph, the twitch caught momentarily at the side of his mouth.

'No one in the Cheka would ever have believed that we followed him along a country road, put a few bullet holes into the car, and he then disappeared in a cloud of smoke. They would have spotted the set-up immediately'

'Siegfeld has, I have to say, proved himself to be most reliable – I think that we may well be able to use him again, and of course the fact that his sister is married to the good Doctor Dilkes, will as we have previously discussed enable us to keep them both in line.'

'The only unknown factor was whether or not the Reichswehr Intelligence man, Mayr, would take the appropriate action and set up a roadblock. Although it was fairly certain that he would - they have been desperately trying to gain control of the Brown Shirts, and the Freikorps for months. I did mention Drexler's name in the phone call because I know that Mayr is in the process of putting him under surveillance. The fact that they opened fire without even issuing a challenge was an absolute bonus, I had thought that we might have to help things along. Petrov's reaction was perfect, we didn't have to fire a shot.'

'That is what bothers me,' Leigh-Hunt gave Gresham a sharp look. 'Whilst the success of your plan has undoubtedly convinced the Russians that Vasily Petrov is now dead, we still do not know where the Yeremin letter is hidden.

Where I have to ask, would we now be if Petrov had in fact been killed in this incident?'

Gresham steepled his fingers, choosing his words carefully.

'Yes if Petrov were to have been killed, in one way it would have been to our disadvantage, however in another it would have absolutely concluded the matter so far as the Russians were concerned. Obviously had that been case, we would have wanted the body found and identified and would not have detonated the vehicle.'

'However, I think that we may be much further forward on that score than you think. Vasily Petrov had the letter in his possession the night that André Tessier was killed. He came directly to England. After removing Fedor Yurkovich, he moved to Manchester and Liverpool for a while, but his fall back position was always Kelsford.'

'So I am fairly certain that he has stashed the letter somewhere in Kelsford. Somewhere safe   not in a biscuit tin in the woods, that only happens in novels – no, I think that he will have lodged it somewhere. A solicitor, bank, something like that, and I think that with the resources that we have to hand, we could find this on our own if necessary.'

Leigh-Hunt sniffed disdainfully. 'I hope that you are right Colonel. Where is our man at present?'

'Will and I came back through France, we dropped him off with a set of fresh documents at a railway station on the Austrian border, he should be back in England within the next few days. I would propose for the time being keeping him on ice at the Clarence until we have sorted things out long term.'

Leigh-Hunt studied the eyepiece swinging rhythmically between his fingers. 'What is your *long term* assessment of the situation?' he asked.

Gresham drummed his fingers together, 'I think that we have at present a very fine balance, which is definitely loaded in our favour. The fact that Vasily Petrov 'no longer exists', is definitely to our advantage. Irrespective of the Yeremin letter, he is a walking encyclopaedia on a part of the world and a régime of which we know virtually nothing. Long term his knowledge of Russia and the Okhrana, or Cheka as it is now known, will be invaluable. His present bargaining coin is the letter, however if I can put my hand on it without his knowledge, then our position will be immensely enhanced.'

Tucking the pince-nez into a waistcoat pocket Leigh-Hunt allowed himself a small smile of satisfaction.

'There is a lot of money swilling around at the moment,' he said fixing his gaze on Gresham. 'The economy is in a very poor state, and with the prevailing industrial unrest the government is making a lot of hidden resources available to organisations such as ours to ensure that once stability has been regained the possibility of revolution will have been eliminated once and for all.'

'If we get the letter from Petrov himself, I am inclined to establish him as a businessman, an impoverished refugee from one of the Baltic states. In depth paperwork, changes to his appearance, and a suitable new identity will be easy.'

The old man's gaze was now on the ceiling, his mind busy with the future. 'The automotive industry will in the next twenty years become one of our major economic lifelines. If we develop a deep cover for him, then build a legitimate concern, based in England - large enough to have offices overseas - we would finish up with a series of legitimate bases across the entire Continent.'

Gresham waited saying nothing. Leigh-Hunt made a small gesture, 'leave that side of things to me. In the meantime, keep him at the Clarence. Put pressure on him to produce the letter, he will expect that, and obviously if you can trace it yourself, so much the better.'

Ralph nodded, these were the instructions that he had been anticipating, what came next he was not prepared for.

'On the subject of funds,' Leigh-Hunt brushed a small fleck from his waistcoat.

'During the war we acquired a small estate by the name of Drumnhuir in the far north of Scotland - Caithness to be precise. Three hundred acres of farmland with a sitting tenant farmer, and a decent sized country house. Nearest neighbours are thirty miles away in one direction, and Scandinavia in the other. It will be extremely useful for a good many things. The original owner was an impoverished Scottish laird who was only too happy to part with its encumbrance for a suitable fee. The farmer is one of our own men, ex-navy, lives with his wife I am told.'

Ralph's brow furrowed in a slight frown, he was not certain where this was leading to.

'For expediency it was bought in your name. Although the department own it, to all intents and purposes, on paper at least, it is yours.'

The frown was replaced by a look of total amazement. 'I don't understand Sir Rowland,' he said.

'It is simple, you have been a serving soldier for almost thirty years now, and so far as the army are concerned, officially you will have to retire sooner or later. An army pension will not I have to say, adequately remunerate you for the services that you have rendered to your country over the years, therefore I have put into place an added pension plan for you. So far as the department are concerned, it will provide a most useful safe house, and as and when required, a secluded training centre.'

'Longman can fly an aeroplane can he not?'

Gresham nodded, he was beginning to warm to his new situation the more he learned about it.

'Yes, we put him through an RFC course during the war.'

Leigh-Hunt began to fiddle once more with the ocular. 'Excellent. Again, the location is perfect. These northern Scots consider themselves to have more affinity with Scandinavia than England. We can, at appropriate times fly an aircraft out from Drunmuir via Kirkwall to either Norway or Denmark - an ideal bridge into Europe which bypasses the usual access points.'

'I will arrange for the necessary paperwork to be dealt with and forwarded to you in due course.'

Almost as an afterthought he added. 'By the way, tell Sergeant Major Longman that I have arranged a commission for him. As from next month he will assume the rank and pay of Lieutenant'.

Chapter 18

Harry stroked his moustache thoughtfully as he read the entry in the daily occurrence book. At 8.20 pm., the previous evening a commercial traveller by the name of Ronald Eales, had called in to the enquiry desk at Long Street in answer to a plea in the Yorkshire Post for information as to the identity of a woman whose body had been found on the railway lines near to Sheffield. Identity was, the report explained complicated by the fact that the lady appeared to have fallen from a moving train only to be hit by another. Harry did not need telling that this in fact meant that what little was left of the body was contained in a bag, and any identification would be done by such things as jewellery and clothing.

The report said that ten days previously, early in the evening of Tuesday 10th July, Eales had been waiting for a colleague on the concourse of Kelsford station when he saw two women talking together, the older of the two was wearing a hat similar to the one described as being recovered from the lines at Sheffield. Her companion a much younger woman, had walked over to him and enquired as to the time, which having consulted his watch he told her, and she then left going down the stairs to the platform. The woman in the hat had meanwhile disappeared, presumably going ahead of her. It was the description of the companion which interested Harry. The younger woman that Eales described was identical to Lisa Abbott.

Closing the occurrence book he stood for a moment deep in thought. If Lisa was in company with and probably on the same train as, a woman who had later mysteriously gone under the wheels of a fast moving express, then it was definitely worth taking a walk out to the basin to see what she had to say about it. Going upstairs he put his head into the detective office to see if any of the Sergeants were available to go with him, the office was however empty, so collecting his hat and stick he set off alone.

'Moses is staying here, I want those bales shifting this morning, before lunch time.' Lisa was in a bad mood. The thought that Gilbert Manton was planning something had been uppermost in her mind since the arrival in Kelsford of Lilian Barstow, and Cole Wade deciding at the last minute this morning to take the entire crew off to the overflow pool at Copinger's Wood did not please her.

'We will be back by about twelve and we'll shift the bales then. The pond needs clearing out so that we can use it.'

Wales's instructions from Gil Manton were specific – he was to take the entire crew out of the way this morning, leaving Lisa at the basin on her own.

Last week whilst Lisa was away in Sheffield, Cole had taken the opportunity to slip off for the day to Leicester. At the Belgrave Wharf he was surprised how ready to discuss matters with him Manton had been. That the haulier knew who he was became quickly apparent, and in view of that, he had been far less reticent to discuss the operation at the basin than Cole had expected. Wade hinted that he would be better able to run the basin than Lisa, something which Manton openly agreed with. He asked Cole if a middle aged woman had arrived at the basin within the last few days, and seemed puzzled when told that she had not. It was at this point that, seeming to make his mind up, he told Wade to go back to Kelsford and wait for a phone call.

The call came earlier that morning. 'Take the men well away, and leave Lisa on her own,' was the instruction.

'If you need an extra man then get your coat off and do some work yourself – I have told you, I want Moses here.'

A few yards away hefting a bale of clothing onto his shoulder, Moses Hawkins grinned to himself, he did not particularly like the American, sooner or later they were going to clash and he would he knew, be unable to keep his hands off of him – it had happened before.

Wade shrugged his shoulders and went off to gather the others together. Whatever was about to take place, or more to the point whoever was coming to the basin, they were going to have to deal with the scouser themselves.

Moses was still shifting the bales when *Gladiator,* one of the Leicester boats glided quietly up to the quay. The motorised boat was a new acquisition, and the pride of Gilbert Manton's small flotilla. Moses did not know any of the five men climbing over the thwarts onto the quay. The first was a middle aged, one legged man, who for all of his disability, supporting himself with a long wooden crutch made the transition onto the loading bay with relatively little effort.

Putting down the bale, Moses regarded the newcomers with both interest and suspicion. He was a brawler and could identify men of a like nature at a glance. That these were trouble was obvious. Apart from the cripple, two were big and heavy in shirt sleeves, one had navy tattoos on his forearms, his companion, carried a faded depiction of the Prince of Wales feathers on the back of his right hand, proclaiming him to have served in the Hussars. The third was thin and slighter of build, with the pallor of someone who worked indoors. At the rear was a portly figure wearing a slightly old fashioned three quarter length morning jacket and a cravat tied close at the neck.

Hawkins turned his attention to the one legged man - because he was disabled did not mean that he was not dangerous. Warily he began to close the distance between the two of them, as yet this was the only one of the crew on the quay. Even so, he misjudged it.

With perfect accuracy and lightning speed, Gimpy Todd lashed the heavy wooden crutch outwards in an arc that resulted in the edge of the tee shaped shoulder support hitting Moses just above the left eye with the force of a kicking horse .

'Is he dead?' asked Gilbert Manton as he joined his henchmen peering down at the inert figure laying on the cobbles.

The thin faced man, Arthur Anderton, a barman from the George III prodded the body with his boot. 'Looks very much like it Mr Manton', he had the thin reedy voice of an habitual gaol bird.

'Shouldn't have been here in the first place,' Manton's voice carried a note of asperity. 'Looks like the Yank might not be as good at following instructions as I had hoped.'

Anderton gave a snigger, 'at least he warned us about the dog,' he said.

Ignoring him, Gilbert Manton strode towards the main warehouse and the office.

Harry liked the summer. Did the sun he wondered, shine on everyone or merely the righteous and himself? As he walked he pondered what had happened between Lisa and the woman on the train. Had there simply been an accident, or was it something more sinister? His deliberations were interrupted by the sight of Gyp sound asleep in the grass by the side of the towpath.

Giving a soft whistle he stopped and waited for her to rouse - for the head to come up and then her usual wag of recognition. When she did not move, he walked slowly over and kneeling down stroked her head. Realizing that something was wrong, he gently lifted an eyelid and for a moment studied the blank, unresponsive pupil. Standing up again he cast around until he found what he was looking for, the remains of a piece of fresh steak. Sniffing it he dropped the meat back into the grass.

Harry covered the last two hundred yards to the basin cautiously, pausing in the cover of the wall of the main warehouse to get his bearings. Ten yards away, tied up was a seventy five foot barge which looked to be unladen, the bows bearing the name *Gladiator*, riding high against the stonework. Laying prone on the loading bay nearby in a pool of blood, he could see the body of the big Liverpudlian, Moses Hawkins.

Treading softly he made his way along the front of the building to the open double doors. From inside came the sound of a deep baritone voice.

'There is a big job coming off Lisa, too big for you to handle. So it seems to me that it is time for a little re-alignment of resources. You understand what I am saying – time for you to disappear from the picture,'

Harry eased in through the doors and moved stealthily towards the office.

'By the way, where is Lilian?' the deep voice carried a note of genuine curiosity.

'If you mean Lil Barstow, I haven't seen that old screw since she was turning tricks, and polishing your prick at the Sailor's.' Lisa's tone was harsh, betraying nothing of the anxiety that she felt. Jesus Christ, she thought, what a time to get caught with no backup.

Taking advantage of the fact that everyone except Lisa was facing away him , Harry moved quickly in through the office door and had pushed his way to the front before any of the men realised what was happening. Lisa was standing behind the desk where she had obviously been working when Manton and his crew walked in. North moved around the desk to stand beside her.

'So,' he asked, 'what have we got here Lisa?'

'Who the fuck are you?' Manton demanded.

'I am Detective Superintendent North, and you mister are on my territory.'

Manton exhaled deeply, a smile of satisfaction lighting up his face.

'Oh, the tame policeman. Don't interfere in things that are out of your league copper. There is about to be a change of management - you will still get you back hander.'

North pushed the heavy silver head of his stick under Manton's meaty jowl, 'I am nobody's tame copper, and I repeat - you are on my territory, turn your arse around and get out of here whilst you still can.'

Despite the strong words, Harry was not at all certain where things were going to go from here. Apart from Gimpy Todd each of the ruffians accompanying Manton was armed with a heavy wooden baton, and obviously prepared to use it.

Harry felt Lisa's hand brush lightly against his leg beneath the desk, as unseen she edged it towards the top drawer.

Manton's grin grew larger. 'Where did you get this comedian from Lisa?' he demanded.

The hand against Harry's leg became more insistent, imperceptibly he moved back an inch or so away from the drawer.

'Everybody stand perfectly still!'

The thick Liverpool accent cut across the room like a knife. Instinctively all eyes turned to look at the figure standing behind them.

Moses Hawkins, the left side of his face a bloody mask, his left eye completely closed, filled the doorway. It was however on the double barrelled shotgun in his hands, that everyone's attention was focussed.

'Nobody does anything unless Mrs Abbott says so. Anyone gets brave and I'll take your legs out first.'

Hawkins was swaying, making an Herculean effort to remain on his feet, and the men in front of him knew that in the enclosed space of the office, whether he discharged the gun intentionally or it went off when he collapsed, there would be little chance of any of them surviving the blast.

From behind the desk Lisa spoke, 'drop your weapons, all of you, and put your hands up where I can see them.'

Turning back to her they saw that pulled from the top drawer of the desk whilst their attention was diverted, she now held Nobby Armstrong's revolver which was pointed at Gilbert Manton. There was a sharp clatter as the batons dropped to the floor, and five pairs of hands raised tentatively in the air.

Something now happened that sent an icy chill through Harry's body.

Lisa's face changed as a realisation hit her. Holding the pistol double handed, she pulled back the hammer and raised it to point between Gilbert Manton's eyes.

Her voice devoid of any emotion she said, 'you've killed my dog.'

Manton licked his lips, unable to speak he was suddenly terrified. Harry knew beyond a shadow of doubt that she was going to pull the trigger.

'Lisa', he said gently, 'Gyp is alright. They have only drugged her. I found her asleep on the towpath, that was how I knew you had got trouble. When she wakes up she will just have a headache – trust me.'

Seconds ticked by before, the pistol held rock steady she said, 'get out, and take your workhouse mongrels with you, if anyone tries anything Moses, blow every one of the bastards to hell.'

Out on the quayside Harry finally regained control of his breathing. He had taken the revolver from Lisa and with Hawkins was now covering the gang's retreat back onto *Gladiator*. How the Liverpudlian was still standing he did not know, the man must, he decided have the constitution of an ox.

The last to board, Gimpy Todd handed his crutch to Arthur Anderton in preparation for manoeuvring over the side.

'You, the cripple,' Hawkins stepped forward, judging his distance carefully, 'let me help you.'

Before Todd realised what was happening, Moses sent the barrels of the shotgun crashing into his face, smashing his nose and mouth and sending him flying backwards into the body of the barge.

Tucking the butt of the gun into his hip Hawkins swung it back and forth across the remainder of the group, 'anyone else,' he asked thickly.

As *Gladiator* disappeared from sight Harry gave the woman next to him a long appraising stare. 'That was interesting', he said.

She nodded, despite her best efforts Lisa's voice sounded strained, 'I owe you'.

'You were going to kill him', Harry said disbelievingly.

'Was I?' she said, 'you're the copper'.

Between them Harry and Lisa assisted Moses Hawkins back into the office and sat him down in the armchair behind the desk, with the adrenalin beginning to drain from his body he was now in a state of near collapse. Before leaving Harry gave Lisa the telephone number of Arthur Mallard's surgery.

'Its best if I was never here,' he said, 'that way things don't get complicated.'

Lisa nodded, against all reason she was finding herself becoming strongly attracted to the detective.

Having phoned the surgery and told the woman who answered that there had been an accident and the doctor was needed, she replaced the receiver with deliberation and stared out of the window onto the recently vacated quay. There were two things in this life that Lisa Abbott did not believe in. One was God, the other was coincidence.

It was not, she mused coincidence that Cole Wade had chosen unexpectedly this morning to take all of the men away from the warehouse down to Copinger's Wood to clear the overflow pool. So, she concluded, it was safe to assume that he knew of the impending visit by Gilbert Manton and obviously stood to benefit from it.

What, she wondered had been planned for her? Once Gil realised that something had undoubtedly happened to Lil Barstow, he must have decided that it was time to take action. Probably, she thought, an accidental drowning. '*Body of local businesswoman found in the canal*', would be the half column report in the Gazette.

Gimpy Todd had a formidable reputation in Leicester for his talent with the crutch that he carried. Moses would not have been expecting the one legged man, awkwardly disembarking from the canal boat to suddenly lash out with the speed and accuracy of a striking cobra. The arrival of Harry North had just tipped the balance. Would the two of them she asked herself have been able to deal with five strong men if Moses had not come round in time.

A groan from Hawkins in the chair brought her attention back, 'Jesus, I'll kill that fucking one legged bastard,' he groaned.

'Oh I think you have done him as much damage as he has done to you,' she replied reassuringly, picking up the shotgun and breaking it. As the cartridges spilled onto the desk she realised with a flash of annoyance that Harry North had taken Nobby's revolver with him.

A footfall outside was followed by the figure of a tall slim man in his mid-thirties standing in the office doorway.

'Dr Dilkes,' he introduced himself. 'I believe there has been some sort of an accident?'

Carefully and with small precise movements Jonathan Dilkes cleaned the area around the wound on Hawkins's face with a cloth and a bowl of warm water provided by Lisa.

Having felt around the injured man's cheek and head he decided that there were no apparent bone fractures, and began the process of stitching up the laceration.

'You said that there had been an accident,' he said flatly. 'This is not an accident, this is the result of a deliberate blow to the head.'

Her hips resting on the desk watching the doctor working, Lisa made a gesture of acknowledgement with her hand. 'Yes, you are right,' she conceded, 'and I am perfectly happy for that to be reflected in your fee.'

Dilkes twisted his mouth uncertainly, he should report this to the police, but his life was complicated enough at the moment. He was under pressure from Ralph Gresham in relation to Heidi's status. Gresham had made it obvious to him that if he did not cooperate in relation to persuading her brother in Germany to participate in some government initiative that Ralph was involved in, then Heidi could find herself on a boat back to Austria. That would mean giving up his position with Arthur Mallard, and returning with her, something that he most certainly did not want to do. He gave a quick nod and tied off the last stitch.

'You have been lucky,' he said to Hawkins. 'A couple of inches to the right and it would have hit you in the temple, which in all probability would have proved fatal. I cannot tell if there is any damage to the eye itself until all of this swelling has gone down, I will need to see you at my surgery in a week's time.'

'He will come in. I will make an appointment,' Lisa said.

Dilkes stared intently into the pupil of Hawkins's good eye. 'Strictly speaking he should go into hospital overnight to be assessed for concussion,' he murmured, 'but I doubt that is going to happen is it ?' He had not failed to notice that the knuckles on both of the man's hands had over the years been broken, and along with the already present scars on the battered face presumed that his patient was no stranger to such injuries.

Hawkins shifted in the chair, the discomfort of having his face treated had served to bring him round considerably.

'Thank you Doctor no, I've been knocked out before, I can take it from here.' Jonathan Dilkes straightened up and re-packed his Gladstone bag.

'How much do I owe you Doctor?' asked Lisa, she had the petty cash tin out on the desk.

Dilkes noticed for the first time that the end of the barrels and foresight of the open shotgun laying beside the cash tin were smeared with fresh blood. Picking the gun up, he threw it up to the light and stared for a long moment down the gleaming barrels. Satisfied that it had not been fired he laid it back on the desk.

'Two pounds should cover it Mrs Abbott,' he said quietly.

Lisa smiled and handed him four pounds from the cash tin. 'I appreciate your skills Doctor, and as I said I expected it to be reflected in your fee.'

Dilkes gave her a slow smile. 'Bring him in when the swelling has subsided and I will look at that eye properly', he said.

As the doctor was leaving Lisa spotted Cole Wade and the other three men coming into sight along the canal bank. Reloading the shotgun she returned to the office where she took a minute to marshal her thoughts and made two decisions.

The first was to follow the time honoured process of binding your enemy to you. Cole Wade, she had no doubt was involved in whatever it was that Gilbert Manton had planned. For the time being it was important that he did not suspect that she knew, and she had her own ways of ensuring that. What to do about Manton was something that she would need to think about.

Second, Moses Hawkins had proved himself to be trustworthy and loyal. From now on she would keep him close to her as a bodyguard. Whether the others were in league with Wade or not only time would reveal, but her instincts told her they were probably not.

Reaching into the cash box again she withdrew the remaining five pounds that was in there and handed the money to Hawkins.

'You have done well today Moses,' she told him. 'Without you I would have been at the bottom of the cut. From now on you work for me personally, do we understand each other?'

Hawkins looked down through his good eye at the money in his hand, 'yes Mrs Abbott, we understand each other perfectly,' he replied.

Harry North listened in the darkness to the rain splashing down from a leaking guttering over the bedroom window. It was not this that was keeping him awake, his mind was too busy turning over what was going on for him to sleep. It was during the quiet hours of the middle of the night, away from any disturbances that he did much of his thinking.

What did he know he asked himself, about the set-up at the canal basin?

That barges were unloading stolen goods there was a certainty - but what sort of goods? Definitely not the bric-a-brac hawked about by petty thieves and burglars. The weakness in Lisa Abbott's planning he decided was that from an early stage it was obvious that it could not simply be the boatmen who were bringing stuff to her. No whatever was going on was with the connivance of the actual hauliers, clearly evidenced by Manton's involvement. They in turn must be working to a coordinated plan, therefore there had to be a common denominator. Harry already knew what that was.

Having set two detectives, Bill Sykes and Laurence Windram, to watch the boats that passed though the town locks, he knew that apart from Manton's barges there were three other companies using the basin. Grigson & Grant of Chesterfield; Retford Haulage; and Don Navigation. Each of them exclusively handled government contracts.

If substantial parts of cargoes were being hidden at the basin, then it should not be difficult to discover exactly where. His mind harkened back to the overheard conversation between Lisa and her manager, the American. '*You blow the charges by pushing the button under the desk … you also need to have the second mains switch down…*'

Tomorrow, he would first telephone Will Mardlin. It was time Will used his new connections at the Home Office to find out something useful for him he decided, instead of the other way round. After that, a trip to the local Record Office might prove useful.

His next problem was what to do about the woman on the railway line at Sheffield. Should he pass on to the local police her name - 'Lil Barstow', and the fact that she was from Leicester, or should he keep the information to himself for the time being? He was now certain of the fact that it was Lisa who was on the Kelsford Station with her, which meant that Lisa also knew how she had died.

Lisa. His mind drifted off in a direction that he had been studiously avoiding. If Lisa was capable of shooting Gilbert Manton because she thought that he had killed Gyp - and Harry was sure that had he not intervened she would have done so - then she was capable of pushing a woman off of a moving train.

The problem was, that she was beginning to get to Harry in a way that had not happened for a good many years. It was not the fact that contrary to all good taste, she habitually dressed in men's riding breeches and boots, or the long blonde hair and good looks that attracted him. The woman had a magnetism that was deeply disturbing. Standing next to her, the Smith & Wesson in her hand about to pull the trigger, Harry had felt a charge running through his body that had nothing to do with the imminent danger that they were in.

He pushed the image to one side and slid his arm around the sleeping woman next to him. Laura stirred and turned over, opening her eyes she looked up at him.

'What's the matter love,' she asked sleepily.

'Nothing, nothing at all,' Harry ran his fingers through the long chestnut hair cascading across the pillow.

Chapter 19

C ole Wade's initial anxiety had begun to ease away. On his return to the basin with the others he had expected to find Gilbert Manton waiting for him. Instead it was a dishevelled Lisa who was standing on the quayside eying him speculatively, a double barrelled twelve bore nestled in the crook of her arm.

Casting a look around he spotted a dark stain on the flag stones near to the edge of the loading dock. 'What's going on Lisa?' he demanded, 'that looks like blood.'

'It is,' she replied, there was a nervous tension in her voice.

'We had a visit from an outside team who thought they could take things over. Fortunately, between us Moses and I convinced them differently, but it was touch and go for a while.' She shot a meaningful look at the others, 'I will explain it to you later.'

Wade nodded, 'where is Moses?' His curiosity was genuine.

'He took a bad beating, but he will be alright. I had a local doctor out to stitch him up, but he won't be doing much for a day or so.'

As if by pre-arranged signal the figure of Moses Hawkins appeared in the doorway of the warehouse. Chesterton, Davies, and Whiteman went over and engaged him in murmured

conversation, eager to be filled in as to what had happened during their absence.

'Are you alright Lisa', asked Wade, a concerned look on his face.

She gave a small nod, 'I think you had better come inside, we need to talk.'

Cole followed her into the warehouse and was surprised when instead of turning into the office she continued towards the wooden staircase which led up into her living quarters.

Breaking the shotgun Lisa allowed the cartridges to spill onto the floor. Without picking them up she propped the gun in a corner before going over to a side table and busying herself pouring two large glasses of whisky.

It was the first time that Wade had been up here since Tom Whiteman had completed the work of converting it from an open storage area into a four roomed flat. To the right he could see a small neat kitchen, on the opposite side was the open door leading to the bedroom and bathroom. The room that they were in measured about twenty feet by fifteen and was tastefully furnished with a three piece suite, dining table and chairs, and along one wall a bookcase, the absence of books being compensated by an array of china ornaments. On the back wall was a watercolour depicting a group of bathers going down into the sea.

Bringing the drinks over to where he had seated himself on the settee she handed him one before settling down at the opposite end of the couch. For the first time since he had known her he was aware that she had lost her poised air of control. Strands of the thick blonde hair, usually tied tightly back in an unfashionable pony tail, were hanging lose around her face, dark patches of sweat stained the collarless man's shirt, and her expression was strained.

'Are you going to tell me what is going on?' he asked.

Swirling the whisky around in her glass, she put it down next to her. 'Yes, I think it is probably time,' she replied.

For the next twenty minutes, Lisa went over the details of how the warehouse setup came into being. How it had started with her and Nobby Armstrong, then following his death, became a deal between herself and Gilbert Manton, and how this morning Manton had made an attempt to remove her. The version that she laid out before Wade was of necessity an edited one. Nobby had died of Spanish flu leaving her fortuitously holding a substantial amount of funds. Manton was an associate of Nobby's who she knew to be one of his drinking cronies. There was no mention of Lilian Barstow's untimely demise, nor was Harry North's part in the recent morning's activities included.

When she was finished she said, 'I am tired of running this setup on my own, ducking and diving, watching my back. If you want in Cole, you can have half.'

Getting up Lisa gave him a tired smile and taking his now empty glass, walked over to the table. Unscrewing the top from the bottle, she poured a generous measure before turning to return to the settee she found him standing beside her.

Cole Wade took the glass and placed it back on the table. They were very close and he could smell the strangely erotic odour of sweat that still lingered from her ordeal. Bending forward he kissed her gently on the lips before saying, 'partners?'

'Partners,' her breath was becoming laboured as he slid his hand across her damp shirt front and traced a finger over the hard nipple. Undoing the buttons he slipped his hand inside.

Head on his shoulder, Lisa allowed herself a quiet smile - he had not even noticed that her whisky glass by the settee was untouched.

Harry scanned the note on his desk from Eric Broughton. It would not now be necessary for him to telephone Will Mardlin as Eric's neatly penned message stated that 'Superintendent Mardlin was going to be in Kelsford after lunch, and would like to talk to him. Could they meet at his house in Lyndon Terrace.'

Excellent, that was one job less to sort out! As a young detective, the first Inspector that Harry worked for was a particularly able man by the name of Tom Norton. One of Norton's adages was that from time to time in order to move things along, it was necessary to 'rattle a few cages' - and that was precisely what Harry intended to do - starting today.

First he intended to pay a visit to the Record Office in Watts Street and have a look at the original plans of the Kelsford Warehouse Project. After that he needed some inside information from Will concerning the government supplies depot at Leicester, obtaining which - depending on what it was that Will wanted from him - might prove easier than he had hoped. If things went as he intended, Gilbert Manton would very soon regret his comment concerning 'tame policemen'.

Then there was the little bombshell he intended to introduce into the morning conference with his Detective Sergeants.

About to start his day off by sending Tommy Bowler out for some coffee and a bacon sandwich, his good humour quickly evaporated when he received a summons from the Chief Constable to join him forthwith in his office.

The morning conference hastily cancelled, Harry reconvened it for lunchtime in the Lamb and Pheasant. Experience had shown that following a meeting with Sidney Hall-Johnson, especially an 'urgent meeting,' he was usually in need of a drink.

On his arrival on the first floor he found Webster Pemberton seated in an armchair, and the Chief Constable pacing up and down his office looking remarkably like an agitated vulture.

'Read this Harry!' Hall-Johnson thrust a typed sheet of foolscap at him.

North took the paper from the outstretched hand, which he noticed was trembling with anger. Dated the previous day it was a memorandum addressed to the Watch Committee.

Monday 14th July 1919.

Memorandum to the Honourable members of the Watch Committee for Kelsford Borough Police Force.

Sirs,

We the undersigned having been elected as a representative committee by a meeting of seventy eight officers and men of the Kelsford Borough Police Force under your command, and which meeting was held in the muster room of the Central Station at 8p.m. today, respectfully beg to inform you that it was resolved, without a dissenting voice, to become members of the National Union of Police and Prison Officers. It was further decided to ask an Executive Member of the above Union to come down from London and address a meeting of the above mentioned officers and men at the earliest opportunity. We therefore respectfully ask that you will grant us permission to carry our resolves into effect.

We are Sirs,

Your obedient servants.

The document was signed by Sgt Joseph Rowell; Sgt Claude Hamilton; PC Simeon Greenwood; PC 84 Frederick Gunn; PC 101 Albert Wales.

'I am going to sack the bloody lot of them!' Hall-Johnson's face was suffused with anger. 'Bloody bastards, how dare they tell me what they are going to do!'

'Other than sack those who have signed this as committee members, what *are* you going to do?' asked Harry quietly.

'I am going to sack every Man-Jack who was at that meeting.' Hall-Johnson pointed an accusing finger at North. 'This man Rowell is one of yours for Christ's sake!'

'Yes he is,' agreed Harry. 'The difficulty is we are trying to avoid a strike, and if we start sacking people at this stage, a strike is exactly what we will finish up with in no time at all.'

'Harry is right', put in Pemberton, 'we need to avoid that at all costs, what do you suggest Harry?'

In no mood for compromise Sidney Hall-Johnson leaned against the ornate fireplace and in his best military style glowered at both of the Superintendents. 'These people have got to learn,' he said decisively. 'I have asked for an emergency meeting of the Watch Committee this afternoon, and I intend to make an initial example of these men who claim to be 'the committee'.

Harry stared at him for several seconds then said, 'That Sir, is a very brave decision. Speaking for myself, I will back you all the way, and you can have every confidence that I will speak for you afterwards, as I am sure will Webster.'

It took a moment for the import of the words to sink in, then, a slightly less assured look on his face the Chief Constable said, 'What do you mean, speak for me afterwards'.

Harry cleared his throat before replying. 'This is essentially a political matter. The government is holding its breath for the time being whilst the police across the country are all poised for someone to light the fuse. Historically, in situations like this, whether it works out or not, they find it safest in the aftermath to replace all of those who were major players - start anew with a clean sheet so to speak. After the strike last year - which was successfully defused, Nott-Bower was replaced as Home Secretary by Edward Shortt, and Sir Edward Henry was replaced as Commissioner of the Met., by Sir Nevil Macready.'

'I suspect that every other Chief Constable in the country has had a similar declaration delivered to him in the last few days. The one who lights the fuse will be a brave man. He will certainly go down in history.'

Hall-Johnson's expression of righteous indignation had been replaced by one of consternation. Webster Pemberton was concentrating on his shoes trying desperately not to burst out laughing.

Regaining his composure the Chief Constable fixed his Detective Superintendent with what he fondly presumed to be a look of utmost composure.

'So, what is your alternative?' he demanded.

North brushed the ends of his moustache and avoided Webster Pemberton's eye. The solution to the situation was simply to wait and see what happened, any fool - other than the one standing in front of him - could see that.

'In a matter of days an Act of Parliament is scheduled to be passed proscribing this union, and making it an offence for any police officer to become a member of such an organisation. At that point we will know whether there is going to be strike action, and that is when we act. Meantime, the government is making all of the decisions - and taking all of the risks - for us.'

'Ask Sergeant Rowell to come and see me please Tommy.' The administration department had taken on a different atmosphere since the departure of Montagu Parfitt. Eric was eminently capable of running the office and young Tommy bustled about cheerfully running errands and making tea, even if as quite a few had noted, for some mysterious reason the only person with whom he could hold a trouble free conversation was Superintendent North

Parfitt had fallen on his feet mused Harry with a mild degree of annoyance. Within less than a week of his ignominious departure from Long Street, he reappeared on the other side of town as general stores manager at Sevastopol Barracks. Army connections surmised North, the old boy network yet again.

A sharp tap on the door heralded the arrival of Joe Rowell, the Sergeant looked tired Harry thought.

'Sit down Joe', he said, 'this is personal, and I don't want us to get into conflict.

They spent the next half an hour arguing back and forth the working conditions, pay, and aspirations of the men who made up rank and file of the police force, and the consequences to the individual of participating in any strike action. Rowell, not for the first time found that Harry's concerns were not so different to his own, simply that the older man was advocating a different approach.

'You are courting disaster Joe. This morning Webster Pemberton and I had to talk that moron upstairs out of persuading the Watch Committee to sack everyone involved in your union declaration. By the end of the week it will have been made an illegal organisation, and if after that you strike, you will be playing straight into the government's hands.'

Harry picked up his cigarettes, then changing his mind dropped them back on the desk.

'The feeling is that Liverpool, and possibly London, is where the strike will take place, which you already know. Let them do it, but hold back yourself. Once the dust has settled it will be negotiation time, then you can legitimately start making the progress that has got to come. It is far better to lose on your terms than win on someone else's. Think of your own future - of Ailma and the youngster she is carrying'

Rowell pulled himself up out of the chair and shook his head. 'I know that you believe what you are saying Harry, but it has gone too far now for me to pull out.'

Walking into the back room of the Lamb and Pheasant just after twelve Harry was once more in good spirits. Having viewed the 1898 plans of the Kelsford Warehouse Basin, he now knew exactly where Lisa Abbot was storing the stolen goods that were passing through her hands. From this point on, it was simply a matter of choosing his own time to close her down.

'Four pints and four chasers please Maria.' He beamed at the buxom young woman behind the bar, his day was getting better by the minute.

'I didn't know you were working here now', he said pleasantly.

What was it Cliff Jarman had said, '*Maria Daley, very good on camera, almost as good as Alice.*'

The barmaid regarded him suspiciously, 'started last week Mr North, its nearer home than the Eagle.' She was uneasy, this was the first time that she had seen the Detective Superintendent in the Lamb, and when Foxy North was unduly friendly it usually spelt trouble.

Bert Conway adopted a more pragmatic approach. 'Fucking hell, Foxy's buying the first round', he said to Clarrie Greasley who was in the process of pulling a chair up to the table, 'the last time I saw him put his hand in his pocket was when he walked into the corner of a table in the Pack Horse.'

'There is nothing wrong with my hearing Bertram, and we will have a little respect for rank if you please', said North as he joined them.

Maria Daley was placing the drinks on the table as Joe Rowell came in through the door, he gave the barmaid a surprised stare followed by a pleasant smile. She glanced uncomfortably around the group, a puzzled look on her face.

'Does Maria know we've seen her fanny', asked Conway. The woman was back behind the bar polishing glasses.

'I think in all truth, she would probably be a bit confused as to who has and who hasn't' replied Clarrie.

'Keep your voices down,' muttered North, 'she knows nothing about anything just yet, and I want it to stay that way.'

The others nodded in agreement, serious once more.

'We have got one or two things to talk about,' Harry said. 'First Joe, what's the score with the Kitson job?'

Rowell took a deep breath. 'We know that Alice was killed with her own scarf, but that won't really figure until we know who did it. Dan, Dan the camera man no longer figures, he is presently in a cell at Skegness looking at a long spell in Lincoln gaol. For my money, the key factor is still this woman Rutherford.'

The others waited whilst he downed his whisky and took a pull at the beer. Who and where Celia Rutherford was, had for some time been a subject of discussion between them.

'Celia left the Cottage Homes around the same time as Alice, and like Alice she went to work for a drapery firm - Howitt's in Chesterfield. She was there for just over two years and in 1910, simply gave in her notice and disappeared. I have been over there. The bloke who was the manager at the time went off to the war and got killed, but a couple of the girls who worked with her are still around. Not much to tell. They say that she was a very quiet, attractive girl who didn't make friends and when she left, simply gave her notice and disappeared.'

'This 'no friends' thing.' Clarrie lit a cigarette and threw the packet into the middle of the table. He looked from Joe to Harry, 'we already know that she probably batted for both sides, could it be that these woman had also got her worked out and kept their distance?'

Joe held his hands out in a gesture of frustration, 'I honestly don't know Clarrie. You could well be right, but they aren't going to tell me that are they? The important thing is they don't know where she went off to.'

Harry picked up the cigarette packet and lit one. 'Alright,' he sighed, 'we just have to keep going with this until we find her. Meanwhile what about the Byram job Clarrie?'

Now it was Greasley's turn to give an embarrassed shrug. 'Nothing Harry, absolutely sod all. No property has surfaced, Bill Sykes and I have turned over every fence and known shop-breaker between here and Derby. It is as tight as the proverbial duck's.'

North cast his eyes up to the ceiling for a few seconds, then looked carefully at each of them.

'Possibly not. Perhaps, if we can work something else out between us, we already hold the key to this whole thing.'

The Sergeants regarded him intently, their attention fully engaged.

'This goes no further than the four of us - understood?' They all nodded, waiting.

'Lew Arthur didn't fall down the stairs, he was helped. The post-mortem showed that before he died Lew was hit over the head twice with a blunt instrument. He was probably dead before he hit the bottom. I am certain that Lew worked out how the Byram job was done, and more importantly, who did it, and that cost him his life. We find out what it was he knew and we crack both the robbery and who murdered him.'

Long moments passed as the others took in what he was saying.

'How long have you known this?' asked Rowell.

'Since the p.m.,' Harry glanced round the table. 'So, get your thinking caps on and put together what I have been trying to fathom out ever since Lew died. We work out what it was that he knew, and we crack both the Byram case and who it was who killed him, because I would like to see the bastard hang.'

There was a lingering silence around the table whilst this latest information sank in.

'What you are saying,' Clarrie spoke slowly, 'is that Lew was killed by another policeman.' He was voicing what the others were thinking.

'I am certain of it,' Harry's voice was flat, his eyes going from one to another of them.

'Then let's say what we are all thinking.' Greasley drew the open cigarette packet towards him and pulled one out.

Bert Conway studied the table to in front of him, with the forefinger of his right hand he began to draw a pattern in a wet patch next to his glass. 'Charlie

O'Keefe. The first two jobs that were suspicious were done when his shift were on nights. We all know that with both the clothing and shoe shop breaks they could not have got the swag away without being seen - so one or more of the night duty men had to be involved. Both times O'Keefe's shift were on duty.'

'With the exception of Joe we have all worked with Charlie. He wasn't a bad detective, but he took liberties - the pen was always mightier than the sword, and easier to write with. Its only a short step to cross over the line. Ignoring the floating element of his shift, his regular men are Ben Gunn, Brad Green, and Albert Wales. All of them idle bastards, just uniform carriers. Thing is, are we really coming up front and saying … 'they are who we are looking for?'

'Gunn and Wales are part of your Union set-up aren't they Joe?' Clarence Greasley held the Scotsman's gaze.

A dangerous glint came into Joe Rowell's eyes. 'What are you saying Clarrie, that this is the doing of the Union men?'

Greasley continued to look at him undeterred. 'This is straight talking time Joe, if Lew was murdered and we are looking for it being done by one or more of our own, I don't give a fuck about treading on toes. You have had a chance to get a closer look at both of them than the rest of us recently, so what I am asking is - what is your opinion?'

'Also Joe, you are involved in the Union for the best of reasons, but it doesn't follow that everyone else is.' Bert Conway's was the voice of reason.

'If what we are talking about is right, then they will be perfectly placed to set up something. Talk up a strike, and set up another job to coincide with it - was that what Lew found out?'

'I don't like either of them.' Rowell glanced at Harry North who remained silent.

Rowell sat for a while in thought, turning over whether to say what was in his mind. Eventually he said, 'Look, I will tell you something. It puts me right on the line, but I have got to trust you.' Again he glanced at the Superintendent, North made no response.

'There have been meetings in Manchester and Liverpool. They both went to one in Manchester recently where there was a foreigner present, a Russian. He is some sort of a communist agitator, and I honestly don't want to know about him. The meeting was very hush-hush, just a handful of influential members. I don't know exactly what was said, but the Russian had a document that he had obtained from a contact at the Home Office. It promises that when we strike the troops sent into Liverpool will lay down their arms and back our lads. When everything is sorted out, we can distance ourselves very quickly from men like that, but at the moment, information is power.'

'I am deeply involved in the Union, and I make no apology for that,' he glared defiantly around the table, 'but I am not privy to that sort of thing, very few of us are. That is wheels-within-wheels, but Albert Wales and Ben Gunn are moving in that circle, so what I am saying is that if you are asking - and I will never say it outside of this room - I would not trust either of those two.'

'Has O'Keefe got any money problems that we know about?' Bert Conway continued to study the table top.

This time it was Harry who shook his head. 'No, I have done all of that. He is as clean as a whistle.'

'What we have to do,' he continued, 'is work on why Lew was killed. Meantime, Bert has made a valid point, if we are right, then the ideal time for the next job is when everything goes up in the air at strike time.'

Harry picked up a beer mat and tapped it thoughtfully against his glass, 'meantime - Bert, make some enquiries about this Yank who works for Lisa Abbott. Get some telegrams off to the police departments in America and Canada - lets see if we can find out who he really is.'

'Where did you get your stick?' It was Will Mardlin himself who opened the door at Lyndon Terrace when North rang the doorbell.

Harry placed the cane carefully in the umbrella stand, 'Laura saw it in an antiques shop and bought it for me as a present,' he lied.

Following Mardlin through into the lounge he greeted Ralph Gresham who was helping himself to a drink from the side trolley.

'Good to see you Harry,' Ralph proffered him a glass of Dewar's then poured himself another.

Harry acknowledged and settled himself down in a deep armchair. Smiling pleasantly he tipped the glass in the direction of the other two and sat back comfortably. It would be wrong to say that things between him and Will had changed, that was not true. What had altered was the fact that they were no longer partners. It was something which happened all of the while. You worked with someone and shared mutual experiences and confidences, then circumstances changed, you both moved to new partners and relationships became slightly skewed. On this occasion Harry was working alone whilst Will was teamed with Ralph. Working alone suited Harry perfectly, no one to watch out for, and no one to second guess what he was doing.

Harry sipped his whisky whilst the pleasantries were disposed of. Whatever it was that Will and Ralph wanted - and he was in no doubt that this meeting was not simply to exchange views on politics - they were going to have to pay a price for it. Harry also had an agenda.

'How tasked up are you at present Harry?' asked Mardlin.

Harry swirled a piece of ice around in the bottom of his glass.

'Two murders, series of shop breaks, a major jewel theft, a King's ransom in cigarettes stored down at Pierpoint's in Chalfont Street, a well organised fencing operation going on that needs watching around the clock - other than that everything is easy Will. What did you have in mind to help me remove some of this burden?'

Mardlin smiled awkwardly. 'Can you spare me a man to do some legwork, probably take just a few days?'

'Let's start from the basis of - you have not got a prayer.' North drained his glass.

'Seriously Harry we need this. There is something that we have to find, it has probably been deposited with a solicitor or bank somewhere in the town, we just need a local man who knows all of the dark corners to ferret it out for us.'

Harry peered into his glass. Suddenly an idea hit him and he suppressed a grin.

'I have got two murder enquiries running, and the press - that barrel of shit Bathurst - on my heels wherever I go. One of the murders, woman by the name of Alice Kitson is just a matter of time. The other however…' he steepled his fingers and crumpled his face into a deeply troubled expression, '… the other is not so straight forward. The body found with the Kitson woman in the kiln. They are separate enquiries that is definite, but until I can identify him I have got to keep a team working on finding out who he is. Once I know that I can free up some manpower.'

Ralph and Will exchanged quick glances before Will said, 'we can help you there Harry, that was one of the things that we came to put you in the picture about.'

Harry accepted another whisky and sipped at it appreciatively. It had been a shot in the dark, but as so often happens, it paid off. He now knew that the body in the kiln was that of Fedir Yurkovich, and that the Russian activist who was stirring the pot in Manchester was in fact Vasily Petrov. So, Bathurst could now be fed a suitably imaginative story about the violent world of tramps and other vagrants, which so often culminated in unsolved deaths of this nature. He would immediately run an issue intended to instil fear and uncertainty into the good people of Kelsford - especially those living in the more exposed outskirts of the town. Sidney Hall-Johnson would in turn, publish figures intended to allay these apprehensions, showing that there were virtually no vagrants passing through the district and that this was an isolated incident. The nett result would be that both of these individuals would be fully occupied spinning their own phantasies, whilst he was free to solve crime.

'It is time,' he said, 'to stop running round in circles, playing games with each other, and lay our cards on the table.'

'Yes Harry, you are right,' Mardlin poured another drink for himself and topped up the other two's glasses. 'Alright Ralph?' Gresham nodded.

North set his glass to one side and said, 'I'll go first then.'

'Will, do you remember a girl called Ada Manners? We turned her up in Leicester living with Frank Kempin during the 'soldier' enquiry. She was using the name Lisa Abbott.'

Will nodded, 'Yes of course I do.' He had good reason to remember the woman, it was she who, however unwillingly, had set them off in the direction of London's East End and an eventual conclusion to the enquiry.

'Lisa is up here now running a very sophisticated operation out of the old canal basin warehouses. She is taking barge loads at a time of government stores, stashing the gear and then moving it out of the district in boats belonging to at least three different companies'

Harry paused to light a cigarette before handing the packet over to Gresham.

'I am ready to close her down, but the hauliers she is tied in with are as far apart as Leicester and Chesterfield. There is no hurry, but I want everything in place to take them all down before I make a move. By everything in place, I mean a swoop on her prime accomplice, a man by the name of Manton who runs an operation out of the Belgrave Wharf at Leicester.'

He had to be careful now, he could not give away his part in the incident at the basin.

'I have got an informant working the boats who says that Manton is about to handle a big deal. I need to know more about that, then I can co-ordinate things with Palmer Osborne at Leicester and we can hit both places at the same time, after that the other hauliers can be reeled in at our convenience.'

'Where do we come into this?' asked Gresham.

'Government stores have to come from government warehouses,' replied Harry.

'The depot manager at Leicester has to be involved up to his neck. I need to know when, in the very near future, something tempting is going to be coming into his hands. Obviously, we nick him as well, then after we have hit the haulier, bring in the Military Police and let them have a look at the book keeping.'

Gresham and Mardlin exchanged glances. 'We have been aware for some time that there is a problem at the Leicester depot,' said Gresham thoughtfully.

'Alright, I can find out in the next couple of days what is likely to be the target. Would you not be best to bring in the Military Police from the outset?'

Both Harry and Will Mardlin's faces broke into smiles. 'No,' said Will, 'the MPs are all right for locking up drunks and deserters, but for this sort of thing, I agree with Harry - do the deed and tell them afterwards.'

'We sort that, and I will find whatever it is that you are looking for,' offered Harry.

Despite the assertions of honesty and openness, Ralph Gresham certainly did not intend disclosing his entire hand to Harry. It was not that he did not trust the detective, or even think that he might constitute a security risk. It was an inbred caution, the result of years of keeping secrets buried deep, only revealing things when it became absolutely necessary, and sometimes never.

For evasion to be successful in Ralph's experience it was necessary in some part to be honest - to inject sufficient verifiable facts into a cover for the story to be totally believable.

'We are looking for an envelope Harry,' he said quietly.

'It contains a document that relates to Russian espionage activities during the war, and could give us a strong hand in defeating the present communist régime. Vasily Petrov was chasing it, he thought that it was in his hands when he caught up with Fedir Yurkovich. Unfortunately, Yurkovich was dead before he realised his mistake. We think that because he was based here, Yurkovich probably deposited it with a solicitor or bank in the town. What we need is someone with local connections to find it for us.'

A slow smile spread across North's face, 'that seems like a job for me to take a look at,' he replied.

Chapter 20

Charlie O'Keefe closed his eyes and raised his face up towards the warm July sunshine. One more job, then no more. After Pierpoint's he would have enough salted away to see him into a comfortable retirement.

Charlie knew that he and the others were lucky to have got away with things this far, he was very much aware that recently suspicion had been growing. He grinned to himself, Byram's had been a big one, and the cigarettes job at Pierpoint's would be equally big. They would have to watch out now for Foxy North, if only the silly old bastard had the sense to go back further - to the beginning of the war, - he would see that they had been at it for years.

The first time was when the Albert pub was bombed at Christmas 1915. He and the lads had been set to guard the premises against looters. That was a joke. Between them he and Brad Green had cleared three cases of Scotch and six hundred cigarettes - straight into the yard, over the wall, and away to Ben Gunn's house, before anyone even thought of counting up how much stock was left. After that it became simple, each time they were on nights and a shop or factory was broken into, then they cleared out as much stock as possible before the detectives came lumbering up on the scene, licking their pencils and making notes. If the burglar was caught it did not matter, who was to believe him when he said that he had not nicked half the property that was missing.

Things really took off after the armistice, when he received a message from the man. He remembered it quite clearly. He came on duty for a night shift and there was a note pushed under the door of his locker telling him to go to the old church in High Street, that had been bombed on the same night as the Albert. Just like that idiot Wade, he had sat in the confessional and listened with interest to the muffled voice in the adjacent cabinet.

Whoever the man was - and although Charlie had one or two ideas, he still could not be certain - he was well informed concerning the shift's activities.

O'Keefe was given two choices, he could carry on in the present vein and rest assured that in the very near future he and his little gang would be arrested, or he could come under the umbrella of a more sophisticated and well organised enterprise that would utilise their skills to the full, and earn for them a lot of money in a very short time.

On reflection the Sergeant thought, it had been a worthwhile bargain. Each job that they had done had been well planned and organised. The Byram setup had been particularly inventive. It would take Foxy a long while to figure out how they had pulled that one off. Now Pierpoint's would be the last - the man had said so. The loot from their previous raids was stored safely away in a warehouse in Nottingham, only he and the man knew where it was - that had been part of the deal. As the man said, pulling the job off was simple, getting rid of the property afterwards was when people got caught. So, there was a rule. Everything was to be held under wraps for at least twelve months, then it would be disposed of by the man and the proceeds split up between them. Actually, there were two rules, the second was that none of Charlie O'Keefe's crew were ever to know that there was someone other than O'Keefe orchestrating their activities. So far as they knew, Charlie was the brains behind the whole thing.

He was aware of a shadow falling across him and opening his eyes he squinted into the afternoon sun. The tall spare figure of Albert Wales was standing in front of the park bench upon which he was seated.

'Sit down, you are blocking the sun,' grunted O'Keefe.

Wales wound his lanky frame down onto the bench next to him. Shading his eyes he peered across the park towards the large double fronted houses opposite in Lyndon Terrace.

'Doesn't Mardlin live across there?' he asked idly.

'Third house from the right,' said his companion, 'and the only reason we are meeting here, is because he is away in London.'

'At least one of them has gone,' muttered Wales. 'If both he and North were here it would be a nightmare trying to keep a step or two ahead. As it is, North has got so much to do with those two murders he hasn't got time to bother about us.'

'That's where you might just be wrong Albert.' O'Keefe gave him a penetrating stare. 'Don't you underestimate Foxy North. He's got eyes where the sun don't shine, and he is sharp as a razor. I know, I worked with him for long enough. And don't think that what he isn't sure about he won't stitch up. You remember Nate Cleaver, he crossed Harry and finished up on a boat to Australia.'

Wales twisted his mouth into a grimace. 'No one ever worked that one out did they. Went into Harry's office all cocky and Jack the Lad, came out looking like he had seen a ghost, just walked out of the building never to be seen again. What do you reckon that was all about Charlie?'

O'Keefe shook his head. 'Its simple, he crossed Harry. It's like putting your hand into an aeroplane propeller. You don't need to know how the engine works - just that if you fuck about with it, you wind up getting hurt.'

They stopped talking at the sight of two men strolling across the open pasture towards them.

Ben Gunn took the stubby pipe from the corner of his mouth and dropped down on the grass, Brad Green, having checked that there was nowhere else on offer for him to sit, joined him.

To any passerby they looked liked four working men spending an afternoon off enjoying the summer weather.

'So what's the rush Charlie?' asked Green.

'The 'rush' is that the timings for the Pierpoint job have altered,' replied O'Keefe.

'The ciggies are still coming in on Friday - in two days time - but instead of sitting there for a week, they are being moved out again on Monday.'

'So I have had to do some very serious thinking, and readjustment of our time scales.'

'I thought we were doing it when the strike took place?' queried Gunn.

So did I thought O'Keefe, but that had changed last night. His new instructions were, that to wait until the weekend of the August bank holiday on the basis that there might be a police strike, was risky and too obvious. He was to tell his men that the cigarettes were being moved out prematurely, they would then hit the bonded warehouse within hours of the consignment arriving, before the soldiers sent in for security had settled down.

'Things have changed,' he said irritably, 'leave that side of the job to me and listen carefully.'

The others looked at him in silence. Of recent Charlie had proved to be much shrewder than they had previously realised, his planning ability was without a doubt extremely sound.

'Firstly, I have brought in outside help. We are going in on Friday night - day after tomorrow - and we can't do this on our own.'

'What do you mean, outside help?' Ben Gunn's voice was hard and challenging. 'Since when do we bring in outsiders?'

It was exactly the question that, seated in the darkness of the confessional of St Edward's Church, Charlie O'Keefe had put to the man.

'This is a big job, £50,000 worth of gear. We can afford to pay out a bit on labour and still come away with a tidy stash.'

'I don't like it…' The pipe in Gunn's hand had ceased burning, he had not noticed.

'I don't care whether you like it or not … I am running this, and you will do as I tell you, now shut up and listen…' Gunn was starting to annoy him. Always questioning, and of recent persistently pushing for an early share out of the proceeds, despite the agreed plan not to touch anything until later. He was going to have to keep a careful eye on Ben.

Word for word, he repeated the briefing that he had been given the previous night.

For the next half an hour he spoke quietly whilst the other three listened in silence. When he had finished, exchanging glances, they nodded to each other. As a plan it was a good one, and as a last job it was worth doing.

'Only thing that bothers me', Brad Green eased his position and scratched at his crutch, the hard ground was far from comfortable. 'The night shift is Claude Hamilton's men. They are a bleeding nuisance. Anyone that moves, they shine their lights on them. How are we going to keep them out of the way?'

O'Keefe grinned, 'not a problem Bradley my son - they won't be there. They will be on the other side of town… at the diversion!'

Cole Wade put the telephone back on its cradle and stared speculatively out of the doors at the placid waters of the canal. With a noisy splash and a deal of quacking, two ducks skidded to a halt on the mirrored surface, then began to swim sedately towards the bank, pushing ripples out in front of them. The man wanted to see him tonight at St Edward's Church. Again the same strictures, come alone, do not bring a firearm. There was this time one additional factor. 'This is a big job, we will be storing the property in your warehouse, so you will need to bring Mrs Abbott on board.' No discussion, no room for argument.

'You alright?' An arm slid around his waist from behind, he had not heard Lisa come into the office.

Wade nodded absently, 'There is something that we need to talk about,' he said.

Unlike the occasion of his previous visit to the bombed out church, there was a pleasant balmy breeze drifting down the High Street as, checking around to make sure that he was not observed, Cole slipped in through the shattered front door of the building. Inside, although dismal, it was lighter than he expected, picking his way carefully between the rubble strewn pews he slipped into the penitent's cubicle of the confessional.

He was seated on the hard bench for some minutes before the sound of the priest's door being opened, accompanied by muffled movements signalled that he was no longer alone.

The partition slid back and a voice asked quietly, 'so, did she agree?'

'Yes, took a bit of work on my part, but she is in.' The truth was, that having listened to Wade's proposition, Lisa had merely nodded and said, 'so be it - but your man had better know what he is doing - and Moses stays here, he is not fit enough yet for a job like this.'

In fact Lisa was neither surprised nor uninterested in this latest development. She had been fairly certain from the descriptions of the men responsible for the Byram job that Cole and the rest of the crew were involved. The point, so far as she was concerned, was that the Byram job appeared to have been a complete success. Whoever organised it was a professional and knew what they were doing with regards to both planning and execution. Nor did the fact that Wade had just chalked up another score on her board for duplicity particularly worry her. At the appropriate time she would wipe the slate clean, it was a skill which she had perfected a long while ago. If this latest job worked out well she might, she decided, consider moving on. Lisa had known from the outset that at some point Gilbert Manton would get greedy. To enter into a running conflict with him was totally within her capabilities, but was unnecessary and would compromise security, something that she did not want. Also her regard for Harry North was becoming more personal than she would have liked, and far from being able to use him for her own ends, she was in fact now in his debt for intervening in the Gil Manton affair.

'Listen closely, because I should tell you right now that if you screw up in any way at all, you will be going through the Town Locks without the benefit of a boat - please do not think that I am making an idle threat, just be very clear.'

When Wade did not respond the voice continued unperturbed, 'I will take that as being understood, so listen very carefully. Firstly, can you get rid of that American accent and speak like a British officer?'

Cole cleared his throat, then in an accent free voice said, 'After four years in the British army, I can pass as English anytime that I choose to do so.'

'Good,' the man seemed satisfied.

'Now, here is what is going to happen.'

The plan was a good one, and so far as Wade could see had no flaws. In two days time, on Friday evening he and Taff Davis were to go to Grange Lane, where at the rear of the Rifleman pub they would find a Dennis three ton army lorry. In the back would be two sets of Military Police uniform, one for a corporal, the other for a Captain. Wearing these, at eight o'clock sharp, they were to drive to Pierpoint's where, having previously received a phone call, the gateman would be expecting them.

Once inside the compound, Wade would speak to the NCO in charge, who would probably be an elderly Sergeant who was relegated to Home Service duties whilst awaiting his discharge, as should be the other three soldiers assigned to security at the premises. In accordance with the plan, Cole would confirm what the caller had told the gateman - that he had come down from Military Headquarters at York to check on security at this and other sites in the region.

Having made a tour of the compound and the warehouses, he would then instruct the Sergeant to gather his men in the canteen for an extra briefing. Once they were in there Wade would assume an informal attitude and instruct Davis to make tea for them - which would be drugged. With the gateman included in the brew it should only be a matter of minutes before the two of them were the only ones on their feet.

Meanwhile Tom Whiteman and Frank Chesterton were to go to the premises of Latimer's removals in Hope Lane where they would find the padlock on the gates undone. They were to steal two of the large furniture vans from the main garage and drive them to Chalfont Street picking up Charlie O'Keefe, Ben Gunn and Albert Wales on the way. On their arrival Taff Davis would be standing sentry guard on the gate and let them in. From there they simply drove across to the far side of the wharf, backed up to the shed doors and loaded the cigarettes onto their lorries.

'By half past nine,' the disembodied voice concluded, 'you will all be back at your cosy little canal basin where you unload and store the goodies, then everyone disappears off into the night.'

'What about the vehicles - you can't just leave them?' asked Wade.

'Once they are unloaded, the men from my team will drive them and the army vehicle to the old flooded quarry on the Derby road. The water there is thirty feet deep, they will never be found.'

'…What about the police? We are going to be at Pierpoint's over an hour, the beatman is bound to walk past…'

'An hour and thirty minutes to be precise,' was the patient reply. '… And no, the beatman will not be coming past, as he and all of the rest of his shift will be engaged elsewhere. Leave that to me.'

The diversion was going to be critical thought the man. Bradley Green would be attending the evening film at the Alhambra Cinema on the opposite side of town. The performance ended at eight o'clock. Green would hide in the toilets whilst the place was locked up, then at half past eight, as the others were loading the lorries, he would start a fire in the projection room. Celluloid film was notoriously inflammable, and it should take only minutes for the building to be alight. By a quarter to nine, the Alhambra should be blazing nicely with the Fire

Brigade in action, and every available policeman needed to close off the adjacent streets and push back the crowds of excited sight see'ers.'

'Right, get those gates, move smartly now !'

Private Herbert Stubbs glowered at the portly Sergeant before muttering a curt, 'Sarn't,' and trotting at the double across the yard to secure the heavy iron gates. Sergeant Hiram Westbury was a pain in the neck. Retired from the army on age in 1912 after 22 years, he along with all of the other 'old sweats' was recalled in August 1914, restored to his previous rank of Sergeant and, on a promise of never having to serve overseas or hear the sound of gunfire other than on a firing range, given the task of training new recruits. With the end of the war, the demobilisation of the Sergeant Westbury's of this world was deferred whilst more productive members of society were released back into the workplace. The delay suited Hiram Westbury nicely, remaining in the army with a cushy posting was preferable to sitting at home waiting for his meagre pension to drop through the letterbox, and he got a chance to continue doing what he had been doing for years - bellowing orders at those he considered inferior to himself.

The gate keeper, a tall elderly man grinned at the soldier through the open door of his tiny cabin. 'Hup two, three, tread lightly, let's see some sparks coming from those boot studs, if you're making some tea I'll have some with you.'

'Tea! Chance would be a fine thing with that old bastard poncing around like a princess with a navvy's tool in her hand!'

Private Stubbs heaved at the heavy gate and began to pull it along its metal rollers into the closed position. It had been a long tiring day. First the cramped rail journey from Nottingham perched on a pile of cardboard boxes containing more smokes than he could consume in a lifetime. The only compensation was that it was a relatively short journey from the Players factory to Kelsford main station and then up here to the old coal wharf on Chalfont Street. Plus he rode in the wagon with his mate, 'Spud' Taylor who was Hir'em - Fir'em's Corporal, whilst 'Ferret Smith, the Sergeant's 'little friend' went in the second wagon with him.

At least they did not have to do any lifting of boxes from the wagons into the secure warehouse, that was taken care of by the Pierpoint loaders, who had now packed up for the day and gone home. Any other sergeant and they would be heading into the canteen where their kitbags were now stacked, leave this old boy on the gate to do what he was paid for, and they could get their heads down with some supper and an evening with their feet up. Not with Sergeant Westbury though - they would get something to eat alright the greedy old sod would see to that - then he would want them out here in the yard marching up and down with a rifle for two hours at a stretch.

'I shouldn't bother closing the gate son, you will only have to open it again.' Clem Waldron got up from his stool and picked up a piece of paper from the wooden desk where he kept a list of everyone coming in and out of the yard.

'Just had a phone call. You have got an officer on his way over to check on security. Better go and tell the Kaiser out there.' Clem cast a practiced eye over the small coke brazier just inside the office door. Despite the summer month it got chilly in the evenings and he was going to be here until tomorrow morning when Arthur Shaw relieved him from duty, although with soldiers marching around the place he could not see the point in having company watchmen on as well. He would stoke the glowing coals up after telling the sergeant that a visitor was on the way.

Sergeant Westbury took the note from Clem's hand, too vain to put on his reading glasses he peered at it myopically. 'Fackin 'ell, I can do without this,' he grumbled, the clipped London vowels grated on the watchman's ears. 'Right, you get back in that 'ut' a bit lively, and tell me as soon as 'e' arrives.'

Clem Waldron took a step closer to the portly sergeant, 'I will tell you this once and once only soldier, I am not one of your conscripted minions. You want to know when your officer arrives, then stand one of your own men at my gate.'

He moved in a little closer, his shoe touching Westbury's left foot, 'and if you tread on my toes again, I might just, accidentally take a bit of the polish off those nice shiny boots of yours, that haven't set foot outside the safety of England's green and pleasant land since well before 1914.'

The sergeant, eyes popping, his face the deep purple colour of a turkey cock, struggled to get his breathing under control. Before he could think of a suitable response the sight of a large Dennis soft back army lorry pulling in through the gate caught his attention. Private Stubbs brought his rifle up smartly to the 'present' and saluted the officer in the passenger seat as the vehicle swept past and came to a halt in the middle of the yard.

'One man on the gate, and you chatting away with a civilian. This is supposed to be a secure area Sergeant!'

The Military Police Captain returned Westbury's salute as he strode over from the vehicle. Shit! thought Westbury, the last thing that he wanted was the MPs rocking his boat.

'Not chatting Sir, briefing the company watchman on his duties. The remainder of my men are 'avin meal before they turn out for guard duty, Sir!'

Cole Wade took in the yard at a glance. If the other two 'Tommies' were anything like this fat pompous old fart and the scruffy individual on the gate, then the job should be a pushover.

'Captain Blandford,' Wade put on his best upper class English voice. 'I am with the Security Section at York Headquarters. The General is particularly keen to ensure that now hostilities are over there is no slackness allowed to develop amongst Home Troops. With that in mind you had better show me around.'

'Sir,' Westbury had drawn himself up to his full five feet six, ramrod straight.

'We have only just arrived Sir. The consignment has been stored securely, men allocated their dispositions and sent to eat the rations we 'av brought with us. When they resume, I shall get mine, Sir!'

It was a lie. As soon as the last of Pierpoint's men left the site, Westbury had sent Corporal Taylor and Ferret Smith into the canteen to raid the larders for a good supper. He just hoped that one of them would spot the newcomers through the window and hide any signs of their depredations.

'Lets see what you have achieved then,' Wade strode off in the direction of the bonded warehouse.

'Not bad, assemble your men in the canteen and I will find out how well they have been briefed.'

Sergeant Westbury was red faced with exertion. The posh MP had walked his legs off, poking into sheds, checking door locks, peering into dustbins, pretentious idiot had even gone through the toilet block checking each cubicle to make sure that no one was hidden away, presumably waiting to pounce.

Walking past his vehicle the Captain indicated to the driver standing smartly at ease by the nearside door, to follow them into the canteen. Inside Corporal Taylor was pacing about uneasily, seated at a wooden table were Privates Smith and Stubbs. All leapt to attention at the sight of the officer.

'Sit down, you too Sergeant,' Cole waved then into the empty chairs at the table.

'Security is not bad considering that you have only just arrived. Where are the keys to the bonded warehouse Sergeant?' he asked, almost as an afterthought.

'Here Sir,' Westbury obligingly dug into his trouser pocket and produced a small bunch of mortise and padlock keys.

'…And they will be kept where ?' demanded the officer.

'I shall keep them on my person Sir,' the Sergeant replied smugly, 'anyone wants these keys, they will have to go through me.'

Now that is something you are going to regret saying, thought Wade grimly. Catching Taff Davis's eye he said abruptly, 'Jackson, go and make some tea, it doesn't look as if these men have had any refreshment since they arrived.'

With a crisply delivered, 'Sir', the Welshman disappeared into the kitchen.

For the next ten minutes Cole Wade lectured the four soldiers on discipline and security until to his immense relief, Davis reappeared carrying a tray laden with mugs of a dark steaming brew which he distributed around the table.

'Take one out to the gate keeper with my compliments,' ordered Wade.

By the time Taff returned from the yard Westbury and his men were all comatose in their chairs. Pushing the Sergeant's inert body to one side, Cole thrust a hand deep into his trouser pocket and withdrew the keys.

'What about the gatekeeper,' he asked.

'Should be drinking it right now,' grinned the stocky Welshman.

'Good, tie these all together just in case they show signs of coming round, O'Keefe promised that whatever was in that powder would keep them out for most of the night, but let's be sure - there is rope in the lorry. Gather up their weapons and chuck them in the wagon, then grab a rifle for yourself and get outside on the gate - just in case someone gets nosey.'

Less than five minutes later, right on schedule, two large pantechnicon lorries pulled quietly into the yard. Taff Davis slid the gates closed behind them and resumed his stance, rifle at his side. Through the tiny window of the gate hut he could see the figure of Clem Waldron slumped over his desk.

'No problems?' Wade asked Tom Whiteman.

Whiteman shook his head, 'no, everything was fine. The padlock on the gate at Latimer's was undone, as he said it would be,' he indicated O'Keefe, 'the rest was easy, the lorries were in the main shed. Ignition switches under the dashboards, full tanks. Drove out and picked these lads up in the next street.'

O'Keefe grinned. He was a big bear of a man with a heavy moustache which when he smiled parted to reveal a set of even white teeth.

'What have you done with the squaddies?' he demanded.

Wade glared at him, the man appeared to consider himself to be in charge, and it irritated the Canadian.

'They are out to the world, and tied up just to be certain - I have done this sort of thing before.' Despite the note of asperity in his voice, he was careful to maintain the English accent.

'Come on let's get moving, we have got half an hour to get out of this place.' O'Keefe was amused at the other man's obvious displeasure. I am the boss here he thought, and you mister are the hired help. As an afterthought he strode over to the wooden hut by the gates. Clem Waldron was still slumped over his desk.

Lifting his keys down from the hook on the end of the desk, O'Keefe closed the door and locked it from the outside. The old man was the biggest danger to them, if however unlikely, he recovered consciousness, he would instantly recognise Charlie and the other policemen.

Walking purposefully across the deserted yard he made his way to the rear of the sheds where the lorries were already being loaded. From somewhere in the distance came the resounding clanging of a fire engine bell.

Chapter 21

'It was a clean, well organised job.' Clarence Greasley pushed his hands deep into his trouser pockets.

'Look at them, short of going up to the workhouse you'd struggle to find four more useless articles than those four.'

Harry North did not even bother to glance across in the direction of the little group of dispirited soldiers, huddled in the doorway of the canteen. 'Poor old Clem', he said sadly, 'turned seventy, just topping up his pension with a nice quiet little job, and then this happens.'

Turning he walked slowly over to the open door of the watchman's hut, it was the first thing that he had seen on his arrival at the yard. The door had been broken open by Claude Hamilton when following the telephone call to the station by an almost distraught Hiram Westbury, at just after 4. a.m., he and the night Inspector, Jack Loakes arrived at the yard.

Sergeant Hamilton and Inspector Loakes were standing by the timber framed hut talking in muted voices with Bert Conway. Inside, slumped across the wooden desk was the prone figure of Clem Waldron, his face and hands an unpleasant shade of dark pink. Detective Constable Laurence Windram was standing just inside the open door, studiously drawing a sketch plan of the body and the layout of the hut.

'When you have finished doing that Lol wait for Aldred Danson to take some pictures, he should be here any minute, then go with the undertakers down to the mortuary. Usual thing strip the body ready for the PM, make an inventory of all of the property and take it down to Long Street.' His voice matched his sombre mood. Whilst the coroner would most likely bring in a verdict of misadventure, so far as Harry was concerned the old man's death was straight forward murder. Murder by mistake ? Murder by omission ? It was irrelevant so far as he was concerned, locking a drugged man in an enclosed space such as the gate hut in close proximity to an open brazier burning coke, amounted to murder.

'What do you think sir, heart attack?' asked Windram.

Harry shook his head absently, his mind elsewhere. The descriptions of the Military Police Captain and his driver, given by Sergeant Westbury did not match up to either Charlie O'Keefe or any of his men. To remove the cigarettes would have required at least three large lorries - the one in which the bogus officer arrived plus two more, so within a short while there should be a report coming in of a further break-in at a company that possessed that sort of transport.

Including O'Keefe himself, his crew numbered four, so there had to have been outside help, plus the fact that Clem would have immediately recognised any of O'Keefe's men as soon as they drove through the gate. Cole Wade was his bet, but he guessed that finding him or any of the rest of Lisa's gang was going to be difficult. They would be well hidden now.

'No, carbon monoxide poisoning.'

Bert Conway's gravelly tones were also muted. Like the rest of the older men, over the years he had known and worked with the Clem Waldron and his death in these circumstances was affecting him deeply.

'He'd stoked the brazier up for the night, then passed out when they slipped him the Mickey Finn and locked the door on him. Coke gives off carbon monoxide which is deadly poisonous, and...' he nodded towards the corpse, '... the body turns a deep pink.'

'Somebody is going to hang for this one...' he was looking directly at the Superintendent.

Lol Windram following his gaze, had a strange feeling that he was missing something.

North did not reply. Pulling out his pocket watch he checked the time, it was five thirty, an hour and a half since Westbury had raised the alarm. There was a lot to do, he and the Detective Sergeants would meet later in the morning to discuss the thing that was on all of their minds, where was Charlie O'Keefe last night?

He was about to speak when the sight of Joe Rowell striding in past the uniformed officer stationed on the gate caught his eye.

'Early morning foreman at Latimer's Removals in Hope Lane has telephoned the nick, they have just arrived for work and two of the big lorries are missing. I have sent a couple of the early morning uniform men down there with instructions that no one is to touch anything,' he said.

Harry gave a brief nod, and waved Clarrie Greasley to join them.

'Right, this is what we are doing,' said in a low voice that only the four of them could hear. 'We all know what we are thinking, but I don't want any speculation until we are on our own away from here.' The other three nodded in agreement.

'Clarrie - you and Bill Sykes make a start on the robbery. Put that fat shit-bag of a Sergeant through the wringer before the MPs arrive from York to cart him off to the glass house.'

'Bert, I want you to take on the investigation into Clem's death yourself - once young Laurence gets back from the mortuary let him work with Clarrie and Bill. Although the death is part and parcel of the robbery, perhaps if we treat it as a separate issue we might just come up with something. You are going to have to sit in on the post mortem - listen to what the new man, Dilkes, has to say - he is very good and doesn't miss a trick.'

Conway grimaced, he hated post mortems and was not looking forward to standing watching the body in the hut being dissected.

'Joe, you and I will go down to Latimer's. With any luck they might have got careless, with a job this complicated there have got to be some loose ends somewhere, its just a matter of finding them.'

Harry parked the Clement Talbot in the street outside of Latimer's yard. His new acquisition was the talk of the station, rumours abounded as to how he had come into possession of it. The most popular opinion was that Cliff Jarman had given it to him as a bribe in a misplaced endeavour to ensure a light prison sentence for himself. Harry was completely aware of the speculation, and not the least phased by it. His activities over the years had often drawn attention to him, and if the current interest centred on how he had mysteriously become the owner of an expensive new touring car, then that was the least of his worries.

Secretly he was quite pleased by the fact that Sidney Hall-Johnson was reported to be highly piqued about the matter, especially as the Chief Constable was so far removed from operational matters that he had never even heard of Clifford Jarman.

Nodding politely to the uniformed officer guarding the gate, Harry and Joe went over to the red faced foreman pacing up and down by the open garage doors.

'Superintendent North,' Harry introduced himself. The foreman was unshaven and reeked of last night's beer.

'Basil Myers sir', the man replied deferentially. Having, on arrival at the yard found the gates wide open and two of his pantechnicons missing, the foreman was not at all certain how much responsibility for the theft would eventually find its way down onto his shoulders.

'So tell me about this Basil,' North had spent a lifetime dealing with men such as Myers. Honest and hard working they usually reached middle age without ever speaking to a policeman, and now confronted with a potential catastrophe at work, along with two men in smart suits, he would be in no doubt that before the day was out they would find a way to get him the sack.

Harry frowned. One step at a time, he was presuming that Basil Myers was 'honest and hard working,' perhaps he was wrong, perhaps Myers was part of the set up. He would revise his opinion and reserve judgement for the time being.

Whilst the foreman launched into an account of how, arriving for work soon after 5.a.m., he had found the yard gates undone and the padlock swinging loose from the hasp, he had gone to the main garages to discover that two of the large furniture removal vans were no longer in their parking places, North's mind was elsewhere.

Waiting until the man had finished telling his story, Harry left Joe Rowell, scribbling busily with a stub of pencil in his note book, and strolled over to the uniform man on the gate who he noted was wearing the red white and blue ribbon of the Military Medal.

Another newcomer. Harry took in the silver numbers on his tunic collar - PC 97.

Adam Larrad, bit on the short side for a policeman, married, joined the Force in 1912 when he came out of the Navy. Recalled as a reservist at the outbreak of war he was lost at sea when the battle cruiser HMS Indefatigable was sunk in May 1916 at Jutland. Every new man he encountered represented someone who was now dead, he reflected sadly.

The officer, whose name was Wainwright, shifted his 'at ease' position slightly and continued to gaze straight ahead. He was used to officers treating him as if he were invisible, it was a daily occurrence in the Guards. They still got killed though he thought. A shell blew them into an unrecognisable package of blood and guts in exactly the same way it did an enlisted man. He had heard about Detective Superintendent Foxy North, but this was the first time that he had encountered him during his six months on the Force. 'Devious and to be avoided' - was the advice given to him in the mess room. Ted Wainwright gave a sideways flick of his eyes. The man looked alright he thought, but you never can tell.

Oblivious to the officer's appraising glance, Harry was lost in deep thought, turning over in his hand the heavy padlock which secured the yard gates.

'Are you on nights or early morning?' he asked absently.

'Early morning sir' came the crisp reply.

'Where was the padlock when you arrived?'

'Exactly where it was when you picked it up sir, through the chain.'

North continued to contemplate the lock, then putting his hand into his jacket pocket he pulled out a jeweller's glass which he screwed into his right eye. For a long moment he examined the lock carefully before hanging it back on the now redundant chain swinging slack through the bars of the gate.

'Why did you join the Force?' he asked.

'I did four years in the Grenadiers sir. Saw a bit of action, didn't want to go back into the printing, thought I might be alright at this.'

Harry nodded slowly. 'I wish you luck, its time we had some new blood.'

Turning he walked slowly back to where Joe Rowell was talking to the foreman. He now knew how the Byram job had been done, and exactly what it was that had got Lew Arthur murdered. He suddenly felt tired beyond his years.

The lunchtime meeting in the Lamb and Pheasant was a sombre affair. There were no guarded asides when Maria Daley set the drinks down on their table, and none of the customary banter between Clarrie Greasley and Bert Conway.

'Are we agreed, this is personal now?' Harry's gaze swept around the table taking in the other three, one by one. Clarrie, big and fat, on the surface jolly, underneath as hard as nails. Bert, square faced and surly, few people other those at this table knew anything of his past history or how much he had done for young Connie Armitage. Big Joe Rowell whose misguided political activities were going to cost him his job before long. Each different, each their own man, but with one thing in common, an unswerving loyalty to each other and to the job that they were doing.

'Is it time we pulled O'Keefe and his mongrels in ?' asked Clarrie.

'And if we do, we have got nothing …' Harry toyed with a beer mat. 'O'Keefe was with his lovely wife at home last night, Gunn was night fishing up by the Town Locks, Wales was off shagging that woman who runs the canteen at Long Street, and Green would you believe it, he went to the pictures.'

'The same pictures that burnt down and pulled every copper in the town off of their beats' said Clarrie.

'Exactly,' Harry's mood was as sour as any of them had ever seen, and they all knew that this was when he was at his most dangerous.

'I didn't know Albert Wales was shagging Bonnie Cassidy,' Conway seemed genuinely shocked. 'I shan't be eating any more food that she's been handling'. The others ignored him.

'We could sort it between the four of us, if you want the job doing Harry.'

Bert looked up suddenly at Joe Rowell. He had a deep respect for the Scotsman's abilities and was slightly startled at the suggestion.

Harry shook his head. 'No Joe. Fitting them up is not the answer. Yes, they could be sorted for some things, but not everything. And that is what I want - everything!'

The three Sergeants remained silent. Had North given the nod to Rowell's offer the other two would have gone along with it, because as Harry said - 'this was personal now.'

'Everything. The robberies, Lew Arthur, now Clem Waldron. When they started killing their own - and make no mistake, locked in that hut being slowly gassed, Clem was murdered - then they made it personal.'

'I want each of them to hang, and to do that it needs to be absolutely watertight and absolutely straight. I need the judge who deals with them to enjoy topping each and every one.'

'What we need to consider,' said Clarrie, ' is the fact that there had to be more than O'Keefe's team involved.'

'Two arrived in the first lorry posing as MPs. Can't be any of O'Keefe's men because Clem would have recognised them. So, they had to be outsiders. Plus, the other two lorries, and sufficient hands to shift the gear quickly. I reckon that we are looking for a team of at least six, probably seven or eight.'

Rowell pushed his empty beer glass to one side, 'add Brad Green onto that, he was obviously given the job of setting the cinema on fire to create a diversion.'

'So,' put in Conway, lighting a cigarette and throwing the packet into the middle of the table, 'where were the 'jolly boaters' whilst all of this was happening?'

Rowell rubbed his eyes, they had all been turned out just after daylight and he was tired.

'I sent Bill and Lol across to the basin just after eight this morning. Wonder of wonders, the only people there were Ma Abbott and that big ugly bastard from Liverpool, oh and the dog.' He allowed himself a wry grin.

'According to her, all of her men have been away up-river for the last two days helping one of the hauliers from Chesterfield to re-float a barge that has gone down and is blocking the waterway. She then basically told them to fuck off, and let the dog take a piece out of Lol's trouser leg.'

'This would be a good time to go back team-handed to turn them over, see where the gear is' suggested Bert.

As an afterthought he added, 'when we go, we are going to have to shoot that fucking mad sheep dog on the way in.'

Again North shook his head. 'Not yet. Without a doubt the cigs are somewhere there or nearby. Thing is, if we go nap too soon and come out empty handed then that is it - game over. No give it a day or two, Joe set a watch on what is happening there and if it looks like anything is moving in or out we have another think. Personally I don't reckon she will attempt to move anything for a while until, the dust settles.'

Harry was loath at the moment to reveal to the others that having examined the original plans, he knew about the tunnels under the warehouse. Things were coming to a head and it would not be long now before he was ready to strike in his own time. He was also very uncomfortable with his personal feelings about the fact that when everything came tumbling down, Lisa Abbott would also crash.

Although nothing was said, the others were puzzled by North's reluctance to get a warrant and raid the warehouse. Now was the obvious time. The woman was on her own with just one of her crew, who according to Laurence Windram and Bill Sykes appeared to have been recently been injured in a fight and was still recovering. If the stolen property was anywhere at the basin they could find it.

'Plus,' said Harry carefully, 'I know why Lew was killed.'

He reached for the cigarette packet on the table and drew one out.

'Go on,' said Clarrie Greasley, 'tell us what you know,'

Harry lit the cigarette and flicked the match stalk onto the table. 'Not yet, when I am absolutely certain, then we will be ready to go - on everything.'

They knew that it was useless to push him. That was the trouble with Harry, he was as good a detective as any of them, probably better, but a total loner. He would keep the knowledge to himself until the last minute.

'Did anything other than the cigs go from Pierpoint's?' He asked suddenly, as if the thought had just occurred to him.

'Actually, yes.' Clarrie was annoyed at North's reluctance to share what was obviously some key information.

'They obviously had a bit of spare room in one of the wagons. Before they left, they ripped open a load of strong boxes in the end warehouse. Not exactly your jeweller's vaults - crow bars and brute force did the job. As yet Stephen Haddow at Pierpoint's hasn't been able to contact the clients who had items on deposit, but it is probably mainly pictures, family heirlooms, that sort of thing, and of course, a selection of items that someone should not have had. All too valuable to leave laying around, but not sufficiently valuable, or clean enough to store in a vault.'

'Get a list from Haddow as soon as possible.' Harry paused. 'Get two lists. One of the clients with stuff on deposit, and one of what they say has gone. Where a client says nothing has gone then we know they were storing hooky.'

Clarrie grinned, 'Already doing it Harry.'

'So when is Moses going to be back working full time?' Cole Wade rolled over onto his side his hand searching the bedside table for his cheroots.

'In a while,' Lisa said noncommittally. Pushing the sheet to one side she got out of bed and pulled a silk wrap around herself before going to the window and looking down at the men unloading one of the Retford Haulage boats. Within days of the incident with Gilbert Manton she had secured assurances from each of the other three hauliers involved in their criminal enterprise that they were with her. Gilbert might have been a link in the Leicester end of the chain, but Bill Grigson, John Capstock, and Sam Wooller were all aware that it was Lisa who controlled the essential factor - the warehouse.

'Manton has been quiet for nearly ten days, we really should start to expect something else from him anytime.' Lisa was turning the matter over in her mind.

Cole came to stand behind her, she felt his erection pressing against her buttocks as his hand slid inside the thin robe and began to caress her breast.

Absently she removed the hand and turned back into the room. Cole was a good lover but she needed to maintain an edge. They had spent the last hour in the flat over the warehouse in a long, leisurely bout of afternoon sex, and he was obviously ready for more, which was exactly the time for her to call a halt. A man with a highly attuned sexual appetite was relatively easy to maintain a hold over, and Cole Wade definitely fell into this category.

'Put some trousers on and start thinking with your head instead of your dick,' she gave him a warm smile.

'Manton has got a big job coming up. Howard Toach the army stores manager at Leicester is about to 'lose' a large consignment of assorted spirits destined for a series of officers messes across the country, I don't know the details. I only know the job is coming off because Gil has been bragging about it to Sam Wooller.'

'When is it happening?' he asked.

It was not such an idle question as it appeared. Yesterday one of Griggs boatmen, Toby Looker unloading Bill Griggs' *Empress* had passed him a whispered message, relayed from Alf Alderton, to the effect that Manton would be in touch with him very soon. Cole was enjoying the relationship with Lisa - who would not he reflected - a good looking woman who was surprisingly experienced in bed. However, business was business, the sooner he received some reinforcements from Manton and took over the basin the better. It was becoming apparent that on the pretext of aiding his recovery, she was keeping Moses Hawkins close to her as a personal bodyguard. He would be interested to find out just how the two of them had turned the tables on Gil. Meanwhile he was going to continue enjoying the hold over her that his present situation as her lover gave him.

'Some time after the bank holiday, that is all that I know.' Lisa was still working out how to deal with the threat posed by Manton. She actually knew from Wooller exactly when the spirits would be delivered - Friday, 1st August, before, not after the bank holiday.

'Its fortunate that you and the lads were down in the vault when those two coppers arrived this morning,' she said. 'Did you get everything in?'

Wade grinned, 'no problem, and we got the other gear in, the pictures and hooky pieces of 'priceless art' that were in the deposits. And of course, the little present for you.'

He indicated the small framed oil painting on the bedroom wall of a classic nude reclining on a divan set amongst a cluster of soft cushions and drapes. With the exception of this and a couple of other items that had caught Lisa's attention, all of the remaining property from the strong boxes was stacked safely in the tunnel.

Lisa gave him an approving look, watching him pull on his trousers and button his shirt, he was certainly a handsome man, and efficient too. What, she wondered was his true background, where was he really from?

'Get down on the dock before they miss you and start talking, I need to take a bath.'

About to demur, Wade was stopped in mid sentence by the bedroom door being pushed half open and Gyp's head poking enquiringly around it. The collie stood glaring at him before padding across the room to lay down beside Lisa, from where she continued to eye Wade suspiciously.

'Does that bloody dog ever give you any privacy?' he demanded testily, keeping a safe distance as he put his hand on the door handle.

'You leave my dog alone, she's paid to look after me,' Lisa retorted good naturedly. Gyp's antipathy towards Wade both amused and pleased her. It gave her one more edge.

As the sound of Cole Wade's footsteps on the bare stair boards receded, Lisa picked up the telephone from the sideboard in the lounge and having first listened to ensure no one was listening on the office extension, began to dial a number.

'For Christ's sake, what do you mean it has been stolen!'

It was the first time that Will had ever seen Ralph Gresham disconcerted. Vasily Petrov spread his hands in a gesture of resignation.

'I had to hide the letter somewhere safe, or at least somewhere I thought it would be safe,' he added bitterly.

'So I took out a safety deposit box at the bonded warehouse in Kelsford and

266

put the letter in it. You know - supposedly safe, anonymous, and in the centre of the area where I was based.

'Just after lunch I saw in an early edition of the Evening Standard that there had been a major robbery up north at Pierpoint's. So I telephoned to make sure that everything was alright. The manager said that mine was one of the boxes that had been broken into.'

The twitch at the side of Gresham's jaw was working overtime.

'Better ring Harry,' Mardlin's voice was perfectly calm, 'we need to be completely honest with him now Ralph, if he knows what he is looking for, we might just stand a chance of getting it back.'

Gresham paced back and forth across the carpeted dining room floor of the Clarence Hotel. Pausing by the window he spent a long while staring down at the traffic in the side street below before turning back to the other two.

'I think you are right Will, can you give him a ring and tell him that we will be up there within the next couple of days, meanwhile impress on him that this is for his ears only.'

Will gave a nod and made his way off to his room to place the call.

Watching Gresham with a certain degree of sympathy, Vasily Petrov tapped with his fingers on the arm of his chair. Ralph was right to be worried he mused. Russian or English, our political masters do not like dangerous situations, someone usually paid a price.

Harry sat back in his arm chair and inhaled deeply on his after dinner cigarette. For years now, he and Laura had got into the habit of eating in the evening when Harry came in from work, and the roast shoulder of lamb with mint sauce and capers had gone down very well. A good end to a busy, and not altogether unproductive day.

The Pierpoint job might just be what he needed to set things moving. He knew who was involved, Charlie O'Keefe and his little gang of renegades, doubtless assisted by Cole Wade. The property was inevitably now sitting in whatever storeroom Lisa had constructed under the warehouse at the canal basin, all he needed to do was judge the time, and of course find the entrance.

He had deliberately thrown a grenade into the group in the Lamb and Pheasant by announcing that he knew why Lew Arthur had been killed. He would not be able to keep the knowledge to himself indefinitely, but there were one or two questions that he still needed to resolve before saying any more.

Finally, the telephone call had made his day. He now held all of the cards in his dealings with Ralph Gresham and Will.

Harry allowed himself a self satisfied smile. So the espionage team had outsmarted themselves. The secret item that made Vasily Petrov so valuable was a letter, which had been stolen from under their noses. Even now he did not know what was in the document, but unless he was much mistaken, Russian script - Cyrillic - was very different to European script, so when he found it - which he was going to - he would recognise it immediately. And now, after this afternoon's phone call from Lisa, he now knew exactly when to even the score with Gilbert Manton. On Monday morning he would speak to Palmer Osborne at Leicester and set up the raid on the Belgrave Wharf.

'Stop grinning Harry, what is amusing you?' Laura was peering at him over the top of the Kelsford Gazette.

'Just thinking that we might have an early night,' North replied impishly.

'Don't make plans,' she replied severely, 'I'm glad you are not a mason love.'

Harry's grin dropped and his eyebrows knitted in a frown.

'Here,' she continued, folding the paper in half and passing it over to him, 'This photograph of Sidney Hall-Johnson and Eva at last night's Masonic ladies evening. Not that you would not look nice in evening dress, but us not being married ...'

Laura stopped talking, Harry she realised was no longer listening. His original smug grin had been replaced by a wide smile.

Chapter 22

Harry looked at his pocket watch, ten thirty exactly. The anonymous phone call made by Joe Rowell to Montague Parfitt a quarter of an hour ago, telling him that there was water running from a burst main into the storeroom at the barracks where he was now the manager, had seen his old adversary trotting off along Wisden Street at a brisk pace.

Harry allowed another two minutes, watching Parfitt's slim figure disappear down the road and turn the corner into St George's Lane. Without the benefit of the Kelsford Police Model T, the walk to the barracks would Harry estimated, take him at least half an hour. another half an hour at the barracks when he found out that he had been the victim of a hoax, and the subsequent walk back, would make an hour and a half. More than ample for his purpose.

Closing the door of the Clement Talbot he strolled the twenty yards to number 15 enjoying the clear Sunday morning sunshine. Despite his ebullient mood, Harry was still slightly puzzled as to how, having left the employment of the Kelsford Police under a cloud, Parfitt had so smoothly made the transition to being stores manager at the barracks. Obviously he mused, there were distinct advantages in being an ex-army officer, as well as a mason.

Pushing open the dark green wicket gate of number fifteen with his stick he walked up to the front door and pressed the bell.

Within seconds it was opened by a smart red haired woman in approaching thirty, almost without realizing it he noticed the small mole beneath her left eye.

It was apparent from the expression on her face that she recognised Harry.

'I know who you are, Superintendent North, and my husband, who is not home at present, does not wish to see or speak to you, now or at any other time.'

Harry gave her one of his most charming smiles.

'Actually, its not your husband that I have come to see - its you Celia.'

The colour drained from the woman's face, leaving it a grey putty shade, from the appalled look in her eyes he knew that she had not even heard the words. Her gaze was riveted on the pasteboard photograph that he was holding up for her to look at.

The coffee house was almost deserted when Harry and Celia Parfitt walked in. Joe Rowell had taken a table at the back of the room although the precaution was hardly necessary, the only other customers were a couple of elderly gentlemen taking a break from an early morning walk.

Once Celia Rutherford or as she now was, Celia Parfitt had recovered from the shock of being identified as the fourth woman in the Jarman photographs, it was almost as if she were relieved to talk to someone about it. Harry suggested that they left the house, in case her husband managed to scrounge a lift from the barracks and returned early, and they drove the short distance to Phipps' where Joe was waiting for them.

'Where did you get the picture from?' she asked.

Harry explained about Jarman's arrest and the discovery of his stock of pornography at Aldred Danson's.

'How did you trace me though, I have been so careful to stay out of the way, and no one had any idea who I was.'

North toyed with a packet of Players, deciding not to light one, he needed to cut down.

'There was a picture in the Gazette of you and your husband, along with the Chief Constable and his wife at a Masonic function. I recognised you immediately'.

'I hated having those pictures taken,' she said.

'Alice loved it though, she said that she wanted to have some mementos of us. She said that the following week we could have some of us - 'doing things'- I knew that it was dangerous, that something like this would happen, so I refused to go there again.'

Harry sipped his coffee. 'Can we go back to the very beginning, when you were Celia Rutherford, in the Cottage Homes, that is where this all started with you and Alice wasn't it?'

Celia Parfitt's titian red hair dipped in acknowledgement.

'Yes, neither of us had any other family, we were close, like sisters. At night we would sneak into bed together and cuddle up. At first there was absolutely nothing in it ... that came later, when we realised that we loved each other.'

'It couldn't continue though, we both knew that. Two young women in love, we would have been crucified if anyone had found out. So, eventually, Alice took a job with that old goat Kitson, and I was 'offered a place' at Howitt's in Chesterfield. That was slave labour. Five of us living over the shop in 'accommodation', ten bob a week less board and keep, I came out with half a crown. But we were from the Homes, so it didn't matter.'

She paused to look at the two men, tears in her eyes. 'Have you any idea how people look down on you when they find out that you were brought up in an institution? They seem to think that it is your fault that your parents died and left you an orphan.'

Joe studied the table cloth before speaking.

'How did you meet your husband?' he asked quietly.

The woman did not answer at first. She sat staring out of the window, her mind elsewhere, thinking of happier times spent with Alice Kitson.

Eventually she said, 'I met Montagu not long after I went to work at Howitt's. It was very casual, I was in a tea room in the town centre in Chesterfield. He came in, he looked so dashing in his uniform and we got chatting. We became friendly and over the next week or so, on my days off we met for afternoon tea. He told me that he was recently divorced, and that he was being posted to India. Then he asked me to marry him, it was as simple as that.'

'I left Howitt's, we got married quietly and took up the overseas posting. That was nine years ago. At the outbreak of war Montie was posted to France and I came back to live in married quarters in York.'

'Something went wrong though didn't it, he left the army under strange circumstances.'

North tapped the cigarette packet on the edge of the table. The woman had an air of honesty that he found appealing. Once she had been shown the photograph it was as if she was pleased that it was over and she could confide in someone, unburden herself of years of guilt.

'Some of that was down to Montie,' she said sadly, 'but mainly it was me.'

'He came from a very middle class family, his father was a senior railway clerk, and when Montie obtained his commission his parents were so proud of him. The difficulty was that he was a terrible snob and couldn't really afford to be an officer.'

'While we were in India, it was alright because everything there was so cheap - even his mess bills were manageable. He was quite a successful gambler, very good at cards, so that eked things out as well. Then during the war years it didn't matter anyway. It was when he came back that the trouble started really, when he had to maintain a standard of living in a peace time English posting.'

She paused again and licked her lips, seeming to search for words.

'He is a weak man and has a lot of faults Superintendent, but he loves me, and always has done. Whereas I have never loved him.'

She smiled wryly. 'That was the difference between me and Alice. She liked both women and men, whereas I, in truth only like other women.'

'Over the years I maintained a pretence with Montie and he never knew. I was always very, very careful, but whilst he was away during the war, I became involved with another officer's wife whose husband was also in France. Stupidly, we carried on seeing each other after the men came back and Montie caught us. He went absolutely mad and threw her out of the house, quite violently. It was all hushed up and everyone thought that it was him who was having the affair with her. At the same time there were problems with the mess accounts, and Montie was asked to resign his commission - which is how we came to be here in Kelsford.

'...And you had kept in contact over the years with Alice hadn't you.'

Celia's head sank and tears began to flow down her face. 'Yes we never lost touch. I loved her, we loved each other. Oh yes she was having sex with that scruffy little photographer, but I didn't mind, and then she was murdered ... who would do that Mr North?'

Montague Parfitt turned his jacket collar up against the steady drizzle which was beginning to soak through his light coat. Grasping the top of the yard gate he hauled himself up, and pausing on the top to check that the ground below was clear, dropped lightly onto the garden path.

Pausing for a minute he checked that the noise of his activities had not been detected. A church clock somewhere in the town centre sounded three o'clock. This was the time that they had gone out on wire cutting patrols, when the enemy was at his lowest ebb. Sentries were tired and sleepy at this time of the night, policemen would be hiding away now in privies, or asleep in empty tramcars, parked at the terminus. Rain was the wire cutter's friend. It deadened sound and kept those who were still wary out of sight in some sheltered place where they could not see what was going on. It was the burglar's friend.

Satisfied that his presence was undetected, Parfitt made his way silently up to the back door of 23 Ludgate Street. Aldred Danson's studio was on the first floor. From the canvas bag over his shoulder he withdrew a tin of Tate & Lyle treacle and a small brush. Within seconds the pane nearest the bottom of the ornamental stained door glass was thickly smeared with the syrup. Placing a small sheet of brown paper over the sticky mess, a quick single tap with the toffee hammer also taken from the bag, resulted in the removal of the glass with a minimum of noise.

Sliding his hand inside the door, Parfitt was relieved to find that, as he had hoped, whoever locked the premises up had left the key in the mortise lock.

Once in the hallway he paused yet again, this time to regain his breath and recover his nerve. His heart he realised was thumping almost audibly in his chest. Calm down he told himself, this is only the first stage. Next I have to get into the studio and find the picture.

This morning he had almost had an heart attack when he saw the letter addressed to Celia from Aldred Danson laying on the hall floor.

'Dear Mrs Parfitt,

In February this year, you had a portrait of yourself taken at my studio, which I hope was to your satisfaction. I am about to make a window display of some of the best recent family and individual photographs taken by the studio, and would be most grateful for your permission to include this picture of you in the display.

Should you wish to look at the picture, it is available along with the other prospective items here at the studio in a cabinet on the first floor. Unfortunately, I cannot send to you a copy as the original negative has been inadvertently destroyed, and the single print item is the only one in my possession.

Yours Sincerely

Aldred Danson.

The police he knew, had taken possession of photographs from Danson's assistant, Clifford Jarman, which included the ones of Celia. He also knew that North was anxious to identify the fourth woman, and as soon as he or one of his men spotted Celia's picture in Danson's window the game would be up, and both he and his stupid wife ruined.

Security in the police was lax, North thought that no one knew about the existence of the photographs they had recovered from Jarman. But he knew - the entire station knew! He should have killed Jarman as well as the Kitson woman and made it look like a double suicide, but it was too late now.

He had known instinctively that Celia was involved with a lover again. She was relaxed and cheerful, just as she had been when she was with Marjorie Stoppard at York. She had even allowed him to make love to her occasionally. Then he found the letters from Alice Kitson, and the photographs, some of Alice, some of Celia.

From the correspondence he quickly came to realise that Alice Kitson was the source of Celia's predilection for members of her own sex, and along with the realisation came an undying hatred of the woman responsible for all his problems.

He began to follow Alice, and it did not take him long to uncover the sordid web of intrigue and deception surrounding Clifford Jarman's pornography enterprise. After that it was relatively easy to get into Jarman's company in the local pub that he frequented - the Shoulder of Mutton in Grant Street. Jarman, under the impression that Parfitt was a potential customer, talked quite readily about his activities, including the fact that he was proposing to leave Kelsford for pastures new.

Once he had established exactly when Jarman was proposing to leave, the rest was easy. The afternoon of the photographer's departure, on the pretext that he needed to talk to her, he simply picked Alice up in the station Model T, took her up to the lime kilns, killed her, and dumped the body. After that everything was safe, a scandal was averted, Celia no longer had a lover, and everyone was looking for Clifford Jarman.

Parfitt's thoughts returned to the job in hand, he needed to concentrate. Men were killed because they let their minds wander from the job in hand, they chanced upon hidden mines and were blown up, or stumbled onto an alert sentry with disastrous results. Not so Captain Parfitt, he had always come sneaking back at dawn into his own lines. Concentration was the keyword.

Inside the studio, he flicked on the small electric torch that he was carrying and shone it around the darkened room. The door from the stairs had been remarkably easy to force. Danson would know in the morning that there had been a burglary but it didn't matter, he would take a selection of other pictures and any cash that was on the premises - God knows, while I am here a few extra quid to pay off Goldman's turf account would be welcome he thought - make it look like a simple break-in. The important thing was that Danson only had one copy of the portrait, the negative no longer existed.

In the far corner, by the wall stood a glass cabinet containing a number of photographs. Slowly, as if in a trance he made his way over to it. Sure enough in the centre, wearing a wide brimmed felt hat and a high necked white blouse with mother of pearl buttons, was a head and shoulders portrait of Celia. He paused, absolutely still, looking at the image in the torch light.

He was still taking in the details of the picture, when he was suddenly dazzled by a blaze of lights being switched on, and the figure of Harry North appeared from behind a tall Chinese screen next to the cabinet.

'Hello Montie,' he said conversationally.

Spinning round Parfitt was presented with the sight of Joe Rowell standing in the kitchen doorway, and Bert Conway covering the exit to the stairs.

'Montague Parfitt, I am arresting you on suspicion of the murder of Alice

274

Kitson,' the words delivered in Joseph Rowell's thick Scottish accent were flat and unemotional.

Harry was tired, he had been on his feet for twenty hours and was now totally worn out. Gratefully he sipped at the cup of tea which Laura had put on the small table by the side of his chair, he was he decided getting too old for this sort of thing. At least Parfitt had not put up a fight, or tried to make a break for it, not that he would have stood a chance with Joe Rowell one side and Bert Conway on the other. He had simply allowed himself to be led away, a defeated look on his face.

Leaving Joe and Bert to interview the prisoner, Harry had snatched a quick nap in his office in readiness for the day, which had turned out to be a busy one.

He began by briefing Sidney Hall-Johnson on the night's events and going over with him what the Chief Constable was going to tell Gilmour Bathurst. Not unexpectedly, Hall-Johnson was appalled at the outcome of the enquiry. His concerns focussed once more on the image of his Force, and of course how it all impacted on him personally. There had already been a degree of speculation in certain quarters concerning the unexpected demise of the Chief Constable's protégé, although fortunately the matter of the missing firearm had been smoothly covered up along with an assurance from Dr Mallard of his own personal discretion.

However this latest incident was potentially disastrous, not only did it bring into question the Chief Constable's own judgement in initially employing the man, and as Harry hinted to him - he would have to handle carefully the potential question of nepotism which might be broached, by a scandal hungry Gilmour Bathurst. After all, he had chosen to employ an old army colleague in the administration post, rather than the obviously better qualified internal candidate. Also there was the rather unfortunate fact that the murderer had used the station motorcar to commit his crime, something that would want a lot of explaining away.

Secure in the knowledge that the Chief Constable had more than sufficient to occupy his day, it was not without some degree of satisfaction that Harry returned to his office.

The remainder of the morning and early afternoon were spent down at Pierpoint's with Clarrie Greasley. Four days after the robbery it was still not possible to draw up an accurate account of the contents of all of the safety deposit boxes.

'This is a list of depositors,' said Stephen Haddow passing over to Harry a neatly typed sheet of names, 'and this is what is missing according to those we have been able to contact.'

Scanning down the first list North's eye came to rest on one particular name. 'Louis Claerebout'.

Where does this one live?' he asked.

The manager shook his head, 'sorry Harry I can't help you with that. By virtue of the nature of the goods stored in those boxes, some depositors prefer to pay in advance and then remain invisible.'

Indicating the second sheet he continued, 'all I know is that he says that the items missing are some paintings and photographs that he brought with him when he escaped the German occupation of Belgium in 1914.'

Greasley frowned, 'if you don't have an address for him, how did you contact him?'

'We didn't' Haddow shrugged his shoulders, ' he telephoned us. Said that he had heard about the raid and wanted to check on his holdings. He was pretty mad when I told him that his box had been cleaned out … but then he is not on his own there, I have been fielding irate phone calls ever since we were hit.'

One more small piece in the puzzle, thought Harry. Not that the name Petrov had used would be of much value now, but it was a start. There was he knew a fifty-fifty chance that the missing letter was sitting on top of a case of cigarettes twenty feet below the main warehouse at the canal basin.

'Are you ready for something to eat love?' Laura picked up the empty tea cup about to replenish it.

'No thanks, I think that I will sit for a while - let my mind settle down - then go and get some sleep, its been a long day.'

Laura smiled, she had seen all of this before many times, he would sit quietly, perhaps talk to her about whatever it was that was on his mind, then drift of to sleep in his chair. Her bit of news would have to wait until later.

'Will Mrs Parfitt be required to give evidence?' she asked.

'I don't know.' It was the same question that had been running through his mind during the day.

'Once we knew who she was, then getting to who killed Alice was easy. It was the scarf that held the clue. Bert spotted it. She was killed on a winter's day and was apparently wearing a light cotton summer scarf. It didn't add up.'

'Oswald Kitson bought Alice the scarf last summer and could therefore be certain when he identified her effects that it was hers. Now according to Celia Rutherford, or Parfitt as she is now, on the one occasion that she and Alice went the studio for Jarman to take their pictures, Alice called at the house for her, and she was wearing the scarf. Parfitt saw her and obviously, noticed what she was wearing.'

'After the photograph session Alice gave Celia the scarf as a keepsake. Celia took it home and put it in a drawer along with some letters that Alice had written to her over the years. Although he didn't know at the time who Alice was, Parfitt must have been suspicious of Celia suddenly having a new female friend. I would presume that knowing as much as he did, he kept a pretty close eye on her all of the time.'

'According to what he has told Joe and Bert, just after Christmas he found the scarf and the letters in Celia's dressing table drawer, along with the photographs that Cliff Jarman took. From the dates on the letters it didn't take him long to work out that not only was Alice Celia's current love, but she was also her first. From that point on Alice was doomed. In actual fact Parfitt may well be right about that - Alice setting Celia on the road to being a lesbian. With her voracious sexual appetite it is more than likely that Alice set out to seduce Celia from the start. One thing I think is certain, Alice liked Celia and was more than happy to have a relationship with her, but by February of this year she was well and truly infatuated with Cliff Jarman.'

' Next he set out to cultivate the photographer. Started to use Jarman's local in Grant Street and befriended him - Jarman never knew who he was, as far as he was concerned 'Montie' was just someone in the pub who bought him the odd pint. Like most of his kind, Jarman liked to brag and told him about Alice, and the fact that he needed to get away from her. Parfitt says he actually bought the rail ticket to Skegness for him - which is something Joe needs to check on - that was how he knew to the hour when Jarman would be leaving.'

'On the afternoon of the day Jarman caught the train to the East Coast, Parfitt rang Alice and told her that he knew all about her sordid little affair with Celia, and needed to talk to her straight away. Then he put Alice's scarf in his pocket, took the station car to collect her and drove up to the Lime Kilns. I'm not sure how he actually managed to strangle her. She was a big woman, slightly taller and heavier than Parfitt. He may persuaded her to get out of the car, then came in from behind her, or more likely did it whilst she was still seated in the car, with her movements restricted it would have been easier.'

Harry paused, that was something the defence would light upon. Alice was a big strong woman, Montague Parfitt was quite slim and lightly built. He would have to speak to Joe, ensure that it was covered in his next interview with the prisoner, get him talking, bring in his wartime experiences, he must have crept up behind a sentry a two somewhere along the line. Hall-Johnson was really going to have some explaining to do in justifying his allowing Montague Parfitt the free use of the Model T to travel back and forth to work.

'Your original question - will Celia have to give evidence - it will depend on whether or not he pleads guilty. Either way she has got to be prepared for a massive scandal. At the moment she is more preoccupied with the fact that it was her husband who killed the woman she loved.'

Harry lapsed into silence, thinking back to Sunday morning, when in answer to the woman's tearful question, '... *who would do that Mr North?*' he had explained to her, exactly who had murdered Alice Kitson.

At first both he and Joe had thought that she might burst into hysterics. They were wrong. A look of shocked incomprehension was after a few moments replaced by one of deep hatred. Hatred not for them, but for the man who had destroyed the one thing that mattered in her life - the only person whom she had ever truly loved.

The two men sat quietly, neither of them speaking, her reaction now would influence their next move.

Eventually, totally calm she said, 'you want me to do something don't you? That is why you have brought me here to tell me this, instead of just coming to the house and arresting him.'

What Harry wanted, was quite simple, although it required Celia Parfitt for the next few days to act as if nothing had happened - something which Harry knew she would be very capable of doing.

She was to go next day to Aldred Danson's studio in a smart suit, and have a studio portrait taken. Danson would then address a letter to her, prepared by North, asking permission to use the picture in a window display, she was to ensure that the letter when delivered, was opened by her husband.

Harry knew that Parfitt would be aware of the photos in Joe Rowell's desk. Despite his strictures that they were to be kept out of sight, word had soon got around the station that Big Joe had a porn collection in his drawer that was part of a major enquiry. The letter was a written invitation to break into Danson's studio and remove the one piece of evidence that would lead the investigating officers to the fourth woman.

Harry had a sense that he ought to feel sorry for Montague Parfitt. Surely the man had loved his wife sufficiently to kill for her?

But Harry was not that naïve. The ex-soldier was not a particularly likable man. Why Harry wondered had his first wife divorced him? He may in the early days of their relationship, have been infatuated with the young and so far as he was aware, innocent shop girl, but that illusion North suspected would have been quickly destroyed when he found out the true nature of his wife's predilections. No, Montague Parfitt, a self made snob, had found himself saddled with a woman who had the potential to destroy his army career - something which he ironically, eventually did for himself.

There would have been opportunities in India for Celia to discreetly satisfy her needs with native girls, but it was probable that he suspected something even then. In 1914 the war came along and for the next four years he was away in France, with no control over his wife's activities. Whilst he was away his worst fears were realised, she established a relationship with the wife of a fellow officer, which was to result, along with his money troubles in him finding himself back on civvy street. Then the ultimate humiliation, discovering Alice, the root of all his troubles and his eventual nemesis.

'Will we still be alright to go to Connie's birthday party on Saturday,' Laura interrupted his train of thought.

'Yes, yes of course, I had forgotten about that.' Harry smiled at her, she put up with a lot from him he thought. Saturday was Connie Armitage's twenty sixth birthday and Bert had booked the church rooms in Rosemary Street for the occasion. It would not be a grand affair, but there was insufficient room at the house.

'What time are we there?'

'Half past seven,' she replied, 'bye the way, I have got my ring back.'

Harry's face took on a puzzled look, 'ring? what ring?'

'My cameo, the one that was at the jeweller's for re-sizing. Mr Byram rang to say it was ready for collection, and then it was stolen in the robbery' Laura said excitedly.

The truth was that she had been bursting to tell him her news since the moment he walked through the door, but knew better than to broach the matter until Harry had got everything off of his mind.

'Where did you find it?' he asked carefully.

'Connie and I went into town this morning. Bert has given her some money for her birthday and she wanted to buy some clothes. We were walking through the Market when I spotted a jewellery stall - you know, one of those that sell antique gold and things - and there it was. I didn't tell the man it was mine, I just asked him where he got it from and he said it was part of a purchase that he made from a pawnbroker's in Derby.'

'I paid him five pounds for it, actually it is worth a lot more than that, but he was satisfied,' she added proudly.

'I was going into Long Street to find you or Clarrie to let you know, in case you wanted to talk to him, but you were both out, and Joe and Bert were tied up with this murder.'

'Did I do wrong?' she asked, suddenly not sure of herself.

'No, no,' he sighed laying a hand over hers, 'I would have liked to have talked to him, but that will have to wait now.'

Inwardly he groaned, they had lost the chance that they had been waiting for. An item of property to surface and someone who was either a witness or a receiver to interview. Itinerant market traders dealing in less than pristine items of cheap jewellery were as difficult to trace as snow that has melted in the morning sun. The man would be miles away now.

'No I am glad you have got it back', he said kindly, 'be sure to wear it at the party.'

Chapter 23

There was something about church halls that made Harry uncomfortable. It was not just the religious connotation, more the guarded atmosphere of disapproval that seemed to pervade them. There was always a lingering tidiness accompanied by an odour of polish and disinfectant that never failed to impart a note of censure along with the silent implication that the rooms were being used for an ungodly purpose.

He pushed his chair back to allow Laura, two plates piled with sandwiches and sausage rolls precariously balanced in one hand, and a glass of milk stout in the other, to work her way in behind the table at which they were sitting.

Placing the stout on the table, she carefully followed suit with the plates.

'I told you not to bother for me,' Harry's voice was pitched at a whisper that only she could hear.

'You have got to eat,' she smiled back at him, 'it's a party, I know that if its not sausage and mash it doesn't interest you, but Connie has gone to a lot of trouble, so be polite, alright?'

Harry knew better than to demur. He was on unsafe ground and Laura was quite capable later on when they got home, of making things very uncomfortable for him. It had happened before on more than one occasion. Demur, and the perfect companion whilst they were out, she could back in her own home manifest her displeasure strongly. The last time was after the two of them had attended Bill Sykes's wedding reception, just before Christmas 1915. Harry and Bert had settled down at a corner table and embarked on a somewhat raucous drinking competition with Clarrie holding the side bets, laid by the not inconsiderable number of bystanders from Long Street.

The outcome was that Harry lost by a whisker, becoming extremely drunk in the process. To Laura's eternal mortification she had to be helped to get him home by Will and Susan Mardlin, something which when he eventually recovered he was made to pay for dearly.

He glanced across at the temporary bar, set up by Reuben Simmonds from the Rifleman, where Clarrie and Joe were in the process of ordering drinks. Searching around the room, Clarrie's gaze first lighted with an enquiring look on Harry who gave a quick nod, before continuing to hunt around for Bert.

Two minutes later the three of them joined Laura and Harry at their table. 'Excellent 'do' Bert,' Harry noticed that both Bert and Clarrie's faces were taking on a deeply mellow colour, they had obviously been indulging enthusiastically from Reuben's barrel of Winstock's bitter.

Bert beamed back at him and took a long pull at his drink. 'Got to give the girl a bit of a do for her birthday,' his steady tone belied the appearance of his face.

Clarrie was looking intently at the ornately set cameo ring on Laura's little finger.

'Laura,' he said, 'I thought you lost that ring in the Byram job. It was on the list of stolen property.'

It was now Laura's turn to beam. 'I found it on the market,' she told him, and then went on to regale them with the tale of her shopping expedition.

The three Sergeants gave Harry guarded looks, 'Connie is waving across at you Laura, I think she wants to talk to you,' Harry pointed to the table recently vacated by Joe and Bert. Connie Armitage and Ailma Rowell were looking across at the group, and signalling to her.

'Back in a minute,' she said, and getting up, made her way across the room.

Harry held his hands up in resignation. 'I know, but she has no idea.'

Clarrie shook his head, 'Bloody hell Harry, we have just lost the break that we have been waiting for.'

'He may come back and stand again next week,' Joe Rowell did not sound hopeful.

'And I might get a season ticket to heaven,' grunted Conway. 'No we have just got to hope that there is some more of the stuff going to surface, I'll put young Laurence in the market on Wednesday just in case…' The others noticed that his attention was on the table where the women were seated. Daniel Scofield had joined them and was being shown the ring by Laura.

'Just as a matter of interest Joe, your lad has been paying a bit of attention to Connie recently. Have a bit of a chat and see what its all about will you.'

'My 'lad' is a grown man Bert, but I take your point. He's a decent bloke and I doubt he would be meaning her any harm.' Rowell deliberately avoided staring across at the other table.

The noncommittal grunt from Bert Conway spoke volumes. He knew that sooner or later Connie was going to find someone and decide to settle down, he was also aware that he was being overprotective.

'Meanwhile,' Harry intervened, determined to lighten the mood, 'it's a party, drop of Scotch?'

'You dozy, greedy bastard! Charlie O'Keefe was beside himself.

'And don't tell me it wasn't you, because I know you Ben Gunn, and all you have been interested in for months is when are you going to get your share!

Gunn shifted uncomfortably in his chair. None of them had known what the problem was when this morning Charlie had summoned them to an emergency meeting in the back room of Wilf Quinlon's beer house in Butt Close, commonly known as 'the Rat and Shafter'.

A blousy woman in her early fifties made her way over from the fireplace where she had been in deep conversation with one of her sisters in trade. Giving O'Keefe what she fondly believed to be a lascivious smile she bent down and whispered something in his ear that the others could not hear. Despite it not being noon yet, she reeked of rum.

'Fuck off Blanche,' he said irritably, 'we are busy, if I do decide that I want to have a spell pissing razor blades, I'll come and see you.'

The woman gave him a dark look but went back to her place by the empty grate without saying anything. She knew better than to antagonise Charlie O'Keefe and his little band. Coppers were dangerous, but bent coppers were poison.

Brad Green reappeared in the kitchen door from the back yard where he had been to relieve himself at the outside drain. Sitting back down again at the rickety table he toyed with his half empty beer glass.

'Alright Charlie, Ben has made a mistake. He kept a piece of tat back and went and hocked it. Wrong, definitely wrong, definitely stupid, but its done. So where do we go from here.'

O'Keefe glared down at the table still angry. Angry at Gunn for being so greedy and breaking the rules, endangering them all. Angry and not a little nervous about the meeting that had taken place in the confessional this morning with the man. His instructions had been very specific. He was to give Harry North a warning. A warning to back off, and at the same time to recover the ring from Laura Percival. North needed to be shown that he was out of his depth, and that if necessary he could be hurt. Finally, if one of O'Keefe's crew was out of control, then he needed to deal with the matter - as the man put it, *'pour encourager les autres.'*

'First of all,' he said grimly, 'Foxy North has to be sent a message.'

Coming back into the High Street out of the cool atmosphere of Marfitt's haberdashery, Laura paused to get her breath and allow her eyes to adjust to the brilliance of the afternoon sunlight.

'I will see you over the weekend then Con.'

Taking a firm grip on Ashleigh's hand in order to prevent the child from running into the road, Connie Armitage gave her a parting smile, 'yes, if you want to come round on Friday, we can have a cup of tea and then go down to the market.'

Connie had walked less than twenty yards, when turning to wave to her friend, who was standing where she had left her, busily counting some change, she saw a large delivery van which had just passed her travelling along the High Street, suddenly swerve across the road heading directly for Laura.

It happened in what seemed less than a second. Connie gave a piercing scream and a startled Laura looked up as the van mounted the pavement. Laura barely had time to leap back, before the van caught her a glancing blow, knocking her to the ground.

Connie hared back down the road towing a frightened Ashleigh behind her. A small group of people had already gathered around Laura and one man was kneeling down holding her hand. Connie pushed her way through the gathering crowd and knelt down beside her friend.

'Laura, are you alright,' she demanded almost distraught. Laura gave a groan, 'yes I think so my leg hurts, if you hadn't screamed he would have killed me.'

A uniformed figure joined them, PC 97 Ted Wainwright, knelt beside her and began to expertly run his hands over her limbs and upper body, asking quietly if she felt any pain and if so where it was. Satisfied that the woman was only bruised and shocked, making sure that she was comfortable with his folded cape under her head he waited patiently for the arrival of the Fire Brigade Ambulance. Looking around, Connie realised that the man who had been holding Laura's hand was nowhere to be seen.

With Laura tucked up in bed, recovering from her narrow escape, Harry sat downstairs in the chair next to the kitchen range deep in thought. That this was no accident was obvious. Every uniform man on duty was out scouring the streets for the delivery van with instructions that if it was sighted the driver was to be arrested and North informed.

Not that he thought that was likely to happen. The van would be reported stolen from some backstreet shop and later found abandoned. He had sent each of the detective teams out with instructions to turn over every pub and drinking stew in the town, and roust every villain they came across until someone told them something about the incident.

They all knew that this was in one way a pointless exercise, no one was going to give any information - primarily because no one actually knew anything, this was not the work of the everyday Kelsford criminal fraternity. However, in another way it was very necessary. Word would have quickly gone around that an attempt had been made to run down Foxy North's common law wife, and irrespective of who had done that, trouble would follow.

The message was clear to Harry, he was getting too close for comfort, and those near to him were vulnerable. He was, he knew, responsible for this whole situation. Having lost the opportunity to find the market trader he had decided to try to flush the thieves out by making it public knowledge that the ring had been recovered. He had told Laura to wear it to Connie's party. Obviously the ruse had been more successful than he anticipated.

What was it Laura said to him, '*all I can remember is jumping out of the path of the van, then I was laying on the pavement and a man was trying to take my ring off of my finger.*'

After a while, Harry came to a decision. It was not one that he relished, however he saw no alternative. Looking up at the kitchen clock he saw that it was half past seven, going into the hall he picked up the telephone handset.

Ben Gunn stood at his point on the corner of the Hadley Lane and Croft Yard. A church clock on the other side of town was striking ten thirty. Screw Charlie O'Keefe he thought. It was ridiculous to steal large amounts of valuable property and then not be able to reap any of the benefits. Charlie said that all of the gear was to be kept hidden away for at least a year, probably more, then when everything had died down they could split the proceeds. 'Charlie said,' everything had to be exactly as 'Charlie said.' Well not any more. He had slipped the ring into his pocket before they left Byrams' and it was pure bad luck that when he didn't reclaim it - as he was never going to do - the pawnbroker in Derby had sold it on to a dealer who stood market. Hard luck, Foxy North was never going to find the dealer in a month of Sundays, those men dealt almost exclusively in pawned gear mixed with stolen property from burglaries. They worked markets all over the country, and never the same one twice, he would be in Durham or Taunton now.

'Alright Ben?'

The bulky figure of the Sergeant loomed up out of the darkness, 'put me ten forty five, Croft Yard,' he continued conversationally.

Gunn grunted, if Charlie thought that everything was 'alright' he was wrong. The others were in agreement, there were going to be no more jobs, North was getting too close to them for that, it was time for a share out of the profits and for them all to go their own separate ways.

'I was thinking,' continued O'Keefe, 'perhaps you are right, realise a little bit of cash - not too much - just enough to make life easier. Only we keep it between ourselves, right?'

'Go on,' he now had Gunn's attention.

'Not everything is stowed that far away. I have deliberately kept some gear handy, just enough for an emergency. Provided the others don't know, we could do a little deal, perhaps a hundred quid between us.'

'Where is it?' Ben could feel a thrill of excitement running through his body.

'Not far, we don't want to talk about it here, let's go round the back and have a drink.' Without waiting for a reply he turned and began to walk slowly away.

It took less than five minutes before they arrived at the entrance to the shell of St Edward's Church, strolling sedately along they were to all intents and purposes a patrolling beat man in the company of the duty Sergeant. As it happened, at this time of night they saw no one, the pubs all closed at ten, and the last tramcar had departed for the terminus half an hour after.

Turning in through the broken gate, O'Keefe made his way purposefully around the side of the church into the overgrown graveyard at the rear. Seating himself on a convenient tombstone, he reached into his tunic pocket and brought out a silver flask.

Making himself comfortable on the next monument Gunn glanced around uneasily. Brought up in the Catholic faith, he had a healthy respect for such places, and a nervous apprehension of the atmosphere shrouding them late at night. Although he would not have admitted it, he never took short cuts through cemeteries during the hours of darkness.

O'Keefe put the flask to his lips, then passed it over, Gunn took a deep swallow, the rum found its way down with a reassuring warmth. Rummaging around inside his tunic he found his pipe and matches.

The Sergeant waited patiently whilst he applied a light to the half smoked contents of the bowl. 'So where is your stash Charlie?' Gunn asked, blowing a cloud of aromatic smoke into the darkness.

O'Keefe grinned, 'just in there,' he inclined his head towards the deserted building, 'in the bell tower, finish your burn and I'll show you.' He was watching the other man intently.

Unscrewing the top of the flask he made to take a swallow, then changing his mind held it out to his companion. Gunn took another pull at the rum before handing it back.

'Jeez Charlie, that's good stuff, its certainly hitting the spot,' Gunn realised that he was starting to feel light headed, the pipe slipped from between his nerveless fingers spilling hot ashes down his tunic before dropping into the grass beside him.

O'Keefe was still watching him, the good natured smile had dropped from his face to be replaced by a more sombre expression. 'It is good stuff Ben, I made it myself.'

It took the Sergeant several minutes to arrange the inert form as he wanted it. Back against the gravestone, legs spread out in front of him, Gunn's shoulders reached the top of the low stone allowing his head to loll back over the top.

Stepping back, O'Keefe reviewed his handiwork. Satisfied, he reached under his tunic and took out a .45 Service revolver which he carefully placed in the man's right hand, then curling the index finger around the trigger he bent the arm into the body and upwards pushing the barrel of the pistol under Gunn's chin. The sound of the explosion when he pulled the trigger was in the stillness of the night deafening, and O'Keefe knew that he had to distance himself from the graveyard quickly. The saving grace was that even if a passerby or nearby resident had heard the shot, it would be difficult for them to place where it had come from.

Laura looked around the living room of Lisa's apartment with interest. To say that she was startled when Harry appeared in the doorway of their bedroom and told her to get up quickly, get dressed, and pack a bag, was an understatement. In all the years they had been together nothing like this had ever happened, but by the same token, no one had ever tried to run her down before either.

Whilst she was packing Harry explained that he was taking her to the canal basin where Lisa Abbott was expecting her. There was a barge going through next morning that would take her secretly along the waterway to Chesterfield, where by early evening she could catch the overnight sleeper train to Glasgow. From there she would take a local train up to her home village of Killin. He would, he promised send a telegram to her sister asking that she meet her from the train and keep her safely out of the way until he had resolved matters in Kelsford.

'Do you really think that this is necessary Harry?' she asked him, pulling tight the leather strap around her suitcase.

'The attempt on you this afternoon was primarily to let me know that they can get at me through you. I can't risk them doing anything else, if you are away up at the farm with Rhoda and Sandy I will rest a lot easier. You are to tell Sandy from me that he is to guard you with his life.'

She smiled at him, touched by his concern, 'I will be safe enough at fortress Campbell,' she said. 'They still shoot first and ask questions afterwards up there. I will ring you from Glasgow when I know what time the train I am catching gets into Killin station, Sandy will come and meet me.'

Twenty minutes later, the car hidden safely amongst some trees off of the road at the back of the basin, Harry smuggled Laura in through the back door of the warehouse and up the staircase into Lisa's quarters.

'This time I owe you Lisa,' Harry held his hand out briefly to her. She clasped it equally briefly, before turning to Laura, 'put your bag in the bedroom and get some sleep love,' she told her, 'you look worn out.'

'It has been a busy day,' Laura replied. In truth she was worn out, and her leg was extremely painful from the fall onto the hard pavement. Gently she ran a hand over Gyp's head and fondled her ears. She knew vaguely that Lisa was someone who Harry had dealt with recently, but other than that the woman was an unknown quantity to her. She can't be that bad she reflected, she has got a lovely dog.

'*Lady Jane* will be going through just after first light, which is in about three hours,' Lisa consulted the man's wristwatch that she wore, then looked at Harry.

'Cole and the men are still away up river, there is only Moses here with me, and he won't say anything.'

In truth at night - the most likely time for a police raid - Cole Wade, with Tom, Frank and Taff were sleeping in an old gipsy lean-to half a mile away in the woods. They would not be back at the basin until breakfast time, and Laura Percival would be long gone then.

Harry nodded, turning to Laura he said, 'take care of yourself, I'll see you when this is sorted and it is safe for you to come back. After a quick embrace he turned and left, he had not failed to notice the painting on the bedroom wall when he took Laura's bag in. It was amongst the items listed as stolen from Pierpoint's.

The truth was that Harry was far more relaxed now that Laura was out of the way. With only himself to worry about, he would be able to pile the pressure on, push those responsible into making wrong moves. This had been personal since Lew Arthur was murdered, with the attack on Laura, if possible it had become more than personal. He now knew almost everything, including the fact that Charlie O'Keefe was merely a link in a very greasy chain.

He had no sooner turned the key in the lock at Tennyson Street when the telephone began to ring. Looking at the hall clock he saw that it was half past one, at this time of the night it could only be Long Street.

The voice on the other end was that of Webster Pemberton. 'Ben Gunn has committed suicide Harry, blown his brains out in the cemetery at the back of St Edwards Church. When he didn't come in to report off from duty at midnight, there was a search of his beat made, Charlie O'Keefe found him'

'Don't touch anything Webster, I will be there in five minutes.' Harry put the phone down on the cradle and rubbed a hand across his jaw, a look of satisfaction on his face. It had begun.

'Thing about suicides Webster, is that there are only two sorts. Clean and messy, and why anyone chooses messy I will never know, because lets face it, dead is dead.'

Ben Gunn was certainly Webster Pemberton decided in the latter category. Propped up with his back against a low tombstone, feet splayed, very little remained of the left side of his face. The heavy calibre bullet travelling up through his jaw had exited through the left eye socket, smashing everything between the nose and left ear.

Kneeling beside the body, Jonathan Dilkes was making a cursory examination, Arthur Mallard had elected to remain in his warm bed and allow his young partner to deal.

'Rigor mortis is only just beginning to set in, so I would say that he has been dead no more than three hours, death appears to be due to a gunshot wound.'

He indicated the revolver still clasped in the corpse's hand, 'apart from anything else, that is a real clue.'

Gallows humour thought Pemberton, even doctors have it, he was conscious that Ducky Mallard's new partner had doubtless seen a lot of gunshot wounds in recent years. What interested him more was that Harry North had answered the telephone on only the second ring, and arrived at the scene less than fifteen minutes later, fully dressed and wide awake. Now why was Harry up and dressed at this time of the morning he wondered.

'Can I ask you Jonathan if it is possible to do the post mortem as a matter of urgency,' Harry gave the doctor a meaningful look.

Dilkes's face carried a thoughtful expression. 'I have every intention of doing so Harry. I will arrange for Arthur to take my surgery in the morning, and make a start on it immediately after we have had breakfast. I think that you need to come along as well.'

Harry grimaced, he hated post mortems and wherever possible delegated someone else to be present. '*After we have had breakfast?*' North's dislike of PMs was an open secret amongst those who new him well.

'Umm, yes, come round about seven, Heidi will do us a spot of bacon and eggs. Get a good start to the morning, it will save us time hanging around.'

Watching Harry's reaction Webster Pemberton had to stop himself bursting out laughing. Oh, I do like this new man, he thought, he will do well!

Jonathan Dilkes was as good as his word, and when Harry arrived at the large palisaded house on Gadsfield Terrace, he was greeted by the smell of frying bacon wafting along the hallway.

Heidi Dilkes her blonde hair tied back in a simple pony tail greeted him with a warm smile, 'Good morning Mr North, how are you today?'

North wondered if she had ever met Lisa Abbot, in some ways the two were quite alike although Heidi was smaller and had brown eyes.

'I am well thank you Mrs Dilkes,' he replied, eyeing cautiously the sizzling pan of bacon and sausage on the hob. Although his breakfast normally consisted of coffee and cigarettes, Harry realised that he had not eat since yesterday morning and was in fact extremely hungry.

'Please, sit down,' she said indicating a place at the table.

No sooner had Harry taken his place than they were joined by Heidi's husband and Arthur Mallard. Placing a plate of food in front of each of them along with a steaming pot of coffee in the middle of the table, Heidi Dilkes sat herself down and they all began to eat. In addition to the bacon, eggs and sausage, North saw that there was fried bread and black pudding, he hoped that he was going to be able to keep it down when the main event of the morning began.

'Eat up Harry, I have never been so well fed in my life,' the older doctor seemed to be enjoying himself immensely.

'By the way, Jonathan knows that you are not good with PMs.'

The three of them burst into laughter, and North realised that Ducky Mallard must have primed his assistant and his wife a long while ago, probably following the post mortem on Lew Arthur, of his aversion to the procedure.

'Don't worry, you have no need to be present,' Dilkes chuckled, 'I really wanted to have a proper look at the body, which I did back here last night with Arthur, and then talk to you.'

North glanced at Heidi Dilkes, not a little embarrassed. She smiled at him, munching a piece of fried bread, and refilled his coffee cup.

'Arthur and I both agree, we don't think that this man killed himself.'

North spiked a ring of black pudding, immensely relieved that his stomach was not going to be tested in the autopsy room.

'Everything is alright, until you look at the entry and exit wounds.' Dilkes accepted another sausage from the plate that his wife held out.

'With any gunshot wound the entry hole is always relatively small, the exit wound considerably larger - and a .45 slug at point blank range will make a hell of a hole when it exits – hence the damage in this case to the face. The entry wound was directly under the chin, for the exit wound to be through the left eye the head must have been tilted backwards.'

'Now I have seen one or two suicides with service revolvers. Usually young officers who simply couldn't go over the top again, and they do it in one of two ways. Either the barrel is placed in the mouth and the trigger pulled, or as in this case it is pushed under the chin and fired. When they do it that way, the natural position to assume is with the head down, trapping the barrel, the last thing the man wants is for the gun to be on the skew and the bullet to go up through his mouth and out of his cheek.'

'So, I think that when this man died he was already unconscious, I will know for certain when I do the stomach contents, but probably some sort of a drug was administered prior to death. Body positioned, gun placed in his hand, and bang. I would not like go into a coroners court and say for definite, but I think that you are looking at a murder.'

Harry pushed his now clean plate to one side and folded his hands on the table.

'That fits in with a lot of things that I know about the man's background,' he said carefully, 'and with a couple of things at the scene.'

'The grass around the grave where we found him was trodden down, as if he had walked around and around, or, more likely, two people were there. His pipe was found near to the gravestone, and there were burn marks on his tunic, as if he was smoking his pipe and simply passed out, so I think that your theory about him being drugged is absolutely correct.'

'What is going on Harry?' asked Arthur Mallard quietly.

'That I cannot tell you at the moment Arthur,' Harry replied, 'and the whole story will probably never be public, but when this is over, if you promise me another breakfast,' he flashed Heidi a smile that had got him into more women's beds than he cared to remember, 'then I will tell you.'

Chapter 24

A small frown creased Will Mardlin's brow as he walked into Harry North's office. His old partner looked tired and drawn. 'Morning Harry, you are looking well,' he said brightly.

'I am in the middle of a major corruption enquiry, yesterday someone tried to kill Laura, and I have been up all night in the cemetery at Saint Edward's with the body of a PC who has had half his head blown off in attempt to make it look as if he committed suicide. I look Will, like shit!'

The frown cleared as Will settled down in the armchair opposite North's desk. 'So everything is normal then, I did think for a moment that you might have been under some pressure. Who is the officer?'

'84 Gunn,' replied Harry .

Taking the opposite chair Ralph Gresham was aware that the young boy who had shown them up to the office, was still hovering in the doorway.

'I.. i.. is there anything else m..m Mr North Sir?' the lad asked casting a wary glance in Ralph's direction. Tommy was nervous in the presence of this new man.

'No that will be all thank you Tommy, close the door if you would please and make sure that we are not disturbed, and that means that I don't want any telephone calls putting through either.'

Mardlin looked at the lad with a renewed interest, Harry was not given to being patient with office boys, usually his conversation with them was conducted at a low bellow.

Tommy gave a deferential nod before disappearing into the corridor and as instructed, closed the door.

'Actually Harry, you do look like shit, are you going to tell me what is going on?'

Harry sighed, and pulling out his cigarettes put one in his mouth and applied a match to it. Over the next half an hour he filled the other two in with everything that had been happening.

'I have been very slow,' he said finally. 'It was looking at us all of the time. The trouble is that we all believed what we were intended to believe instead of questioning what we knew to be wrong'.

'Lew Arthur worked out how the Byram robbery was done almost from the beginning, and it was that which cost him his life'.

He blew a thin stream of smoke from a freshly lit cigarette, towards the ceiling.

'We, or rather I, assumed that it couldn't be O'Keefe's team because they weren't working on the night of the robbery. They finished night duty on Saturday and were nicely tucked up in bed whilst the burglary was being committed on Sunday night'.

'But the fact is, the robbery wasn't done on *Sunday* night, it was done the night before, on *Saturday* - O'Keefe's last night on duty'.

Perplexed, Will Mardlin shook his head. 'You are way ahead of me Harry'.

'The key repository'.

A look of comprehension dawned in Mardlin's eyes. 'Oh my God, of course', he breathed.

Ralph Gresham glanced from one to the other waiting for an explanation.

Harry stubbed the half smoked cigarette out in the glass ashtray in front of him.

'Twenty years ago Robert Archer Robson, when he was Head Constable initiated a scheme to help the police, or the Fire Brigade going to premises at night, to gain entry quickly. For the sum of two guineas a year, owners of businesses were invited to lodge a spare key to their premises with the police in 'the key repository'. Any incident at their premises and the police could gain access quickly instead of waiting hours for a key holder to attend.'

'It's not a good system, I have been trying for the last two years to get Hall-Johnson to do away with it – he most certainly will now', interposed Will.

'The incident on Sunday night at the Byram house was a blind'. Absently Harry lit another cigarette, pushing the packet towards Gresham.

'O'Keefe and his gang had the spare key from the repository in their possession on Saturday night. They screwed the shop nice and quietly – undisturbed – and moved the stolen gear away at their leisure. Then they locked up again, knowing that, in the normal course of events, no one would be going near the place until Monday morning. The key was then simply replaced in the key repository'.

'Cole Wade and his team were paid to set up the fake raid on the Byram's house on Sunday night, terrorise them and make David Byram hand over the keys to the shop and to the main safe. After that everyone thought that the robbery was done on the same night that the keys were stolen - Sunday. I would think that on Sunday night, Wade handed over the keys to O'Keefe, who simply walked past the shop, made sure no one was about, unlocked the door and left it open, then walked on and dropped them in the river'.

'How did Lew work it out?' asked Mardlin.

'Lew was always shrewd', replied Harry sadly. 'I sat down and went through his pocket book for the period before he died. Early on that Saturday evening PC 74 Griffin reported an unusual light burning at the back of Butresses's china factory in Norman Street, and Lew went upstairs to get the key'.

'The keys are hung in alphabetical order of the key holder, so Butress hangs next to Byram. Each has a label written out by the Admin Inspector, or Eric Broughton as it is now, who has responsibility for the repository, so the majority would have been made out a long while ago by Caldwell Frazer or his predecessor, before he finished.'

'Whoever took Byram's key away would have put a temporary replacement on the hook until the genuine key was returned later in the night. I think that Lew must have registered that the tag was written out in a different handwriting – one that he recognised. After the robbery, he would have put two and two together and come up with the correct answer'.

'So what would have got him killed?' asked Gresham.

Harry slumped down in his seat. 'It wasn't O'Keefe's writing that Lew recognised', he said simply.

'O'Keefe is not bright enough to set up something like this. Whoever swapped the keys wrote the dummy label – Lew Arthur knew who it was and they found out. That is why he was killed'.

'So what do you plan to do next?' asked Will.

'Whoever it is that is masterminding what is going on is both clever and ruthless.' Harry stood up and looked out of the window.

'This thing with Ben Gunn, he was shot in the head and made to look like a suicide, it was done to keep the others in line. He broke the rules and was responsible for the one and only item of jewellery from the Byram job surfacing. By coincidence it was a ring belonging to Laura, and an attempt was made yesterday to run her down and recover it.'

'So … I am going to flush them out, but I need a bit of help from you . In half an hour I am catching the fast train up to Glasgow, then I will take a local connection to Killin. I will be there late tonight. If all goes well, I should be back in two days, three at the outside.'

'In the meantime I would like you to take over the reins here Will and be at the end of a telephone. Plus, in a couple of hours time, put this note on Joe Rowell's desk.'

From underneath his blotter he drew a single sheet of paper.

'Joe, I missed the significance of the ring. The market trader bought it from a pawnshop in Derby. Pawnbrokers always scratch their identity mark on jewellery. I am going up to Killin to get the ring back from Laura. If you need me, I will be at the Bridge of Lochay. Should be back by Thursday.' Harry.

Harry knew that he was taking an immense risk. The truth was that he had overlooked the possibility of a pawn mark leading them to the pawn broker. That was the reason that the man behind O'Keefe was desperate to get it back. The apparently careless reference to the Bridge of Lochay should flush them out, and he would be waiting.

'I don't like this Harry,' Mardlin was fully aware of the risks involved in what North was proposing to do. 'These people are dangerous, you could wind up getting killed.'

'My decision Will, you left me to run the shop months ago, and we all have to die one day.'

Ralph Gresham lifted a hand in a gesture of interruption. 'That is settled then. If you like Harry, you can forget the train and whilst Will deals with things here, I'll run you over to Nottingham, Percy is there and he can fly you up to Scotland after lunch. Much quicker than the train, and no changes at Glasgow. Meanwhile, would there be any whisky about?'

Clarrie Greasley dropped the file of statements relating to the Pierpoint case on his desk, it was half past ten and the office was deserted. Bert had left a couple of hours ago on the eight thirty train to sort out with Palmer Osborne the detective Inspector at Leicester, the details of the raid that they were planning on Gilbert Manton's premises, and where Joe was he had no idea.

On the other side of the office he spotted a piece of paper on Joe's desk, hopefully saying where he had gone to. Walking across to the desk he saw that the note was in Harry North's neat hand.

Picking it up he read, and then re-read the contents. Glancing around the office he saw that Joe Rowell's hat and coat were missing. Clarrie went into the passage, his pace quickening to almost a run as he approached the door to the administration office.

'Where is Sergeant Rowell?' he demanded of a startled Eric Broughton.

'He's not here Clarrie, he came in about an hour ago and said that he was going out of town on an urgent enquiry, and wouldn't be back for a couple of days, he was in a hell of a rush …'

Eric was talking to himself, Clarrie Greasley was already flying down the passage towards the staircase and out into the street.

The train journey to Killin had been a nightmare. The longest leg, the two hundred and fifty mile journey from Kelsford to Glasgow had taken four hours. It was then that his problems started.

The connection to Stirling was delayed by two hours due to work being done on the line, and then he had to wait a further forty five minutes before the slow local train to Killin departed. It was now ten fifteen and Clarrie was feeling fraught. At the tiny stop in Killin, he chanced upon a farmer who, having spent the evening in one of the local hostelries was on his way home and offered him a lift on the mile trip out of the village to the Bridge of Lochay Hotel.

Watching the farmer's pony and trap disappearing around the bend a hundred yards away, Clarrie stood in the darkness and pondered his next move.

The title 'hotel' was he thought somewhat ambitious. The 'Bridge of Lochay' was rather a very large pub. Stone built with a white painted frontage, the lights burning behind the curtained windows of the bar made it a very welcoming prospect to the weary traveller. Surprisingly, despite the lateness of the hour the night was not quiet, the inky black waters of the River Dochart thundering under the bridge immediately behind the inn provided an imposing backdrop to the scene.

Straightening his tie and picking up his hurriedly packed overnight bag, Clarrie walked through the front door into the entrance hall. He was very much aware that after travelling for over eight hours he was dishevelled and in need of a shave. Not the best image to present when booking in at an hotel.

Avoiding the reception desk he made his way through into the bar suddenly realising how hungry he was, and more importantly how much he needed a drink. A momentary silence fell amongst the locals seated around the room as the presence of the stranger was noted, then the low hubbub of conversation resumed.

Clarrie ordered a large dram and a pint of Usher's Sixty Shilling mild. It was not until it was placed in front of him that he realised that a Scottish dram was almost double that of an English tot.

Sinking the whisky in one, he picked up the pint and took a deep swallow. The small sandy haired barman watched him, impressed.

'You're a thirsty man sir,' the Highland burr carried a soothing note, and Clarrie pushed the glass back towards him.

'I'll have another of those please, and I would be happy if you would join me.'

Graciously, the barman complied and set the two single malts on the bar in front of them.

'Slangevar' he said taking down half of the dram.

'I am late arriving,' said Clarrie, the whisky circulating around his system was beginning to relax him down. 'I had arranged to meet a business colleague, another Englishman and his wife, he is slim, white hair and moustache, she is quite small red haired, have they booked in as yet?'

The barman gave him a slow smile. 'Aye, I ken the gentleman you mean, but he is not with his wife. He was going to book in, but we are full up with the salmon fishers.' He waved his hand towards the room.

'No he went away up to Blair's cottage, about half a mile along the track at the back there you'ken. Its an old shepherd's place that we rent out occasionally.'

Clarrie took a long pull at the Scottish ale. 'Actually, there were three of us meeting, my other colleague is a Scotsman, big fellow, name of Rowell, has he arrived yet?'

The barman's face screwed up as he examined the question. 'No there has been no Scotsman arrived during the day.'

Where was Joe Rowell? He had an hour's start on Clarrie, but had not yet arrived.

He would, Greasley presumed have encountered the same delay as himself at Stirling. Probably he had attempted to take an alternative route which had proved even longer, plus the fact that, not knowing that he was being pursued, he would not realize the urgency.

On the other hand, he might be here already, waiting somewhere in the darkness.

Turning left out of the hotel door, Clarrie crossed the stone bridge and took the cart track leading past an old toll house along the bank of the Dochart. It was a long dark walk and had it not been for the full moon shining down from a cloudless sky he would probably have missed the cottage.

It was larger than he had expected, more a farmhouse than a cottage, the pale moonlight glinting coldly off of white stuccoed walls giving its position away. Pausing in the shelter of a large oak tree, Greasley waited, checking for any signs of movement. The building was in darkness except for the illumination of a dim oil lamp in an upstairs back window.

After fifteen minutes, satisfied that he had not been followed, he made his way softly around to the back of the cottage. The kitchen door was unlocked and opened to his touch, he was he remembered in a part of the world where doors were rarely bolted and barred.

Slipping the gun out of his belt - Montague Parfitt was not the only one to take advantage of the armistice - he stepped into the darkened kitchen then waited, listening intently for any sound coming from the upstairs room.

Clarrie moved cautiously through into the living room, checking for signs of anything unusual. Everything downstairs was in darkness. Nothing disturbed the quiet and, his eyes becoming accustomed to the darkness he felt his way stealthily along the wall through into the passageway, again he stopped to listen and allow his eyes to adjust to the gloom, the last thing he wanted, was to signal his presence by bumping into a piece of furniture or knocking over an ornament.

At the end of the passage was the front door, a patch of pale moonlight shining in through the quarter light at the top. To his right a narrow staircase led up to the first floor. The thin gleam of the oil lamp showed under the door to the bedroom at the head of the stairs. Keeping close to the wall and treading on the edge of the stair boards in the hope of avoiding one that might creak Clarrie slowly inched his way up.

Reaching the head of the stairs he placed his left hand on the door knob and gently turned it, in his other hand the butt of the pistol was slippery with sweat - the door was locked from the inside.

'Harry, are you in there?' he whispered.

As he spoke a slight noise at the foot of the stairs made him spin round. Clearly silhouetted in the moonlight was the figure of Joseph Rowell pointing an automatic pistol at him. In one smooth movement, without pausing to think, Greasley fired three times.

In the fleeting second before Rowell fired back, Clarrie Greasley remained motionless by the bedroom door, gun held out in front of him. Rowell' first shot hit him in the chest sending him crashing back against the door, his second through the bridge of Greasley's nose took the back of his head off. The impact of the body hitting the door smashed the lock from its keep and propelled it into the bedroom.

Sitting motionless in an armchair beside the bed, Harry North stared down momentarily at the inert figure, the shotgun in his hands was cocked and pointing unwaveringly at the doorway, Nobby Armstrong's revolver lay on the night stand beside him. Turned down low on the far side of the room the oil lamp illuminated the doorway whilst throwing him into deep shadow.

The laboured breathing and heavy footfall of the man slowly mounting the stairs told him that at least one of Greasley's bullets had found its mark.

Momentarily the doorway darkened before Rowell stepped into the lamplight. His right arm hung limply by his side, blood soaking the front of his chest, the automatic in his left swept the room before coming to rest on Harry North.

'Was he alone?' Harry stood up dropping the hammers back down on the shotgun and laying it on the bed. Rowell nodded, his face contorted with pain.

'Jesus, you cut it close Joe, where did he get you?'

Rowell sank down on the bed. His face was ashen and it was obvious that he was losing a lot of blood. he was Harry knew about to pass out.

The sound of the back door crashing open and heavy footsteps running up the stairs was followed by the appearance in the doorway of a big capable looking man in his early sixties accompanied by Percy Longman, both were carrying hunting rifles. The older man Harry noted bore a striking resemblance to Joe.

'MacIntyre will have heard the shots and be on the way up with the doctor,' the man said grimly.

'Thanks dad,' Joe muttered, it was good he thought just before he passed out, to be home again.

Laying in the hospital bed, his chest swathed in bandages Joe looked, Harry thought very weak. He had lost a lot of blood, but of the two bullets that hit him, because of the heavy calibre of the weapon and the relatively close range at which it was fired, the first had gone through his right shoulder, and the other into his side just below the ribcage, exiting without hitting any bones or vital organs. He was, the doctor told Harry on his arrival at Stirling Infirmary, a very lucky man to be alive. Which North thought grimly was more than could be said for Clarence Greasley.

'How are you feeling?' he asked.

Joe smiled wanly from the depths of the crisply laundered sheets.

'Not good, but it worked out as we planned.'

Laura Percival glared at Harry from the opposite side of the bed where she was busily arranging the flowers that she had insisted they bought on the way in from the stall outside of the hospital. Despite Harry's assurances that it was all part of a carefully prepared plan she was furious with both of them.

Harry had sent her up to Killin to ensure her safety. That he had also, without her knowledge spoken to her brother-in-law over his concerns for her safety, became immediately apparent when on arrival at her sister's farm she was greeted by sufficient men of the Campbell clan, all armed to the teeth with shotguns and rifles to withstand a siege by the entire British army.

Things were, he explained to her when he arrived in the meadow at the back of the farm with Joe, in an aeroplane flown by a man who answered solely to the name of Percy, 'coming to a head, and he couldn't afford to take any risks.'

What he had not explained was that 'coming to a head' involved himself and Joe setting themselves up as targets in order to flush out the gang leader.

'There wasn't the time,' Harry explained evasively. 'We knew that he would be hours behind us and needed to set up the cottage and a bit of back-up

'A bit of back-up,' was he thought gratefully something of an understatement. In setting things up to flush Greasley out he knew from the outset that they were both taking an immense risk.

Initially, flying up to Scotland with Joe, the best Harry had hoped for was that he could keep Laura out of the way, and then see what happened. He had reckoned without the nature of the place and the people with whom he was to become involved.

'We need to see my father - tell him everything, and tell him what you need,' Joe was emphatic as they discussed in the kitchen of the Campbell farmhouse how they were going to set the trap.

Within two hours of their arrival, Angus Rowell and Laura's brother-in-law Sandy Campbell had laid the ground for the plan to deal with Clarrie Greasley.

When he arrived in the bar of the Bridge of Lochay, the barman Willie McNabb carefully directed Greasley to the cottage a mile away down the track. Joe was already in the deep kitchen larder, his father and Percy - who had been instructed by Ralph Gresham that once he had delivered them to the Campbell farm, he was to remain and 'lend a hand'- were hidden away in the cow byre. As soon as Clarrie left to set off up the track, the hotel bar emptied and he was trailed at a safe distance by Sandy Campbell and a half dozen heavily armed clansmen, including Douglas McIntyre the local Constable, and Dr Tam McOwen, both of whom had been brought in at an early stage by Angus Rowell.

'So you see, there was really no danger at all,' Harry was aware that he sounded slightly lame.

Laura's expression made it very apparent that she did not '*see*'.

'An Inspector and two Constables arrived from Stirling just after breakfast,' Harry glanced uneasily at Laura, he had never seen her this angry before.

'They have taken charge of the body. I telegraphed Hall-Johnson and everything is being sorted.'

He gave the figure under the bedclothes a reassuring smile, 'I should be on the way back home as soon as possible … I think that Laura is staying for a while.'

Laura gave him an icy stare. 'I think that I will be here for quite a while,' she said, 'first of all to look after you Joseph, because you may have lost sight of the fact that Ailma is in no condition to make a two day train journey, and secondly because I don't quite know how long it will take me to forgive you for what you have done this time Harry.'

Wincing, Joe eased his position under the sheets. It was he thought ironic that having survived four years of war he had come so near to being killed in his home village.

Catching his breath he said, 'can I ask you both something?'

They turned to look at him.

'When you eventually get married, can I be best man?'

Waiting on the platform for the Glasgow train Harry was lost in thought. Greasley's death was only the beginning. Everything would now start to unravel, and he needed to keep a tight control of events. His underlying sadness that Clarrie Greasley, a friend of so many years, had turned bad, was to an extent mitigated by his relief that he could now go back to giving his implicit trust to Bert Conway.

At first, when he realised that it was one of his Sergeants who was behind everything, he had not been certain which of them it was. It was fairly obvious that this had been going on for some time, and that with all of the opportunities the war presented the corruption went back much further than the heady days of the armistice. By a process of elimination, that effectively took Joseph Rowell out of the equation. Joe, he was fairly certain would still have been away in the army when all of this had begun. Which meant that he was left with Bert Conway and Clarence Greasley, both friends of over twenty years, the two men with whom he would have trusted his life. After the Pierpoint robbery, with the undamaged padlock on Latimer's gates, he went back and had a quiet chat with David Byram.

Had either Bert or Clarrie been to see him for anything in the time preceding the robbery, he asked? David Byram's response was an immediate, 'yes,' Sergeant Greasley came to see him just after Christmas to conduct a security check on the premises. Was Sergeant Greasley, at any time during that visit left on his own in Byram's office? Again after a moment's consideration, the jeweller remembered that he had left Clarrie for a few minutes whilst he went into the shop to deal with a client.

It was the final piece in the puzzle. When Wade's men conducted the bogus raid on Byram's house they took away all of the keys, including the crucial key to the vault. However, if the burglary was committed the night before, then the gang must have already been in possession of the vault key.

So, it was simple, on his own in the office, Clarrie made a quick impression of the vault key, probably on a lump of putty brought with him for the purpose and then later had a duplicate cut.

From that point on, Harry knew who his adversary was.

In Harry's experience, most situations carried a positive element somewhere. Before leaving the hospital he had spent a short while with the consultant who was dealing with Joe. Sergeant Rowell, the consultant assured him would make a full recovery and be back to duty in around six to eight weeks provided he took it easy. He was somewhat surprised and extremely gratified by the offer Harry made to him of a case of single malt whisky, to be delivered to him from a merchant of his choice in Prince's Street, provided Joe was not allowed to get out of his bed for at least another week.

The Superintendent's concern for his officer was, thought Mr MacAlpine, a thing to be commended. Harry for his part was immensely pleased that he had found a way to keep his Sergeant safely tucked away in Scotland until after the forthcoming police strike.

Chapter 25

It was late evening when Harry stepped down onto the platform at Kelsford Station from the Glasgow train. Having slept away most of the journey he was not particularly tired, which was just as well because his day was far from over.

Allowing himself the luxury of a taxi cab from the station to Tennyson Street, he was back home in a matter of minutes. Going through to the kitchen he found a two day old loaf in the bread bin, and the remains of a gammon joint and a piece of Stilton in the larder. Having made himself a sandwich he put it on a plate with a thick wedge of the cheese, before taking the top off of a bottle of light ale.

The kitchen clock said half past nine, leaving the food on one side Harry went through to the hall and picked up the telephone receiver. A minute later his call was answered by a familiar voice.

'I need to see you, urgently,' he said, 'half past eleven, in the back lane, and make sure no one sees you.'

Replacing the handset he made his way back into the kitchen, and sitting down by the empty range took a long pull at the beer. This was without a doubt the most difficult decision he had ever made. Was it, he kept asking himself purely to repay a debt, to clear the board once and for all, or was there something else, something that he could not admit even to himself?

Finishing the beer he opened a second and took a bite of the sandwich. He had chosen his course of action and now he decided, he would have to play the cards whichever way they fell.

Bert Conway was still in the sergeants office when he arrived at the first floor. He waved a hand to Harry as the Superintendent went into his own office. Harry waved back and leaving the door open slumped down in his chair. Will had been busy during his absence he noted. The stack of files awaiting decisions whether to prosecute or not was gone, there were no messages waiting for immediate attention, and a brief note told him that nothing of any consequence had taken place in the last couple of days - an assertion with which Harry did not entirely concur.

'You thought it might have been me didn't you?' Conway's stocky frame filled the doorway.

'Honest answer Bert - I didn't want it to be either of you, but it had to Clarrie because of the visit he made to get a copy of the vault key.'

'But I could have been in partners with him though, couldn't I?'

Harry nodded slowly, 'you could have been, but I didn't have him down for taking a partner, and I didn't have you down for being bent. Plus the fact that you borrowed twenty quid from me to pay for Connie's birthday party, if you had just robbed Pierpoint's you wouldn't have been short.'

Both men smiled at each other the tension easing away, 'how do you know what has happened anyway?' asked North.

'Laura rang me to say that she is staying up in the porridge swamps - Stirling or somewhere - she explained about Clarrie being dead and that he shot Joe up pretty badly, and that you were on the way home. She said that she had given you a bit of a hard time, and could Connie help out by doing a bit of cooking and washing for you until she gets back.'

North held up a cautionary finger, 'this is important Bert, not a word to anyone about Clarrie. I do not want O'Keefe or any of his team to get the slightest whisper. I doubt if in reality Charlie O'Keefe actually knew who he was working for, and I want it to stay that way until I am ready.'

Conway gave a nod of agreement, 'do you think that Clarrie ordered Ben Gunn's execution?'

'Without a doubt,' North reached into his desk drawer and brought out a bottle of Famous Grouse, from a second he produced two glasses.

'Clarrie and O'Keefe have been bang at it for a long while. Once he had killed Lew Arthur, Clarrie had nothing to lose - you can only hang a man once. Clem Waldron was a mistake, but at the end of the day, so far as they were concerned, he was expendable. Clarrie must have been beside himself when he saw Laura flashing her ring around. The hit and run was a genuine attempt to get the ring back and to send me a clear message at the same time.'

'I knew that Joe was not involved, and if I am truthful, I was sure that you weren't either. I chose Joe to partner me partly because we were going to Scotland, and partly because I hoped that I might find a way to keep him up there until after the weekend - away from this strike.'

'You certainly succeeded in doing that,' replied Conway ruefully.

'However, with Joe out of the frame there will be no strike here. Webster called an open meeting last night and laid it out for the lads. Strike, and irrespective of age, service, or rank, you will never work again. No strike, and you will quite quickly get what you want and everybody lives happily ever after. There was an open vote, show of hands and it was unanimous'

He held his glass out for a re-fill and gave Harry a quizzical look when having replenished it he replaced the stopper and returned the bottle to the drawer.

'I am not finished yet,' Harry said, 'one more job to do, then home to bed, in case you are not aware of it, I have had a pretty shitty couple of days.'

Conway knew better than to ask where he was going at this time of night. Instead he reached into his jacket pocket and pulled out a typed sheet of paper.

'Got a reply from the New York Police Department. Cole Wade, or to give him his correct name, James Dinwoodie, is a number one bad bugger.'

Reaching over he handed North the paper, the Superintendent scrutinised the list of offences that Wade was wanted for.

'Can I keep this?' he asked. Conway waved a meaty fist, 'yes, it a copy I had typed up for you.'

'Which brings us to the next main event, have you got everything in place for raiding the basin warehouses?'

Conway eased his position in the chair and lit a cigarette before passing the packet to Harry.

'Day after tomorrow, dawn swoop, six a.m. Webster has drawn up a list of twenty good men, we will bring them in tomorrow night, then nobody leaves the station or communicates with anybody outside until after the job is done. Meanwhile, Will Mardlin and that 'army type' have gone down to Leicester to be with Palmer Osborne's team when they knock out Manton at the same time we go into the basin. They are particularly interested in the manager of the army depot'

'Firearms?' North was mentally ticking off a shopping list.

'Ten of the men will be armed, especially now we know that the yank is so dangerous.'

'I want him alive,' instructed North, 'Detectives?'

'Bill, Lol, and Daniel will be with me, we will start a search of the buildings as soon as we have secured the place.'

'No,' Harry frowned, 'no, I want you and your men to hang back and deal with the prisoners. I will take care of searching the warehouses. Did you do as I said and made sure that O'Keefe and his men are included in the raiding party?'

Bert gave an affirmative nod, 'Exactly as you said.'

It would have been normal for the detectives to conduct the search, but Harry knew what he was doing, and securing the prisoners was equally important.

After a few more minutes spent discussing details Harry, checking his watch saw that it was a quarter past eleven. Making his excuses, on the spur of the moment he leaned over and taking Bert's hambone fist in his, they shook hands. The sentiment between the two old friends was unspoken.

'I don't suppose,' Harry asked, ' Laura happened to say when she was coming home?'

As he pulled to a halt and switched off his lights, just for a moment Harry caught a glimpse of a white shirt and riding breeches standing by a tree next to the lane.

Climbing out of the car he closed the door quietly and made his way over, Gyp came trotting forward to meet him, nuzzling his hand.

'This had better be worthwhile,' Lisa said.

'Are you certain no one has followed you?' he asked.

'No one has followed me,' she replied tersely, 'I am taking the dog out before we go to bed, now what is this about?'

'This is about the fact that I owe you,' said Harry, 'this is about clearing the slate once and for all. On Friday morning just after daylight, I am coming in here to take this place apart and recover the property that was stolen from Pierpoint's and anything else on offer - everything, cigarettes, spirits, jewellery, oil paintings, you name it, if it is down in your little hidey hole under the water I am having it back. At the same time the police at Leicester will be turning over Gilbert Manton's premises.'

North registered the startled look on her face, 'you, and only you can disappear without a trace. That wipes the slate clean.'

'You said that there were two things,' she said cautiously.

'Cole Wade, if I am letting you go, then I want him. Other than you he is the only person who knows everything that is going on. That is the deal, take it or leave it. I have got a surveillance team watching the basin right now, if you attempt to move anything out then we will hit you straight away.' He had to gamble on her believing his bluff, as to put a watch on the premises now would risk blowing the raid.

Lisa frowned, her mind was racing, how did North know about the underground vault? Gyp stirred restively by her feet. From the outset she had known that this moment would come sooner or later, and twenty four hours would be more than sufficient time for her to implement her escape plan.

The stuff in the vault was valuable, but during the time that the basin had been in operation Lisa had stashed away equal amounts of money in three separate bank accounts across the country, one in Liverpool, a second in London, and the third at Folkestone. The first two would provide her with ready access to money should she need to flee to America, the third would serve the same purpose in seeing her evade capture into Europe. On a weekly basis she received lists of all sailings to North America and cross channel ferry timetables. She could walk out of the basin at five minutes notice and disappear without trace.

'Wade, or as he is really, James Dinwoodie, is extremely dangerous Lisa.' Without realising he had moved closer to her, his voice barely above a whisper.

'He is a Canadian, and he is wanted all over Canada and the States. In both countries there are warrants in existence for his arrest for the murder of police officers killed in shoot-outs.'

'I want him, and I don't want you hurt simply because you got in the way. If push comes to shove he will go down shooting. Believe me, you are out of your league with him, this is not a question of pushing Lily Barstow off of a train in the middle of the night - he is more than capable of killing you.'

Harry was now so close to Lisa that her he felt her body stiffen at the mention of the woman's name. This time she did not attempt to conceal the startled expression on her face.

Lisa quickly recovered herself, how in hell's name did he know about Lil Barstow? So far as she knew the body had not even been identified.

Licking her lips, she swallowed hard, the saliva had suddenly dried in her mouth.

'Alright,' she said quietly, 'you want me to give you the only person other than me who knows everything - that I will do.'

'Just tell me one thing though - I need to know, is this only about clearing the slate?'

Harry held her gaze in silence, she was tall for a woman and their eyes were almost on a level. He could smell a faint muskiness mixed with perspiration on the still warm evening air, she was without question the most sensual woman he had ever met. Leaning forward he kissed her, gently at first then as she responded, with a deep passion that surprised them both.

'We could be so good together Harry North,' she breathed. This was the first time that she could ever remember being so excited by a man.

Harry put his hand behind her head, twining his fingers in the thick blonde hair and pulled it gently into his shoulder.

'And we would destroy each other Lisa,' he whispered.

They remained motionless for some time before she lifted her head and gave him a sad smile, tears were streaming down her face.

'We have both been around too long, seen and done too many things,' she said softly.

'I will be gone by Friday morning, and I will do as you ask.'

Reaching up she kissed him once more, a long hard passionate kiss that both of them would remember before turning and walking purposefully away into the darkness.

'When we get there, Sgt Lyner's men will deal with anyone on the dockside or the towpath area. Detectives Sykes, Windram and Scofield, will be with Sergeant Conway. We go in, in one hour's time at five thirty sharp.'

It was half past four in the morning and the muster room at Long Street was crowded with men who had been brought in at short notice the night before to take part in the raid on the canal basin.

Harry looked around the twenty or so officers gathered in the muster room, there were three new men in Cedric Lyner's group. Men who had joined since the war, each one an ex-soldier wearing decorations attesting to their experience in combat. Standing to one side was PC 97 Ted Wainwright, the red white and blue of the Military Medal taking precedence over his campaign ribbons. Harry noted that he was one of the group of Constables carrying .303 Lee Enfield Service rifles, Harry's instinct was that if Wainwright stayed the distance he would be an asset to the force. Along with the rest of the new men this was going to be his first opportunity to show his real capabilities.

Harry took up the briefing, 'Sergeant Lyner is in charge of the uniform men who are armed. I want your men Cedric to do an initial sweep of the loading bay and the buildings, work together, I am sure I don't need to tell you how to do it.'

'There is one man in particular, a Canadian who goes by the name of Cole Wade, his real name is James Dinwoodie. He has previous in both America and Canada for shooting his way out of situations, and he has previously killed police officers, he also spent four years in the British Army in France, so believe me he is no amateur. Whilst I want him alive, that will not be at the expense of any police officer's safety. You do what is necessary - I will give you my full backing.'

A ripple of assent ran through the ranks. Bert Conway's eyes held a gleam of anticipation. This was going to be a day of reckoning, these people had played fast and loose for long enough. He felt the weight of the Colt automatic tucked into the back of his belt.

Conway was however slightly puzzled. Firstly when, prior to the briefing he and Harry went down to the armoury for North to sign the firearms authorisations, he was surprised that the Superintendent did not draw a weapon himself. 'What about you Harry', he asked? Shaking his head North simply said, 'I won't need one.'

The second thing that was bothering him was the fact that included in the raiding party were Charlie O'Keefe, Brad Green, and Albert Wales. He had worked with Foxy long enough to know that this was definitely not by accident. Harry had something planned to make Charlie tip his hand, and when he did, he and his little team of villains would be marching in alongside the other prisoners. If anything happened to Harry, then he, Bert Conway would ensure that.

His train of thought was interrupted by North's voice.

'Sergeant O'Keefe, you and your men will be with me. As soon as Sergeant Lyner's men have closed the quay and ensured that the buildings are clear, Sergeant Conway and his detectives will arrest everyone on site. Meanwhile you will come with me and we will make a search of the premises from top to bottom.

O'Keefe held up a hand in a gesture of understanding.

Harry pursed his lips and looked around at the assembled men. Lisa would have been gone for several hours by now he estimated.

By the middle of the morning, once Wade and the others realised that she had double crossed them, they would be falling over themselves to incriminate her, and in doing so put their own heads into the noose.

Will Mardlin had been in Leicester since the previous day working with Palmer Osborne, and his men on the raid that was going to take place simultaneously at the Belgrave Wharf. Will and Gresham's plan was to be present when the Leicester police went in, seize anything that related to the Kelsford end of the operation, and give to Gilbert Manton a personal, if somewhat cryptic message from Detective Superintendent North that, 'there was no such thing as a tame tiger.'

As the men fell out he spoke quietly to Cedric Lyner and Bert Conway.

'These are devious bastards, once we have secured the place I want you to put a close guard on the site, Cedric, make sure that the access to and from the road at the back is closed, I don't want a car suddenly appearing from nowhere and whipping them off.'

'Wouldn't it be better if I did the search of the buildings with Dan and Lol?' Conway asked in a low voice.

North looked at him sharply, 'No. If all goes well you will be busy rounding up prisoners. Any property that is recovered inside can be accounted for by the uniform men with me. I don't want afterwards for you to be interviewing these buggers and when we go to court someone saying that you went into the warehouse and 'found' things that weren't there.'

Bert gave him a long hard stare. 'Alright,' he agreed. 'You might have a point.' His voice did not carry any conviction.

Something was very wrong. Standing on the quayside, Harry North stared around him stone faced.

The raid had gone like clockwork, the armed men coming in from opposite ends of the wharf, searching and clearing each building individually with military precision. The hut at the far end which was the living quarters for Wade's men was deserted, as were the rest of the buildings. The straw palliasses had not been slept on, there was not a soul on the wharf other than the policemen.

'Do exactly as you were instructed, keep a tight ring around the place, either they have been warned, or there is something else going on. Either way, nothing now moves in or out, any barge tries to come through, nick everybody on it!'

North was furious, at the very end, Lisa had double crossed him. She could not have cleared the vault, of that he was certain, there simply had not been sufficient time. No, she had dispersed the gang before making good her own escape. In his mind's eye he could see her melting away through the trees into the darkness. What a bloody fool he thought, trusting a woman with her track record!

'Sergeant O'Keefe,' he snapped , 'bring your men into the warehouse, 'lets see if we can at least salvage something.'

Striding into the warehouse, he pressed the switch inside the door flooding the dim interior with bright light. 'Turn over every bale, box, bit of furniture,' he growled, 'the gear is in here somewhere.'

Mounting the bare boards of the wooden staircase, he pushed open the door to Lisa's living quarters, and stood for a moment not certain what he was looking for.

The room was exactly as it had been the last time he was there. Away to his right through the open doorway into the bedroom he could see the neatly made double bed with the small oil painting on the wall.

Casting his eye around the living room it was apparent that nothing had been touched, it was as if she had just stepped out and would be returning any time.

A scrabbling sound caught his attention, and seconds later Gyp's face peered around the dining table to look enquiringly at him. Tail wagging gently from side to side she came around from the back of the table and sat on the rug in the middle of the room.

Slowly a realisation hit him, and a wry smile broke out across his face.

Lisa had agreed to give him the only other person who knew everything. Wade did not know everything, he only knew as much as Lisa chose to let him know.

The only person apart from Lisa who knew everything was sitting in front of him - Gyp!

Harry's eyes moved to the table, in the centre, weighted down with a small Chinese ornament was a single sheet of paper. Picking it up he quickly read the note in Lisa's bold handwriting.

'White Star Line, SS Asconia.
Arrives New York, 7th August.'
Lisa.

Back in the warehouse North regarded the three policeman, now standing in a bemused group by the office door. In truth, Brad Green and Albert Wales, were still reeling from the fact that the fourth member of the gang had been summarily dispatched by Charlie O'Keefe for stepping outside of the agreed rules. That he would be punished they had no doubt, but to simply take him into the graveyard and shoot him was totally unexpected, and despite his almost casual assurance that 'three ways was better than four,' they now regarded O'Keefe with more than a degree of mistrust.

'So, what have you found?' demanded North.

'Nothing Sir, the place is clean.' Charlie O'Keefe had entered the building with high hopes of uncovering the haul of property undoubtedly hidden somewhere on the premises. Once they uncovered it, the man would come up with a plan to bring it back into their hands.

It had not happened though, whilst Harry was upstairs rifling through the knickers in 'my ladies boudoir' they had found nothing. A sudden, staggering thought came into O'Keefe's head. Could Foxy North be 'the man'? It would explain so much if he was.

'It's here somewhere - that crate over there, what's under it?' Harry strode over to the large wooden box and put his shoulder against it. The crate slide smoothly to one side revealing the steel plate covering the entrance to the vault.

'I thought you had searched the place,' he snarled at the Sergeant, 'get that lid up', he pointed to a long steel bar with an hook on the end.

The plate slid backwards easily along the greased runners in which it was set, revealing a perpendicular metal ladder descending into the tunnel.

'Get down there and have a look, shout up if you find anything,' Harry was secretly elated that his deductions had proved to be correct.

Led by Brad Green the three of them cautiously descended the ladder. The drop was Green estimated about fifteen feet. Switching on the lamp that hung from his belt, he shone it along the wall of the tunnel which appeared to run away for some distance towards where the canal should be.

A second lamp, and then a third appeared as O'Keefe and Wales joined him. Swinging his light back and forth, O'Keefe revealed the stacks of boxes and crates piled neatly down the centre.

'Fucking hell Charlie, its an Aladdin's cave,' breathed Albert Wales.

O'Keefe was running his fingers along a large cardboard box bearing the Players Navy Cut trade mark. He held a finger to his lips, 'shh, not so loud, we need to think about this.'

'There's not a lot to think about Charlie, we are down here, Foxy is up top, and the only way out is past him, we can hardly take this lot up in our pockets can we?' O'Keefe's thoughts were however running down a different track, if North was 'the man', then it was eminently do-able, but he would have to break his cover. They could seal the chamber back up, replace the crate over the entrance, tell Conway and the others that there was nothing here, and come back later.

His train of thought was disrupted by the unexpected sound of the heavy metal shutter being slid back into place above them. The shaft of light coming through the aperture was suddenly extinguished and other than for the light from their lamps, they were in total darkness.

'What the bloody hell,' O'Keefe's lack of understanding was mirrored in the faces of the other two.

Bert Conway and Cedric Lyner were standing by the edge of the water conversing in quiet voices when they were almost thrown off of their feet by a tremor that shook the entire quayside followed by a deep rumbling sound from somewhere underground.

'Mine!' shouted Ted Wainwright as he and the other ex-soldiers instinctively threw themselves to the ground, hands over their heads, rifles thrown out in front of them.

Conway and Lyner grabbed onto each other managing to retain their balance, Lol Windram and Dan Scofield, along with several of the other policemen caught unawares were thrown to the ground.

Conway began to run towards the double doors of the warehouse from which a cloud of dust was now pouring, he skidded to a halt at the sight of a dishevelled Harry North staggering back out into the daylight.

Chapter 26

After the cooling sea breezes blowing across the Atlantic, the heat coming up from the dockside was overbearing. It had been a pleasant voyage Lisa reflected, it was difficult to realise that less than a week ago she had been throwing things into a suitcase prior to abandoning the Kelsford basin.

As soon as she left Harry Lisa had woken Cole Wade and the members of her crew. Having given each of the men twenty pounds travelling money she told them to separate and disperse as quickly as possible. A hastily consulted White Star sailing list showed that the SS Asconia was due to depart from Liverpool in forty eight hours. Sufficient time for her to obtain tickets to America for her and Cole.

Within an hour the basin was deserted, it was as if Lisa Abbott and her gang had never been there. It had taken only a few minutes to convince Cole that the contents of the vault were lost to them, that any attempt to put together a boatload of gear and sail it up the canal was to court certain disaster.

As part of her escape plans Lisa had some time previously acquired two sets of travel documents from a contact in Nottingham, one in the name of Evelyn Boulter the second Edith Hill. Both women the forger, assured her were in their mid thirties and had died two years previously in a typhoid epidemic at Southall workhouse. Buried anonymously in a double pauper's coffin they had then been signed out in the discharge register by an unscrupulous deputy, and to all appearances disappeared back onto the streets of Nottingham. At a hundred pounds each it had been an expensive but worthwhile outlay. Essentially the documents were genuine, so far as the authorities were aware Edith Hill and Evelyn Boulter were still alive and well. Lisa had already decided that she would travel to America as Evelyn, then immediately destroy that identity and become Edith Hill. Next year when the government started to issue a document that they were calling a 'passport' she would apply for one in Hill's name.

Similarly, Wade's army discharge papers had been altered into the name of Chas. Warren, and would, he assured her be sufficient to get him through American immigration as a British citizen. She smiled grimly to herself, he would be most surprised she thought if he knew that she was aware that he was not American.

Taking him with her was she had decided a necessary precaution. If he were arrested anywhere in England - which left to his own inept devices was a certainty - he would she knew attempt to buy his way out of trouble by telling the police everything he knew about the canal basin operation. That was something that she could not allow to happen because, once things had quietened down, after a good long holiday Lisa Abbott had every intention of returning to England - there were too many opportunities not to.

Lisa allowed herself another quiet smile, this time much gentler, that Harry North would give Gyp a good home she was certain. He was right of course, they would have destroyed each other, although she felt a deep satisfaction that she had read him correctly, that he was as attracted to her as she was to him.

During the voyage she had insisted that she and Cole Wade travelled separately and had no contact other than late at night when she visited him in his cabin. The dark haired Mrs Boulter, recently widowed and on her way to visit friends in Chicago, bore no resemblance to Lisa Abbott and would not at a later date be connected with her.

On the quayside below, amongst the throng of people milling around she spotted two thickset men who despite the warmth of the day were wearing suits and soft hats. They were moving unobtrusively through the crowd, pausing at the bottom of each gangway to speak quietly to other men discretely positioned next to the attendants bidding farewell to the disembarking passengers and collecting their tips.

 Turning she made her way up the narrow stair to the next deck and tapped softly on Wade's cabin door, without waiting for a response she stepped into the cool interior of the cabin.

Cole Wade looked every inch the English gentleman. Light grey travelling suit with a mustard coloured waistcoat and tie to match, he was even wearing fashionable brown and cream 'correspondents' brogues.

'What do you think then my dear?' he asked in a well modulated English accent.

Lisa looked appraisingly at him, 'I think you will do,' she replied softly, moving close and kissing him on the lips. 'Just be careful with your papers and watch the accent.'

'Don't worry, it will be fine,' once more the American twang was back in his voice.

'Unless things have changed dramatically, these guys are not the brightest in the world and if it does look like it can go wrong ...' like a music hall magician, Wade flipped his hand in an upwards gesture and a fifty dollar bill appeared between his fingers.

'Alright, but still be careful,' Lisa turned to go, with her hand on the door handle she paused and as an afterthought added, 'It is going to take at least an hour for everyone to clear the ship, give it twenty minutes before you send your luggage down, that way it will be the busiest time.'

'Whatever you say lady,' he smiled confidently, 'but trust me, I'm on my own territory now.'

Blowing him a kiss Lisa stepped outside onto the deck and closed the cabin door behind her. She breathed a sigh of relief, Wade had not seen her slip the key out of the door. Carefully she inserted it back in the lock, to her intense relief it turned silently. Slipping it into her purse she descended to the lower deck where a steward was waiting with her sea trunk.

At the foot of the gangway she handed the man a five dollar tip. Giving her a polite, 'Thank you Ma'am,' he was about to depart when she laid a hand on the arm of his immaculate cream jacket and a second bill, this time a twenty, was slipped into his hand.

'The two men over there, the detectives,' the man followed her eyes and nodded.

'Tell them that the man they are looking for is in cabin 23 on 'B' deck.'

The pince-nez dangling from Leigh-Hunt's fingers was swinging back and forth in a slow arc which, thought Ralph Gresham bore an uncanny resemblance to the tail of an annoyed cat.

'Are you totally satisfied that the Yeremin letter is now a lost cause Colonel Gresham?'

Ralph knew from the icy tones and the use of his full title, that the politician was intensely annoyed. He was still stunned by the fact that Harry North had chosen to deal with O'Keefe and his men in such an arbitrary manner. It was obvious that Cole Wade had utilised his demolition skills to set up a fail safe system in the underground vault by placing explosives at either end of the tunnel which could be blown remotely from in the office, placing any evidence stored in there beyond recovery. That Ralph would himself have done the same thing without a second thought temporarily escaped him. Although he knew much of Harry, he would never have credited him with possessing the degree of ruthlessness required to press the switches and walk away.

'Yes Sir Rowland, regrettably when the chamber containing the stores of stolen property was detonated, not only were the men in there killed instantly by the blast, but as was intended the chamber flooded. It is doubtful if even at a later date it will be possible recover anything.'

The diplomat sat in silence, lips tightly compressed into a thin line. 'Ah well, spilt milk and all that,' he said finally. If nothing else Rowland Leigh-Hunt was a realist. It was unfortunate that such a unique bargaining chip should be lost as the result of a bungled criminal venture, however if it were lost to him it was also lost to anyone else.

'Keep Petrov at the Clarence for the time being,' he instructed, 'so far as the Russians are concerned he died in Germany, we will now start to look at setting him up with a new identity and running him ourselves.'

Changing the subject he asked, 'This explosion thing, is it possible that it was in fact an accident?'

Ralph shook his head. 'No, not the remotest. Wade was an expert in dealing with explosives. We now know that apart from any wartime experience, he was trained as a civil engineer and before the war worked on the construction of the Canadian Pacific Railway.'

The quick flick caught at the side of his jaw. 'To tidy things up, I volunteered 'as a serving army engineer, accredited in the handling and use of explosives,' to survey the scene.'

'Wade had set charges at each end of the tunnel sufficient to blow out the retaining walls without bringing down the building above. The charges were activated from the office, as a fail safe to prevent accidents, setting them off required two specific actions. A mains switch on the wall had to thrown, then a button behind the desk pressed. No way that it could have been an accident.'

'I left a signed statement under the name '*Colonel Sheldon, Royal Engineers*' for the Coroner to the effect that the explosion was due to the inadvertent detonation of a booby trap from within the vault by one of the officers conducting the search.'

'Interesting man, Superintendent North, we must bear him in mind.' Leigh-Hunt tucked the pince-nez carefully away in his waistcoat pocket.

'Meanwhile there is a small problem that requires attention.'

Ralph raised a quizzical eyebrow.

'The man you suggested we infiltrate into MI5 - Parfitt - has turned out not to be one of your better ideas.'

'At the time Sir Rowland, we did not know that he was responsible for murdering a woman,' murmured Gresham. At the time he thought, you considered it to be a very good idea indeed.

Ignoring the remark Leigh-Hunt continued, 'He is currently on remand in

Lincoln Prison and has got word out to his new employers that unless he is acquitted of this charge he will make things very embarrassing for them. Vernon Kell is furious and is blaming us for foisting onto him someone who is proving to be a potential security risk.'

'What does he want?' asked Gresham.

The old man steepled his fingers as if considering his response.

'In one respect, Vernon is correct. We did slip Parfitt sideways into his little group of Boy Scouts. More importantly, I have at present got one or two things boiling away in the pot which require Kell's good will, so I have told him that we will take care of the matter for him - as a favour.'

A quick twitch caught at Gresham's mouth, 'Lincoln Prison. That should not be too difficult.'

'Tommy, I wonder if you would be so good as to look after Gyp for me, and take her back to Tennyson Street at lunch time.'

Eric Broughton glanced up from the list of overtime figures that he was trying to balance. During the last week this had become a daily routine. Harry would walk Gyp in to work with him and deposit her in the admin office in young Tommy's care. During his lunch break the office boy would then walk her back to Tennyson Street, let himself in with a key which Harry had given him, and feed her. She would then spend the afternoon dozing in the kitchen until North returned in the early evening.

'Yes Mr North Sir,' the lad replied brightly, he looked at the new leather lead that Harry held out to him and hesitated a moment before saying, 'if you don't mind sir, she doesn't like the lead, and doesn't really need it, she will do exactly as I tell her.'

'That is perfectly alright Tom, I don't use the lead either, just thought that you might be more comfortable with it.' So far as Harry was aware, Eric did not see the sixpence which he slid into Tommy's hand.

'When Mrs Percival is back from seeing her relatives in Scotland it won't be necessary for me to bring the dog in with me.'

Eric grinned pleasantly, 'absolutely no problem sir.' By now, everyone was aware that for some unknown reason 'Mrs Percival' was away in Scotland and Foxy was having his dinners at Sergeant Conway's house'.

As the door closed behind North, Eric laid his pen down and watched Tommy Bowler, who oblivious to the attention was busy settling the dog on an old police greatcoat beside his desk. It had not gone without notice around the station that for some mysterious reason the office boy ceased to stammer when speaking to Superintendent North. What Eric had noticed during the last week was that whenever anyone came into the office with a query, or it was necessary for Tommy to answer the telephone, his hand automatically dropped to the dog's head which he would stroke gently whilst speaking perfectly normally.

'Tom, have you got a dog of your own at home?' Tommy was Eric knew, the youngest of four children and came in to Kelsford each morning on the bus from his father's small holding near Monckton village.

'Yy' yes Eric,' he straightened up satisfied that the collie was settled and sat back on the office stool. 'I have got a rrr'retriever, her name is bb'Beth.' Reaching down his right hand began to caress Gyp's ear. 'She is three, about the same age as Gyp I would say.'

Eric nodded and returned to adding up his figures, later in the morning he would have a word with Harry North. It was unheard of for an office boy to bring his dog in to work with him, and how the Superintendent was going to arrange it he could not begin to imagine.

Harry had hardly sat down at his desk when Tommy Bowler's head poked around the door, 'Please sir, Mr Mardlin and a gentleman to see you sir.'

Waving them into comfortable seats Harry thought how tired they both looked, it was not he realised, only himself who had been under pressure these last few days.

'Have you got everything you needed from the Leicester job?' he asked, going to the door and calling after Tommy for him to make some coffee.

Will nodded, 'yes, everything there is tidied up. Manton is in custody at Leicester gaol, and the Military Police have shipped the manager from the army depot off up to York.'

'At present, Manton is saying nothing and denying everything, but Palmer Osborne said something interesting. Apparently Manton and Lisa had a fallout recently. The word is that Manton came up here team handed to try to take back his holdings, timed it when most of her crew were off of the site and she was on her own with just one man. Seems there was a fight, she and her bodyguard both pulled guns, have you heard anything?'

Mardlin paused, what Palmer Osborne actually said was that Manton was alleging that the scales were tipped by the arrival of Lisa's 'tame copper', who weighed in and allowed the 'Scouser', armed with a shotgun to catch them off balance.

Harry rubbed a hand across his jaw, 'I had heard much the same, seems that she and her man, Moses Hawkins got lucky.'

'Which is more than can be said for Manton's crew,' replied Mardlin pointedly, 'Hawkins pistol whipped one of his men - a particularly evil bastard by the name of Todd - with a shotgun, took his eye out.

North nodded and accepted the packet of Passing Cloud that Ralph Gresham held out to him. 'Well, thieves fall out and all that,' he said philosophically, 'if you are afraid of wolves, don't go into the forest.'

Will Mardlin fixed his old friend with a long hard stare. … Afraid of wolves, no one can ever say that of you Harry he mused. First Clarrie Greasley, then Charlie O'Keefe. Greasley was a risk, but a worthwhile risk. Detonating the vault, that took more than nerve, that took something that he knew he did not possess.

'Bad job about Clarrie,' he said quietly.

'Yes, I am hoping that we can keep it under wraps. 'Soapy Syd' upstairs is beside himself. He can see his less than luminary career going straight down the pan. I don't give a toss about him, but if we can keep this away from the public we might just get things back on an even keel. We survived the strike, but the Parfitt thing when it goes to trial will be embarrassing, especially as he used the station car to take her out to the lime kiln, but if this last one with Greasley gets out…'

'I think I might be able to help Harry,' Ralph stubbed his cigarette out.

'I know a man who has connections, on nodding terms with the Home office, that sort of thing, it is as they say 'do-able.'

North gave him a grateful nod, 'Thank you Ralph, I would be very grateful.'

'You can forget about the Petrov thing as well Harry,' Gresham stood up ready to leave.

'When the vault went up, so did the Yeremin letter. I have no problem with a bunch of bent coppers going up in smoke, but after all of the trouble it has caused it would have been nice to have salvaged the letter.'

A bright smile lit up Harry North's face, 'ah, the letter, I had forgotten about that - not a problem - I've got it.'

As the other two watched with stunned expressions on their faces, he reached into the top drawer of his desk and produced a single sheet of paper covered in typed Cyrillic symbols.

Taking it from his outstretched hand Ralph Gresham studied the cyphers in amazement.

'Where did you get this from?' Gresham's voice was little more than a whisper.

Still smiling, Harry gently retrieved it from his grasp and turned it over, on the back in bright blue ink was written,

'*White Star Line, SS Asconia.*
Arrives New York, 7th August.'
Lisa.

Postscript

As was anticipated, the police strike of August 1919 was a failure. The recommendations of the Desborough Committee, hastily set up after an initial police strike twelve months earlier had already gone a long way towards resolving the men's grievances.

Other than in London and Liverpool where following a short period of civil disorder which was dealt with by the military, there was little support amongst the rank and file police for militant action. In the period following August 1919 government reprisals were Draconian. Every man, irrespective of rank or length of service who had failed to turn in for duty was dismissed and never allowed to again work as a police officer. Any thoughts of a police union were proscribed and a 'Police Federation' instituted which was by law prohibited from engaging or affiliating with any industrial union or going of ever on strike. As had been its intention from the outset, the government having rid itself of all traces of militancy, created in the words of Harry North 'a tame tiger.'

In Kelsford, with Joseph Rowell the main advocate for industrial action, two hundred miles away in a hospital bed in Stirling, there was no strike. In common with most other provincial Forces, not a single man participated in the industrial action, electing to allow the establishment processes to take their course.

In the confusion of the times it was not difficult to ensure that the corruption issue within the Kelsford Police Force was kept safely out of the public eye. The untimely death of Detective Sergeant Clarence Greasley in a hunting accident whilst on leave in the Scottish Highlands, was reported by the blissfully unaware editor of the Kelsford Gazette, in a glowing obituary provided by Detective Superintendent Harry North.

A large and very public funeral attended by several hundred people was held at St John's Church in Kelsford for the three officers tragically killed by a booby trap bomb whilst searching for stolen property at the old warehousing complex on the outskirts of the town. The site was subsequently declared unsafe and closed off pending demolition.

Whilst the problems of 1919 were never made public, and the Greasley affair kept a close secret known only to certain senior officers of the Force itself, there was one unavoidable repercussion. Following a series of damning articles in the Kelsford Gazette, deep concern was expressed by the Home Secretary at the lack of discretion - verging on nepotism - on the part of the Chief Constable, which resulted in the employment by the Force in a responsible position of the accused murderer Montague Parfitt.

In October1919 Sidney Hall-Johnson bowed to public censure and resigned as Chief Constable of the Kelsford Police Force. Anxious to restore the image of the Force a decision was taken by the Home Office that rather than advertise the post, they would seek a suitable internal candidate, and at the end of the month William Mardlin was appointed as Chief Constable.

Celia Parfitt was spared the indignity of testifying as to the details of her sordid relationship which led to the murder of Alice Kitson, when her husband died unexpectedly of a heart attack whilst on remand in Lincoln gaol.

Lisa Abbott after spending six months touring around the United States, as had always been her intention, returned to England at the end of January 1920 - exactly two weeks after, under the 18th Amendment to the United States Constitution, the prohibition of the sale and manufacture of alcohol in America became law. her travels had taken her across the border into Canada where she made substantial investments in several distilleries.

Cole wade never stood trial for the crimes committed by James Dinwoodie in America and Canada. He was shot and killed resisting arrest in his cabin on the SS Asconia in New York Harbour by agents of the Bureau of Investigation acting on information supplied by the British police.

So far as concerns the Yeremin Letter, its history after it passed into the possession of British Intelligence has become shrouded in mystery. For many years it lay unused, retained as a bargaining chip should the need ever arise. Following Leigh-Hunt's death in the 1930s', sightings of the letter, or alleged copies of it, were reported as far apart as China and America until it eventually disappeared entirely in the 1950s'.

The real mystery - whether or not Josef Stalin was in fact a traitor to the communist cause, which created of him one of the most powerful dictators in history - always hung upon the evidence of this single intelligence report, and will probably never be resolved.

ND - #0251 - 270225 - C0 - 234/156/21 - PB - 9781780914152 - Gloss Lamination